品味莎士比亞

英◇文◇名◇作◇選

BEAUTIFUL STORIES FROM SHAKESPEARE

E. Nesbit－著
李璞良－譯

CONTENTS

CONTENTS

Preface

The writings of Shakespeare have been justly termed "the richest, the purest, the fairest, that genius uninspired ever penned." Shakespeare instructed by delighting. His plays alone (leaving mere science out of the question), contain more actual wisdom than the whole body of English learning.

He is the teacher of all good—pity, generosity, true courage, love. His bright wit is cut out "into little stars." His solid masses of knowledge are meted out in morsels and proverbs, and thus distributed, there is scarcely a corner of the English-speaking world to-day which he does not illuminate, or a cottage which he does not enrich.

His bounty is like the sea, which, though often unacknowledged, is everywhere felt. As his friend, Ben Jonson, wrote of him, "He was not of an age but for all time." He ever kept the highroad of human life whereon all travel. He did not pick out by-paths of feeling and sentiment.

In his creations we have no moral highwaymen, sentimental thieves, interesting villains, and amiable, elegant adventuresses—no delicate entanglements of situation, in which the grossest images are presented to the mind disguised under the superficial attraction of style and sentiment.

He flattered no bad passion, disguised no vice in the garb of virtue, trifled with no just and generous principle. While causing us to laugh at folly, and shudder at crime, he still preserves our love for our fellow-beings, and our reverence for ourselves.

Shakespeare was familiar with all beautiful forms and images, with all that is sweet or majestic in the simple aspects of nature, of that indestructible love of flowers and fragrance, and dews, and clear waters—and soft airs and sounds, and bright skies and woodland solitudes, and moon-light bowers, which are the material elements of poetry,—and with that fine sense of their indefinable relation to mental emotion, which is its essence and vivifying soul—and which, in the midst of his most busy and tragical scenes, falls like gleams of sunshine on rocks and ruins—contrasting with all that is rugged or repulsive, and reminding us of the existence of purer and brighter elements.

These things considered, what wonder is it that the works of Shakespeare, next to the Bible, are the most highly esteemed of all the classics of English literature. "So extensively have the characters of Shakespeare been drawn upon by artists, poets, and writers of fiction," says an American author,—"So interwoven are these characters in the great body of English literature, that to be ignorant of the plot of these dramas is often a cause of embarrassment." But Shakespeare wrote for grown-up people, for men and women, and in words that little folks cannot understand.

Hence this volume. To reproduce the entertaining stories contained in the plays of Shakespeare, in a form so simple that young people can understand and enjoy them, was the object had in view by the author of these Beautiful Stories from Shakespeare.

E.T.R.

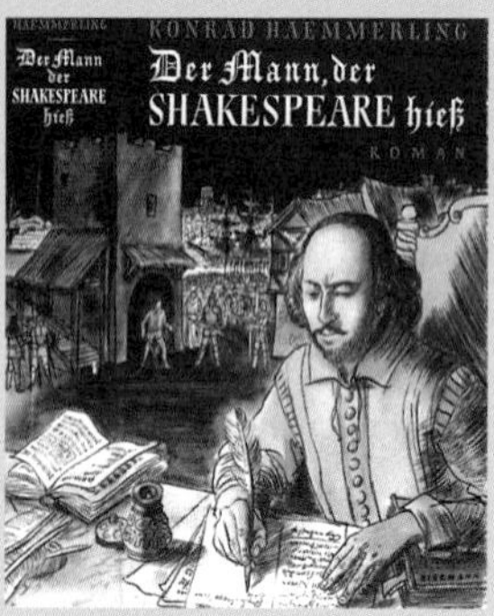

William Shakespeare
(1564-1616)

It may be said of Shakespeare, that from his works may be collected a system of civil and economical prudence. He has been imitated by all succeeding writers; and it may be doubted whether from all his successors more maxims of theoretical knowledge, or more rules of practical prudence can be collected than he alone has given to his country.

—*Dr. Samuel Johnson*

Samuel Johnson
(1709-1784)

Shakespeare's birthplace in Stratford

A BRIEF LIFE OF SHAKESPEARE

In the register of baptisms of the parish church of Stratford-upon-Avon, a market town in Warwickshire, England, appears, under date of April 26, 1564, the entry of the baptism of William, the son of John Shakespeare. The entry is in Latin—"Gulielmus filius Johannis Shakespeare."

The date of William Shakespeare's birth has usually been taken as three days before his baptism, but there is certainly no evidence of this fact. The family name was variously spelled, the dramatist himself not always spelling it in the same way. While in the baptismal record the name is spelled "Shakespeare," in several authentic autographs of the dramatist it reads "Shakspere," and in the first edition of his works it is printed “Shakespeare.”

Halliwell tells us, that there are not less than thirty-four ways in which the various members of the Shakespeare family wrote the name.

Shakespeare’s father, while an alderman at Stratford, appears to have been unable to write his name, but as at that time nine men out of ten were content to make their mark for a signature, the fact is not specially to his discredit.

The traditions and other sources of information about the occupation of Shakespeare’s father differ. He is described as a butcher, a wool-stapler, and a glover, and it is not impossible that he may have been all of these simultaneously or at different times, or that if he could not properly be called any one of them, the nature of his occupation was such as to make it easy to understand how the various traditions sprang up.

He was a landed proprietor and cultivator of his own land even before his marriage, and he received with his wife, who was Mary Arden, daughter of a country gentleman, the estate of Asbies, 56 acres in extent.

William was the third child. The two older than he were daughters, and both probably died in infancy. After him was born three sons and a daughter. For ten or twelve years at least, after Shakespeare’s birth his father continued to be in easy circumstances. In the year 1568 he was the high bailiff or chief magistrate of Stratford, and for many years afterwards he held the position of alderman as he had done for three years before.

To the completion of his tenth year, therefore, it is natural to suppose that William Shakespeare would get the best education that Stratford could afford. The free school of the town was open to all boys and like all the grammar-schools of that time, was under the direction of men who, as graduates of the universities, were qualified to diffuse that sound scholarship which was once the boast of England.

There is no record of Shakespeare's having been at this school, but there can be no rational doubt that he was educated there. His father could not have procured for him a better education anywhere. To those who have studied Shakespeare's works without being influenced by the old traditional theory that he had received a very narrow education, they abound with evidences that he must have been solidly grounded in the learning, properly so called, was taught in the grammar schools.

Nor was Stratford shut out from the general world, as many country towns are. It was a great highway, and dealers with every variety of merchandise resorted to its markets. The eyes of the poet dramatist must always have been open for observation. But nothing is known positively of Shakespeare from his birth to his marriage to Anne Hathaway in 1582, and from that date nothing but the birth of three children until we find him an actor in London about 1589.

How long acting continued to be Shakespeare's sole profession we have no means of knowing, but it is in the highest degree probable that very soon after arriving in London he began that work of adaptation by which he is known to have begun his literary career.

To improve and alter older plays not up to the standard that was required at the time was a common practice even among the best dramatists of the day, and Shakespeare's abilities would speedily mark him out as eminently fitted for this kind of work. When the alterations in plays originally composed by other writers became very extensive, the work of adaptation would become in reality a work of creation. And this is exactly what we have examples of in a few of Shakespeare's early works, which are known to have been founded on older plays.

It is unnecessary here to extol the published works of the world's greatest dramatist. Criticism has been exhausted upon them, and the finest minds of England, Germany, and America have devoted their powers to an elucidation of their worth.

Shakespeare died at Stratford on the 23rd of April, 1616. Shakespeare's fellow-actors, fellow-dramatists, and those who knew him in other ways, agree in expressing not only admiration of his genius, but their respect and love for the man. Ben Jonson said, "I love the man, and do honor his memory, on this side idolatry, as much as any. He was indeed honest, and of an open and free nature."

He was buried on the second day after his death, on the north side of the chancel of Stratford church. Over his grave there is a flat stone with this inscription, said to have been written by himself:

Good friend for Jesus sake forbeare
To digg the dust encloased heare:
Blest be ye man yt spares these stone,
And curst be he yt moves my bones.

Shakespeare's funerary monument

1 Hamlet

001 Hamlet was the only son of the King of Denmark. He loved his father and mother dearly—and was happy in the love of a sweet lady named Ophelia. Her father, Polonius, was the King's Chamberlain.

While Hamlet was away studying at Wittenberg, his father died. Young Hamlet hastened home in great grief to hear that a serpent[1] had stung the King, and that he was dead. The young Prince had loved his father so tenderly that you may judge what he felt when he found that the Queen, before yet the King had been laid in the ground a month, had determined to marry again—and to marry the dead King's brother.

Hamlet refused to put off mourning[2] for the wedding.

"It is not only the black I wear on my body," he said, "that proves my loss. I wear mourning in my heart for my dead father. His son at least remembers him, and grieves[3] still."

Then said Claudius the King's brother, "This grief is unreasonable. Of course you must sorrow at the loss of your father, but . . ."

"Ah," said Hamlet, bitterly, "I cannot in one little month forget those I love."

1 serpent ['sɜːrpənt] (n.) a snake, especially a large one 大蛇
2 mourning ['mɔːrnɪŋ] (n.) the period during which somebody's death is mourned 服喪
3 grieve [griːv] (v.) to feel or express great sadness 悲傷

002 With that the Queen and Claudius left him, to make merry over their wedding, forgetting the poor good King who had been so kind to them both.

And Hamlet, left alone, began to wonder and to question as to what he ought to do. For he could not believe the story about the snake-bite. It seemed to him all too plain that the wicked Claudius had killed the King, so as to get the crown and marry the Queen. Yet he had no proof, and could not accuse Claudius. And while he was thus thinking came Horatio, a fellow student of his, from Wittenberg.

"What brought you here?" asked Hamlet, when he had greeted his friend kindly.

Hamlet, Prince of Denmark

003 "I came, my lord, to see your father's funeral[4]."

"I think it was to see my mother's wedding," said Hamlet, bitterly. "My father! We shall not look upon his like again."

"My lord," answered Horatio, "I think I saw him yesternight[5]."

Then, while Hamlet listened in surprise, Horatio told how he, with two gentlemen of the guard, had seen the King's ghost on the battlements[6].

Hamlet went that night, and true enough, at midnight, the ghost of the King, in the armor he had been wont[7] to wear, appeared on the battlements in the chill[8] moonlight.

Hamlet was a brave youth. Instead of running away from the ghost he spoke to it—and when it beckoned[9] him he followed it to a quiet place, and there the ghost told him that what he had suspected was true.

4 funeral ['fju:nərəl] (n.) a ceremony for burying or burning the body of a dead person 喪禮

5 yesternight ['jestərnaɪt] (ad.) on the last night〔古〕昨天夜裡

6 battlements ['bætlmənts] (n.) (pl.) a low wall around the top of a castle, that has spaces to shoot guns or arrows through 設有槍砲眼的城垛

7 wont [wɑ:nt] (a.) be accustomed 習慣於

8 chill [tʃɪl] (a.) unpleasantly cold 寒冷的

9 beckon ['bekən] (v.) to move your hand or head in a way that tells someone to come nearer 招手示意

Hamlet and his father's ghost

004 The wicked Claudius had indeed killed his good brother the King, by dropping poison into his ear as he slept in his orchard[10] in the afternoon.

"And you," said the ghost, "must avenge[11] this cruel murder—on my wicked brother. But do nothing against the Queen—for I have loved her, and she is your mother. Remember me."

Then seeing the morning approach[12], the ghost vanished[13].

10 orchard ['ɔːrtʃərd] (n.) area of fruit or nut trees 果樹園
11 avenge [ə'vendʒ] (v.) to inflict injury in return for 報仇
12 approach [ə'proutʃ] (v.) come near 接近
13 vanish ['vænɪʃ] (v.) to disappear suddenly 突然不見

005 "Now," said Hamlet, "there is nothing left but revenge[14]. Remember thee[15]—I will remember nothing else—books, pleasure, youth—let all go—and your commands[16] alone live on my brain."

So when his friends came back he made them swear to keep the secret of the ghost, and then went in from the battlements, now gray with mingled[17] dawn and moonlight, to think how he might best avenge his murdered father.

The shock of seeing and hearing his father's ghost made him feel almost mad, and for fear that his uncle might notice that he was not himself, he determined to hide his mad longing for revenge under a pretended madness in other matters.

And when he met Ophelia, who loved him—and to whom he had given gifts, and letters, and many loving words—he behaved so wildly to her, that she could not but think him mad.

Hamlet, Ophelia, Queen and Claudius

006 For she loved him so that she could not believe he would be as cruel as this, unless he were quite mad. So she told her father, and showed him a pretty letter from Hamlet. And in the letter was much folly[18], and this pretty verse[19]—

Hamlet and Ophelia

Doubt that the stars are
fire;
Doubt that the sun doth
move;
Doubt truth to be a liar;
But never doubt I love.

And from that time everyone believed that the cause of Hamlet's supposed madness was love.

14 revenge [rɪ'vendʒ] (n.) harm done to someone as a punishment for harm that they have done to someone else 報仇
15 thee [ði:] (n.) objective case of thou〔古〕(thou 的受格) 你
16 command [kə'mænd] (n.) an order given by somebody in authority 命令
17 mingle ['mɪŋgəl] (v.) to mix or combine 混合
18 folly ['fɑ:li] (n.) stupidity, or a stupid action, idea 愚蠢
19 verse [vɜːrs] (n.) writing which is arranged in short lines with a regular rhythm; poetry 韻文

(007) Poor Hamlet was very unhappy. He longed to obey his father's ghost—and yet he was too gentle and kindly to wish to kill another man, even his father's murderer. And sometimes he wondered whether, after all, the ghost spoke truly.

Just at this time some actors came to the Court.

Just at this time some actors came to the Court, and Hamlet ordered them to perform a certain play before the King and Queen. Now, this play was the story of a man who had been murdered in his garden by a near relation, who afterwards married the dead man's wife.

You may imagine the feelings of the wicked King, as he sat on his throne, with the Queen beside him and all his Court around, and saw, acted on the stage, the very wickedness that he had himself done.

And when, in the play, the wicked relation poured poison into the ear of the sleeping man, the wicked Claudius suddenly rose, and staggered[20] from the room—the Queen and others following.

008 Then said Hamlet to his friends—"Now I am sure the ghost spoke true. For if Claudius had not done this murder, he could not have been so distressed[21] to see it in a play."

In the play, the wicked relation poured poison into the ear of the sleeping man.

Now the Queen sent for Hamlet, by the King's desire, to scold him for his conduct[22] during the play, and for other matters; and Claudius, wishing to know exactly what happened, told old Polonius to hide himself behind the hangings[23] in the Queen's room.

And as they talked, the Queen got frightened at Hamlet's rough, strange words, and cried for help, and Polonius behind the curtain cried out too.

20 stagger ['stægər] (v.) to walk or move with a lack of balance as if you are going to fall 搖搖晃晃

21 distressed [dɪ'strest] (a.) very upset 痛苦的

22 conduct [kən'dʌkt] (n.) the way someone behaves 行為

23 hangings ['hæŋɪŋz] (n.) (pl.) a large piece of cloth, often with a picture on it, that is hung on a wall for decoration 簾子

009 Hamlet, thinking it was the King who was hidden there, thrust with his sword at the hangings, and killed, not the King, but poor old Polonius.

Hamlet thought it was the King who was hidden there.

So now Hamlet had offended his uncle and his mother, and by bad hap[24] killed his true love's father.

"Oh! what a rash[25] and bloody deed is this," cried the Queen.

And Hamlet answered bitterly, "Almost as bad as to kill a king, and marry his brother."

Then Hamlet told the Queen plainly all his thoughts and how he knew of the murder, and begged her, at least, to have no more friendship or kindness of the base[26] Claudius, who had killed the good King.

And as they spoke the King's ghost again appeared before Hamlet, but the Queen could not see it. So when the ghost had gone, they parted.

24 hap [hæp] (n.) chance 機會
25 rash [ræʃ] (a.) careless or unwise, without thought for what might happen or result 行為魯莽的
26 base [beɪs] (a.) not honorable and lacking in morals 卑鄙的

010 When the Queen told Claudius what had passed, and how Polonius was dead, he said, "This shows plainly that Hamlet is mad, and since he has killed the Chancellor, it is for his own safety that we must carry out our plan, and send him away to England."

So Hamlet was sent, under charge[27] of two courtiers[28] who served the King, and these bore letters to the English Court, requiring that Hamlet should be put to death.

But Hamlet had the good sense to get at these letters, and put in others instead, with the names of the two courtiers who were so ready to betray him.

Then, as the vessel went to England, Hamlet escaped on board a pirate ship, and the two wicked courtiers left him to his fate, and went on to meet theirs.

Hamlet escaped on board a pirate ship.

27 charge [tʃɑːrdʒ] (n.) the responsibility or duty of looking after somebody or something 看管

28 courtier [ˈkɔːrtɪr] (n.) one who is attached to a royal court 朝臣

011 Hamlet hurried home, but in the meantime a dreadful thing had happened. Poor pretty Ophelia, having lost her lover and her father, lost her wits[29] too, and went in sad madness about the Court, with straws, and weeds, and flowers in her hair, singing strange scraps[30] of songs, and talking poor, foolish, pretty talk with no heart of meaning to it.

Ophelia has lost her wits.

And one day, coming to a stream where willows[31] grew, she tried to bang a flowery garland[32] on a willow, and fell into the water with all her flowers, and so died.

29 wits [wɪts] (n.) (pl.) the basic human power of intelligent thought and perception 理智

30 scrap [skræp] (n.) a small irregular piece of something or a small amount of information 片段

31 willow ['wɪloʊ] (n.) a tree that grows near water and has long, thin branches that hang down 柳樹

32 garland ['gɑːrlənd] (n.) a circle made of flowers and leaves worn around the neck or head as a decoration 花環

Ophelia put straws, weeds, and flowers in her hair.

Ophelia

012 And Hamlet had loved her, though his plan of seeming madness had made him hide it; and when he came back, he found the King and Queen, and the Court, weeping at the funeral of his dear love and lady.

Ophelia and Laertes

Ophelia's brother, Laertes, had also just come to Court to ask justice for the death of his father, old Polonius; and now, wild with grief, he leaped into his sister's grave, to clasp[33] her in his arms once more.

"I loved her more than forty thousand brothers," cried Hamlet, and leapt into the grave after him, and they fought till they were parted.

Afterwards Hamlet begged Laertes to forgive him. "I could not bear," he said, "that any, even a brother, should seem to love her more than I."

But the wicked Claudius would not let them be friends. He told Laertes how Hamlet had killed old Polonius, and between them they made a plot to slay Hamlet by treachery[34].

33 clasp [klæsp] (v.) to embrace 緊抱

34 treachery [ˈtretʃəri] (n.) an act of betrayal or deceit 背叛

Ophelia

013 Laertes challenged him to a fencing match, and all the Court were present.

Hamlet had the blunt[35] foil[36] always used in fencing, but Laertes had prepared for himself a sword, sharp, and tipped with poison.

And the wicked King had made ready a bowl of poisoned wine, which he meant to give poor Hamlet when he should grow warm with the sword play, and should call for drink.

So Laertes and Hamlet fought, and Laertes, after some fencing, gave Hamlet a sharp sword thrust.

Hamlet, angry at this treachery—for they had been fencing, not as men fight, but as they play—closed with Laertes in a struggle; both dropped their swords, and when they picked them up again, Hamlet, without noticing it, had exchanged his own blunt sword for Laertes' sharp and poisoned one.

And with one thrust of it he pierced Laertes, who fell dead by his own treachery.

At this moment the Queen cried out, "The drink, the drink! Oh, my dear Hamlet! I am poisoned!"

She had drunk of the poisoned bowl the King had prepared for Hamlet, and the King saw the Queen, whom, wicked as he was, he really loved, fall dead by his means[37].

35 blunt [blʌnt] (a.) not sharp or pointed 鈍的

36 foil [fɔɪl] (n.) metal in a very thin flexible sheet 金屬薄片

37 means [miːnz] (n.) (pl.) a method of doing something 手段

014 Then Ophelia being dead, and Polonius, and the Queen, and Laertes, and the two courtiers who had been sent to England, Hamlet at last found courage to do the ghost's bidding and avenge his father's murder—which, if he had braced[38] up his heart to do long before, all these lives had been spared, and none had suffered but the wicked King, who well deserved to die.

Hamlet, his heart at last being great enough to do the deed he ought, turned the poisoned sword on the false King.

"Then—venom[39]—do thy work!" he cried, and the King died. So Hamlet in the end kept the promise he had made his father. And all being now accomplished, he himself died.

And those who stood by saw him die, with prayers and tears, for his friends and his people loved him with their whole hearts. Thus ends the tragic tale of Hamlet, Prince of Denmark.

38 brace [breɪs] (v.) to rouse oneself to greater effort 振奮
39 venom ['venəm] (n.) liquid poison that some snakes, insects etc produce when they bite or sting you 毒液

2 A Midsummer Night's Dream

015 Hermia and Lysander were lovers; but Hermia's father wished her to marry another man, named Demetrius.

Now, in Athens, where they lived, there was a wicked[1] law, by which any girl who refused to marry according to her father's wishes, might be put to death[2].

Hermia's father was so angry with her for refusing to do as he wished, that he actually brought her before the Duke[3] of Athens to ask that she might be killed, if she still refused to obey[4] him.

The Duke gave her four days to think about it, and, at the end of that time, if she still refused to marry Demetrius, she would have to die.

016 Lysander of course was nearly mad with grief, and the best thing to do seemed to him for Hermia to run away to his aunt's house at a place beyond the reach of that cruel law; and there he would come to her and marry her. But before she started, she told her friend, Helena, what she was going to do.

Hermia and Helena

Helena had been Demetrius' sweetheart long before his marriage with Hermia had been thought of, and being very silly, like all jealous people, she could not see that it was not poor Hermia's fault that Demetrius wished to marry her instead of his own lady, Helena.

She knew that if she told Demetrius that Hermia was going, as she was, to the wood outside Athens, he would follow her, "and I can follow him, and at least I shall see him," she said to herself.

1 wicked ['wɪkɪd] (a.) morally wrong and bad 惡劣的
2 put to death: to kill; execute 處死
3 duke [dju:k] (n.) a nobleman of high rank 公爵
4 obey [oʊ'beɪ] (v.) do as told 聽從

So she went to him, and betrayed[5] her friend's secret.

Now this wood where Lysander was to meet Hermia, and where the other two had decided to follow them, was full of fairies, as most woods are, if one only had the eyes to see them, and in this wood on this night were the King and Queen of the fairies, Oberon and Titania.

Now fairies are very wise people, but now and then they can be quite as foolish as mortal[6] folk[7]. Oberon and Titania, who might have been as happy as the days were long, had thrown away all their joy in a foolish quarrel.

They never met without saying disagreeable things to each other, and scolded each other so dreadfully that all their little fairy followers, for fear, would creep into acorn[8] cups and hide them there.

So, instead of keeping one happy Court[9] and dancing all night through in the moonlight as is fairies' use, the King with his attendants wandered through one part of the wood, while the Queen with hers kept state in another.

5 betray [bɪ'treɪ] (v.) reveal something 洩露
6 mortal ['mɔːrtəl] (a.) having to die 會死的
7 folk [fouk] (n.) people in general 人
8 acorn ['eɪkɔːrn] (n.) fruit of oak 橡實

9 court [kɔːrt] (n.) the official home of a queen or king 宮廷

The Quarrel of Oberon and Titania

018 And the cause of all this trouble was a little Indian boy whom Titania had taken to be one of her followers. Oberon wanted the child to follow him and be one of his fairy knights[10]; but the Queen would not give him up.

On this night, in a mossy[11] moonlit glade[12], the King and Queen of the fairies met.

"Ill met by moonlight, proud Titania," said the King.

"What! jealous, Oberon?" answered the Queen. "You spoil everything with your quarreling. Come, fairies, let us leave him. I am not friends with him now."

"It rests with you to make up the quarrel," said the King. "Give me that little Indian boy, and I will again be your humble servant and suitor[13]."

10 knight [naɪt] (n.) a man with a high rank in the past who was trained to fight while riding a horse 騎士
11 mossy ['mɔːsi] (a.) similar to moss, e.g. in texture or color 似苔的
12 glade [gleɪd] (n.) an open space or passage in a wood or forest 林間空地
13 suitor ['suːtər] (n.) man wooing woman 追求者

019 "Set your mind at rest[14]," said the Queen. "Your whole fairy kingdom buys not that boy from me. Come, fairies."

And she and her train[15] rode off down the moonbeams.

"Well, go your ways," said Oberon. "But I'll be even with you before you leave this wood."

Titania

Then Oberon called his favorite fairy, Puck. Puck was the spirit[16] of mischief.

He used to slip into the dairies[17] and take the cream away, and get into the churn[18] so that the butter would not come, and turn the beer sour, and lead people out of their way on dark nights and then laugh at them, and tumble[19] people's stools[20] from under them when they were going to sit down, and upset their hot ale[21] over their chins when they were going to drink.

14 set your mind at rest: to stop someone from worrying about something 別操心
15 train [treɪn] (n.) a long moving line of people or animals 隊列
16 spirit ['spɪrɪt] (n.) a supernatural being 精靈
17 dairy ['deri] (n.) farm for milk production 製酪場
18 churn [tʃɜːrn] (n.) a container used for shaking milk in order to make it into butter 攪乳器
19 tumble ['tʌmbəl] (v.) to cause to fall 使跌倒
20 stool ['stuːl] (n.) a seat usually without back or arms 凳子
21 ale [eɪl] (n.) any of various types of beer 麥芽酒

"Now," said Oberon to this little sprite, "fetch me the flower called Love-in-idleness[22]. The juice of that little purple flower laid on the eyes of those who sleep will make them, when they wake, to love the first thing they see. I will put some of the juice of that flower on my Titania's eyes, and when she wakes she will love the first thing she sees, were it lion, bear, or wolf, or bull, or meddling[23] monkey, or a busy ape[24]."

Puck

While Puck was gone, Demetrius passed through the glade followed by poor Helena, and still she told him how she loved him and reminded him of all his promises, and still he told her that he did not and could not love her, and that his promises were nothing.

22 love-in-idleness (n.) a common and long cultivated European herb〔古〕三色堇

23 meddle ['medl] (v.) interfere in somebody else's concerns 管閒事

24 ape [eɪp] (n.) a tailless monkey resembling man 人猿

021 Oberon was sorry for poor Helena, and when Puck returned with the flower, he bade him follow Demetrius and put some of the juice on his eyes, so that he might love Helena when he woke and looked on her, as much as she loved him.

So Puck set off[25]., and wandering through the wood found, not Demetrius, but Lysander, on whose eyes he put the juice; but when Lysander woke, he saw not his own Hermia, but Helena, who was walking through the wood looking for the cruel Demetrius; and directly lie saw her he loved her and left his own lady, under the spell[26]. of the purple flower.

Puck and Lysander

When Hermia woke she found Lysander gone, and wandered about the wood trying to find him. Puck went back and told Oberon what lie had done, and Oberon soon found that he had made a mistake, and set about[27]. looking for Demetrius, and having found him, put some of the juice on his eyes.

25 set off: set out; start off 出發

26 spell [spel] (n.) the influence that a spell has over somebody or something 咒語；魔力

27 set about: begin to deal with 開始做

022 And the first thing Demetrius saw when he woke was also Helena. So now Demetrius and Lysander were both following her through the wood, and it was Hermia's turn to follow her lover as Helena had done before.

The end of it was that Helena and Hermia began to quarrel, and Demetrius and Lysander went off to fight. Oberon was very sorry to see his kind scheme to help these lovers turn out so badly. So he said to Puck—

"These two young men are going to fight. You must overhang[28] the night with drooping[29] fog, and lead them so astray[30], that one will never find the other. When they are tired out, they will fall asleep. Then drop this other herb on Lysander's eyes. That will give him his old sight and his old love. Then each man will have the lady who loves him, and they will all think that this has been only a Midsummer Night's Dream. Then when this is done, all will be well with them."

So Puck went and did as he was told, and when the two had fallen asleep without meeting each other, Puck poured the juice on Lysander's eyes, and said:

28 overhang [ˌoʊvərˈhæŋ] (v.) to hang over 懸於……之上
29 droop [druːp] (v.) to hang down 低垂
30 astray [əˈstreɪ] (a.) away from the correct path or correct way of doing something 迷路的

(023) *When thou[31] wakest,*
Thou takest
True delight
In the sight
Of thy former lady's eye:
Jack shall have Jill[32];
Nought[33] shall go ill."

Meanwhile Oberon found Titania asleep on a bank where grew wild thyme[34], oxlips[35], and violets, and woodbine[36], musk-roses[37] and eglantine[38]. There Titania always slept a part of the night, wrapped in the enameled[39] skin of a snake.

Oberon stooped[40] over her and laid the juice on her eyes, saying:—

What thou seest when thou wake,
Do it for thy[41] true love take.

Now, it happened that when Titania woke the first thing she saw was a stupid clown, one of a party of players who had come out into the wood to rehearse[42] their play. This clown had met with Puck, who had clapped an ass's head on his shoulders so that it looked as if it grew there.

31 thou [ðaʊ] (pron.) nominative singular of the personal pronoun of the second person〔古〕(第二人稱單數主格)你
32 Jill [dʒɪl] (n.) a young woman 情人

024 Directly Titania woke and saw this dreadful monster, she said, "What angel is this? Are you as wise as you are beautiful?"

"What angel is this?"

"If I am wise enough to find my way out of this wood, that's enough for me," said the foolish clown.

"Do not desire to go out of the wood," said Titania. The spell of the love-juice was on her, and to her the clown seemed the most beautiful and delightful creature on all the earth.

"I love you," she went on. "Come with me, and I will give you fairies to attend on you."

33 nought [nɑːt] (n.) nothing; zero 沒有什麼
34 thyme [taɪm] (n.) aromatic bush 百里香
35 oxlip ['ɑːkslɪp] (n.) woodland plant with yellow flower 一種櫻草
36 woodbine ['wʊdbaɪn] (n.) climbing plant with fragrant flowers 一種忍冬屬植物

37 musk-rose (n.) musk-scented rose 麝香薔薇
38 eglantine (n.) ['egləntaɪn] rose with single flowers 多花薔薇
39 enameled [ɪ'næməld] (a.) something with enamel coating 琺瑯質的
40 stoop [stuːp] (v.) to bend your body forward and down 屈身
41 thy [ðaɪ] (pron.) the singular possessive case of the personal pronoun thou〔古〕你的（thou 的所有格）
42 rehearse [rɪ'hɜːrs] (v.) to practice a play, a piece of music, etc. 排練

025 So she called four fairies, whose names were Peaseblossom, Cobweb, Moth, and Mustardseed.

"You must attend this gentleman," said the Queen. "Feed him with apricots[43] and dewberries[44], purple grapes, green figs[45], and mulberries[46]. Steal honey-bags for him from the bumblebees[47], and with the wings of painted butterflies fan the moonbeams from his sleeping eyes."

"I will," said one of the fairies, and all the others said, "I will."

"Now, sit down with me."

026 "Now, sit down with me," said the Queen to the clown, "and let me stroke[48] your dear cheeks, and stick musk-roses in your smooth, sleek[49] head, and kiss your fair large ears, my gentle joy."

"Where's Peaseblossom?" asked the clown with the ass's head. He did not care much about the Queen's affection, but he was very proud of having fairies to wait on him.

"Scratch my head, Peaseblossom," said the clown. "Where's Cobweb?"

"Ready," said Cobweb.

"Ready," said Peaseblossom.

"Kill me," said the clown, "the red bumblebee on the top of the thistle[50] yonder[51], and bring me the honey-bag. "Where's Mustardseed?"

43 apricot ['æprɪkɑːt] (n.) a small round soft fruit with a pale orange furry skin 杏仁

44 dewberry ['duːberi] (n.) an edible bluish black blackberry 懸鉤子屬植物之果實

45 fig [fɪg] (n.) a pear-shaped fruit with sweet flesh and many seeds 無花果

46 mulberry ['mʌlberi] (n.) a small sweet fruit resembling a berry 桑椹

47 bumblebee ['bʌmblbiː] (n.) a large hairy bee 大黃蜂

48 stroke [strouk] (v.) to rub gently with the hand 用手輕撫

49 sleek [sliːk] (a.) smooth; glossy 光滑的

50 thistle ['θɪsəl] (n.) a plant with prickly stems and leaves 薊

51 yonder ['jɑːndər] (adv.) in or to that place over there 那邊的

027 "Ready," said Mustardseed.

"Oh, I want nothing," said the clown. "Only just help Cobweb to scratch. I must go to the barber's, for methinks[52] I am marvelous hairy about the face."

" I must go to the barber's."

"Would you like anything to eat?" said the fairy Queen. "I should like some good dry oats," said the clown—for his donkey's head made him desire donkey's food—"and some hay to follow."

"Shall some of my fairies fetch you new nuts from the squirrel's house?" asked the Queen.

"I'd rather have a handful or two of good dried peas," said the clown. "But please don't let any of your people disturb me; I am going to sleep."

Then said the Queen, "And I will wind thee[53] in my arms."

And so when Oberon came along he found his beautiful Queen lavishing[54] kisses and endearments[55] on a clown with a donkey's head.

028 And before he released her from the enchantment[56], he persuaded her to give him the little Indian boy he so much desired to have.

Then he took pity on her, and threw some juice of the disenchanting[57] flower on her pretty eyes; and then in a moment she saw plainly the donkey-headed clown she had been loving, and knew how foolish she had been.

Oberon took off the ass's head from the clown, and left him to finish his sleep with his own silly head lying on the thyme and violets.

Oberon took pity on Titania.

52 methinks [mɪ'θɪŋks] (v.) (old use) I think〔古〕據我看來
53 thee [ði:] (pron.) objective case of thou〔古〕(thou 的受格) 你
54 lavish ['lævɪʃ] (v.) to expend or bestow liberally 濫施
55 endearment [ɪn'dɪrmənt] (n.) an expression of affection 愛意
56 enchantment [ɪn'tʃæntmənt] (n.) a change caused by magic 魔力
57 disenchant [ˌdɪsɪn'tʃænt] (v.) free somebody from spell 使醒悟

The Reconciliation of Oberon and Titania

029 Thus all was made plain and straight again. Oberon and Titania loved each other more than ever. Demetrius thought of no one but Helena, and Helena had never had any thought of anyone but Demetrius.

As for Hermia and Lysander, they were as loving a couple as you could meet in a day's march, even through a fairy wood.

So the four mortal lovers went back to Athens and were married; and the fairy King and Queen live happily together in that very wood at this very day.

3 King Lear

030 King Lear was old and tired. He was aweary[1] of the business of his kingdom, and wished only to end his days quietly near his three daughters.

King Lear wished only to end his days quietly near his three daughters.

Two of his daughters were married to the Dukes of Albany and Cornwall; and the Duke of Burgundy and the King of France were both suitors for the hand of Cordelia, his youngest daughter.

Lear called his three daughters together, and told them that he proposed to divide his kingdom between them.

"But first," said he, "I should like to know much you love me."

Goneril, who was really a very wicked woman, and did not love her father at all, said she loved him more than words could say; she loved him dearer than eyesight, space or liberty, more than life, grace, health, beauty, and honor.

"I love you as much as my sister and more," professed Regan, "since I care for nothing but my father's love."

031 Lear was very much pleased with Regan's professions[2], and turned to his youngest daughter, Cordelia.

"Now, our joy, though last not least," he said, "the best part of my kingdom have I kept for you. What can you say?"

"Nothing, my lord," answered Cordelia.

"Nothing can come of nothing. Speak again," said the King.

And Cordelia answered, "I love your Majesty[3] according to my duty—no more, no less."

And this she said, because she was disgusted with the way in which her sisters professed love, when really they had not even a right sense of duty to their old father.

"I love your Majesty according to my duty—no more, no less."

1 aweary [ə'wɪri] (a.) feeling very tired (archaic or literary) 疲倦的
2 profession [prə'feʃən] (n.) a statement of your belief, opinion, or feeling 表白
3 Majesty ['mædʒəsti] (n.) title applied to a reigning sovereign (preceded by his, her, or your)（大寫）陛下

(032) "I am your daughter," she went on, "and you have brought me up and loved me, and I return you those duties back as are right and fit, obey you, love you, and most honor you."

"Go! Be forever a stranger to my heart and me."

Lear, who loved Cordelia best, had wished her to make more extravagant[4] professions of love than her sisters.

"Go," he said, "be forever a stranger to my heart and me."

The Earl[5] of Kent, one of Lear's favorite courtiers[6] and captains, tried to say a word for Cordelia's sake, but Lear would not listen.

He divided the kingdom between Goneril and Regan, and told them that he should only keep a hundred knights at arms, and would live with his daughters by turns.

When the Duke of Burgundy knew that Cordelia would have no share of the kingdom, he gave up his courtship of her. But the King of France was wiser, and said, "Thy dowerless[7] daughter, King, is Queen of us—of ours, and our fair France."

Cordelia's Farewell

033 "Take her, take her," said the King; "for I will never see that face of hers again."

So Cordelia became Queen of France, and the Earl of Kent, for having ventured[8] to take her part, was banished from the kingdom.

The King now went to stay with his daughter Goneril, who had got everything from her father that he had to give, and now began to grudge[9] even the hundred knights that he had reserved for himself.

4 extravagant [ɪk'strævəgənt] (a.) doing or using something too much 過度的
5 earl [ɜːrl] (n.) a British nobleman next below a marquis 伯爵
6 courtier ['kɔːrtɪr] (n.) companion of a queen, king or other ruler in their official home 朝臣
7 dowerless ['daʊərləs] (a.) lacking a dowry 沒有嫁妝的
8 venture ['ventʃər] (v.) to assume the risk of 敢於
9 grudge [grʌdʒ] (v.) to do or give something very unwillingly 不情願做

(034) She was harsh and undutiful[10] to him, and her servants either refused to obey his orders or pretended that they did not hear them.

Now the Earl of Kent, when he was banished, made as though he would go into another country, but instead he came back in the disguise[11] of a servingman and took service with the King.

The King had now two friends—the Earl of Kent, whom he only knew as his servant, and his Fool[12], who was faithful to him.

Goneril told her father plainly that his knights only served to fill her Court with riot[13] and feasting; and so she begged him only to keep a few old men about him such as himself.

"My train[14] are men who know all parts of duty," said Lear. "Goneril, I will not trouble you further—yet I have left another daughter."

King's Fool

10 undutiful [ʌn'du:tɪfəl] (a.) lacking due respect or dutifulness 不孝的

11 disguise [dɪs'gaɪz] (n.) something done to prevent recognition 偽裝

12 fool [fu:l] (n.) a court jester 弄臣

13 riot ['raɪət] (n.) a very amusing or entertaining occasion 狂歡

14 train [treɪn] (n.) a group of servants or officers following an important person 隨從

035 And his horses being saddled[15], he set out with his followers for the castle of Regan. But she, who had formerly outdone[16] her sister in professions of attachment[17] to the King, now seemed to outdo her in undutiful conduct, saying that fifty knights were too many to wait on him, and Goneril (who had hurried thither[18] to prevent Regan showing any kindness to the old King) said five were too many, since her servants could wait on him.

Then when Lear saw that what they really wanted was to drive him away, he left them.

15 saddle ['sædəl] (v.) to put a saddle on a horse 裝馬鞍

16 outdo [aut'du:] (v.) to surpass 超過

17 attachment [ə'tætʃmənt] (n.) a feeling that you like or love someone or something 情感

18 thither ['θɪðər] (ad.) to that place 到那邊

It was a wild and stormy night,
and with no companion
but the poor Fool.

036 It was a wild and stormy night, and he wandered about the heath[19] half mad with misery, and with no companion but the poor Fool. But presently his servant, the good Earl of Kent, met him, and at last persuaded him to lie down in a wretched[20] little hovel[21].

At daybreak the Earl of Kent removed his royal master to Dover, and hurried to the Court of France to tell Cordelia what had happened.

Cordelia's husband gave her an army and with it she landed at Dover. Here she found poor King Lear, wandering about the fields, wearing a crown of nettles[22] and weeds.

They brought him back and fed and clothed him, and Cordelia came to him and kissed him.

"You must bear with me," said Lear; "forget and forgive. I am old and foolish."

And now he knew at last which of his children it was that had loved him best.

037 And now he knew at last which of his children it was that had loved him best, and who was worthy of his love.

Goneril and Regan joined their armies to fight Cordelia's army, and were successful; and Cordelia and her father were thrown into prison.

Then Goneril's husband, the Duke of Albany, who was a good man, and had not known how wicked his wife was, heard the truth of the whole story.

19 heath [hiːθ] (n.) an area of open land where grass, bushes, and other small plants grow 荒原

20 wretched ['retʃɪd] (a.) extremely bad or unpleasant 破落的

21 hovel ['hɑːvəl] (n.) a poor cottage, hut, or cabin 茅舍

22 nettle ['netl] (n.) a wild plant with heart-shaped leaves that are covered in hairs which sting 蕁麻

(038) And when Goneril found that her husband knew her for the wicked woman she was, she killed herself, having a little time before given a deadly poison to her sister, Regan, out of a spirit of jealousy.

But they had arranged that Cordelia should be hanged in prison, and though the Duke of Albany sent messengers at once, it was too late.

The old King came staggering[23] into the tent of the Duke of Albany, carrying the body of his dear daughter Cordelia, in his arms.

And soon after, with words of love for her upon his lips, he fell with her still in his arms, and died.

23 stagger ['stægər] (v.) to walk or move unsteadily, almost falling over 蹣跚

4 The Taming of the Shrew

039 There lived in Padua a gentleman named Baptista, who had two fair daughters. The eldest, Katharine, was so very cross[1] and ill-tempered, and unmannerly[2], that no one ever dreamed of marrying her, while her sister, Bianca, was so sweet and pretty, and pleasant-spoken, that more than one suitor asked her father for her hand.

Katharine was very cross and ill-tempered, and unmannerly.

But Baptista said the elder daughter must marry first. So Bianca's suitors decided among themselves to try and get some one to marry Katharine—and then the father could at least be got to listen to their suit for Bianca.

A gentleman from Verona, named Petruchio, was the one they thought of, and, half in jest[3], they asked him if he would marry Katharine, the disagreeable scold[4].

Much to their surprise he said yes, that was just the sort of wife for him, and if Katharine were handsome and rich, he himself would undertake soon to make her good-tempered.

Petruchio began by asking Baptista's permission to
pay court to his gentle daughter Katharine.

040 Petruchio began by asking Baptista's permission to pay court to[5] his gentle daughter Katharine—and Baptista was obliged to[6] own[7] that she was anything but gentle.

And just then her music master rushed in, complaining that the naughty girl had broken her lute[8] over his head, because he told her she was not playing correctly.

"Never mind," said Petruchio, "I love her better than ever, and long to have some chat with her."

1 cross [krɑ:s] (a.) annoyed or angry 脾氣壞的
2 unmannerly [ʌn'mænərli] (ad.) socially incorrect in behavior 無禮貌地
3 jest [dʒest] (n.) something you say that is intended to be funny, not serious 俏皮話
4 scold [skoʊld] (n.) person who rebukes others 愛罵人的人
5 pay court to: to try to win somebody's love 追求
6 be obliged to: feel that you have a duty to do something 使不得不
7 own [oʊn] (v.) to admit that something is true 承認
8 lute [lu:t] (n.) a musical instrument like a guitar with a round body, played with the fingers or a plectrum 魯特琴

041 When Katharine came, he said, "Good-morrow, Kate—for that, I hear, is your name."

"You've only heard half," said Katharine, rudely.

"Oh, no," said Petruchio, "they call you plain Kate, and bonny[9] Kate, and sometimes Kate the shrew[10], and so, hearing your mildness praised in every town, and your beauty too, I ask you for my wife."

"Your wife!" cried Kate. "Never!" She said some extremely disagreeable things to him, and, I am sorry to say, ended by boxing his ears.

"If you do that again, I'll cuff[11] you," he said quietly; and still protested, with many compliments, that he would marry none but her.

When Baptista came back, he asked at once—"How speed you with my daughter?"

"How should I speed but well," replied Petruchio—"how, but well?"

"If you do that again, I'll cuff you."

(042) "How now, daughter Katharine?" the father went on.

"I don't think," said Katharine, angrily, "you are acting a father's part in wishing me to marry this madcap[12] ruffian[13]."

"Ah!" said Petruchio, "you and all the world would talk amiss[14] of her. You should see how kind she is to me when we are alone. In short, I will go off to Venice to buy fine things for our wedding—for—kiss me, Kate! we will be married on Sunday."

With that, Katharine flounced[15] out of the room by one door in a violent temper, and he, laughing, went out by the other.

9 bonny ['bɑːni] (a.) attractively lively and graceful 健康活潑的

10 shrew [ʃruː] (n.) an unpleasant woman who is easily annoyed and who argues a lot 悍婦

11 cuff [kʌf] (v.) to hit someone lightly, especially in a friendly way 摑；打

12 madcap ['mædkæp] (a.) acting or behaving without caring or stopping to think about possible consequences 魯莽的

13 ruffian ['rʌfiən] (n.) a violent man, involved in crime 惡棍

14 amiss [ə'mɪs] (ad.) incorrectly or inappropriately 錯誤地

15 flounce [flaʊns] (v.) to walk in a quick determined way without looking at people because you are angry 斷然離去

Katharine did indeed marry Petruchio on Sunday.

043 But whether she fell in love with Petruchio, or whether she was only glad to meet a man who was not afraid of her, or whether she was flattered[16] that, in spite of her rough words and spiteful[17] usage[18], he still desired her for his wife—she did indeed marry him on Sunday, as he had sworn she should.

To vex[19] and humble Katharine's naughty, proud spirit, he was late at the wedding, and when he came, came wearing such shabby[20] clothes that she was ashamed to be seen with him. His servant was dressed in the same shabby way, and the horses they rode were the sport[21] of everyone they passed.

16 flatter ['flætər] (v.) to praise someone in order to please them or get something from them 奉承
17 spiteful ['spaɪtfəl] (a.) full of ill will 惡意的
18 usage ['ju:sɪdʒ] (n.) the way something is treated or used 對待
19 vex [veks] (v.) to cause somebody anxiety or distress 使挫敗
20 shabby ['ʃæbi] (a.) threadbare or worn, as clothes 破爛的
21 sport [spɔ:rt] (n.) a subject for laughter 笑柄

Petruchio behaved all through his wedding
in so mad and dreadful a manner.

044 And, after the marriage, when should have been the wedding breakfast, Petruchio carried his wife away, not allowing her to eat or drink—saying that she was his now, and he could do as he liked with her.

And his manner was so violent, and he behaved all through his wedding in so mad and dreadful a manner, that Katharine trembled and went with him.

045 He mounted her on a stumbling[22], lean, old horse, and they journeyed by rough muddy ways to Petruchio's house, he scolding and snarling[23] all the way.

She was terribly tired when she reached her new home, but Petruchio was determined that she should neither eat nor sleep that night, for he had made up his mind to teach his bad-tempered wife a lesson she would never forget.

At last Katharine went supperless to bed.

So he welcomed her kindly to his house, but when supper was served he found fault with[24] everything—the meat was burnt, he said, and ill-served, and he loved her far too much to let her eat anything but the best. At last Katharine, tired out with her journey, went supperless to bed.

22 stumble ['stʌmbəl] (v.) to walk in an unsteady way and often almost fall 踉蹌

23 snarl [snɑːrl] (v.) to speak or say something in a nasty, angry way 咆哮

24 to find fault with: to criticize or complain of 挑剔；抱怨

046 Then her husband, still telling her how he loved her, and how anxious he was that she should sleep well, pulled her bed to pieces, throwing the pillows and bedclothes on the floor, so that she could not go to bed at all, and still kept growling[25] and scolding at the servants so that Kate might see how unbeautiful a thing ill-temper was.

The next day, too, Katharine's food was all found fault with, and caught away before she could touch a mouthful, and she was sick and giddy[26] for want of sleep.

Then she said to one of the servants—"I pray thee go and get me some repast[27]. I care not what."

"What say you to a neat's[28] foot?" said the servant.

Katharine said "Yes," eagerly; but the servant, who was in his master's secret, said he feared it was not good for hasty-tempered people. Would she like tripe[29]?

"Bring it me," said Katharine.

"I don't think that is good for hasty-tempered people," said the servant. "What do you say to a dish of beef and mustard?"

25 growl ['graʊl] (v.) to make a low rough sound, usually in anger 咆哮

26 giddy ['gɪdi] (a.) feeling slightly sick and unable to balance 暈眩的

27 repast [rɪ'pæst] (n.) a meal 飲食

28 neat [niːt] (n.) an animal in the cattle family 牛類動物

29 tripe [traɪp] (n.) the covering of the inside of the stomach of an animal, such as a cow or sheep, used for food 可食用動物的肚子

Katharine was sick and giddy for want of sleep.

047 "I love it," said Kate. "But mustard is too hot."

"Why, then, the beef, and let the mustard go," cried Katharine, who was getting hungrier and hungrier.

"No," said the servant, "you must have the mustard, or you get no beef from me."

Katharine saw servant was making fun of her.

"Then," cried Katharine, losing patience, "let it be both, or one, or anything thou wilt."

"Why, then," said the servant, "the mustard without the beef!"

Then Katharine saw he was making fun of her, and boxed his ears.

Just then Petruchio brought her some food—but she had scarcely begun to satisfy her hunger, before he called for the tailor to bring her new clothes, and the table was cleared, leaving her still hungry.

Katharine was pleased with the pretty new dress and cap that the tailor had made for her, but Petruchio found fault with everything, flung[30] the cap and gown on the floor vowing his dear wife should not wear any such foolish things.

30 fling [flɪŋ] (v.) to throw something or someone suddenly and with a lot of force 扔擲

0048 "I will have them," cried Katharine. "All gentlewomen wear such caps as these—"

"When you are gentle you shall have one too," he answered, "and not till then."

"Come, Kate, let's go to your father's, shabby as we are, for as the sun breaks through the darkest clouds, so honor peereth in the meanest habit. It is about seven o'clock now. We shall easily get there by dinner-time." Petruchio said.

"It's nearly two," said Kate, but civilly[31] enough, for she had grown to see that she could not bully her husband, as she had done her father and her sister; "it's nearly two, and it will be supper-time before we get there."

"It shall be seven," said Petruchio, obstinately[32], "before I start. Why, whatever I say or do, or think, you do nothing but contradict[33]. I won't go today, and before I do go, it shall be what o'clock I say it is."

At last they started for her father's house.

"Look at the moon," said he.

"It's the sun," said Katharine, and indeed it was.

31 civilly ['sɪvəli] (ad.) politely and formally 有禮貌地

32 obstinately ['ɑːbstɪnɪtli] (ad.) unwilling to change or give up something such as an idea or attitude 固執地

33 contradict [ˌkɑːntrə'dɪkt] (v.) to argue against the truth or correctness of somebody's statement or claim 反駁

Bianca and Lucentio's wedding

049 "I say it is the moon. Contradicting again! It shall be sun or moon, or whatever I choose, or I won't take you to your father's."

Then Katharine gave in[34], once and for all[35]. "What you will have it named," she said, "it is, and so it shall be so for Katharine."

So they journeyed on to Baptista's house, and arriving there, they found all folks keeping Bianca's wedding feast, and that of another newly married couple, Hortensio and his wife.

They were made welcome, and sat down to the feast.

After dinner, when the ladies had retired, Baptista joined in a laugh against Petruchio, saying "Now in good sadness, son Petruchio, I fear you have got the veriest[36] shrew of all."

(050) "You are wrong," said Petruchio, "let me prove it to you. Each of us shall send a message to his wife, desiring her to come to him, and the one whose wife comes most readily shall win a wager[37] which we will agree on."

The others said yes readily enough, for each thought his own wife the most dutiful, and each thought he was quite sure to win the wager. They proposed a wager of twenty crowns[38].

"Twenty crowns," said Petruchio, "I'll venture so much on my hawk or hound, but twenty times as much upon my wife."

"A hundred then," cried Lucentio, Bianca's husband.

"Content," cried the others.

Then Lucentio sent a message to the fair Bianca bidding her to come to him. And Baptista said he was certain his daughter would come.

But the servant coming back, said, "Sir, my mistress is busy, and she cannot come."

34 give in: submit or yield to another's wish or opinion 讓步

35 once and for all: finally, permanently, conclusively 永遠地

36 veriest ['verist] (a.) utmost; most complete; superlative of very 完全的（very 的最高級）

37 wager ['weɪdʒər] (n.) an agreement in which you win or lose money according to the result of something such as a race 賭注

38 crown [kraʊn] (n.) a former British coin worth five shillings 克朗（英國 25 便士的貨幣）

051 "There's an answer for you," said Petruchio.

"You may think yourself fortunate if your wife does not send you a worse."

Then Hortensio said, "Go and entreat[39] my wife to come to me at once."

"Oh—if you entreat her," said Petruchio.

"I am afraid," answered Hortensio, sharply, "do what you can, yours will not be entreated."

But now the servant came in, and said, "She says you are playing some jest, she will not come."

"Better and better," cried Petruchio; "now go to your mistress and say I command her to come to me."

They all began to laugh, saying they knew what her answer would be, and that she would not come.

Then suddenly Baptista cried—

"Here comes Katharine!"

And sure enough—there she was.

"What do you wish, sir?" she asked her husband.

"Where are your sister and Hortensio's wife?"

"Talking by the parlor[40] fire."

"Fetch them here."

When she was gone to fetch them, Lucentio said—"Here is a wonder!"

"I wonder what it means," said Hortensio.

39 entreat [ɪn'triːt] (v.) to try very hard to persuade someone to do something 懇求

40 parlor ['pɑːrlər] (n.) a room in a private house used for relaxing, especially one which was kept tidy for the entertaining of guests 起居室；客廳

052 "It means peace," said Petruchio, "and love, and quiet life."

"Well," said Baptista, "you have won the wager, and I will add another twenty thousand crowns to her dowry[41]—another dowry for another daughter—for she is as changed as if she were someone else."

There was nothing ever but love between Katharine and Petruchio.

So Petruchio won his wager, and had in Katharine always a loving wife and true, and now he had broken her proud and angry spirit he loved her well, and there was nothing ever but love between those two. And so they lived happy ever afterwards.

41 dowry ['daʊri] (n.) property and money that a woman gives to her husband when they marry in some societies 嫁妝

5 The Tempest

053 Prospero, the Duke of Milan, was a learned and studious[1] man, who lived among his books, leaving the management of his dukedom to his brother Antonio, in whom indeed he had complete trust.

But that trust was ill-rewarded, for Antonio wanted to wear the duke's crown himself, and, to gain his ends, would have killed his brother but for the love the people bore him.

However, with the help of Prospero's great enemy, Alonso, King of Naples, he managed to get into his hands the dukedom with all its honor, power, and riches.

For they took Prospero to sea, and when they were far away from land, forced him into a little boat with no tackle[2], mast[3], or sail.

In their cruelty and hatred they put his little daughter, Miranda (not yet three years old), into the boat with him, and sailed away, leaving them to their fate.

1 studious ['stu:diəs] (a.) spending a lot of time studying and reading 勤奮好學的

2 tackle ['tækəl] (n.) all the objects needed for a particular activity 裝備

3 mast [mæst] (n.) a tall pole on a boat or ship that supports its sails 桅杆

054 But one among the courtiers with Antonio was true to his rightful master, Prospero. To save the duke from his enemies was impossible, but much could be done to remind him of a subject's[4] love.

So this worthy lord, whose name was Gonzalo, secretly placed in the boat some fresh water, provisions[5], and clothes, and what Prospero valued most of all, some of his precious books.

Prospero and Miranda in the little boat

The boat was cast on an island, and Prospero and his little one landed in safety. Now this island was enchanted, and for years had lain under the spell of a fell[6] witch, Sycorax, who had imprisoned in the trunks of trees all the good spirits she found there.

She died shortly before Prospero was cast on those shores, but the spirits, of whom Ariel was the chief, still remained in their prisons.

4 subject ['sʌbdʒɪkt] (n.) somebody who is ruled by a king, queen, or other authority 臣民

5 provisions [prə'vɪʒənz] (n.) (pl.) the things supplied, esp. a stock of food 糧食

6 fell [fel] (a.) having an extremely vicious character 邪惡的

055 Prospero was a great magician, for he had devoted himself almost entirely to the study of magic during the years in which he allowed his brother to manage the affairs of Milan.

By his art he set free the imprisoned spirits, yet kept them obedient to his will, and they were more truly his subjects than his people in Milan had been.

For he treated them kindly as long as they did his bidding[7], and he exercised his power over them wisely and well. One creature alone he found it necessary to treat with harshness: this was Caliban, the son of the wicked old witch, a hideous[8], deformed[9] monster, horrible to look on, and vicious[10] and brutal[11] in all his habits.

Caliban

7 bidding [ˈbɪdɪŋ] (n.) an order; command 命令
8 hideous [ˈhɪdiəs] (a.) extremely ugly or bad 醜陋的；可怕的
9 deformed [dɪˈfɔːrmd] (a.) something that is deformed has the wrong shape 畸形的
10 vicious [ˈvɪʃəs] (a.) very unkind in a way that is intended to hurt someone's feelings 邪惡的
11 brutal [ˈbruːtəl] (a.) cruel, violent and completely without feelings 粗暴的

(056) When Miranda was grown up into a maiden, sweet and fair to see, it chanced that Antonio and Alonso, with Sebastian, his brother, and Ferdinand, his son, were at sea together with old Gonzalo, and their ship came near Prospero's island.

Miranda

Prospero, knowing they were there, raised by his art a great storm, so that even the sailors on board gave themselves up for lost; and first among them all Prince Ferdinand leaped into the sea, and, as his father thought in his grief, was drowned.

But Ariel brought him safe ashore; and all the rest of the crew, although they were washed overboard, were landed unhurt in different parts of the island, and the good ship herself, which they all thought had been wrecked[12], lay at anchor in the harbor whither Ariel had brought her. Such wonders could Prospero and his spirits perform.

12 wreck [rek] (v.) if a ship is wrecked, it is badly damaged and sinks 遇難

Miranda and the Tempest

057 While yet the tempest was raging[13], Prospero showed his daughter the brave ship laboring in the trough[14] of the sea, and told her that it was filled with living human beings like themselves.

She, in pity of their lives, prayed him who had raised this storm to quell[15] it. Then her father bade her to have no fear, for he intended to save every one of them.

13 rage ['reɪdʒ] (v.) to happen in a strong or violent way 肆虐
14 trough [trɑːf] (n.) a long hollow area in the surface of the ground or the sea bed, or between waves 波谷
15 quell [kwel] (v.) to stop something, especially by using force 平息

(058) Then, for the first time, he told her the story of his life and hers, and that he had caused this storm to rise in order that his enemies, Antonio and Alonso, who were on board, might be delivered into his hands.

When he had made an end of his story he charmed her into sleep, for Ariel was at hand, and he had work for him to do.

Prospero charmed Miranda into sleep, for Ariel was at hand.

Ariel, who longed for his complete freedom, grumbled[16] to be kept in drudgery[17], but on being threateningly reminded of all the sufferings he had undergone when Sycorax ruled in the land, and of the debt of gratitude[18] he owed to the master who had made those sufferings to end, he ceased to complain, and promised faithfully to do whatever Prospero might command.

"Do so," said Prospero, "and in two days I will discharge[19] thee."

16 grumble ['grʌmbəl] (v.) to keep complaining in an unhappy way 發牢騷

17 drudgery ['drʌdʒəri] (n.) hard, disagreeable, or servile work 苦工

18 gratitude ['grætɪtu:d] (n.) the feeling of being grateful 感恩

19 discharge [dɪs'tʃɑ:rdʒ] (v.) to officially allow someone to leave somewhere 釋放

Ferdinand Lured by Ariel

059 And then he bade Ariel take the form of a water nymph[20] and sent him in search of the young prince. And Ariel, invisible to Ferdinand, hovered near him, singing the while—

Come unto these yellow sands
And then take hands:
Court'sied when you have, and kiss'd
(The wild waves whist),
Foot it featly[21] here and there;
And, sweet sprites, the burden bear!

060 And Ferdinand followed the magic singing, as the song changed to a solemn[22] air, and the words brought grief to his heart, and tears to his eyes, for thus they ran—

Full fathom[23] five thy father lies;
Of his bones are coral[24] made.
Those are pearls that were his eyes,
Nothing of him that doth[25] fade,
But doth suffer a sea-change
Into something rich and strange.
Sea-nymphs hourly ring his knell[26].
Hark[27]! now I hear them,— ding dong bell!

20 nymph [nɪmf] (n.) (in ancient Greek and Roman traditional stories) a goddess or spirit in the form of a young woman, living in a tree, river, mountain, etc 山林水澤的仙女

21 featly [ˈfiːtli] (ad.) quick and exact either in movement 靈巧地

22 solemn [ˈsɑːləm] (a.) very serious and not happy 嚴肅的

23 fathom [ˈfæðəm] (n.) a unit for measuring the depth of water, equal to 1.8 meters or 6 feet 噚（測水深的單位）

24 coral [ˈkɑːrəl] (n.) a marine organism that lives in colonies and has an external skeleton 珊瑚

25 doth [dʌθ] (v.) does: archaic or poetic 3rd person singular, present tense of do 古時 do 的第三人稱單數現在式

26 knell [nel] (n.) the sound of a bell being rung slowly because someone has died 喪鐘聲

27 hark [hɑːrk] (v.) to listen (often used in exclamation) 聽！

061 And so singing, Ariel led the spellbound[28] prince into the presence of Prospero and Miranda.

Then, behold[29]! all happened as Prospero desired. For Miranda, who had never, since she could first remember, seen any human being save her father, looked on the youthful prince with reverence[30] in her eyes, and love in her secret heart.

"I might call him," she said, "a thing divine[31], for nothing natural I ever saw so noble!"

And Ferdinand, beholding her beauty with wonder and delight, exclaimed—"Most sure the goddess on whom these airs attend!"

Nor did he attempt to hide the passion which she inspired in him, for scarcely had they exchanged half a dozen sentences, before he vowed to make her his queen if she were willing.

But Prospero, though secretly delighted, pretended wrath[32]. "You come here as a spy," he said to Ferdinand. "I will manacle[33] your neck and feet together, and you shall feed on fresh water mussels[34], withered[35] roots and husk[36], and have sea-water to drink. Follow."

28 spellbound ['spelbaʊnd] (a.) extremely interested in something you are listening to 入迷的

29 behold [bɪ'hould] (int.) to see or to look at something 瞧！

30 reverence ['revərəns] (n.) great respect and admiration for someone or something 崇敬

He vowed to make her his queen if she were willing.

31 divine [dɪ'vaɪn] (a.) connected with a god, or like a god 神聖的
32 wrath [ræθ] (n.) extreme anger 憤怒
33 manacle ['mænəkəl] (v.) to restrain somebody using manacles 上鐐銬
34 mussel ['mʌsəl] (n.) a small sea animal, with a soft body that can be eaten and a black shell that is divided into two parts 淡菜

35 withered ['wɪðərd] (a.) dry and decaying 枯萎的
36 husk [hʌsk] (n.) the dry outer covering of certain fruits or seeds 外皮；殼

(062) "No," said Ferdinand, and drew his sword. But on the instant Prospero charmed him so that he stood there like a statue, still as stone; and Miranda in terror prayed her father to have mercy on her lover.

Miranda in very pity would have helped him in his hard work, but he would not let her do it.

But he harshly refused her, and made Ferdinand follow him to his cell[37]. There he set the Prince to work, making him remove thousands of heavy logs of timber and pile them up; and Ferdinand patiently obeyed, and thought his toil all too well repaid by the sympathy of the sweet Miranda.

She in very pity would have helped him in his hard work, but he would not let her, yet he could not keep from her the secret of his love, and she, hearing it, rejoiced and promised to be his wife.

37 cell [sel] (n.) a small, close room, as in a monastery or prison
單人小室

063 Then Prospero released him from his servitude[38], and glad at heart, he gave his consent to their marriage.

"Take her," he said, "she is thine[39] own."

In the meantime, Antonio and Sebastian in another part of the island were plotting the murder of Alonso, the King of Naples, for Ferdinand being dead, as they thought, Sebastian would succeed to the throne on Alonso's death. And they would have carried out their wicked purpose while their victim was asleep, but that Ariel woke him in good time.

Many tricks did Ariel play them. Once he set a banquet before them, and just as they were going to fall to, he appeared to them amid thunder and lightning in the form of a Harpy[40], and immediately the banquet disappeared. Then Ariel upbraided[41] them with their sins and vanished too.

Ariel appeared to them in the form of a harpy.

38 servitude ['sɜːrvɪtuːd] (n.) the condition of a slave 奴役
39 thine [ðaɪn] (pron.) belonging to thee（thou 的所有格）你的
40 Harpy ['hɑːrpi] (n.) in Greek mythology, a creature with the head of a woman and the body of a bird 鳥身女妖
41 upbraid [ʌp'breɪd] (v.) to tell someone angrily that they have done something wrong 訓斥

064 Prospero by his enchantments drew them all to the grove[42] without his cell, where they waited, trembling and afraid, and now at last bitterly repenting them of their sins.

Prospero determined to make one last use of his magic power, "And then," said he, "I'll break my staff[43] and deeper than did ever plummet[44] sound I'll drown my book."

So he made heavenly music to sound in the air, and appeared to them in his proper shape as the Duke of Milan. Because they repented, he forgave them and told them the story of his life since they had cruelly committed him and his baby daughter to the mercy of wind and waves.

Alonso, who seemed sorriest of them all for his past crimes, lamented[45] the loss of his heir[46].

But Prospero drew back a curtain and showed them Ferdinand and Miranda playing at chess. Great was Alonso's joy to greet his loved son again, and when he heard that the fair maid with whom Ferdinand was playing was Prospero's daughter, and that the young folks had plighted their troth[47], he said—

42 grove [ɡroʊv] (n.) a small wood 小樹林
43 staff [stæf] (n.) a stick or rod used as a symbol of authority 權杖
44 plummet ['plʌmɪt] (v.) drop downward fast 筆直落下

065 "Give me your hands, let grief and sorrow still embrace his heart that doth not wish you joy."

So all ended happily. The ship was safe in the harbor, and next day they all set sail for Naples, where Ferdinand and Miranda were to be married. Ariel gave them calm seas and auspicious[48] gales[49]; and many were the rejoicings at the wedding.

45 lament [lə'ment] (v.) to express feelings of great sadness about something 悲痛

46 heir [er] (n.) person who will legally receive money, property or a title from another person 嗣子

47 plight one's troth: to promise something solemnly, especially to marry somebody 山盟海誓

48 auspicious [ɑː'spɪʃəs] (a.) showing that something is likely to be successful 吉兆的

49 gale [geɪl] (n.) a very strong wind 強風

066 Then Prospero, after many years of absence, went back to his own dukedom, where he was welcomed with great joy by his faithful subjects.

He practiced the arts of magic no more, but his life was happy, and not only because he had found his own again, but chiefly because, when his bitterest foes who had done him deadly wrong lay at his mercy, he took no vengeance[50] on them, but nobly forgave them.

As for Ariel, Prospero made him free as air, so that he could wander where he would, and sing with a light heart his sweet song—

Where the bee sucks, there suck I:
In a cowslip's[51] bell I lie;
There I couch when owls do cry.
On the bat's back I do fly
After summer, merrily:
Merrily, merrily, shall I live now,
Under the blossom that hangs on the bough[52].

50 vengeance ['vendʒəns] (n.) punishment that is inflicted in return for a wrong 報復

51 cowslip ['kaʊˌslɪp] (n.) a small plant with yellow flowers that smell sweet 櫻草

52 bough [baʊ] (n.) a large branch of a tree 大樹枝

6 Cymbeline

067 Cymbeline was the King of Britain. He had three children. The two sons were stolen away from him when they were quite little children, and he was left with only one daughter, Imogen.

The King married a second time, and brought up Leonatus, the son of a dear friend, as Imogen's playfellow; and when Leonatus was old enough, Imogen secretly married him. This made the King and Queen very angry, and the King, to punish Leonatus, banished[1] him from Britain.

Poor Imogen was nearly heart-broken at parting from Leonatus, and he was not less unhappy. For they were not only lovers and husband and wife, but they had been friends and comrades[2] ever since they were quite little children.

With many tears and kisses they said "Good-bye." They promised never to forget each other, and that they would never care for anyone else as long as they lived.

1 banish ['bæniʃ] (v.) to send someone away, especially from their country, and forbid them to come back 流放
2 comrade ['kɑːmræd] (n.) an intimate friend; a companion 夥伴

"Sweetest, fairest, wear this bracelet for my sake."

068 "This diamond was my mother's, love," said Imogen; "take it, my heart, and keep it as long as you love me."

"Sweetest, fairest," answered Leonatus, "wear this bracelet for my sake."

"Ah!" cried Imogen, weeping, "when shall we meet again?"

And while they were still in each other's arms, the King came in, and Leonatus had to leave without more farewell.

When he was come to Rome, where he had gone to stay with an old friend of his father's, he spent his days still in thinking of his dear Imogen, and his nights in dreaming of her.

One day at a feast some Italian and French noblemen were talking of their sweethearts, and swearing that they were the most faithful and honorable and beautiful ladies in the world.

And a Frenchman reminded Leonatus how he had said many times that his wife Imogen was more fair, wise, and constant[3] than any of the ladies in France.

"I say so still," said Leonatus.

"She is not so good but that she would deceive[4]," said Iachimo, one of the Italian nobles.

3 constant [ˈkɑːnstənt] (a.) faithful and loyal 忠貞的

4 deceive [dɪˈsiːv] (v.) to cheat; mislead or cause to err 欺騙

069 "She never would deceive," said Leonatus.

"I wager[5]," said Iachimo, "that, if I go to Britain, I can persuade your wife to do whatever I wish, even if it should be against your wishes."

"I wager that I can persuade your wife to do whatever I wish."

"That you will never do," said Leonatus. "I wager this ring upon my finger," which was the very ring Imogen had given him at parting, "that my wife will keep all her vows[6] to me, and that you will never persuade her to do otherwise."

So Iachimo wagered half his estate[7] against the ring on Leonatus's finger, and started forthwith[8] for Britain, with a letter of introduction to Leonatus's wife.

When he reached there he was received with all kindness; but he was still determined to win his wager.

5 wager ['weɪdʒər] (v.) to bet 打賭
6 vow [vaʊ] (n.) a serious promise or decision 誓約
7 estate [ɪ'steɪt] (n.) all of someone's property and money 財產
8 forthwith [fɔːrθ'wɪð] (ad.) immediately; at once 馬上

070 He told Imogen that her husband thought no more of her, and went on to tell many cruel lies about him.

Imogen listened at first, but presently perceived[9] what a wicked person Iachimo was, and ordered him to leave her.

Then he said—"Pardon me, fair lady, all that I have said is untrue. I only told you this to see whether you would believe me, or whether you were as much to be trusted as your husband thinks. Will you forgive me?"

"I forgive you freely," said Imogen.

Imogen perceived what a wicked person Iachimo was, and ordered him to leave her.

9 perceive [pər'si:v] (v.) to understand or think of something or someone in a particular way 察覺到

071 "Then," went on Iachimo, "perhaps you will prove it by taking charge of a trunk[10], containing a number of jewels which your husband and I and some other gentlemen have bought as a present for the Emperor of Rome."

"I will indeed," said Imogen, "do anything for my husband and a friend of my husband's. Have the jewels sent into my room, and I will take care of them."

"It is only for one night," said Iachimo, "for I leave Britain again tomorrow."

So the trunk was carried into Imogen's room, and that night she went to bed and to sleep. When she was fast asleep, the lid of the trunk opened and a man got out. It was Iachimo.

The story about the jewels was as untrue as the rest of the things he had said. He had only wished to get into her room to win his wicked wager.

He looked about him and noticed the furniture, and then crept[11] to the side of the bed where Imogen was asleep and took from her arm the gold bracelet which had been the parting gift of her husband. Then he crept back to the trunk, and next morning sailed for Rome.

10 trunk [trʌŋk] (n.) a very large box made of wood or metal, in which clothes, books etc are stored or packed for travel 大皮箱

11 creep [kriːp] (v.) to move slowly, quietly and carefully, usually in order to avoid being noticed 潛入

072

When he met Leonatus, he said—"I have been to Britain and I have won the wager, for your wife no longer thinks about you. She stayed talking with me all one night in her room, which is hung with tapestry[12] and has a carved chimney-piece, and silver andirons[13] in the shape of two winking[14] Cupids."

"I do not believe she has forgotten me; I do not believe she stayed talking with you in her room. You have heard her room described by the servants."

"Ah!" said Iachimo, "but she gave me this bracelet. She took it from her arm. I see her yet. Her pretty action did outsell[15] her gift, and yet enriched it too. She gave it me, and said she prized[16] it once."

"Take the ring," cried Leonatus, "you have won; and you might have won my life as well, for I care nothing for it now I know my lady has forgotten me."

073 And mad with anger, he wrote letters to Britain to his old servant, Pisanio, ordering him to take Imogen to Milford Haven, and to murder her, because she had forgotten him and given away his gift.

When Pisanio got this letter, he was too good to carry out its orders.

At the same time he wrote to Imogen herself, telling her to go with Pisanio, his old servant, to Milford Haven, and that he, her husband, would be there to meet her.

Now when Pisanio got this letter he was too good to carry out its orders, and too wise to let them alone altogether. So he gave Imogen the letter from her husband, and started with her for Milford Haven.

12 tapestry [ˈtæpɪstri] (n.) a heavy piece of fabric with a woven pattern or picture 掛毯

13 andiron [ˈændaɪən] (n.) metal holder for fireplace logs 壁爐的鐵製柴架

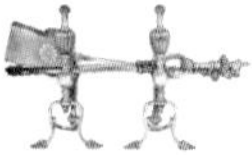

14 wink [wɪŋk] (v.) to close and open one eye quickly 眨眼

15 outsell [aʊtˈsel] (v.) to sell more than something else 銷售勝過……

16 prize [praɪz] (v.) to think that someone or something is very important or valuable 珍視

0074 Before he left, the wicked Queen gave him a drink which, she said, would be useful in sickness. She hoped he would give it to Imogen, and that Imogen would die, and the wicked Queen's son could be King. For the Queen thought this drink was a poison, but really and truly it was only a sleeping-draft[17].

When Pisanio and Imogen came near to Milford Haven, he told her what was really in the letter he had had from her husband.

"I must go on to Rome, and see him myself," said Imogen.

And then Pisanio helped her to dress in boy's clothes, and sent her on her way, and went back to the Court. Before he went he gave her the drink he had had from the Queen.

Pisanio gave Imogen the drink he had had from the Queen.

Imogen went on, getting more and more tired, and at last came to a cave. Someone seemed to live there, but no one was in just then. So she went in, and as she was almost dying of hunger, she took some food she saw there, and had just done so, when an old man and two boys came into the cave.

075 She was very much frightened when she saw them, for she thought that they would be angry with her for taking their food, though she had meant to leave money for it on the table.

As Imogen was almost dying of hunger, she took some food.

But to her surprise they welcomed her kindly. She looked very pretty in her boy's clothes and her face was good, as well as pretty.

"You shall be our brother," said both the boys; and so she stayed with them, and helped to cook the food, and make things comfortable.

But one day when the old man, whose name was Bellarius, was out hunting with the two boys, Imogen felt ill, and thought she would try the medicine Pisanio had given her.

So she took it, and at once became like a dead creature, so that when Bellarius and the boys came back from hunting, they thought she was dead, and with many tears and funeral songs, they carried her away and laid her in the wood, covered with flowers.

17 draft [dræft] (n.) the amount of air, liquid, or smoke taken in in a single breath or swallow 藥水等一次的服用量

076 They sang sweet songs to her, and strewed[18] flowers on her, pale primroses[19], and the azure[20] harebell[21], and eglantine[22], and furred moss, and went away sorrowful.

No sooner had they gone than Imogen awoke, and not knowing how she came there, nor where she was, went wandering through the wood.

Now while Imogen had been living in the cave, the Romans had decided to attack Britain, and their army had come over, and with them Leonatus, who had grown sorry for his wickedness against Imogen, so had come back, not to fight with the Romans against Britain, but with the Britons against Rome.

Imogen

So as Imogen wandered alone, she met with Lucius, the Roman General, and took service with him as his page[23].

When the battle was fought between the Romans and Britons, Bellarius and his two boys fought for their own country, and Leonatus, disguised as a British peasant, fought beside them.

077 The Romans had taken Cymbeline prisoner, and old Bellarius, with his sons and Leonatus, bravely rescued the King.

Then the Britons won the battle, and among the prisoners brought before the King were Lucius, with Imogen, Iachimo, and Leonatus, who had put on the uniform of a Roman soldier.

He was tired of his life since he had cruelly ordered his wife to be killed, and he hoped that, as a Roman soldier, he would be put to death.

When they were brought before the King, Lucius spoke out—"A Roman with a Roman's heart can suffer," he said. "If I must die, so be it. This one thing only will I entreat. My boy, a Briton born, let him be ransomed[24]. Never master had a page so kind, so duteous, diligent, true. He has done no Briton harm, though he has served a Roman. Save him, Sir."

18 strew [stru:] (v.) to scatter, or let fall loosely 撒

19 primrose ['pri:mrouz] (n.) a flowering plant from the family that includes the cowslip, cyclamen, and pimpernel 櫻草花

20 azure ['æʒər] (a.) having a bright blue color like the sky 天藍色的

21 harebell ['herbel] (n.) a small, branching plant, having blue, bellshaped flowers 風信子

22 eglantine ['egləntaɪn] (n.) rose with single flowers 多花薔薇

23 page [peɪdʒ] (n.) boy attendant 侍從

24 ransom ['rænsəm] (v.) pay money for somebody's release 贖回

078 Then Cymbeline looked on the page, who was his own daughter, Imogen, in disguise, and though he did not recognize her, he felt such a kindness that he not only spared the boy's life, but he said—"He shall have any boon[25] he likes to ask of me, even though he ask a prisoner, the noblest taken."

Then Imogen said, "The boon I ask is that this gentleman shall say from whom he got the ring he has on his finger," and she pointed to Iachimo.

"Speak," said Cymbeline, "how did you get that diamond?"

Then Iachimo told the whole truth of his villainy[26]. At this, Leonatus was unable to contain[27] himself, and casting aside all thought of disguise, he came forward, cursing himself for his folly[28] in having believed Iachimo's lying story, and calling again and again on his wife whom he believed dead.

"Oh, Imogen, my love, my life!" he cried. "Oh, Imogen!" Then Imogen, forgetting she was disguised, cried out, "Peace, my lord—here, here!"

Leonatus turned to strike the forward page who thus interfered in his great trouble, and then he saw that it was his wife, Imogen, and they fell into each other's arms.

25 boon [buːn] (n.) something that is very helpful and improves the quality of life 恩惠

26 villainy ['vɪləni] (n.) evil act 惡行

079 The King was so glad to see his dear daughter again, and so grateful to the man who had rescued him (whom he now found to be Leonatus), that he gave his blessing on their marriage, and then he turned to Bellarius, and the two boys.

Now Bellarius spoke—"I am your old servant, Bellarius. You accused me of treason[29] when I had only been loyal to you, and to be doubted, made me disloyal. So I stole your two sons, and see,—they are here!"

And he brought forward the two boys, who had sworn to be brothers to Imogen when they thought she was a boy like themselves.

The wicked Queen was dead of some of her own poisons, and the King, with his three children about him, lived to a happy old age. So the wicked were punished, and the good and true lived happy ever after.

So may the wicked suffer, and honest folk prosper[30] till the world's end.

27 contain [kən'teɪn] (v.) to control or hide a strong emotion 控制

28 folly ['fɑ:li] (n.) a stupid thing 蠢事

29 treason ['tri:zən] (n.) betrayal of country 叛國罪

30 prosper ['prɑ:spər] (v.) to be or become successful 繁榮

7 As You Like It

080 There was once a wicked Duke named Frederick, who took the dukedom that should have belonged to his brother, sending him into exile[1].

His brother went into the Forest of Arden, where he lived the life of a bold forester, as Robin Hood did in Sherwood Forest in merry England.

The banished Duke's daughter, Rosalind, remained with Celia, Frederick's daughter, and the two loved each other more than most sisters.

One day there was a wrestling[2] match at Court, and Rosalind and Celia went to see it. Charles, a celebrated wrestler, was there, who had killed many men in contests of this kind.

Orlando, the young man he was to wrestle with, was so slender and youthful, that Rosalind and Celia thought he would surely be killed, as others had been; so they spoke to him, and asked him not to attempt so dangerous an adventure; but the only effect of their words was to make him wish more to come off[3] well in the encounter[4], so as to win praise from such sweet ladies.

1 exile ['eksaɪl] (n.) unwilling absence from a home country or place of residence 流放
2 wrestling ['reslɪŋ] (n.) sport with two contestants fighting 摔角
3 come off: to acquit oneself 表現
4 encounter [ɪn'kaʊntər] (n.) an occasion when two teams play against each other 衝突

Rosalind and Celia loved each other more than most sisters.

At last, Orlando threw Charles to the ground.

081 Orlando, like Rosalind's father, was being kept out of his inheritance[5] by his brother, and was so sad at his brother's unkindness that, until he saw Rosalind, he did not care much whether he lived or died.

But now the sight of the fair Rosalind gave him strength and courage, so that he did marvelously, and at last, threw Charles to such a tune, that the wrestler had to be carried off the ground.

Duke Frederick was pleased with his courage, and asked his name.

"My name is Orlando, and I am the youngest son of Sir Rowland de Boys," said the young man.

5 inheritance [ɪn'herɪtəns] (n.) money or objects that someone gives you when they die 遺產

082 Now Sir Rowland de Boys, when he was alive, had been a good friend to the banished Duke, so that Frederick heard with regret whose son Orlando was, and would not befriend[6] him.

But Rosalind was delighted to hear that this handsome young stranger was the son of her father's old friend, and as they were going away, she turned back more than once to say another kind word to the brave young man.

"Gentleman," she said, giving him a chain from her neck, "wear this for me. I could give more, but that my hand lacks means[7]."

Rosalind and Celia, when they were alone, began to talk about the handsome wrestler, and Rosalind confessed that she loved him at first sight.

"Come, come," said Celia, "wrestle with thy affections."

"Oh," answered Rosalind, "they take the part of a better wrestler than myself. Look, here comes the Duke."

"With his eyes full of anger," said Celia.

"You must leave the Court at once," he said to Rosalind.

"Why?" she asked.

"Never mind why," answered the Duke, "you are banished. If within ten days you are found within twenty miles of my Court, you die."

6 befriend [bɪ'frend] (v.) to act as a friend to 以朋友相待

7 means [mi:nz] (n.) (pl.) available money（作複數）財產；資力

083 So Rosalind set out to seek her father, the banished Duke, in the Forest of Arden.

Celia loved her too much to let her go alone, and as it was rather a dangerous journey, Rosalind, being the taller, dressed up as a young countryman, and her cousin as a country girl, and Rosalind said that she would be called Ganymede, and Celia, Aliena.

They were very tired when at last they came to the Forest of Arden, and as they were sitting on the grass a countryman passed that way, and Ganymede asked him if he could get them food.

He did so, and told them that a shepherd's flocks and house were to be sold. They bought these and settled down as shepherd and shepherdess in the forest.

In the meantime, Oliver having sought to take his brother Orlando's life, Orlando also wandered into the forest, and there met with the rightful Duke, and being kindly received, stayed with him.

084 Now, Orlando could think of nothing but Rosalind, and he went about the forest carving her name on trees, and writing love sonnets[8] and hanging them on the bushes, and there Rosalind and Celia found them.

Orlando liked the pretty shepherd youth, because he fancied a likeness in him to Rosalind.

One day Orlando met them, but he did not know Rosalind in her boy's clothes, though he liked the pretty shepherd youth, because he fancied[9] a likeness in him to her he loved.

"There is a foolish lover," said Rosalind, "who haunts[10] these woods and hangs sonnets on the trees. If I could find him, I would soon cure him of his folly."

8 sonnet ['sɑːnɪt] (n.) a poem that has 14 lines and a particular pattern of rhyme 十四行詩
9 fancy ['fænsi] (v.) to imagine 想像
10 haunt [hɔːnt] (v.) to go often to a place 經常去某地

085 Orlando confessed that he was the foolish lover, and Rosalind said—"If you will come and see me every day, I will pretend to be Rosalind, and I will take her part, and be wayward[11] and contrary[12], as is the way of women, till I make you ashamed of your folly in loving her."

And so every day he went to her house, and took a pleasure in saying to her all the pretty things he would have said to Rosalind; and she had the fine and secret joy of knowing that all his love-words came to the right ears. Thus many days passed pleasantly away.

One morning, as Orlando was going to visit Ganymede, he saw a man asleep on the ground, and that there was a lioness crouching near, waiting for the man who was asleep to wake: for they say that lions will not prey on anything that is dead or sleeping.

Then Orlando looked at the man, and saw that it was his wicked brother, Oliver, who had tried to take his life. He fought with the lioness and killed her, and saved his brother's life.

While Orlando was fighting the lioness, Oliver woke to see his brother, whom he had treated so badly, saving him from a wild beast at the risk of his own life.

11 wayward ['weɪwərd] (a.) behaving badly, in a way that is difficult to control 任性的；反覆無常的

12 contrary ['kɑːntreri] (a.) describes a person who intentionally wants to disagree with and annoy other people 愛唱反調的

Orlando took a pleasure in saying to "him" all the pretty things
he would have said to Rosalind.

086 This made him repent of his wickedness, and he begged Orlando's pardon, and from thenceforth[13] they were dear brothers.

The lioness had wounded[14] Orlando's arm so much, that he could not go on to see the shepherd, so he sent his brother to ask Ganymede to come to him.

Oliver went and told the whole story to Ganymede and Aliena, and Aliena was so charmed with his manly way of confessing[15] his faults, that she fell in love with him at once.

But when Ganymede heard of the danger Orlando had been in she fainted; and when she came to herself, said truly enough, "I should have been a woman by right."

Aliena was charmed with Oliver's manly way of confessing his faults.

13 thenceforth ['ðensfɔːrθ] (ad.) from that time on 從那時起
14 wound [wuːnd] (v.) to injure someone with a knife, gun etc 傷害
15 confess [kən'fes] (v.) to admit that you have done something wrong or illegal 坦白

(087) Oliver went back to his brother and told him all this, saying, "I love Aliena so well that I will give up my estates[16] to you and marry her, and live here as a shepherd."

"Let your wedding be tomorrow," said Orlando, "and I will ask the Duke and his friends."

When Orlando told Ganymede how his brother was to be married on the morrow[17], he added: "Oh, how bitter a thing it is to look into happiness through another man's eyes."

Then answered Rosalind, still in Ganymede's dress and speaking with his voice—"If you do love Rosalind so near the heart, then when your brother marries Aliena, shall you marry her."

Now the next day the Duke and his followers, and Orlando, and Oliver, and Aliena, were all gathered together for the wedding.

Then Ganymede came in and said to the Duke, "If I bring in your daughter Rosalind, will you give her to Orlando here?"

"That I would," said the Duke, "if I had all kingdoms to give with her."

16 estates [ɪ'steɪts] (n.) property in land or buildings 地產，房屋
17 morrow ['mɔːroʊ] (n.) the next day 翌日

088 "And you say you will have her when I bring her?" she said to Orlando.

"That would I," he answered, "were I king of all kingdoms."

Then Rosalind and Celia went out, and Rosalind put on her pretty woman's clothes again, and after a while came back.

She turned to her father—"I give myself to you, for I am yours."

"If there be truth in sight," he said, "you are my daughter."

Then she said to Orlando, "I give myself to you, for I am yours."

Rosalind put on her pretty woman's clothes again.

089 "If there be truth in sight," he said, "you are my Rosalind."

"I will have no father if you be not he," she said to the Duke, and to Orlando, "I will have no husband if you be not he."

So Orlando and Rosalind were married, and Oliver and Celia, and they lived happy ever after, returning with the Duke to the kingdom.

090

For Frederick had been shown by a holy hermit[18] the wickedness of his ways, and so gave back the dukedom of his brother, and himself went into a monastery[19] to pray for forgiveness.

The wedding was a merry one, in the mossy glades of the forest. A shepherd and shepherdess who had been friends with Rosalind, when she was herself disguised as a shepherd, were married on the same day, and all with such pretty feastings and merrymakings[20] as could be nowhere within four walls, but only in the beautiful green wood.

18 hermit ['hɜːrmɪt] (n.) someone who lives alone and has a simple way of life 隱士

19 monastery ['mɑːnəsteri] (n.) a building in which monks live and worship 修道院

20 merrymaking ['meriˌmeɪkɪŋ] (n.) fun and enjoyment, especially drinking, dancing, and singing 歡慶活動

8 The Comedy of Errors

091 Aegeon was a merchant of Syracuse, which is a seaport in Sicily. His wife was Aemilia, and they were very happy until Aegeon's manager died, and he was obliged to go by himself to a place called Epidamnum on the Adriatic.

As soon as she could Aemilia followed him, and after they had been together some time two baby boys were born to them. The babies were exactly alike; even when they were dressed differently they looked the same.

And now you must believe a very strange thing. At the same inn[1] where these children were born, and on the same day, two baby boys were born to a much poorer couple than Aemilia and Aegeon; so poor, indeed, were the parents of these twins that they sold them to the parents of the other twins.

Aemilia was eager to show her children to her friends in Syracuse, and in treacherous[2] weather she and Aegeon and the four babies sailed homewards. They were still far from Syracuse when their ship sprang[3] a leak.

Aemilia fastened one of her children to a mast[4] and tied one of the slave-children to her; Aegeon followed her example with the remaining children. Then the parents secured themselves to the same masts, and hoped for safety.

1 inn [ɪn] (n.) a small hotel or pub, especially an old one in the countryside 旅舍

2 treacherous ['tretʃərəs] (a.) if the ground or sea is treacherous, it is extremely dangerous 危險的

3 spring [sprɪŋ] (v.) to crack, split, or warp 破裂

4 mast [mæst] (n.) a tall pole on a boat or ship that supports its sails 桅杆

092 The ship, however, suddenly struck a rock and was split[5] in two, and Aemilia, and the two children whom she had tied, floated away from Aegeon and the other children.

Aemilia and her charges[6] were picked up by some people of Epidamnum, but some fishermen of Corinth took the babies from her by force, and she returned to Epidamnum alone, and very miserable. Afterwards she settled in Ephesus, a famous town in Asia Minor.

5 split [splɪt] (v.) to divide or separate something into different parts or groups 破裂

6 charge [tʃɑːrdʒ] (n.) somebody being taken care of 被照顧的人或物

093 Aegeon and his charges were also saved; and, more fortunate than Aemilia, he was able to return to Syracuse and keep them till they were eighteen.

His own child he called Antipholus, and the slavechild he called Dromio; and, strangely enough, these were the names given to the children who floated away from him.

At the age of eighteen the son who was with Aegeon grew restless with a desire to find his brother. Aegeon let him depart with his servant, and the young men are henceforth known as Antipholus of Syracuse and Dromio of Syracuse.

Let alone, Aegeon found his home too dreary[7] to dwell in, and traveled for five years. He did not, during his absence, learn all the news of Syracuse, or he would never have gone to Ephesus.

As it was, his melancholy[8] wandering ceased in that town, where he was arrested almost as soon as he arrived.

7 dreary ['drɪri] (a.) dull and making you feel sad or bored 陰鬱的
8 melancholy ['melənkɑ:li] (a.) very sad 鬱悶的

094 He then found that the Duke of Syracuse had been acting in so tyrannical a manner to Ephesians unlucky enough to fall into his hands, that the Government of Ephesus had angrily passed a law which punished by death or a fine of a thousand pounds any Syracusan who should come to Ephesus.

Aegeon was brought before Solinus, Duke of Ephesus, who told him that he must die or pay a thousand pounds before the end of the day.

You will think there was fate in this when I tell you that the children who were kidnaped[9] by the fishermen of Corinth were now citizens of Ephesus, whither they had been brought by Duke Menaphon, an uncle of Duke Solinus. They will henceforth be called Antipholus of Ephesus and Dromio of Ephesus.

9 kidnap [ˈkɪdnæp] (v) to take somebody away by force, usually for ransom 綁架

095 Moreover, on the very day when Aegeon was arrested, Antipholus of Syracuse landed in Ephesus and pretended that he came from Epidamnum in order to avoid a penalty[10].

He handed his money to his servant Dromio of Syracuse, and bade him take it to the Centaur[11] Inn and remain there till he came. In less than ten minutes he was met on the Mart by Dromio of Ephesus, his brother's slave, and immediately mistook him for his own Dromio.

"Why are you back so soon? Where did you leave the money?" asked Antipholus of Syracuse.

This Drornio knew of no money except sixpence, which he had received on the previous Wednesday and given to the saddler[12]; but he did know that his mistress was annoyed because his master was not in to dinner, and he asked Antipholus of Syracuse to go to a house called The Phoenix[13] without delay.

096 His speech angered the hearer, who would have beaten him if he had not fled. Antipholus of Syracuse then went to The Centaur, found that his gold had been deposited[14] there, and walked out of the inn.

He was wandering about Ephesus when two beautiful ladies signaled to him with their hands. They were sisters, and their names were Adriana and Luciana.

Adriana was the wife of his brother Antipholus of Ephesus, and she had made up her mind, from the strange account given her by Dromio of Ephesus, that her husband preferred another woman to his wife.

"Ay, you may look as if you did not know me," she said to the man who was really her brother-in-law, "but I can remember when no words were sweet unless I said them, no meat flavorsome unless I carved[15] it."

10 penalty ['penəlti] (n.) a punishment for breaking a law, rule, or legal agreement 處罰
11 centaur ['sentɔːr] (n.) one of a race of beings, half man and half horse 半人半馬的怪物
12 saddler ['sædlər] (n.) a maker or seller of saddlery 馬具商
13 phoenix ['fiːnɪks] (n.) mythological bird 鳳凰
14 deposit [dɪ'pɑːzɪt] (v.) to put or set down 放置
15 carve [kɑːrv] (v.) to cut into slices 切開

097

"Is it I you address?" said Antipholus of Syracuse stiffly[16]. "I do not know you."

"Fine, brother," said Luciana. "You know perfectly well that she sent Dromio to you to bid you come to dinner."

Adriana said, "Come, come; I have been made a fool of long enough. My truant[17] husband shall dine with me and confess his silly pranks[18] and be forgiven."

They were determined ladies, and Antipholus of Syracuse grew weary of disputing with them, and followed them obediently to The Phoenix, where a very late "mid-day" dinner awaited them.

They were at dinner when Antipholus of Ephesus and his slave Dromio demanded admittance.

"Maud, Bridget, Marian, Cecily, Gillian, Ginn!" shouted Dromio of Ephesus, who knew all his fellow-servants' names by heart.

16 stiffly ['stɪfli] (ad.) in a stiff way or manner 拘謹地
17 truant ['tru:ənt] (a.) not working or being used 懶散的
18 prank [præŋk] (n.) a mischievous trick 惡作劇

098 From within came the reply, "Fool, dray[19] horse, coxcomb[20], idiot!" It was Dromio of Syracuse unconsciously insulting[21] his brother.

Master and man did their best to get in, short of using a crowbar[22], and finally went away; but Antipholus of Ephesus felt so annoyed with his wife that he decided to give a gold chain which he had promised her, to another woman.

Inside The Phoenix, Luciana, who believed Antipholus of Syracuse to be her sister's husband, attempted, by a discourse[23] in rhyme, when alone with him, to make him kinder to Adriana.

In reply he told her that he was not married, but that he loved her so much that, if Luciana were a mermaid, he would gladly lie on the sea if he might feel beneath him her floating golden hair.

Luciana was shocked and left him, and reported his lovemaking to Adriana, who said that her husband was old and ugly, and not fit to be seen or heard, though secretly she was very fond of him.

19 dray [dreɪ] (n.) a large low horse-drawn cart with no fixed sides, designed for heavy loads 板車

20 coxcomb ['kɑːkskoʊm] (n.) a man who is too proud of his appearance 花花公子

21 insult [ɪn'sʌlt] (v.) be offensive to somebody 羞辱

22 crowbar ['kroʊbɑːr] (n.) strong metal lever 鐵橇

23 discourse ['dɪskɔːrs] (n.) a speech about a particular, usually serious, subject 談話

If Luciana were a mermaid, he would gladly lie on the sea
if he might feel beneath him her floating golden hair.

099 Antipholus of Syracuse soon received a visitor in the shape of Angelo the goldsmith, of whom Antipholus of Ephesus had ordered the chain which he had promised his wife and intended to give to another woman.

The goldsmith handed the chain to Antipholus of Syracuse, and treated his "I bespoke it not" as mere fun, so that the puzzled merchant took the chain as good-humoredly as he had partaken[24] of Adriana's dinner. He offered payment, but Angelo foolishly said he would call again.

The goldsmith

The consequence was that Angelo was without money when a creditor[25] of the sort that stands no nonsense, threatened him with arrest unless he paid his debt immediately.

This creditor had brought a police officer with him, and Angelo was relieved to see Antipholus of Ephesus coming out of the house where he had been dining because he had been locked out of The Phoenix.

Bitter was Angelo's dismay[26] when Antipholus denied receipt of the chain. Angelo could have sent his mother to prison if she had said that, and he gave Antipholus of Ephesus in charge.

(100) At this moment up came Dromio of Syracuse and told the wrong Antipholus that he had shipped his goods, and that a favorable wind was blowing. To the ears of Antipholus of Ephesus this talk was simple nonsense.

He would gladly have beaten the slave, but contented himself with crossly[27] telling him to hurry to Adriana and bid her send to her arrested husband a purse of money which she would find in his desk.

Though Adriana was furious with her husband because she thought he had been making love to her sister, she did not prevent Luciana from getting the purse, and she bade Dromio of Syracuse bring home his master immediately.

Unfortunately, before Dromio could reach the police station he met his real master, who had never been arrested, and did not understand what he meant by offering him a purse.

Antipholus of Syracuse was further surprised when a lady whom he did not know asked him for a chain that he had promised her.

24 partake [pɑːr'teɪk] (v.) to take part 參加
25 creditor ['kredɪtər] (n.) person or organization owed money by another 債主
26 dismay [dɪs'meɪ] (n.) a feeling of unhappiness and disappointment 沮喪
27 crossly ['krɑːsli] (ad.) in a cross manner 不高興地

101 She was, of course, the lady with whom Antipholus of Ephesus had dined when his brother was occupying his place at table. "Avaunt[28], thou[29] witch!" was the answer which, to her astonishment, she received.

Meanwhile Antipholus of Ephesus waited vainly for the money which was to have released him. Never a good-tempered man, he was crazy with anger when Dromio of Ephesus, who, of course, had not been instructed to fetch a purse, appeared with nothing more useful than a rope.

He beat the slave in the street despite the remonstrance[30] of the police officer; and his temper did not mend when Adriana, Luciana, and a doctor arrived under the impression that he was mad and must have his pulse felt.

He raged so much that men came forward to bind him. But the kindness of Adriana spared him this shame. She promised to pay the sum demanded of him, and asked the doctor to lead him to The Phoenix.

28 avaunt [ə'vɔːnt] (int.) Away! expressing contempt or abhorrence〔古〕滾！

29 thou [ðaʊ] (n.) nominative singular of the personal pronoun of the second person〔古〕你（第二人稱單數主格）

30 remonstrance [rɪ'mɑːnstrəns] (n.) the act of expressing earnest opposition or protest 告誡

(102) Angelo's merchant creditor being paid, the two were friendly again, and might soon have been seen chatting before an abbey[31] about the odd behavior of Antipholus of Ephesus.

"Softly," said the merchant at last, "that's he, I think."

It was not; it was Antipholus of Syracuse with his servant Dromio, and he wore Angelo's chain round his neck!

The reconciled[32] pair fairly pounced[33] upon him to know what he meant by denying the receipt of the chain he had the impudence[34] to wear.

Antipholus of Syracuse lost his temper, and drew his sword, and at that moment Adriana and several others appeared.

"Hold!" shouted the careful wife. "Hurt him not; he is mad. Take his sword away. Bind him—and Dromio too."

31 abbey ['æbi] (n.) monastery or convent 大修道院
32 reconcile ['rekənsaɪl] (v.) to solve a dispute or end a quarrel 和解
33 pounce [paʊns] (v.) to more quickly in order to catch something 一把抓住
34 impudence ['ɪmpjʊdəns] (n.) showing a lack of respect and excessive boldness 厚臉皮

"People, why do you gather here?"

103 Dromio of Syracuse did not wish to be bound, and he said to his master, "Run, master! Into that abbey, quick, or we shall be robbed!" They accordingly retreated[35] into the abbey.

Adriana, Luciana, and a crowd remained outside, and the Abbess[36] came out, and said, "People, why do you gather here?"

"To fetch my poor distracted[37] husband," replied Adriana.

Angelo and the merchant remarked that they had not known that he was mad. Adriana then told the Abbess rather too much about her wifely worries, for the Abbess received the idea that Adriana was a shrew, and that if her husband was distracted he had better not return to her for the present.

104 Adriana determined, therefore, to complain to Duke Solinus, and, lo and behold! a minute afterwards the great man appeared with officers and two others. The others were Aegeon and the headsman. The thousand marks had not been found, and Aegeon's fate seemed sealed.

Ere the Duke could pass the abbey Adriana knelt before him, and told a woeful[38] tale of a mad husband rushing about stealing jewelry and drawing his sword, adding that the Abbess refused to allow her to lead him home.

The Duke bade the Abbess be summoned[39], and no sooner had he given the order than a servant from The Phoenix ran to Adriana with the tale that his master had singed off the doctor's beard.

"Nonsense!" said Adriana, "he's in the abbey."

"As sure as I live I speak the truth," said the servant.

35 retreat [riː'triːt] (v.) to go away from a place or person in order to escape from fighting or danger 撤退

36 abbess ['æbɪs] (n.) the nun in charge of a convent 女修道院院長

37 distracted [dɪ'stræktɪd] (a.) anxious and unable to think clearly 發狂的

38 woeful ['woʊfəl] (a.) very bad or serious 不幸的

39 summon ['sʌmən] (v.) to call by authority 召喚

105 Antipholus of Syracuse had not come out of the abbey, before his brother of Ephesus prostrated[40] himself in front of the Duke, exclaiming, "Justice, most gracious Duke, against that woman." He pointed to Adriana. "She has treated another man like her husband in my own house."

Even while he was speaking Aegeon said, "Unless I am delirious[41], I see my son Antipholus."

No one noticed him, and Antipholus of Ephesus went on to say how the doctor, whom he called "a threadbare[42] juggler[43]," had been one of a gang who tied him to his slave Dromio, and thrust them into a vault[44] whence he had escaped by gnawing[45] through his bonds.

The Duke could not understand how the same man who spoke to him was seen to go into the abbey, and he was still wondering when Aegeon asked Antipholus of Ephesus if he was not his son.

He replied, "I never saw my father in my life;" but so deceived was Aegeon by his likeness to the brother whom he had brought up, that he said, "Thou art[46] ashamed to acknowledge me in misery."

40 prostrate [prɑː'streɪt] (v.) lay somebody or something on ground 俯臥

41 delirious [dɪ'lɪriəs] (a.) unable to think or speak clearly because of fever, excitement or mental confusion 精神錯亂的

42 threadbare ['θredber] (a.) overused so no longer convincing 老套的

43 juggler ['dʒʌglər] (n.) a deceiver; a fraud 騙子

44 vault [vɑːlt] (n.) any subterranean chamber 地窖

45 gnaw [nɔː] (v.) to bite or chew something repeatedly 啃咬

46 art [ɑːrt] present 2nd singular form of be 〔古〕be 的第二人稱單數現在式

106 Soon, however, the Abbess advanced[47] with Antipholus of Syracuse and Dromio of Syracuse.

Then cried Adriana, "I see two husbands or mine eyes deceive me;" and Antipholus, espying[48] his father, said, "Thou art Aegeon or his ghost."

It was a day of surprises, for the Abbess said, "I will free that man by paying his fine, and gain my husband whom I lost. Speak, Aegeon, for I am thy wife Aemilia."

The Duke was touched. "He is free without a fine," he said.

So Aegeon and Aemilia were reunited, and Adriana and her husband reconciled; but no one was happier than Antipholus of Syracuse, who, in the Duke's presence, went to Luciana and said, "I told you I loved you. Will you be my wife?"

Her answer was given by a look, and therefore is not written.

The two Dromios were glad to think they would receive no more beatings.

47 advance [əd'væns] (v.) to go forward 向前進

48 espy [ɪ'spaɪ] (v.) to discover (something hidden) 發現

9 Romeo and Juliet

107 Once upon a time there lived in Verona two great families named Montagu and Capulet. They were both rich, and I suppose they were as sensible[1], in most things, as other rich people. But in one thing they were extremely silly. There was an old, old quarrel between the two families, and instead of making it up like reasonable folks, they made a sort of pet[2] of their quarrel, and would not let it die out[3].

So that a Montagu wouldn't speak to a Capulet if he met one in the street—nor a Capulet to a Montagu—or if they did speak, it was to say rude and unpleasant things, which often ended in a fight.

And their relations and servants were just as foolish, so that street fights and duels[4] and uncomfortablenesses of that kind were always growing out of the Montagu-and-Capulet quarrel.

Now Lord Capulet, the head of that family, gave a party—a grand[5] supper and a dance—and he was so hospitable[6] that he said anyone might come to it except (of course) the Montagues.

108 But there was a young Montagu named Romeo, who very much wanted to be there, because Rosaline, the lady he loved, had been asked.

This lady had never been at all kind to him, and he had no reason to love her; but the fact was that he wanted to love somebody, and as he hadn't seen the right lady, he was obliged to love the wrong one. So to the Capulet's grand party he came, with his friends Mercutio and Benvolio.

1 sensible ['sensɪbəl] (a.) having sound reason and judgment 明智的
2 pet [pet] (n.) a fit of sulkiness 慍怒
3 die out: to become less common and finally stop existing 逐漸消失
4 duel ['du:əl] (n.) a fight with weapons between two people, used in the past to settle a quarrel 決鬥
5 grand [grænd] (a.) splendid in style and appearance 盛大的
6 hospitable ['hɑ:spɪtəbəl] (a.) friendly, welcoming, and generous to guests or strangers 好客的

109 Old Capulet welcomed him and his two friends very kindly—and young Romeo moved about among the crowd of courtly[7] folk dressed in their velvets[8] and satins[9], the men with jeweled[10] sword hilts[11] and collars, and the ladies with brilliant gems on breast and arms, and stones of price set in their bright girdles[12].

The ladies with brilliant gems on breast and arms, and stones of price set in their bright girdles

Romeo was in his best too, and though he wore a black mask over his eyes and nose, everyone could see by his mouth and his hair, and the way he held his head, that he was twelve times handsomer than anyone else in the room.

Presently amid the dancers he saw a lady so beautiful and so lovable that from that moment he never again gave one thought to that Rosaline whom he had thought he loved.

7 courtly ['kɔːrtlɪ] (a.) polite, graceful and formal in behaviour 宮廷式的
8 velvet ['velvɪt] (n.) fabric with soft lustrous pile 天鵝絨

(110) And he looked at this other fair lady, as she moved in the dance in her satin and pearls, and all the world seemed vain and worthless to him compared with her.

And he was saying this, or something like it, when Tybalt, Lady Capulet's nephew, hearing his voice, knew him to be Romeo.

Tybalt, being very angry, went at once to his uncle, and told him how a Montagu had come uninvited to the feast; but old Capulet was too fine a gentleman to be discourteous[13] to any man under his own roof, and he bade Tybalt be quiet. But this young man only waited for a chance to quarrel with Romeo.

9 satin ['sætn] (n.) a type of cloth that is very smooth and shiny 緞
10 jeweled ['dʒu:əld] (a.) decorated with jewels 有寶石的
11 hilt [hɪlt] (n.) the handle of a sword or knife, where the blade is attached 劍柄

12 girdle ['gɜ:rdl] (n.) a long strip of cloth worn tied around the waist 腰帶
13 discourteous [dɪs'kɜ:rtiəs] (a.) behavior or an action that is bad mannered or impolite 失禮的

111 In the meantime Romeo made his way to the fair lady, and told her in sweet words that he loved her, and kissed her. Just then her mother sent for[14] her, and then Romeo found out that the lady on whom he had set his heart's hopes was Juliet, the daughter of Lord Capulet, his sworn foe. So he went away, sorrowing indeed, but loving her none the less.

Then Juliet said to her nurse, "Who is that gentleman that would not dance?"

"His name is Romeo, and a Montagu, the only son of your great enemy," answered the nurse.

Then Juliet went to her room, and looked out of her window, over the beautiful green-grey garden, where the moon was shining. And Romeo was hidden in that garden among the trees—because he could not bear to go right away without trying to see her again.

So she—not knowing him to be there—spoke her secret thought aloud, and told the quiet garden how she loved Romeo.

112 And Romeo heard and was glad beyond measure. Hidden below, he looked up and saw her fair face in the moonlight, framed in the blossoming creepers[15] that grew round her window, and as he looked and listened, he felt as though he had been carried away in a dream, and set down by some magician in that beautiful and enchanted garden.

"Ah—why are you called Romeo?" said Juliet. "Since I love you, what does it matter what you are called?"

"Call me but love, and I'll be new baptized[16]—henceforth I never will be Romeo," he cried, stepping into the full white moonlight from the shade of the cypresses[17] and oleanders[18] that had hidden him.

She was frightened at first, but when she saw that it was Romeo himself, and no stranger, she too was glad, and, he standing in the garden below and she leaning from the window, they spoke long together, each one trying to find the sweetest words in the world, to make that pleasant talk that lovers use.

14 sent for: order, request, or command to come 派人去叫來

15 creeper ['kriːpər] (n.) a plant that grows along the ground, or up walls or trees 匍匐植物

16 baptize ['bæptaɪz] (v.) to perform the ceremony of baptism on someone 受洗

17 cypress ['aɪprɪs] (n.) a tree with dark green leaves and hard wood, which does not lose its leaves in winter 白扁柏

18 oleander [ˌoʊli'ændər] (n.) an evergreen Mediterranean tree or bush with strong leaves and white, red or pink flowers 歐洲夾竹桃

113 And the tale of all they said, and the sweet music their voices made together, is all set down in a golden book, where you may read it for yourselves some day. And the time passed so quickly, as it does for folk who love each other and are together, that when the time came to part, it seemed as though they had met but that moment—and indeed they hardly knew how to part.

They tried to find the sweetest words in the world, to make that pleasant talk that lovers use.

"I will send to you tomorrow," said Juliet.

And so at last, with lingering[19] and longing, they said good-bye. Juliet went into her room, and a dark curtain hid her bright window. Romeo went away through the still and dewy[20] garden like a man in a dream.

19 lingering ['lɪŋgərɪŋ] (n.) to delay leaving somewhere because of reluctance to go 徘徊

20 dewy ['du:ɪ] (a.) wet with drops of dew 帶露水的

114 The next morning, very early, Romeo went to Friar[21] Laurence, a priest, and, telling him all the story, begged him to marry him to Juliet without delay. And this, after some talk, the priest consented[22] to do.

So when Juliet sent her old nurse to Romeo that day to know what he purposed to do, the old woman took back a message that all was well, and all things ready for the marriage of Juliet and Romeo on the next morning.

Juliet and her nurse

The young lovers were afraid to ask their parents' consent to their marriage, as young people should do, because of this foolish old quarrel between the Capulets and the Montagues.

And Friar Laurence was willing to help the young lovers secretly, because he thought that when they were once married their parents might soon be told, and that the match might put a happy end to the old quarrel.

21 friar ['fraər] (n.) a man belonging to one of several Roman Catholic religious groups, whose members often promise to stay poor 天主教的苦行僧

22 consent [kən'sent] (v.) to give formal permission for something to happen 答應

115 So the next morning early, Romeo and Juliet were married at Friar Laurence's cell, and parted with tears and kisses. And Romeo promised to come into the garden that evening, and the nurse got ready a rope-ladder to let down from the window, so that Romeo could climb up and talk to his dear wife quietly and alone.

Romeo and Juliet were married at Friar Laurence's cell.

But that very day a dreadful thing happened.

Tybalt, the young man who had been so vexed[23] at Romeo's going to the Capulet's feast, met him and his two friends, Mercutio and Benvolio, in the street, called Romeo a villain[24], and asked him to fight.

Romeo had no wish to fight with Juliet's cousin, but Mercutio drew his sword, and he and Tybalt fought. And Mercutio was killed.

When Romeo saw that this friend was dead, he forgot everything except anger at the man who had killed him, and he and Tybalt fought till Tybalt fell dead.

23 vexed [vekst] (a.) provoked to slight annoyance or anxiety 生氣的

24 villain ['vɪlən] (n.) a bad person who harms other people or breaks the law 惡棍

116 So, on the very day of his wedding, Romeo killed his dear Juliet's cousin, and was sentenced to be banished[25].

Poor Juliet and her young husband met that night.

Poor Juliet and her young husband met that night indeed; he climbed the rope-ladder among the flowers, and found her window, but their meeting was a sad one, and they parted with bitter tears and hearts heavy, because they could not know when they should meet again.

Now Juliet's father, who, of course, had no idea that she was married, wished her to wed a gentleman named Paris, and was so angry when she refused, that she hurried away to ask Friar Laurence what she should do.

25 banish [ˈbænɪʃ] (v.) to send someone away, especially from their country, and forbid them to come back 流放

Romeo and Juliet parted with bitter tears and hearts heavy.

117 He advised her to pretend to consent, and then he said, "I will give you a draught[26] that will make you seem to be dead for two days, and then when they take you to church it will be to bury you, and not to marry you. They will put you in the vault[27] thinking you are dead, and before you wake up Romeo and I will be there to take care of you. Will you do this, or are you afraid?"

"Will you do this, or are you afraid?"

"I will do it; talk not to me of fear!" said Juliet.

And she went home and told her father she would marry Paris. If she had spoken out and told her father the truth . . . well, then this would have been a different story.

Lord Capulet was very much pleased to get his own way, and set about inviting his friends and getting the wedding feast ready. Everyone stayed up all night, for there was a great deal to do, and very little time to do it in.

26 draught [dræft] (n.) the amount of air, liquid, or smoke taken in in a single breath or swallow（一劑藥的）服用量

27 vault [vɑːlt] (n.) a room where people from the same family are buried, often under the floor of a church（教堂下的）墓穴

"I will do it; talk not to me of fear!" said Juliet.

118 Lord Capulet was anxious to get Juliet married because he saw she was very unhappy. Of course she was really fretting[28] about her husband Romeo, but her father thought she was grieving for the death of her cousin Tybalt, and he thought marriage would give her something else to think about.

Early in the morning the nurse came to call Juliet, and to dress her for her wedding; but she would not wake, and at last the nurse cried out suddenly—

"Alas[29]! alas! help! help! my lady's dead! Oh, well-a-day that ever I was born!"

Lady Capulet came running in, and then Lord Capulet, and Lord Paris, the bridegroom. There lay Juliet cold and white and lifeless, and all their weeping could not wake her. So it was a burying that day instead of a marrying.

Meantime Friar Laurence had sent a messenger to Mantua with a letter to Romeo telling him of all these things; and all would have been well, only the messenger was delayed, and could not go.

But ill news travels fast. Romeo's servant who knew the secret of the marriage, but not of Juliet's pretended death, heard of her funeral, and hurried to Mantua to tell Romeo how his young wife was dead and lying in the grave.

28 fret [fret] (v.) to be anxious or worried 擔心

29 alas [ə'læs] (int.) used to express sadness, shame, or fear 哎呀

119 "Is it so?" cried Romeo, heart-broken. "Then I will lie by Juliet's side tonight."

And he bought himself a poison, and went straight back to Verona. He hastened to the tomb where Juliet was lying. It was not a grave, but a vault.

He broke open the door, and was just going down the stone steps that led to the vault where all the dead Capulets lay, when he heard a voice behind him calling on him to stop. It was the Count Paris, who was to have married Juliet that very day.

"How dare you come here and disturb the dead bodies of the Capulets, you vile Montagu?" cried Paris.

Poor Romeo, half mad with sorrow, yet tried to answer gently.

"You were told," said Paris, "that if you returned to Verona you must die."

"I must indeed," said Romeo. "I came here for nothing else. Good, gentle youth—leave me! Oh, go—before I do you any harm! I love you better than myself—go—leave me here—"

Then Paris said, "I defy[30] you, and I arrest you as a felon[31]," and Romeo, in his anger and despair, drew his sword.

30 defy [dɪˈfaɪ] (v.) to act or be against, a person, decision, law, situation, etc 挑戰

31 felon [ˈfelən] (n.) someone who is guilty of a serious crime 犯重罪者

120 They fought, and Paris was killed. As Romeo's sword pierced him, Paris cried—

"Oh, I am slain[32]! If thou[33] be merciful[34], open the tomb, and lay me with Juliet!"

And Romeo said, "In faith I will."

And he carried the dead man into the tomb and laid him by the dear Juliet's side.

Then he kneeled by Juliet and spoke to her, and held her in his arms, and kissed her cold lips, believing that she was dead, while all the while she was coming nearer and nearer to the time of her awakening. Then he drank the poison, and died beside his sweetheart and wife.

Romeo kneeled by Juliet and spoke to her.

32 slain [sleɪn] past participle of slay 「slay」(殺死)的過去分詞

33 thou [ðaʊ] (pron.) nominative singular of the personal pronoun of the second person; you〔古〕(第二人稱單數主格)汝

34 merciful ['mɜːrsɪfəl] (a.) showing mercy or compassion to somebody 仁慈的

Now came Friar Laurence when it was too late, and saw all that had happened—and then poor Juliet woke out of her sleep to find her husband and her friend both dead beside her.

The noise of the fight had brought other folks to the place too, and Friar Laurence, hearing them, ran away, and Juliet was left alone.

She saw the cup that had held the poison, and knew how all had happened, and since no poison was left for her, she drew her Romeo's dagger[35] and thrust it through her heart—and so, falling with her head on her Romeo's breast, she died.

And here ends the story of these faithful and most unhappy lovers.

35 dagger ['dægər] (n.) a short pointed knife used as a weapon 短劍，匕首

Falling with her head on her Romeo's breast, she died.

122 And when the old folks knew from Friar Laurence of all that had befallen[36], they sorrowed exceedingly, and now, seeing all the mischief[37] their wicked quarrel had wrought[38], they repented them of it, and over the bodies of their dead children they clasped[39] hands at last, in friendship and forgiveness.

36 befall [bɪ'fɑ:l] (v.) to happen, or happen to somebody, especially through the unexpected workings of chance or fate（尤指不幸）降臨於
37 mischief ['mɪstʃɪf] (n.) to deliberately cause quarrels or unfriendly feelings between people 不和
38 wrought [rɑ:t] (v.) past tense & past participle of work 〔古〕work 的過去式和過去分詞
39 clasp [klæsp] (v.) to hold someone or something tightly, closing your fingers or arms around them 緊握

10 The Merchant of Venice

Antonio was a rich and prosperous[1] merchant of Venice. His ships were on nearly every sea, and he traded with Portugal, with Mexico, with England, and with India.

Although proud of his riches, he was very generous with them, and delighted to use them in relieving[2] the wants of his friends, among whom his relation, Bassanio, held the first place.

Now Bassanio, like many another gay and gallant[3] gentleman, was reckless[4] and extravagant[5], and finding that he had not only come to the end of his fortune, but was also unable to pay his creditors[6], he went to Antonio for further help.

1 prosperous ['prɑːspərəs] (a.) to be or become successful, especially financially 富有的
2 relieve [rɪ'liːv] (v.) to remove something such as a burden or difficulty from the person on whom it is imposed 接濟
3 gallant ['gælənt] (a.) grand and majestic 堂皇的
4 reckless ['rekləs] (a.) doing something dangerous and not caring about the risks and the possible results 不顧後果的
5 extravagant [ɪk'strævəgənt] (a.) spending, using or doing more than necessary in an uncontrolled way 奢侈的
6 creditor ['kredɪtər] (a.) a person, bank, or company that you owe money to 債主

124 "To you, Antonio," he said, "I owe the most in money and in love: and I have thought of a plan to pay everything I owe if you will but help me."

"Say what I can do, and it shall be done," answered his friend.

Then said Bassanio, "In Belmont is a lady richly left, and from all quarters of the globe renowned[7] suitors come to woo her, not only because she is rich, but because she is beautiful and good as well. She looked on me with such favor when last we met, that I feel sure that I should win her away from all rivals[8] for her love had I but the means to go to Belmont, where she lives."

"All my fortunes," said Antonio, "are at sea, and so I have no ready money; but luckily my credit is good in Venice, and I will borrow for you what you need."

7 renowned [rɪ'naʊnd] (a.) well known or famous, especially for a skill or expertise 有聲譽的

8 rival ['raɪvəl] (n.) a person, group, etc. competing with others for the same thing or in the same area 競爭者

9 despise [dɪ'spaɪz] (v.) to dislike somebody or something intensely and with contempt 鄙視

10 scorn [skɔ:rn] (n.) a very great lack of respect for someone or something that you think is stupid or worthless 輕蔑

11 cur [kɜ:r] (n.) an offensive term for somebody regarded as mean, cowardly, or otherwise unpleasant 無賴

12 threshold ['θreʃoʊld] (n.) the entrance to a room or building, or the area of floor or ground at the entrance 門檻

125 There was living in Venice at this time a rich money-lender, named Shylock. Antonio despised[9] and disliked this man very much, and treated him with the greatest harshness and scorn[10]. He would thrust him, like a cur[11], over his threshold[12], and would even spit[13] on him.

There was living in Venice at this time a rich money-lender, named Shylock.

Shylock submitted[14] to all these indignities[15] with a patient shrug[16]; but deep in his heart he cherished[17] a desire for revenge on the rich, smug[18] merchant.

13 spit [spɪt] to force out the contents of the mouth, especially saliva (v.) 吐口水

14 submit [səb'mɪt] (v.) to accept somebody else's authority or will, especially reluctantly or under pressure 忍受

15 indignity [ɪn'dɪgnɪti] (n.) loss of respect or self-respect, or something which causes this 屈辱

16 shrug [ʃrʌg] (n.) to raise and drop the shoulders briefly, especially to indicate indifference or lack of knowledge 聳肩（以表示無奈等）

17 cherish ['tʃerɪʃ] (v.) retain something in mind 懷有

18 smug [smʌg] (a.) showing too much satisfaction with your own cleverness or success, used to show disapproval 自鳴得意的

126 For Antonio both hurt his pride and injured his business. "But for him," thought Shylock, "I should be richer by half a million ducats[19]. On the market place, and wherever he can, he denounces[20] the rate of interest I charge, and—worse than that—he lends out money freely."

So when Bassanio came to him to ask for a loan of three thousand ducats to Antonio for three months, Shylock hid his hatred, and turning to Antonio, said—

"Harshly as you have treated me, I would be friends with you and have your love. So I will lend you the money and charge you no interest. But, just for fun, you shall sign a bond[21] in which it shall be agreed that if you do not repay me in three months' time, then I shall have the right to a pound of your flesh, to be cut from what part of your body I choose."

"No," cried Bassanio to his friend, "you shall run no such risk for me."

"Why, fear not," said Antonio, "my ships will be home a month before the time. I will sign the bond."

127 Thus Bassanio was furnished with the means to go to Belmont, there to woo[22] the lovely Portia.

The very night he started, the money-lender's pretty daughter, Jessica, ran away from her father's house with her lover, and she took with her from her father's hoards[23] some bags of ducats and precious stones.

Jessica

Shylock's grief and anger were terrible to see. His love for her changed to hate. "I would she were dead at my feet and the jewels in her ear," he cried.

His only comfort now was in hearing of the serious losses which had befallen Antonio, some of whose ships were wrecked. "Let him look to his bond," said Shylock, "let him look to his bond."

19 ducat ['dʌkət] (n.) a gold or silver coin formerly used in some European countries 硬幣

20 denounce [dɪ'naʊns] (v.) to criticize something or someone strongly and publicly 譴責

21 bond [bɑːnd] (n.) document promising to pay 字據；借據

22 woo [wuː] (v.) to seek the affection or love of a woman in order to marry her 追求

23 hoard [hɔːrd] (n.) a collection of things that someone hides somewhere, especially so they can use them later 貯藏的錢財

128 Meanwhile Bassanio had reached Belmont, and had visited the fair Portia. He found, as he had told Antonio, that the rumor of her wealth and beauty had drawn to her suitors from far and near.

But to all of them Portia had but one reply. She would only accept that suitor who would pledge[24] himself to abide[25] by the terms[26] of her father's will.

These were conditions that frightened away many an ardent[27] wooer. For he who would win Portia's heart and hand, had to guess which of three caskets[28] held her portrait. If he guessed aright, then Portia would be his bride; if wrong, then he was bound by oath[29] never to reveal which casket he chose, never to marry, and to go away at once.

24 pledge [pledʒ] (v.) to make a serious or formal promise to give or do something 發誓
25 abide [ə'baɪd] (v.) to endure or withstand something 忍受
26 terms [tɜːrmz] (n.) (pl.) the conditions that are set for an agreement, contract, arrangement etc〔複〕條件
27 ardent ['ɑːrdənt] (a.) showing strong feelings 熱烈的
28 casket ['kæskɪt] (n.) a small decorated box in which you keep Jewellery and other valuable objects 首飾盒
29 oath [oʊθ] (n.) a promise, especially that you will tell the truth in a law court 宣誓

129 The caskets were of gold, silver, and lead. The gold one bore this inscription[30]:—

"Who chooseth me shall gain what many men desire"; the silver one had this:—

"Who chooseth me shall get as much as he deserves"; while on the lead one were these words:—

"Who chooseth me must give and hazard all he hath."

The Prince of Morocco, as brave as he was black, was among the first to submit to this test. He chose the gold casket, for he said neither base lead nor silver could contain her picture.

So he chose the gold casket, and found inside the likeness of what many men desire—death.

30 inscription [ɪn'skrɪpʃən] (n.) a sequence of words or letters written, printed, or engraved on a surface 銘文

31 haughty ['hɑːti] (a.) unfriendly and seeming to consider yourself better than other people 傲慢的

32 rack [ræk] (n.) a torture device used to stretch the body of somebody strapped horizontally onto it 拷問臺；折磨

130 After him came the haughty[31] Prince of Arragon, and saying, "Let me have what I deserve—surely I deserve the lady," he chose the silver one, and found inside a fool's head.

"Did I deserve no more than a fool's head?" he cried.

Then at last came Bassanio, and Portia would have delayed him from making his choice from very fear of his choosing wrong. For she loved him dearly, even as he loved her.

"But," said Bassanio, "let me choose at once, for as I am, I live upon the rack[32]."

131 Then Portia bade her servants to bring music and play while her gallant lover made his choice. And Bassanio took the oath and walked up to the caskets—the musicians playing softly the while.

"Mere outward show," he said, "is to be despised. The world is still deceived with ornament, and so no gaudy[33] gold or shining silver for me. I choose the lead casket; joy be the consequence!"

And opening it, he found fair Portia's portrait inside, and he turned to her and asked if it were true that she was his.

"Yes," said Portia, "I am yours, and this house is yours, and with them I give you this ring, from which you must never part."

33 gaudy ['gɑːdi] (a.) unpleasantly bright in color or decoration 俗艷的

34 dash [dæʃ] (v.) to disappoint someone by telling them that what they want is not possible 使（希望）破滅

35 entitle [ɪn'taɪtəl] (v.) to give someone the right to do or have something 給某人權力或資格

36 celebrated ['selɪbreɪtɪd] (a.) famous and admired 著名的

132 And Bassanio, saying that he could hardly speak for joy, found words to swear that he would never part with the ring while he lived.

Then suddenly all his happiness was dashed[34] with sorrow, for messengers came from Venice to tell him that Antonio was ruined, and that Shylock demanded from the Duke the fulfilment of the bond, under which he was entitled[35] to a pound of the merchant's flesh.

Portia was as grieved as Bassanio to hear of the danger which threatened his friend.

"First," she said, "take me to church and make me your wife, and then go to Venice at once to help your friend. You shall take with you money enough to pay his debt twenty times over."

But when her newly-made husband had gone, Portia went after him, and arrived in Venice disguised as a lawyer, and with an introduction from a celebrated[36] lawyer Bellario, whom the Duke of Venice had called in to decide the legal questions raised by Shylock's claim to a pound of Antonio's flesh.

Portia went after Bassanio, and arrived in Venice disguised as a lawyer.

133 When the Court met, Bassanio offered Shylock twice the money borrowed, if he would withdraw[37] his claim.

But the money-lender's only answer was—

"If every ducat in six thousand ducats,
Were in six parts, and every part a ducat,
I would not draw them,—I would have my bond."

It was then that Portia arrived in her disguise, and not even her own husband knew her. The Duke gave her welcome on account of the great Bellario's introduction, and left the settlement of the case to her.

"I would have my bond."

Then in noble words she bade Shylock have mercy. But he was deaf to her entreaties.

"I will have the pound of flesh," was his reply.

"What have you to say?" asked Portia of the merchant.

134 "But little," he answered; "I am armed and well prepared."

"The Court awards you a pound of Antonio's flesh," said Portia to the money-lender.

"Most righteous judge!" cried Shylock. "A sentence: come, prepare."

"Tarry[38] a little. This bond gives you no right to Antonio's blood, only to his flesh. If, then, you spill a drop of his blood, all your property will be forfeited[39] to the State. Such is the Law."

And Shylock, in his fear, said, "Then I will take Bassanio's offer."

"No," said Portia sternly[40], "you shall have nothing but your bond. Take your pound of flesh, but remember, that if you take more or less, even by the weight of a hair, you will lose your property and your life."

Shylock now grew very much frightened. "Give me my three thousand ducats that I lent him, and let him go."

Bassanio would have paid it to him, but said Portia, "No! He shall have nothing but his bond."

37 withdraw [wɪð'drɔː] (v.) to take or move out or back, or to remove 撤銷

38 tarry ['tæri] (v.) to delay or be slow in going somewhere 等等

39 forfeit ['fɔːrfit] (v.) to lose a right, position, possession etc or have it taken away from you because you have broken a law or rule 沒收

40 sternly ['stɜːrnli] (adv.) in a way that shows disapproval 堅決地

135 "You, a foreigner," she added, "have sought to take the life of a Venetian[41] citizen, and thus by the Venetian law, your life and goods are forfeited. Down, therefore, and beg mercy of the Duke."

Thus were the tables turned, and no mercy would have been shown to Shylock had it not been for Antonio. As it was, the money-lender forfeited half his fortune to the State, and he had to settle the other half on his daughter's husband, and with this he had to be content.

Bassanio, in his gratitude to the clever lawyer, was induced to part with the ring his wife had given him, and with which he had promised never to part, and when on his return to Belmont he confessed as much to Portia, she seemed very angry, and vowed she would not be friends with him until she had her ring again.

But at last she told him that it was she who, in the disguise of the lawyer, had saved his friend's life, and got the ring from him.

So Bassanio was forgiven, and made happier than ever, to know how rich a prize he had drawn in the lottery[42] of the caskets.

41 Venetian [vɪ'niːʃən] (a.) relating to the Italian city of Venice, or its people or culture 威尼斯的

42 lottery ['lɑːtəri] (n.) an activity, situation, or enterprise with an outcome dependent on chance 抽籤

11 Macbeth

(136) When a person is asked to tell the story of Macbeth, he can tell two stories. One is of a man called Macbeth who came to the throne of Scotland by a crime in the year of our Lord 1039, and reigned justly and well, on the whole, for fifteen years or more. This story is part of Scottish history.

The other story issues[1] from a place called Imagination; it is gloomy and wonderful, and you shall hear it.

A year or two before Edward the Confessor began to rule England, a battle was won in Scotland against a Norwegian[2] King by two generals named Macbeth and Banquo.

Edward the Confessor
(ca. 1003-1066)

After the battle, the generals walked together towards Forres, in Elginshire, where Duncan, King of Scotland, was awaiting them.

While they were crossing a lonely heath[3], they saw three bearded women, sisters, hand in hand, withered[4] in appearance and wild in their attire[5].

"Hail, Macbeth, King that is to be!"

137

"Speak, who are you?" demanded Macbeth.

"Hail[6], Macbeth, chieftain[7] of Glamis," said the first woman.

"Hail, Macbeth, chieftain of Cawdor," said the second woman.

1 issue ['ɪʃuː] (v.) to emerge or come out from somewhere 來自
2 Norwegian [nɔːr'wiːdʒən] (a.) pertaining to Norway, its language, or people 挪威的
3 heath [hiːθ] (n.) shrubby uncultivated land 荒原
4 withered ['wɪðərd] (a.) dry and decaying 憔悴的
5 attire [ə'taɪr] (n.) clothes, especially of a particular or formal type 衣著
6 hail [heɪl] (int.) used to greet, welcome, or acclaim somebody（表示歡呼）好啊
7 chieftain ['tʃiːftɪn] (n.) the leader of a tribe 首領

138 "Hail, Macbeth, King that is to be," said the third woman.

Then Banquo asked, "What of me?" and the third woman replied, "Thou[8] shalt[9] be the father of kings."

"Tell me more," said Macbeth. "By my father's death I am chieftain of Glamis, but the chieftain of Cawdor lives, and the King lives, and his children live. Speak, I charge you!"

The women replied only by vanishing.

The women replied only by vanishing, as though suddenly mixed with the air.

Banquo and Macbeth knew then that they had been addressed by witches, and were discussing their prophecies[10] when two nobles approached. One of them thanked Macbeth, in the King's name, for his military services, and the other said, "He bade[11] me call you chieftain of Cawdor."

8 thou [ðaʊ] (pron.) nominative singular of the personal pronoun of the second person〔古〕(第二人稱單數主格)你

9 shalt [ʃəlt] (v.aux.) the second person singular, present indicative, of shall〔古〕shall 的第二人稱單數(與 thou 連用)

10 prophecy ['prɑːfɪsi] (n.) prediction of a future event that is believed to reveal the will of a deity 預言

11 bade [beɪd] past tense of bid 「bid」(吩咐)的過去式

139 Macbeth then learned that the man who had yesterday borne[12] that title was to die for treason[13], and he could not help thinking, "The third witch called me, 'King that is to be.'"

"Banquo," he said, "you see that the witches spoke truth concerning me. Do you not believe, therefore, that your child and grandchild will be kings?"

Banquo frowned[14]. Duncan had two sons, Malcolm and Donalbain, and he deemed it disloyal to hope that his son Fleance should rule Scotland. He told Macbeth that the witches might have intended to tempt them both into villainy[15] by their prophecies concerning the throne.

The witches might have intended to tempt them both into villainy.

Macbeth, however, thought the prophecy that he should be King too pleasant to keep to himself, and he mentioned it to his wife in a letter.

12 borne [bɔːrn] past participle of bear「bear」（擁有）的過去分詞

13 treason ['triːzən] (n.) the crime of lack of loyalty to your country, especially by helping its enemies 叛國罪

14 frown ['fraʊn] (v.) to show a facial expression of displeasure or concentration by wrinkling the brow 皺眉頭

15 villainy ['vɪləni] (n.) evil or criminal behaviour 邪惡

140 Lady Macbeth was the grand-daughter of a King of Scotland who had died in defending his crown against the King who preceded[16] Duncan, and by whose order her only brother was slain[17].

To her, Duncan was a reminder[18] of bitter wrongs. Her husband had royal blood in his veins[19], and when she read his letter, she was determined that he should be King.

When a messenger arrived to inform her that Duncan would pass a night in Macbeth's castle, she nerved herself for a very base[20] action.

She told Macbeth almost as soon as she saw him that Duncan must spend a sunless morrow. She meant that Duncan must die, and that the dead are blind.

"We will speak further," said Macbeth uneasily, and at night, with his memory full of Duncan's kind words, he would fain[21] have spared his guest.

16 precede [prɪ'si:d] (v.) to be or go before something or someone in time or space 先於

17 slain [sleɪn] past participle of slay 「slay」(殺死)的過去分詞

18 reminder [rɪ'maɪndər] (n.) something that makes you notice, remember, or think about something 提醒者

19 vein [veɪn] (n.) a tube that carries blood to the heart from the other parts of the body 血管

20 base [beɪs] (a.) lacking moral principles 卑鄙的

21 fain [feɪn] (adv.) with gladness or eagerness 樂意地

22 morality [mɔ'ræləti] (n.) beliefs or ideas about what is right and wrong and about how people should behave 道德

23 egg [eg] (n.) to encourage someone to do something, especially something that they do not want to do or should not do 慫恿

Lady Macbeth was the grand-daughter of a King of Scotland.

141 "Would you live a coward?" demanded Lady Macbeth, who seems to have thought that morality[22] and cowardice were the same.

"I dare do all that may become a man," replied Macbeth; "who dare do more is none."

"Why did you write that letter to me?" she inquired fiercely, and with bitter words she egged[23] him on to murder, and with cunning words she showed him how to do it.

142 After supper Duncan went to bed, and two grooms[24] were placed on guard at his bedroom door. Lady Macbeth caused them to drink wine till they were stupefied[25].

She then took their daggers and would have killed the King herself if his sleeping face had not looked like her father's.

Macbeth came later, and found the daggers lying by the grooms; and soon with red hands he appeared before his wife, saying, "Methought I heard a voice cry, 'Sleep no more! Macbeth destroys the sleeping.'"

"Wash your hands," said she. "Why did you not leave the daggers by the grooms? Take them back, and smear[26] the grooms with blood."

"I dare not," said Macbeth.

His wife dared, and she returned to him with hands red as his own, but a heart less white, she proudly told him, for she scorned his fear.

"Take the daggers back, and smear the grooms with blood."

143 The murderers heard a knocking, and Macbeth wished it was a knocking which could wake the dead. It was the knocking of Macduff, the chieftain of Fife, who had been told by Duncan to visit him early. Macbeth went to him, and showed him the door of the King's room.

Macduff entered, and came out again crying, "O horror! horror! horror!"

Macbeth appeared as horror-stricken as Macduff, and pretending that he could not bear to see life in Duncan's murderers, he slew the two grooms with their own daggers before they could proclaim[27] their innocence.

24 groom [grʊm] (n.) an officer in a royal household 侍從官

25 stupefied ['stu:pɪfaɪd] (a.) so surprised, tired, or bored that you cannot think clearly 昏昏沉沉的

26 smear [smɪr] (v.) to spread a liquid or a thick substance over a surface 塗抹

27 proclaim [proʊ'klem] (v.) to say publicly or officially that something important is true 聲明

144 These murders did not shriek[28] out, and Macbeth was crowned at Scone. One of Duncan's sons went to Ireland, the other to England.

Macbeth was King. But he was discontented. The prophecy concerning Banquo oppressed his mind. If Fleance were to rule, a son of Macbeth would not rule. Macbeth determined, therefore, to murder both Banquo and his son Fleance.

He hired two ruffians[29], who slew Banquo one night when he was on his way with Fleance to a banquet which Macbeth was giving to his nobles. Fleance escaped.

Meanwhile Macbeth and his Queen received their guests very graciously, and he expressed a wish for them which has been uttered thousands of times since his day—"Now good digestion wait on appetite, and health on both."

28 shriek [ʃriːk] (v.) a short, loud, high cry, especially one produced suddenly as an expression of a powerful emotion 尖叫

29 ruffian ['rʌfiən] (n.) a violent man, involved in crime 暴徒

Macbeth and his Queen received their guests very graciously.

145 "We pray your Majesty to sit with us," said Lennox, a Scotch noble; but ere Macbeth could reply, the ghost of Banquo entered the banqueting hall[30] and sat in Macbeth's place.

Not noticing the ghost, Macbeth observed that, if Banquo were present, he could say that he had collected under his roof the choicest chivalry[31] of Scotland. Macduff, however, had curtly[32] declined his invitation.

The King was again pressed to take a seat, and Lennox, to whom Banquo's ghost was invisible, showed him the chair where it sat.

30 banqueting hall: hall where banquets are held 宴會廳
31 chivalry [ˈʃɪvəlri] (n.) knights, noblemen, or armed mounted soldiers, collectively or in a group 騎士
32 curtly [ˈkɜːrtli] (adv.) using very few words in a way that seems rude 草率地

Macbeth saw the ghost like a form of mist and blood.

146 But Macbeth, with his eyes of genius, saw the ghost. He saw it like a form of mist and blood, and he demanded passionately, "Which of you have done this?"

Still none saw the ghost but he, and to the ghost Macbeth said, "Thou canst[33] not say I did it."

The ghost glided[34] out, and Macbeth was impudent[35] enough to raise a glass of wine "to the general joy of the whole table, and to our dear friend Banquo, whom we miss."

The toast was drunk as the ghost of Banquo entered for the second time.

"Begone[36]!" cried Macbeth. "You are senseless, mindless! Hide in the earth, thou horrible shadow."

Again none saw the ghost but he.

"What is it your Majesty sees?" asked one of the nobles.

147 The Queen dared not permit an answer to be given to this question. She hurriedly begged her guests to quit a sick man who was likely to grow worse if he was obliged to talk.

Macbeth, however, was well enough next day to converse with the witches whose prophecies had so depraved[37] him.

He found them in a cavern[38] on a thunderous day. They were revolving[39] round a cauldron[40] in which were boiling particles[41] of many strange and horrible creatures, and they knew he was coming before he arrived.

"Answer me what I ask you," said the King.

"Would you rather hear it from us or our masters?" asked the first witch.

33 canst [kənst] (v.aux.) an archaic form of the verb "can" used with "thou"〔古〕can 之第二人稱單數現在式（僅與 thou 連用）

34 glide [glaɪd] (v.) to move easily without stopping and without effort or noise 滑動

35 impudent ['ɪmpjʊdənt] (a.) rude and showing no respect to other people 放肆的

36 begone [bɪ'gɑːn] (int.) Go away! 走開！

37 deprave [dɪ'preɪv] (v.) corrupt somebody 使墮落

38 cavern ['kævərn] (n.) a large cave 大洞穴

39 revolve [rɪ'vɑːlv] (v.) to move or cause something to move round a central point or line 旋轉

40 cauldron ['kɑːldrən] (n.) a large round metal pot for boiling liquids over a fire 大鍋

41 particle ['pɑːrtɪkəl] (n.) a very small piece of something 微粒；顆粒

148

"Call them," replied Macbeth.

Thereupon the witches poured blood into the cauldron and grease into the flame that licked it, and a helmeted head appeared with the visor[42] on, so that Macbeth could only see its eyes.

He was speaking to the head, when the first witch said gravely[43], "He knows thy[44] thought," and a voice in the head said, "Macbeth, beware Macduff, the chieftain of Fife." The head then descended into the cauldron till it disappeared.

"One word more," pleaded Macbeth.

"He will not be commanded," said the first witch, and then a crowned child ascended from the cauldron bearing a tree in his hand. The child said—

"Macbeth shall be unconquerable till The Wood of Birnam climbs Dunsinane Hill."

"That will never be," said Macbeth; and he asked to be told if Banquo's descendants[45] would ever rule Scotland.

42 visor ['vaɪzər] (n.) transparent front of helmet 頭盔的面甲

43 gravely ['greɪvli] (adv.) solemn and serious in manner 嚴肅地

44 thy [ðaɪ] (pron.) belonging or relating to you, the second person singular possessive corresponding to "thou"〔古〕你的（thou 的所有格）

149 The cauldron sank into the earth; music was heard, and a procession of phantom kings filed[46] past Macbeth; behind them was Banquo's ghost.

In each king, Macbeth saw a likeness to Banquo, and he counted eight kings. Then he was suddenly left alone.

His next proceeding was to send murderers to Macduff's castle. They did not find Macduff, and asked Lady Macduff where he was. She gave a stinging[47] answer, and her questioner called Macduff a traitor[48].

"Thou liest!" shouted Macduff's little son, who was immediately stabbed[49], and with his last breath entreated[50] his mother to fly. The murderers did not leave the castle while one of its inmates[51] remained alive.

Macduff was in England listening, with Malcolm, to a doctor's tale of cures wrought by Edward the Confessor when his friend Ross came to tell him that his wife and children were no more.

45 descendant [dɪ'sendənt] (n.) a person, animal, or plant related to one that lived in the past 後代；子孫

46 file [faɪl] (v.) to move in line one behind the other 排成縱隊行進

47 stinging ['stɪŋɪŋ] (a.) harsh or hurtful in tone or character 刺耳的

48 traitor ['trɪtər] (n.) person who is not loyal or stops being loyal to their own country, social class, beliefs, etc 叛徒

49 stab [stæb] (v.) to push a knife into someone or something 刺殺

50 entreat [ɪn'triːt] (v.) an attempt to persuade someone to do something 懇求

51 inmate ['ɪnmeɪt] (n.) someone who is being kept in a prison 囚犯

150 At first Ross dared not speak the truth, and turn Macduff's bright sympathy with sufferers relieved by royal virtue into sorrow and hatred.

But when Malcolm said that England was sending an army into Scotland against Macbeth, Ross blurted out[52] his news, and Macduff cried, "All dead, did you say? All my pretty ones and their mother? Did you say all?"

His sorry hope was in revenge, but if he could have looked into Macbeth's castle on Dunsinane Hill, he would have seen at work a force more solemn than revenge.

Retribution[53] was working, for Lady Macbeth was mad. She walked in her sleep amid ghastly[54] dreams.

Lady Macbeth walked in her sleep amid ghastly dreams.

52 blurt out: to speak out suddenly and without thought 脱口而出

53 retribution [ˌretrɪ'bjuːʃən] (n.) deserved and severe punishment 報應，懲罰

54 ghastly ['gæstli] (a.) making you very frightened, upset, or shocked 恐怖的

Lady Macbeth was mad.

151 She was wont[55] to wash her hands for a quarter of an hour at a time; but after all her washing, would still see a red spot of blood upon her skin.

It was pitiful to hear her cry that all the perfumes of Arabia could not sweeten her little hand.

"Canst thou not minister to a mind diseased?" inquired Macbeth of the doctor, but the doctor replied that his patient must minister to her own mind.

This reply gave Macbeth a scorn of medicine. "Throw physic[56] to the dogs," he said; "I'll none of it."

One day he heard a sound of women crying. An officer approached him and said, "The Queen, your Majesty, is dead."

"Out, brief candle," muttered Macbeth, meaning that life was like a candle, at the mercy of a puff[57] of air. He did not weep; he was too familiar with death.

Presently a messenger told him that he saw Birnam Wood on the march. Macbeth called him a liar and a slave, and threatened to hang him if he had made a mistake. "If you are right you can hang me," he said.

55 wont [wɑːnt] (a.) accustomed or likely to do something 慣於

56 physic ['fɪzɪk] (n.) (archaic) a medicine, especially a purgative〔古〕藥劑

57 puff [pʌf] (n.) a short sudden rush of air, wind, gas, or smoke 一陣陣地吹

Life was like a candle, at the mercy of a puff of air.

152 From the turret[58] windows of Dunsinane Castle, Birnam Wood did indeed appear to be marching. Every soldier of the English army held aloft a bough which he had cut from a tree in that wood, and like human trees they climbed Dunsinane Hill.

Macbeth had still his courage. He went to battle to conquer or die, and the first thing he did was to kill the English general's son in single combat.

Macbeth then felt that no man could fight him and live, and when Macduff came to him blazing[59] for revenge, Macbeth said to him, "Go back; I have spilt too much of your blood already."

"My voice is in my sword," replied Macduff, and hacked[60] at him and bade him yield.

"I will not yield!" said Macbeth, but his last hour had struck. He fell.

Macbeth's men were in retreat when Macduff came before Malcolm holding a King's head by the hair.

"Hail, King!" he said; and the new King looked at the old.

So Malcolm reigned after Macbeth; but in years that came afterwards the descendants of Banquo were kings.

58 turret ['tʌrɪt] (n.) a small rounded tower that projects from a wall or corner of a large building such as a castle 塔樓
59 blazing ['bleɪzɪŋ] (a.) feeling or showing intense emotions 熾烈的
60 hack [hæk] (v.) to cut something roughly or violently 砍

12 Twelfth Night

153 Orsino, the Duke of Illyria, was deeply in love with a beautiful Countess[1] named Olivia. Yet was all his love in vain, for she disdained[2] his suit; and when her brother died, she sent back a messenger from the Duke, bidding him tell his master that for seven years she would not let the very air behold her face, but that, like a nun, she would walk veiled; and all this for the sake of a dead brother's love, which she would keep fresh and lasting in her sad remembrance.

The Duke longed for someone to whom he could tell his sorrow, and repeat over and over again the story of his love. And chance brought him such a companion.

For about this time a goodly ship was wrecked on the Illyrian coast, and among those who reached land in safety were the captain and a fair young maid, named Viola. But she was little grateful for being rescued from the perils[3] of the sea, since she feared that her twin brother was drowned, Sebastian, as dear to her as the heart in her bosom[4], and so like her that, but for the difference in their manner of dress, one could hardly be told from the other.

1 countess ['kaʊntɪs] (n.) a woman who holds the rank of count or earl 女伯爵

2 disdain [dɪs'deɪn] (v.) extreme contempt or disgust for something or somebody 鄙視

3 peril ['perəl] (n.) great danger 重大危險

4 bosom ['bʊzəm] (n.) the place where emotions are felt 內心

Olivia would not let the very air behold her face for seven years.
She would walk veiled.

154 The captain, for her comfort, told her that he had seen her brother bind himself "to a strong mast[5] that lived upon the sea," and that thus there was hope that he might be saved.

Viola now asked in whose country she was, and learning that the young Duke Orsino ruled there, and was as noble in his nature as in his name, she decided to disguise herself in male attire[6], and seek for employment with him as a page[7].

In this she succeeded, and now from day to day she had to listen to the story of Orsino's love.

At first she sympathized very truly with him, but soon her sympathy grew to love. At last it occurred to Orsino that his hopeless love-suit might prosper[8] better if he sent this pretty lad to woo Olivia for him.

Viola unwillingly went on this errand[9], but when she came to the house, Malvolio, Olivia's steward, a vain[10], officious[11] man, sick, as his mistress told him, of self-love, forbade the messenger admittance.

5 mast [mæst] (n.) a tall pole on a boat or ship that supports its sails 桅杆

6 attire [ə'taɪr] (n.) clothes, especially of a particular or formal type 衣著

7 page [peɪdʒ] (n.) boy servant in medieval times 年輕侍從

8 prosper ['prɑːspər] (v.) to be successful 成功

9 errand ['erənd] (n.) short journey either to take a message or to deliver or collect something 差事

Viola disguise herself in male attire.

155 Viola, however (who was now called Cesario), refused to take any denial, and vowed to have speech with the Countess.

Olivia, hearing how her instructions were defied[12] and curious to see this daring youth, said, "We'll once more hear Orsino's embassy[13]."

10 vain [veɪn] (a.) excessively proud, especially of personal appearance 自負的

11 officious [ə'fɪʃəs] (a.) too eager to tell people what to do 多管閒事的

12 defy [dɪ'faɪ] (v.) to refuse to obey 公然反抗

13 embassy ['embəsɪ] (n.) the mission, rank, or function of an ambassador 大使的地位

156 When Viola was admitted to her presence and the servants had been sent away, she listened patiently to the reproaches[14] which this bold messenger from the Duke poured upon her, and listening she fell in love with the supposed Cesario; and when Cesario had gone, Olivia longed to send some love-token[15] after him. So, calling Malvolio, she bade him follow the boy.

"He left this ring behind him," she said, taking one from her finger. "Tell him I will none of it."

Malvolio did as he was bid, and then Viola, who of course knew perfectly well that she had left no ring behind her, saw with a woman's quickness that Olivia loved her. Then she went back to the Duke, very sad at heart for her lover, and for Olivia, and for herself.

It was but cold comfort[16] she could give Orsino, who now sought to ease the pangs[17] of despised love by listening to sweet music, while Cesario stood by his side.

"Ah," said the Duke to his page that night, "you too have been in love."

"A little," answered Viola.

14 reproach [rɪ'proʊtʃ] (n.) criticism or disapproval for having done something wrong 斥責的話

15 token ['toʊkən] (n.) an object kept in memory of somebody or something 紀念物

16 cold comfort: very limited consolation or empathy 不太起作用的安慰

17 pang [pæŋ] (n.) a sudden sharp feeling, especially of painful emotion 苦痛

It was but cold comfort Cesario could give Orsino.

157 "What kind of woman is it?" he asked.

"Of your complexion[18]," she answered.

"What years, i' faith?" was his next question.

To this came the pretty answer, "About your years, my lord."

"Too old, by Heaven!" cried the Duke. "Let still the woman take an elder than herself."

And Viola very meekly[19] said, "I think it well, my lord."

18 complexion [kəm'plekʃən] (n.) the character of something or the way it appears 樣子；性質

19 meekly [mi:kli] (adv.) very quiet and gentle and unwilling to argue with people 溫順地

158 By and by Orsino begged Cesario once more to visit Olivia and to plead his love-suit.

But she, thinking to dissuade him, said—"If some lady loved you as you love Olivia?"

"Ah! that cannot be," said the Duke.

"But I know," Viola went on, "what love woman may have for a man. My father had a daughter loved a man, as it might be," she added blushing, "perhaps, were I a woman, I should love your lordship."

"And what is her history?" he asked.

"A blank, my lord," Viola answered. "She never told her love, but let concealment[20] like a worm in the bud feed on her damask[21] cheek: she pined[22] in thought, and with a green and yellow melancholy[23] she sat, like Patience on a monument, smiling at grief. Was not this love indeed?"

"But died thy sister of her love, my boy?" the Duke asked; and Viola, who had all the time been telling her own love for him in this pretty fashion, said—

"I am all the daughters my father has and all the brothers—Sir, shall I go to the lady?"

20 concealment [kən'si:lmənt] (n.) when something is hidden 隱藏

21 damask ['dæməsk] (a.) grayish-pink color 淡紅色的

22 pine [paɪn] (v.) to become weak and lose vitality as a result of grief or longing 憔悴

23 melancholy ['melənkɑ:li] (n.) a feeling of sadness for no particular reason 憂愁

She let concealment like a worm in the bud feed on her damask cheek.

159 "To her in haste," said the Duke, at once forgetting all about the story, "and give her this jewel."

So Viola went, and this time poor Olivia was unable to hide her love, and openly confessed it with such passionate truth, that Viola left her hastily, saying—

"Nevermore will I deplore[24] my master's tears to you."

But in vowing this, Viola did not know the tender pity she would feel for other's suffering.

So when Olivia, in the violence of her love, sent a messenger, praying Cesario to visit her once more, Cesario had no heart to refuse the request.

24 deplore [dɪ'plɔːr] (v.) to regret or feel grief about something 哀嘆

160 But the favors which Olivia bestowed[25] upon this mere page aroused the jealousy of Sir Andrew Aguecheek, a foolish, rejected lover of hers, who at that time was staying at her house with her merry old uncle Sir Toby.

Sir Andrew Aguecheek

This same Sir Toby dearly loved a practical joke, and knowing Sir Andrew to be an arrant[26] coward, he thought that if he could bring off a duel[27] between him and Cesario, there would be rare sport indeed.

So he induced Sir Andrew to send a challenge, which he himself took to Cesario. The poor page, in great terror, said—"I will return again to the house, I am no fighter."

"Back you shall not to the house," said Sir Toby, "unless you fight me first."

And as he looked a very fierce old gentleman, Viola thought it best to await Sir Andrew's coming; and when he at last made his appearance, in a great fright, if the truth had been known, she tremblingly drew her sword, and Sir Andrew in like fear followed her example.

161 Happily for them both, at this moment some officers of the Court came on the scene, and stopped the intended duel. Viola gladly made off[28] with what speed she might, while Sir Toby called after her—

"A very paltry[29] boy, and more a coward than a hare[30]!"

Now, while these things were happening, Sebastian had escaped all the dangers of the deep, and had landed safely in Illyria, where he determined to make his way to the Duke's Court.

On his way thither he passed Olivia's house just as Viola had left it in such a hurry, and whom should he meet but Sir Andrew and Sir Toby. Sir Andrew, mistaking Sebastian for the cowardly Cesario, took his courage in both hands, and walking up to him struck him, saying, "There's for you."

"Why, there's for you; and there, and there!" said Sebastian, hitting back a great deal harder, and again and again, till Sir Toby came to the rescue of his friend.

25 bestow [bɪ'stoʊ] (v.) to give someone something of great value or importance 贈與

26 arrant ['ærənt] (a.) used to emphasize how bad something is 徹底的

27 duel ['du:əl] (n.) formal fight over matter of honor 決鬥

28 make off: to leave a place quickly, usually with good reason 匆匆離開；逃走

29 paltry ['pɔ:ltri] (a.) unimportant or worthless 無用的

30 hare [her] (n.) an animal like a rabbit but larger, which can run very quickly 野兔

(162) Sebastian, however, tore himself free from Sir Toby's clutches[31], and drawing his sword would have fought them both, but that Olivia herself, having heard of the quarrel, came running in, and with many reproaches sent Sir Toby and his friend away.

Olivia besought Sebastian to come into the house with her.

Then turning to Sebastian, whom she too thought to be Cesario, she besought[32] him with many a pretty speech to come into the house with her.

Sebastian, half dazed[33] and all delighted with her beauty and grace, readily consented, and that very day, so great was Olivia's haste, they were married before she had discovered that he was not Cesario, or Sebastian was quite certain whether or not he was in a dream.

Meanwhile Orsino, hearing how ill Cesario sped with Olivia, visited her himself, taking Cesario with him.

31 clutches ['klʌtʃɪz] (n.) (pl.) the power, influence, or control that someone has〔複〕掌握
32 beseech [bɪ'siːtʃ] (v.) to ask earnestly 懇求
33 dazed [deɪzd] (a.) unable to think clearly, especially because of a shock, accident etc 暈暈然的

Olivia and Sebastian were married before she had discovered that he was not Cesario.

163 Olivia met them both before her door, and seeing, as she thought, her husband there, reproached him for leaving her, while to the Duke she said that his suit was as fat and wholesome to her as howling[34] after music.

34 howling ['haʊlɪŋ] (n.) a long, wailing cry 哀號聲

164 "Still so cruel?" said Orsino.

"Still so constant," she answered.

Then Orsino's anger growing to cruelty, he vowed that, to be revenged on her, he would kill Cesario, whom he knew she loved.

"Come, boy," he said to the page.

And Viola, following him as he moved away, said, "I, to do you rest, a thousand deaths would die."

A great fear took hold on Olivia, and she cried aloud, "Cesario, husband, stay!"

"Her husband?" asked the Duke angrily.

"No, my lord, not I," said Viola.

"Call forth the holy father," cried Olivia.

And the priest who had married Sebastian and Olivia, coming in, declared Cesario to be the bridegroom.

"O thou dissembling[35] cub[36]!" the Duke exclaimed. "Farewell, and take her, but go where thou and I henceforth may never meet."

At this moment Sir Andrew came up with bleeding crown, complaining that Cesario had broken his head, and Sir Toby's as well.

"I never hurt you," said Viola, very positively; "you drew your sword on me, but I bespoke[37] you fair, and hurt you not."

165 Yet, for all her protesting, no one there believed her; but all their thoughts were on a sudden changed to wonder, when Sebastian came in.

"I am sorry, madam," he said to his wife, "I have hurt your kinsman. Pardon me, sweet, even for the vows we made each other so late ago."

"One face, one voice, one habit, and two persons!" cried the Duke, looking first at Viola, and then at Sebastian.

"An apple cleft in two," said one who knew Sebastian, "is not more twin than these two creatures. Which is Sebastian?"

"I never had a brother," said Sebastian. "I had a sister, whom the blind waves and surges[38] have devoured[39]."

"Were you a woman," he said to Viola, "I should let my tears fall upon your cheek, and say, "Thrice welcome, drowned Viola!"

Then Viola, rejoicing to see her dear brother alive, confessed that she was indeed his sister, Viola.

35 dissemble [dɪ'sembəl] (v.) to hide your true feelings, thoughts etc 隱藏真心

36 cub [kʌb] (n.) the young of certain animal as the fox, bear, etc. 幼獸

37 bespeak [bɪ'spiːk] (v.) to ask for beforehand 預先要求

38 surge [sɜːrdʒ] (n.) a sudden quick movement of a liquid, electricity, chemical etc through something 大浪

39 devour [dɪ'vaʊr] (v.) to eat something quickly and hungrily 吞沒

“Thou shalt be my wife, and my fancy’s queen.”

166 As she spoke, Orsino felt the pity that is akin[40] to love.

“Boy,” he said, “thou hast said to me a thousand times thou never shouldst love woman like to me.”

“And all those sayings will I overswear,” Viola replied, “and all those swearings keep true.”

“Give me thy hand,” Orsino cried in gladness. “Thou shalt be my wife, and my fancy’s queen.”

Thus was the gentle Viola made happy, while Olivia found in Sebastian a constant lover, and a good husband, and he in her a true and loving wife.

40 akin [əˈkɪn] (a.) very similar to something 近似的

13 Othello

Othello, Desdemona and Brabantio

167 Four hundred years ago there lived in Venice an ensign[1] named Iago, who hated his general, Othello, for not making him a lieutenant[2]. Instead of Iago, who was strongly recommended, Othello had chosen Michael Cassio, whose smooth tongue had helped him to win the heart of Desdemona.

Iago had a friend called Roderigo, who supplied him with money and felt he could not be happy unless Desdemona was his wife.

Othello was a Moor[3], but of so dark a complexion that his enemies called him a Blackamoor. His life had been hard and exciting. He had been vanquished in battle and sold into slavery; and he had been a great traveler and seen men whose shoulders were higher than their heads.

168 Brave as a lion, he had one great fault—jealousy. His love was a terrible selfishness. To love a woman meant with him to possess her as absolutely as he possessed something that did not live and think. The story of Othello is a story of jealousy.

The story of Othello
is a story of jealousy.

One night Iago told Roderigo that Othello had carried off Desdemona without the knowledge of her father, Brabantio.

He persuaded Roderigo to arouse Brabantio, and when that senator[4] appeared Iago told him of Desdemona's elopement[5] in the most unpleasant way. Though he was Othello's officer, he termed him a thief and a Barbary[6] horse.

1 ensign ['ensən] (n.) below lieutenant junior grade 少尉
2 lieutenant [luː'tenənt] (n.)) a commissioned military officer 中尉；少尉
3 Moor [mʊr] (n.) a swarthy race of north Africa 非洲摩爾人
4 senator ['seɪnətər] (n.) a member of the Senate or a senate 元老院議員
5 elopement [ɪ'loʊpmənt] (n.) to leave your home secretly in order to get married 私奔
6 Barbary ['bɑːrbərɪ] (n.) former region of North Africa stretching from the Atlantic coast to western Egypt（北非）巴巴利

I saw Othello's visage in his mind.

169 Brabantio accused Othello before the Duke of Venice of using sorcery[7] to fascinate his daughter, but Othello said that the only sorcery he used was his voice, which told Desdemona his adventures and hair-breadth escapes.

Desdemona was led into the council-chamber, and she explained how she could love Othello despite his almost black face by saying, "I saw Othello's visage[8] in his mind."

As Othello had married Desdemona, and she was glad to be his wife, there was no more to be said against him, especially as the Duke wished him to go to Cyprus to defend it against the Turks.

Othello was quite ready to go, and Desdemona, who pleaded to go with him, was permitted to join him at Cyprus.

Othello's feelings on landing in this island were intensely joyful. "Oh, my sweet," he said to Desdemona, who arrived with Iago, his wife, and Roderigo before him, "I hardly know what I say to you. I am in love with my own happiness."

7 sorcery ['sɔːrsəri] (n.) magic that uses the power of evil forces 巫術

8 visage ['vɪzɪdʒ] (n.) somebody's face or facial expression 容貌；表情

Cassio was on duty in the Castle where Othello ruled Cyprus.

170 News coming presently that the Turkish fleet[9] was out of action, he proclaimed a festival in Cyprus from five to eleven at night.

Cassio was on duty in the Castle where Othello ruled Cyprus, so Iago decided to make the lieutenant drink too much. He had some difficulty, as Cassio knew that wine soon went to his head, but servants brought wine into the room where Cassio was, and Iago sang a drinking song, and so Cassio lifted a glass too often to the health of the general.

When Cassio was inclined to be quarrelsome, Iago told Roderigo to say something unpleasant to him. Cassio cudgeled[10] Roderigo, who ran into the presence of Montano, the ex-governor.

171 Montano civilly interceded for Roderigo, but received so rude an answer from Cassio that he said, "Come, come, you're drunk!"

Cassio then wounded him, and Iago sent Roderigo out to scare the town with a cry of mutiny[11].

The uproar[12] aroused Othello, who, on learning its cause, said, "Cassio, I love thee[13], but never more be officer of mine."

On Cassio and Iago being alone together, the disgraced man moaned[14] about his reputation. Iago said reputation and humbug[15] were the same thing.

"O God," exclaimed Cassio, without heeding him, "that men should put an enemy in their mouths to steal away their brains!"

Iago advised him to beg Desdemona to ask Othello to pardon him.

9 fleet [fliːt] (n.) a group of ships, or all the ships in a navy 艦隊
10 cudgel [ˈkʌdʒəl] (v.) to beat somebody with a cudgel 用棍棒打
11 mutiny [ˈmjuːtni] (n.) open rebellion against constituted authority (especially by seamen or soldiers against their officers) 叛亂
12 uproar [ˈʌprɔːr] (n.) a loud or noisy disturbance 騷動
13 thee [ðiː] (n.) objective case of thou〔古〕(thou 的受格) 你
14 moan [moʊn] (v.) to complain in an annoying way, especially in an unhappy voice and without good reason 抱怨
15 humbug [ˈhʌmbʌg] (n.) something that is silly or makes no sense 騙人、無用的東西

172 Cassio was pleased with the advice, and next morning made his request to Desdemona in the garden of the castle.

She was kindness itself, and said, "Be merry, Cassio, for I would rather die than forsake your cause."

Cassio at that moment saw Othello advancing with Iago, and retired hurriedly.

Iago said, "I don't like that."

"What did you say?" asked Othello, who felt that he had meant something unpleasant, but Iago pretended he had said nothing.

"Was not that Cassio who went from my wife?" asked Othello, and Iago, who knew that it was Cassio and why it was Cassio, said, "I cannot think it was Cassio who stole away in that guilty manner."

Desdemona told Othello that it was grief and humility which made Cassio retreat[16] at his approach[17]. She reminded him how Cassio had taken his part when she was still heart-free[18], and found fault with her Moorish lover.

173 Othello was melted, and said, "I will deny thee nothing," but Desdemona told him that what she asked was as much for his good as dining.

Desdemona left the garden, and Iago asked if it was really true that Cassio had known Desdemona before her marriage.

"Yes," said Othello.

"Indeed," said Iago, as though something that had mystified[19] him was now very clear.

"Is he not honest?" demanded Othello, and Iago repeated the adjective inquiringly, as though he were afraid to say "No."

"What do you mean?" insisted Othello.

To this Iago would only say the flat opposite of what he said to Cassio. He had told Cassio that reputation was humbug.

To Othello he said, "Who steals my purse steals trash, but he who filches from me my good name ruins me."

At this Othello almost leapt into the air, and Iago was so confident of his jealousy that he ventured to warn him against it.

16 retreat [riːˈtriːt] (v.) to move away or backward 退下

17 approach [əˈproutʃ] (n.) a coming nearer in space or time 接近

18 heart-free (a.) not in love 不為情所困的

19 mystify [ˈmɪstɪfaɪ] (v.) to make somebody unable to understand or explain something 使困惑

Iago called jealousy "the green-eyed monster which doth mock the meat it feeds on."

174 Yes, it was no other than Iago who called jealousy "the green-eyed monster which doth[20] mock[21] the meat it feeds on."

Iago having given jealousy one blow, proceeded to feed it with the remark that Desdemona deceived her father when she eloped[22] with Othello. "If she deceived him, why not you?" was his meaning.

Presently Desdemona re-entered to tell Othello that dinner was ready. She saw that he was ill at ease[23]. He explained it by a pain in his forehead. Desdemona then produced[24] a handkerchief, which Othello had given her.

175 A prophetess[25], two hundred years old, had made this handkerchief from the silk of sacred silkworms, dyed[26] it in a liquid prepared from the hearts of maidens, and embroidered[27] it with strawberries.

Gentle Desdemona thought of it simply as a cool, soft thing for a throbbing[28] brow; she knew of no spell upon it that would work destruction for her who lost it.

A prophetess had made this handkerchief from the silk of sacred silkworms.

20 doth [dʌθ] (v. aux.) does: archaic or poetic 3rd person singular, present tense of do〔古〕do 的第三人稱單數現在式

21 mock [mɑːk] (v.) to treat somebody or something with scorn or contempt 嘲笑

22 elope [ɪ'loʊp] (v.) to leave your home secretly in order to get married 私奔

23 ill at ease: uncomfortable and nervous 侷促不安

24 produce [prə'duːs] (v.) take something out 拿出

25 prophetess ['prɑːfɪtəs] (n.) a female prophet 女先知

26 dye [daɪ] (v.) to give something a different color using a dye 染色

27 embroider [ɪm'brɔɪdər] (v.) to decorate with needlework 刺繡

28 throb [θrɑːb] (v.) to beat in a rapid forceful way 跳動

176 "Let me tie it round your head," she said to Othello; "you will be well in an hour."

But Othello pettishly[29] said it was too small, and let it fall.

Desdemona and he then went indoors to dinner, and Emilia picked up the handkerchief which Iago had often asked her to steal.

She was looking at it when Iago came in. After a few words about it he snatched it from her, and bade her leave him.

In the garden he was joined by Othello, who seemed hungry for the worst lies he could offer. He therefore told Othello that he had seen Cassio wipe his mouth with a handkerchief, which, because it was spotted with strawberries, he guessed to be one that Othello had given his wife.

The unhappy Moor went mad with fury, and Iago bade the heavens witness that he devoted his hand and heart and brain to Othello's service.

"I accept your love," said Othello. "Within three days let me hear that Cassio is dead."

Iago's next step was to leave Desdemona's handkerchief in Cassio's room. Cassio saw it, and knew it was not his, but he liked the strawberry pattern on it, and he gave it to his sweetheart Bianca and asked her to copy it for him.

177 Iago's next move was to induce[30] Othello, who had been bullying[31] Desdemona about the handkerchief, to play the eavesdropper[32] to a conversation between Cassio and himself. His intention was to talk about Cassio's sweetheart, and allow Othello to suppose that the lady spoken of was Desdemona.

"How are you, lieutenant?" asked Iago when Cassio appeared.

"The worse for being called what I am not," replied Cassio, gloomily. "Keep on reminding Desdemona, and you'll soon be restored," said Iago, adding, in a tone too low for Othello to hear, "If Bianca could set the matter right, how quickly it would mend!"

29 pettishly ['petɪʃli] (adv.) with a freak of ill temper 怒氣沖沖地

30 induce [ɪn'duːs] (v.) to persuade or influence somebody to do or think something 引誘

31 bully ['bʊli] (v.) to threaten to hurt someone or frighten them, especially someone smaller or weaker 威嚇；欺侮

32 eavesdropper ['iːvzdrɑːpər] (n.) a secret listener to private conversations 偷聽者

178 "Alas! poor rogue[33]," said Cassio, "I really think she loves me," and like the talkative coxcomb[34] he was, Cassio was led on to boast of Bianca's fondness for him, while Othello imagined, with choked[35] rage, that he prattled[36] of Desdemona, and thought, "I see your nose, Cassio, but not the dog I shall throw it to."

Othello was still spying when Bianca entered, boiling over with the idea that Cassio, whom she considered her property, had asked her to copy the embroidery[37] on the handkerchief of a new sweetheart. She tossed[38] him the handkerchief with scornful words, and Cassio departed with her.

Othello had seen Bianca, who was in station lower, in beauty and speech inferior far, to Desdemona and he began in spite of himself to praise his wife to the villain before him. He praised her skill with the needle, her voice that could "sing the savageness out of a bear," her wit, her sweetness, the fairness of her skin.

33 rogue [roʊg] (n.) a man or boy who behaves badly, but who you like in spite of this, often used humorously 調皮鬼

34 coxcomb ['kɑːkskoʊm] (n.) stupid man who is too proud of his clothes and appearance 花花公子

179 Every time he praised her Iago said something that made him remember his anger and utter it foully[39], and yet he must needs praise her, and say, "The pity of it, Iago! O Iago, the pity of it, Iago!"

There was never in all Iago's villainy one moment of wavering. If there had been he might have wavered then.

"Strangle[40] her," he said; and "Good, good!" said his miserable dupe[41].

The pair were still talking murder when Desdemona appeared with a relative of Desdemona's father, called Lodovico, who bore a letter for Othello from the Duke of Venice. The letter recalled Othello from Cyprus, and gave the governorship to Cassio.

35 choked [tʃoʊkt] (a.) very upset 惱怒的
36 prattle ['prætl] (v.) to talk in a silly, idle, or childish way 幼稚地說話
37 embroidery [ɪm'brɔɪdəri] (n.) something with decorative needlework 刺繡品
38 toss [tɔ:s] (v.) throw carelessly 拋擲
39 foully [faʊlli] (adv.) in a wicked and shameful manner 卑鄙地
40 strangle ['stræŋgəl] (v.) to kill someone by pressing their throat with your hands, a rope etc 勒死
41 dupe [du:p] (n.) someone who is tricked, especially into becoming involved in something illegal 容易受騙的人

180 Luckless Desdemona seized this unhappy moment to urge once more the suit of Cassio.

"Fire and brimstone[42]!" shouted Othello.

"It may be the letter agitates[43] him," explained Lodovico to Desdemona, and he told her what it contained.

"I am glad," said Desdemona. It was the first bitter speech that Othello's unkindness had wrung[44] out of her.

"I am glad to see you lose your temper," said Othello.

"Why, sweet Othello?" she asked, sarcastically[45]; and Othello slapped her face.

Now was the time for Desdemona to have saved her life by separation, but she knew not her peril—only that her love was wounded to the core[46].

"I have not deserved this," she said, and the tears rolled slowly down her face.

42 fire and brimstone: in the Christian religion, eternal punishment in hell 地獄裡的磨難

43 agitate ['ædʒɪteɪt] (v.) make somebody anxious 激怒

181 Lodovico was shocked and disgusted. "My lord," he said, "this would not be believed in Venice. Make her amends[47]."

But, like a madman talking in his nightmare, Othello poured out his foul[48] thought in ugly speech, and roared, "Out of my sight!"

"I will not stay to offend you," said his wife, but she lingered even in going, and only when he shouted "Avaunt[49]!" did she leave her husband and his guests.

Othello then invited Lodovico to supper, adding, "You are welcome, sir, to Cyprus. Goats and monkeys!" Without waiting for a reply he left the company.

Distinguished visitors detest[50] being obliged to look on at family quarrels, and dislike being called either goats or monkeys, and Lodovico asked Iago for an explanation.

44 wring [rɪŋ] (v.) to succeed in getting something from someone, but only after a lot of effort 強迫取得

45 sarcastically [sɑːr'kæstɪkli] (adv.) in a sarcastic manner 挖苦地

46 to the core: in every part 徹底地

47 amends [ə'mendz] (n.) something done or given as compensation for a wrong 賠罪

48 foul [faʊl] (a.) disgustingly dirty; filled with offensive matter 邪惡的

49 avaunt [ə'vɔːnt] (int.) Away! Depart! Begone! 〔古〕滾！

50 detest [dɪ'test] (v.) to hate something or someone very much 憎惡

182 True to himself, Iago, in a round-about way, said that Othello was worse than he seemed, and advised them to study his behavior and save him from the discomfort of answering any more questions.

He proceeded to tell Roderigo to murder Cassio. Roderigo was out of tune with his friend. He had given Iago quantities of jewels for Desdemona without effect; Desdemona had seen none of them, for Iago was a thief.

Iago smoothed him with a lie, and when Cassio was leaving Bianca's house, Roderigo wounded him, and was wounded in return.

Cassio shouted, and Lodovico and a friend came running up. Cassio pointed out Roderigo as his assailant[51], and Iago, hoping to rid himself of an inconvenient friend, called him "Villain!" and stabbed him, but not to death.

183 At the Castle, Desdemona was in a sad mood. She told Emilia that she must leave her; her husband wished it.

"Dismiss[52] me!" exclaimed Emilia.

"It was his bidding, said Desdemona; we must not displease him now."

She sang a song which a girl had sung whose lover had been base to her—a song of a maiden crying by that tree whose boughs droop[53] as though it weeps, and she went to bed and slept.

She woke with her husband's wild eyes upon her.

"Have you prayed tonight?" he asked; and he told this blameless and sweet woman to ask God's pardon for any sin she might have on her conscience.

"I would not kill thy soul," he said.

He told her that Cassio had confessed, but she knew Cassio had nought[54] to confess that concerned her. She said that Cassio could not say anything that would damage her. Othello said his mouth was stopped.

51 assailant [ə'seɪlənt] (n.) someone who attacks 襲擊者

52 dismiss [dɪs'mɪs] (v.) to remove someone from their job 遣散

53 droop [dru:p] (v.) to hang or bend down 低垂

54 nought [nɑ:t] (variant of naught) used in some expressions to mean nothing 無

Desdemona wept.

184 Then Desdemona wept, but with violent words, in spite of all her pleading, Othello pressed upon her throat and mortally[55] hurt her.

Then with boding[56] heart came Emilia, and besought[57] entrance at the door, and Othello unlocked it, and a voice came from the bed saying, "A guiltless death I die."

"Who did it?" cried Emilia; and the voice said, "Nobody—I myself. Farewell!"

"'Twas[58] I that killed her," said Othello.

He poured out his evidence by that sad bed to the people who came running in, Iago among them; but when he spoke of the handkerchief, Emilia told the truth. And Othello knew.

"Are there no stones in heaven but thunderbolts?" he exclaimed, and ran at Iago, who gave Emilia her death-blow and fled.

185 But they brought him back, and the death that came to him later on was a relief from torture[59].

They would have taken Othello back to Venice to try him there, but he escaped them on his sword.

"A word or two before you go," he said to the Venetians in the chamber. "Speak of me as I was—no better, no worse. Say I cast away the pearl of pearls, and wept with these hard eyes; and say that, when in Aleppo years ago I saw a Turk beating a Venetian, I took him by the throat and smote[60] him thus."

With his own hand he stabbed himself to the heart; and ere[61] he died his lips touched the face of Desdemona with despairing love.

55 mortally ['mɔːrtəlʒ] (adv.) in a deadly or fatal manner 致命地
56 boding ['boudɪŋ] (a.) a feeling of evil to come 不祥的
57 beseech [bɪ'siːtʃ] (v.) ask for or request earnestly 懇求
58 twas [twɑːz] abbreviation of "it was"〔詩〕it was 的縮寫
59 torture ['tɔːrtʃər] (n.) intense feelings of suffering; acute mental or physical pain 痛苦
60 smite [smɪt] (v.) to destroy, attack, or punish someone 殺死
61 ere [er] (conj.) before 在……以前

14 The Winter's Tale

Leontes and Polixenes had been brought up together.

186 Leontes was the King of Sicily, and his dearest friend was Polixenes, King of Bohemia. They had been brought up together, and only separated when they reached man's estate[1] and each had to go and rule over his kingdom.

After many years, when each was married and had a son, Polixenes came to stay with Leontes in Sicily.

187 Leontes was a violent-tempered man and rather silly, and he took it into his stupid head that his wife, Hermione, liked Polixenes better than she did him, her own husband.

When once he had got this into his head, nothing could put it out; and he ordered one of his lords, Camillo, to put a poison in Polixenes' wine.

Camillo tried to dissuade him from this wicked action, but finding he was not to be moved, pretended to consent. He then told Polixenes what was proposed against him, and they fled from the Court of Sicily that night, and returned to Bohemia, where Camillo lived on as Polixenes' friend and counselor[2].

Leontes threw the Queen into prison; and her son, the heir to the throne, died of sorrow to see his mother so unjustly and cruelly treated.

While the Queen was in prison she had a little baby, and a friend of hers, named Paulina, had the baby dressed in its best, and took it to show the King, thinking that the sight of his helpless little daughter would soften his heart towards his dear Queen, who had never done him any wrong, and who loved him a great deal more than he deserved.

1 estate [ɪ'steɪt] (n.) the period, circumstances, or condition in which somebody lives 人生階段

2 counselor ['kaʊnsələr] (n.) one who gives advice or counsel 顧問

Leontes thought his wife, Hermione, liked Polixenes better than she did her own husband.

188 But the King would not look at the baby, and ordered Paulina's husband to take it away in a ship, and leave it in the most desert[3] and dreadful place he could find, which Paulina's husband, very much against his will, was obliged to do.

Then the poor Queen was brought up to be tried for treason[4] in preferring Polixenes to her King; but really she had never thought of anyone except Leontes, her husband.

Leontes had sent some messengers to ask the god, Apollo, whether he was not right in his cruel thoughts of the Queen. But he had not patience to wait till they came back, and so it happened that they arrived in the middle of the trial. The Oracle said—

Leontes had sent some messengers to ask the god, Apollo.

189 *Hermione is innocent, Polixenes blameless,*
Camillo a true subject, Leontes a jealous tyrant,
and the King shall live without an heir,
if that which is lost be not found.

Then a man came and told them that the little Prince was dead. The poor Queen, hearing this, fell down in a fit[5]; and then the King saw how wicked and wrong he had been.

He ordered Paulina and the ladies who were with the Queen to take her away, and try to restore[6] her. But Paulina came back in a few moments, and told the King that Hermione was dead.

3 desert ['dezərt] (a.) abandoned 無人居住的
4 treason ['tri:zən] (n.) the crime of lack of loyalty to your country, especially by helping its enemies 叛國罪
5 fit [fɪt] (n.) lose consciousness 昏厥
6 restore [rɪ'stɔ:r] (v.) to bring back to health 使恢復健康

190 Now Leontes' eyes were at last opened to his folly. His Queen was dead, and the little daughter who might have been a comfort to him he had sent away to be the prey of wolves and kites[7].

Life had nothing left for him now. He gave himself up to his grief, and passed in many sad years in prayer and remorse[8]. The baby Princess was left on the seacoast of Bohemia, the very kingdom where Polixenes reigned.

Paulina's husband never went home to tell Leontes where he had left the baby; for as he was going back to the ship, he met a bear and was torn to pieces. So there was an end of him.

But the poor deserted[9] little baby was found by a shepherd. She was richly dressed, and had with her some jewels, and a paper was pinned to her cloak, saying that her name was Perdita, and that she came of noble parents.

The shepherd, being a kind-hearted man, took home the little baby to his wife, and they brought her up as their own child.

7 kite [kaɪt] (n.) a small slim hawk with long pointed wings and a forked 鳶

8 remorse [rɪ'mɔːrs] (n.) strong feeling of being sorry that you have done something very bad 悔恨

9 deserted [dɪ'zɜːrtɪd] (a.) left desolate or empty 被遺棄的

191 She had no more teaching than a shepherd's child generally has, but she inherited from her royal mother many graces and charms, so that she was quite different from the other maidens in the village where she lived.

Perdita inherited from her royal mother many graces and charms.

One day Prince Florizel, the son of the good King of Bohemia, was bunting near the shepherd's house and saw Perdita, now grown up to a charming woman.

He made friends with the shepherd, not telling him that he was the Prince, but saying that his name was Doricles, and that he was a private gentleman; and then, being deeply in love with the pretty Perdita, he came almost daily to see her.

The King could not understand what it was that took his son nearly every day from home; so he set people to watch him, and then found out that the heir of the King of Bohemia was in love with Perdita, the pretty shepherd girl. Polixenes, wishing to see whether this was true, disguised himself, and went with the faithful Camillo, in disguise too, to the old shepherd's house.

A peddler was selling ribbons and laces and gloves.

192 They arrived at the feast of sheep-shearing, and, though strangers, they were made very welcome. There was dancing going on, and a peddler[10] was selling ribbons and laces and gloves, which the young men bought for their sweethearts.

Florizel and Perdita, however, were taking no part in this gay scene, but sat quietly together talking.

The King noticed the charming manners and great beauty of Perdita, never guessing that she was the daughter of his old friend, Leontes.

He said to Camillo, "This is the prettiest low-born lass[11] that ever ran on the green sward[12]. Nothing she does or seems but smacks[13] of something greater than herself—too noble for this place."

And Camillo answered, "In truth she is the Queen of curds[14] and cream."

193 But when Florizel, who did not recognize his father, called upon the strangers to witness his betrothal[15] with the pretty shepherdess, the King made himself known and forbade the marriage, adding that if ever she saw Florizel again, he would kill her and her old father, the shepherd; and with that he left them.

"She is the Queen of curds and cream."

But Camillo remained behind, for he was charmed with Perdita, and wished to befriend her.

10 peddler ['pedlər] (n.) someone who travels about selling his wares (as on the streets or at carnivals) 小販

11 lass [læs] (n.) a girl or young woman who is unmarried 小姑娘

12 sward [swɔːd] (n.) an area of land covered with grass 草地

13 smack [smæk] (v.) to have a unique flavor or taste 有特別的味道

14 curd [kɜːrd] (n.) solid part of sour milk 凝乳狀食品

15 betrothal [bɪ'troʊðəl] (n.) an engagement to marry 訂婚

194 Camillo had long known how sorry Leontes was for that foolish madness of his, and he longed to go back to Sicily to see his old master. He now proposed that the young people should go there and claim the protection of Leontes.

So they went, and the shepherd went with them, taking Perdita's jewels, her baby clothes, and the paper he had found pinned to her cloak. Leontes received them with great kindness.

"Such a sweet creature my daughter might have been, if I had not cruelly sent her from me."

He was very polite to Prince Florizel, but all his looks were for Perdita. He saw how much she was like the Queen Hermione, and said again and again—

"Such a sweet creature my daughter might have been, if I had not cruelly sent her from me."

195 When the old shepherd heard that the King had lost a baby daughter, who had been left upon the coast of Bohemia, he felt sure that Perdita, the child he had reared[16], must be the King's daughter, and when he told his tale and showed the jewels and the paper, the King perceived that Perdita was indeed his long-lost child. He welcomed her with joy, and rewarded the good shepherd.

Polixenes had hastened after his son to prevent his marriage with Perdita, but when he found that she was the daughter of his old friend, he was only too glad to give his consent.

Yet Leontes could not be happy. He remembered how his fair Queen, who should have been at his side to share his joy in his daughter's happiness, was dead through his unkindness, and he could say nothing for a long time but—

"Oh, thy[17] mother! thy mother!" and ask forgiveness of the King of Bohemia, and then kiss his daughter again, and then the Prince Florizel, and then thank the old shepherd for all his goodness.

16 rear [rɪr] (v.) to bring up 撫養

17 thy [ðaɪ] (pron.) the singular possessive case of the personal pronoun thou: used as a possessive adjective〔古〕汝的；你的（thou 的所有格）

196 Then Paulina, who had been high all these years in the King's favor, because of her kindness to the dead Queen Hermione, said—

"I have a statue made in the likeness of the dead Queen, a piece many years in doing, and performed by the rare Italian master, Giulio Romano. I keep it in a private house apart, and there, ever since you lost your Queen, I have gone twice or thrice a day. Will it please your Majesty to go and see the statue?"

So Leontes and Polixenes, and Florizel and Perdita, with Camillo and their attendants[18], went to Paulina's house where there was a heavy purple curtain screening[19] off an alcove[20]; and Paulina, with her hand on the curtain, said—

"She was peerless[21] when she was alive, and I do believe that her dead likeness excels[22] whatever yet you have looked upon, or that the hand of man hath[23] done. Therefore I keep it lonely, apart. But here it is—behold, and say, 'tis well."

18 attendant [ə'tendənt] (n.) someone who waits on or tends to or attends to the needs of another 隨從

19 screen [skriːn] (v.) if something screens something else, it is in front of it and hides it 掩蔽

20 alcove ['ælkouv] (n.) a place in the wall of a room that is built further back than the rest of the wall 凹室；壁龕

21 peerless ['pɪrləs] (a.) so good as to have no equal 無與倫比的

197 And with that she drew back the curtain and showed them the statue. The King gazed and gazed on the beautiful statue of his dead wife, but said nothing.

"I like your silence," said Paulina; "it the more shows off your wonder. But speak, is it not like her?"

"It is almost herself," said the King, "and yet, Paulina, Hermione was not so much wrinkled[24], nothing so old as this seems."

"Oh, not by much," said Polixenes.

"Ah," said Paulina, "that is the cleverness of the carver[25], who shows her to us as she would have been had she lived till now."

And still Leontes looked at the statue and could not take his eyes away.

Paulina drew back the curtain and showed them the statue.

22 excel [ɪk'sel] (v.) to do something very well, or much better than most people 勝過

23 hath [hæθ] (v.) (v. aux.) present 3rd pers sg of have〔古〕have 的第三人稱單數現在式

24 wrinkled ['rɪŋkəld] (a.) skin or cloth that is wrinkled has small lines or folds in it 有皺紋的

25 carver ['kɑːrvər] (n.) someone who carves wood or stone 雕刻者

198 "If I had known," said Paulina, "that this poor image would so have stirred your grief, and love, I would not have shown it to you."

But he only answered, "Do not draw the curtain."

"No, you must not look any longer," said Paulina, "or you will think it moves."

"Let be! let be!" said the King. "Would you not think it breathed?"

"I will draw the curtain," said Paulina; " you will think it lives presently."

"Ah, sweet Paulina," said Leontes, "make me to think so twenty years together."

"If you can bear it," said Paulina, "I can make the statue move, make it come down and take you by the hand. Only you would think it was by wicked magic."

"Whatever you can make her do, I am content to look on," said the King.

And then, all folks there admiring and beholding, the statue moved from its pedestal[26], and came down the steps and put its arms round the King's neck, and he held her face and kissed her many times, for this was no statue, but the real living Queen Hermione herself.

26 pedestal ['pedɪstəl] (n.) a base or support for a column or statue（雕像等的）臺座

Quoon Hcrmionc had lived hidden all these years.

199 She had lived hidden, by Paulina's kindness, all these years, and would not discover herself to her husband, though she knew he had repented, because she could not quite forgive him till she knew what had become of her little baby.

Now that Perdita was found, she forgave her husband everything, and it was like a new and beautiful marriage to them, to be together once more. Florizel and Perdita were married and lived long and happily.

To Leontes his many years of suffering were well paid for in the moment when, after long grief and pain, he felt the arms of his true love around him once again.

15 Much Ado About Nothing

Don Pedro came for a holiday to Messina, a town in Sicily.

200 It began with sunshine. Don Pedro, Prince of Arragon, in Spain, had gained so complete a victory over his foes that the very land whence they came is forgotten.

Feeling happy and playful after the fatigues of war, Don Pedro came for a holiday to Messina, a town in Sicily; and in his suite were his stepbrother Don John and two young Italian lords, Benedick and Claudio.

Benedick was a merry chatterbox[1], who had determined to live a bachelor[2]. Claudio, on the other hand, no sooner arrived at Messina than he fell in love with Hero, the daughter of Leonato, Governor of Messina.

One July day, a perfumer called Borachio was burning dried lavender[3] in a musty room in Leonato's house, when the sound of conversation floated through the open window.

201 "Give me your candid[4] opinion of Hero," Claudio asked.

"Too short and brown for praise," was Benedick's reply; "but alter[5] her color or height, and you spoil her."

"In my eyes she is the sweetest of women," said Claudio.

"Not in mine," retorted Benedick, "and I have no need for glasses. She is like the last day of December compared with the first of May if you set her beside her cousin. Unfortunately, the Lady Beatrice is a fury."

"Too short and brown for praise."

Beatrice was Leonato's niece. She amused herself by saying witty and severe things about Benedick, who called her Dear Lady Disdain[6].

1 chatterbox ['tʃætərbɑːks] (n.) somebody who talks a lot, especially about unimportant things 喋喋不休的人
2 bachelor ['bætʃələr] (n.) a man who has never been married 單身漢
3 lavender ['lævɪndər] (n.) plant that has grey-green leaves and purple flowers with a strong pleasant smell 薰衣草
4 candid ['kændɪd] (a.) honest or direct 直言的
5 alter ['ɑːltər] (v.) cause to change 改變
6 disdain [dɪs'deɪn] (n.) extreme contempt or disgust for something or somebody 鄙視

202 Claudio and Benedick were still talking when Don Pedro came up and said good-humoredly, "Well, gentlemen, what's the secret?"

"I am longing," answered Benedick, "for your Grace to command me to tell."

"I charge you, then, on your allegiance[7] to tell me," said Don Pedro, falling in with his humor.

"Claudio is in love with Hero, Leonato's short daughter," said Benedick.

Don Pedro was pleased, for he admired Hero and was fond of Claudio. When Benedick had departed, he said to Claudio—

"Be steadfast[8] in your love for Hero, and I will help you to win her. Tonight her father gives a masquerade[9], and I will pretend I am Claudio, and tell her how Claudio loves her, and if she be pleased, I will go to her father and ask his consent to your union."

7 allegiance [ə'liːdʒəns] (n.) loyalty to a leader, country etc 忠誠
8 steadfast ['stɛdfæst] (a.) faithful and very loyal 堅定的
9 masquerade [ˌmæskə'reɪd] (n.) a party of guests wearing costumes and masks 化裝舞會

203 However, Claudio had an enemy who was outwardly a friend. This enemy was Don Pedro's stepbrother Don John, who was jealous of Claudio because Don Pedro preferred him to Don John.

It was to Don John that Borachio came with the interesting conversation which he had overheard.

"I shall have some fun at that masquerade myself," said Don John when Borachio ceased speaking.

On the night of the masquerade, Don Pedro, masked and pretending he was Claudio, asked Hero if he might walk with her.

They moved away together, and Don John went up to Claudio and said, "Signor[10] Benedick, I believe?"

"The same," fibbed[11] Claudio.

10 signor ['siːnjɔːr] (n.) the usual Italian form of title or address for a man. It is the equivalent of English "Mr." 閣下

11 fib [fɪb] (v.) to tell an insignificant or harmless lie 撒小謊

204 "I should be much obliged then," said Don John, "if you would use your influence with my brother to cure him of his love for Hero. She is beneath him in rank."

"How do you know he loves her?" inquired Claudio.

"I heard him swear his affection," was the reply, and Borachio chimed[12] in with, "So did I too."

Claudio was then left to himself, and his thought was that his Prince had betrayed him.

"Farewell, Hero," he muttered; "I was a fool to trust to an agent[13]."

Meanwhile Beatrice and Benedick (who was masked) were having a brisk[14] exchange of opinions.

"Did Benedick ever make you laugh?" asked she.

"Who is Benedick?" he inquired.

"A Prince's jester[15]," replied Beatrice, and she spoke so sharply that "I would not marry her," he declared afterwards, "if her estate were the Garden of Eden."

But the principal speaker at the masquerade was neither Beatrice nor Benedick. It was Don Pedro, who carried out his plan to the letter, and brought the light back to Claudio's face in a twinkling, by appearing before him with Leonato and Hero, and saying, "Claudio, when would you like to go to church?"

12 chime [tʃaɪm] (v.) be in agreement with something else 同意

13 agent ['eɪdʒənt] (n.) a spy 密探

14 brisk [brɪsk] (a.) quick, energetic and active 快的

15 jester ['dʒestər] (n.) a man employed in the past by a ruler to entertain people with jokes, stories etc 弄臣

205 "Tomorrow," was the prompt[16] answer. "Time goes on crutches[17] till I marry Hero."

"Give her a week, my dear son," said Leonato, and Claudio's heart thumped[18] with joy.

"And now," said the amiable[19] Don Pedro, "we must find a wife for Signor Benedick. It is a task for Hercules[20]."

"I will help you," said Leonato, "if I have to sit up ten nights."

Then Hero spoke. "I will do what I can, my lord, to find a good husband for Beatrice."

Borachio cheered up Don John by laying a plan before him with which he was confident he could persuade both Claudio and Don Pedro that Hero was a fickle[21] girl who had two strings to her bow. Don John agreed to this plan of hate.

16 prompt [prɑːmpt] (a.) done quickly and without delay 迅速的

17 crutch [krʌtʃ] (n.) one of a pair of long sticks that you put under your arms to help you walk when you have hurt your leg 丁字形拐杖

18 thump [θʌmp] (v.) make dull heavy sound 砰然作聲

19 amiable ['eɪmiəbəl] (a.) friendly and easy to like 和藹可親的

20 Hercules: Roman mythological hero, noted for his courage and great strength〔羅馬神話〕大力士海克力斯

21 fickle ['fɪkəl] (a.) likely to change, especially in affections, intentions, loyalties, or preferences 善變的

206 Don Pedro, on the other hand, had devised[22] a cunning plan of love. "If," he said to Leonato, "we pretend, when Beatrice is near enough to overhear us, that Benedick is pining[23] for her love, she will pity him, see his good qualities, and love him. And if, when Benedick thinks we don't know he is listening, we say how sad it is that the beautiful Beatrice should be in love with a heartless scoffer[24] like Benedick, he will certainly be on his knees before her in a week or less."

So one day, when Benedick was reading in a summer-house, Claudio sat down outside it with Leonato, and said, "Your daughter told me something about a letter Beatrice wrote."

"She will get up twenty times in the night and write goodness knows what. But once Hero peeped, and saw the words 'Benedick and Beatrice' on the sheet, and then Beatrice tore it up," exclaimed Leonato.

"Hero told me," said Claudio, "that she cried, 'O sweet Benedick!'"

207 Benedick was touched to the core by this improbable story, which he was vain enough to believe. "She is fair and good," he said to himself. "I must not seem proud. I feel that I love her. People will laugh, of course; but their paper bullets will do me no harm."

Benedick in the summer-house

At this moment Beatrice came to the summerhouse[25], and said, "Against my will, I have come to tell you that dinner is ready."

"Fair Beatrice, I thank you," said Benedick.

"I took no more pains to come than you take pains to thank me," was the rejoinder, intended to freeze him.

But it did not freeze him. It warmed him. The meaning he squeezed out of her rude speech was that she was delighted to come to him.

22 devise [dɪ'vaɪz] (v.) think something up 想出

23 pine [paɪn] (v.) to long for somebody or something, especially somebody or something unattainable 渴望

24 scoffer (n.) someone who jeers or mocks or treats something with contempt 嘲笑者

25 summerhouse ['sʌmərhaʊs] (n.) a small roofed building affording shade and rest 涼亭

208 Hero, who had undertaken the task of melting the heart of Beatrice, took no trouble to seek an occasion. She simply said to her maid Margaret one day, "Run into the parlor[26] and whisper to Beatrice that Ursula and I are talking about her in the orchard[27]."

Benedick called Beatrice "Dear Lady Disdain".

Having said this, she felt as sure that Beatrice would overhear what was meant for her ears as if she had made an appointment with her cousin.

In the orchard was a bower[28], screened from the sun by honeysuckles[29], and Beatrice entered it a few minutes after Margaret had gone on her errand[30].

26 parlor ['pɑːrlər] (n.) a living room that is set aside for entertaining guests 起居室

27 orchard ['ɔːrtʃərd] (n.) a place where fruit trees are grown 果樹園

28 bower ['bauər] (n.) a pleasant place in the shade under a tree 樹蔭處

29 honeysuckle ['hʌniˌsʌkəl] (n.) a climbing bush with twining stems 忍冬屬植物

30 errand ['erənd] (n.) short journey either to take a message or to deliver or collect something 差事

209 "But are you sure," asked Ursula, who was one of Hero's attendants, "that Benedick loves Beatrice so devotedly?"

"So say the Prince and my betrothed[31]," replied Hero, "and they wished me to tell her, but I said, 'No! Let Benedick get over it.'"

"Why did you say that?"

"Because Beatrice is unbearably proud. Her eyes sparkle with disdain and scorn. She is too conceited[32] to love. I should not like to see her making game of poor Benedick's love. I would rather see Benedick waste away like a covered fire."

"I don't agree with you," said Ursula. "I think your cousin is too clear-sighted not to see the merits of Benedick."

"He is the one man in Italy, except Claudio," said Hero.

The talkers then left the orchard, and Beatrice, excited and tender, stepped out of the summer-house, saying to herself, "Poor dear Benedick, be true to me, and your love shall tame this wild heart of mine."

31 betrothed [bɪˈtroʊðd] (n.) the person that someone has agreed to marry 未婚夫（妻）

32 conceited [kənˈsiːtɪd] (a.) having an exaggerated sense of self-importance 驕傲自大的

210 We now return to the plan of hate.

The night before the day fixed for Claudio's wedding, Don John entered a room in which Don Pedro and Claudio were conversing, and asked Claudio if he intended to be married tomorrow.

"You know he does!" said Don Pedro.

"He may know differently," said Don John, "when he has seen what I will show him if he will follow me."

They followed him into the garden; and they saw a lady leaning out of Hero's window talking love to Borachio.

Claudio thought the lady was Hero, and said, "I will shame her for it tomorrow!"

Don Pedro thought she was Hero, too; but she was not Hero; she was Margaret.

Don John chuckled[33] noiselessly when Claudio and Don Pedro quitted[34] the garden; he gave Borachio a purse containing a thousand ducats[35].

The money made Borachio feel very gay, and when he was walking in the street with his friend Conrade, he boasted of his wealth and the giver, and told what he had done.

33 chuckle ['tʃʌkəl] (v.) to laugh quietly 暗自發笑

34 quit [kwɪt] (v.) to depart from 離開

35 ducat ['dʌkət] (n.) formerly a gold coin of various European countries 硬幣

211

A watchman overheard them, and thought that a man who had been paid a thousand ducats for villainy[36] was worth taking in charge. He therefore arrested Borachio and Conrade, who spent the rest of the night in prison.

Before noon of the next day half of the aristocrats[37] in Messina were at church. Hero thought it was her wedding day, and she was there in her wedding dress, no cloud on her pretty face or in her frank and shining eyes. The priest was Friar[38] Francis.

Turning to Claudio, he said, "You come hither, my lord, to marry this lady?"

"No!" contradicted[39] Claudio.

Leonato thought he was quibbling[40] over grammar. "You should have said, Friar," said he, "'You come to be married to her.'"

Friar Francis turned to Hero. "Lady," he said, "you come hither to be married to this Count?"

"I do," replied Hero.

36 villainy ['vɪləni] (n.) an evil or immoral act 惡行

37 aristocrat [ə'rɪstəkræt] (n.) a class of people who hold high social rank 貴族

38 friar ['fraər] (n.) a man belonging to one of several Roman Catholic religious groups, whose members often promise to stay poor 天主教的苦行僧

39 contradict [ˌkɑːntrə'dɪkt] (v.) to disagree with something, especially by saying that the opposite is true 反駁

40 quibble ['kwɪbəl] (v.) to argue about, or say you disapprove of, something very small and unimportant 推託

212 "If either of you know any impediment[41] to this marriage, I charge you to utter it," said the Friar.

"Do you know of any, Hero?" asked Claudio.

"None," said she.

"Know you of any, Count?" demanded the Friar.

"I dare reply for him, 'None,'" said Leonato.

Claudio exclaimed bitterly, "O! what will not men dare say! Father," he continued, "will you give me your daughter?"

"As freely," replied Leonato, "as God gave her to me."

"And what can I give you," asked Claudio, "which is worthy of this gift?"

"Nothing," said Don Pedro, "unless you give the gift back to the giver."

"Sweet Prince, you teach me," said Claudio. "There, Leonato, take her back." These brutal words were followed by others which flew from Claudio, Don Pedro and Don John.

213 The church seemed no longer sacred. Hero took her own part as long as she could, then she swooned[42].

All her persecutors[43] left the church, except her father, who was befooled by the accusations against her, and cried, "Hence from her! Let her die!"

But Friar Francis saw Hero blameless with his clear eyes that probed[44] the soul.

"She is innocent," he said; "a thousand signs have told me so."

Hero revived under his kind gaze. Her father, flurried[45] and angry, knew not what to think, and the Friar said, "They have left her as one dead with shame. Let us pretend that she is dead until the truth is declared, and slander[46] turns to remorse[47]."

"The Friar advises well," said Benedick.

41 impediment [ɪm'pedɪmənt] (n.) something that hinders progress 阻礙

42 swoon [swuːn] (v.) to experience a sudden and usually brief loss of consciousness 昏倒

43 persecutor ['pɜːrsɪkjuːtər] (n.) a person or thing that persecutes or harasses 迫害者

44 probe [proʊb] (v.) to conduct a thorough investigation of something 探查

45 flurried ['flɜːrid] (a.) confused and nervous or excited 激動的

46 slander ['slændər] (n.) a false and malicious statement that damages somebody's reputation 造謠中傷

47 remorse [rɪ'mɔːrs] (v.) a strong feeling of guilt and regret about something you have done 痛悔

214 Then Hero was led away into a retreat, and Beatrice and Benedick remained alone in the church.

Benedick knew she had been weeping bitterly and long. "Surely I do believe your fair cousin is wronged," he said.

She still wept.

"Is it not strange," asked Benedick, gently, "that I love nothing in the world as well as you?"

"It were as possible for me to say I loved nothing as well as you," said Beatrice, "but I do not say it. I am sorry for my cousin."

"Tell me what to do for her," said Benedick. "Kill Claudio."

"Ha! not for the wide world," said Benedick.

"Your refusal kills me," said Beatrice. "Farewell."

"Enough! I will challenge him," cried Benedick.

215 During this scene Borachio and Conrade were in prison. There they were examined by a constable[48] called Dogberry.

The watchman gave evidence to the effect that Borachio had said that he had received a thousand ducats for conspiring[49] against Hero.

Leonato was not present at this examination, but he was nevertheless now thoroughly convinced Of Hero's innocence. He played the part of bereaved[50] father very well, and when Don Pedro and Claudio called on him in a friendly way, he said to the Italian, "You have slandered my child to death, and I challenge you to combat."

"I cannot fight an old man," said Claudio.

"You could kill a girl," sneered[51] Leonato, and Claudio crimsoned[52].

48 constable ['kɑːnstəbəl] (n.) a royal household official in Middle Ages 總管

49 conspire [kən'spaɪr] (v.) to secretly plan with someone else to do something illegal 密謀

50 bereaved [bɪ'riːvd] (a.) having a close relative or friend who has recently died 失去所愛的人的

51 sneer [snɪr] (v.) express through a scornful smile 冷笑

52 crimson ['krɪmzən] (v.) redden in face 臉紅

216 Hot words grew from hot words, and both Don Pedro and Claudio were feeling scorched[53] when Leonato left the room and Benedick entered.

"The old man," said Claudio, "was like to have snapped[54] my nose off."

"You are a villain[55]!" said Benedick, shortly. "Fight me when and with what weapon you please, or I call you a coward."

Claudio was astounded, but said, "I'll meet you. Nobody shall say I can't carve[56] a calf's head."

Benedick smiled, and as it was time for Don Pedro to receive officials, the Prince sat down in a chair of state and prepared his mind for justice. The door soon opened to admit Dogberry and his prisoners.

"What offence," said Don Pedro, "are these men charged with?"

217 Borachio thought the moment a happy one for making a clean breast of it. He laid the whole blame on Don John, who had disappeared. "The lady Hero being dead," he said, "I desire nothing but the reward of a murderer."

Claudio heard with anguish and deep repentance. Upon the re-entrance of Leonato be said to him, "This slave makes clear your daughter's innocence. Choose your revenge."

"Leonato," said Don Pedro, humbly, "I am ready for any penance[57] you may impose."

"I ask you both, then," said Leonato, "to proclaim my daughter's innocence, and to honor her tomb by singing her praise before it. As for you, Claudio, I have this to say: my brother has a daughter so like Hero that she might be a copy of her. Marry her, and my vengeful[58] feelings die."

"Noble sir," said Claudio, "I am yours."

53 scorch [skɔːrtʃ] (v.) to subject somebody to severe criticism 挖苦

54 snap [snæp] (v.) break suddenly and abruptly, as under tension 猛咬

55 villain ['vɪlən] (n.) any person regarded as evil 惡棍

56 carve [kɑːrv] (v.) to make an object or pattern by cutting a piece of wood or stone 雕刻

57 penance ['penəns] (n.) self-punishment for sin 贖罪

58 vengeful ['vendʒfəl] (a.) very eager to punish someone who has done something bad 報復的

218 Claudio then went to his room and composed a solemn song. Going to the church with Don Pedro and his attendants, he sang it before the monument[59] of Leonato's family.

When he had ended he said, "Good night, Hero. Yearly will I do this."

He then gravely, as became a gentleman whose heart was Hero's, made ready to marry a girl whom he did not love. He was told to meet her in Leonato's house, and was faithful to his appointment.

He was shown into a room where Antonio (Leonato's brother) and several masked ladies entered after him. Friar Francis, Leonato, and Benedick were present. Antonio led one of the ladies towards Claudio.

"Sweet," said the young man, "let me see your face."

"Swear first to marry her," said Leonato.

"Give me your hand," said Claudio to the lady; "before this holy friar I swear to marry you if you will be my wife."

"Alive I was your wife," said the lady, as she drew off her mask.

59 monument ['mɑːnjʊmənt] (n.) a structure erected to commemorate persons or events 紀念碑

219 "Another Hero!" exclaimed Claudio.

"Hero died," explained Leonato, "only while slander lived."

The Friar was then going to marry the reconciled[60] pair, but Benedick interrupted him with, "Softly, Friar; which of these ladies is Beatrice?"

Hereat[61] Beatrice unmasked, and Benedick said, "You love me, don't you?"

"Only moderately," was the reply. "Do you love me?"

"Moderately," answered Benedick.

"I was told you were well-nigh[62] dead for me," remarked Beatrice.

"Of you I was told the same," said Benedick.

"Here's your own hand in evidence of your love," said Claudio, producing a feeble sonnet[63] which Benedick had written to his sweetheart.

"And here," said Hero, "is a tribute to Benedick, which I picked out of the pocket of Beatrice."

"A miracle!" exclaimed Benedick. "Our hands are against our hearts! Come, I will marry you, Beatrice."

"You shall be my husband to save your life," was the rejoinder[64].

Benedick kissed her on the mouth; and the Friar married them after he had married Claudio and Hero.

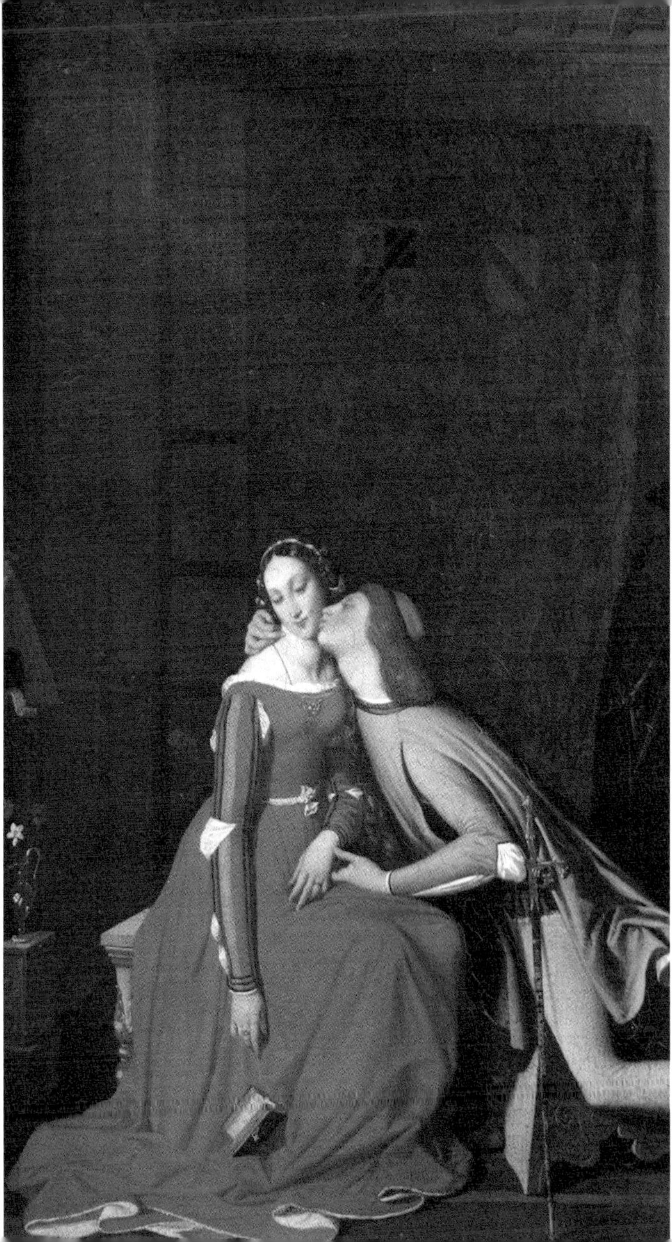

220 "How is Benedick the married man?" asked Don Pedro.

"Too happy to be made unhappy," replied Benedick. "Crack what jokes you will. As for you, Claudio, I had hoped to run you through the body, but as you are now my kinsman, live whole and love my cousin."

"My cudgel[65] was in love with you, Benedick, until today," said Claudio; but, "Come, come, let's dance," said Benedick.

And dance they did. Not even the news of the capture of Don John was able to stop the flying feet of the happy lovers, for revenge is not sweet against an evil man who has failed to do harm.

60 reconcile ['rekənsaɪl] (v.) to restore peace of friendship between 和解

61 hereat (n.) at this point 此際

62 well-nigh ['welnaɪ] (adv.) very nearly 幾乎

63 sonnet ['sɑːnɪt] (n.) a poem that has 14 lines and a particular pattern of rhyme 十四行詩

64 rejoinder [rɪ'dʒɔɪndər] (n.) a quick reply to a question or remark 回答

65 cudgel ['kʌdʒəl] (n.) a heavy stick used as a weapon 棍棒

16 Measure for Measure

Vienna

221 More centuries ago than I care to say, the people of Vienna[1] were governed too mildly. The reason was that the reigning[2] Duke Vicentio was excessively good-natured, and disliked to see offenders[3] made unhappy.

The consequence was that the number of ill-behaved persons in Vienna was enough to make the Duke shake his head in sorrow when his chief secretary showed him it at the end of a list.

222 He decided, therefore, that wrongdoers[4] must be punished. But popularity was dear to him. He knew that, if he were suddenly strict after being lax[5], he would cause people to call him a tyrant. For this reason he told his Privy[6] Council[7] that he must go to Poland on important business of state.

"I have chosen Angelo to rule in my absence," said he.

Now this Angelo, although he appeared to be noble, was really a mean man.

Duke Vicentio was excessively good-natured, and disliked to see offenders made unhappy.

1 Vienna [vɪ'enə] (n.) the capital and largest city of Austria 維也納
2 reigning ['reɪnɪŋ] (a.) exercising power or authority 在位的
3 offender [ə'fendər] (n.) someone who is guilty of a crime 違法者
4 wrongdoer ['rɔːŋduər] (n.) a person who does something bad or illegal 違法犯罪者
5 lax [læks] (a.) not severe or strong enough 鬆弛的
6 privy ['prɪvi] (a.) sharing knowledge of something secret or private 祕密參與的
7 council ['kaʊnsəl] (n.) an appointed or elected body of people with an administrative, advisory, or representative function 顧問班子

223 He had promised to marry a girl called Mariana, and now would have nothing to say to her, because her dowry[8] had been lost. So poor Mariana lived forlornly[9], waiting every day for the footstep of her stingy[10] lover, and loving him still.

Having appointed Angelo his deputy[11], the Duke went to a friar called Thomas and asked him for a friar's dress and instruction in the art of giving religious counsel, for he did not intend to go to Poland, but to stay at home and see how Angelo governed.

Angelo had not been a day in office when he condemned[12] to death a young man named Claudio for an act of rash selfishness which nowadays would only be punished by severe reproof[13].

8 dowry ['daʊri] (n.) money or property brought by a woman to her husband at marriage 嫁妝

9 forlornly [fər'lɔːrnli] (adv.) lonely because of isolation or desertion 孤苦伶仃地

10 stingy ['stɪndʒi] (a.) selfishly unwilling to share with others 吝嗇的

11 deputy ['depjʊti] (n.) one appointed to act for another 代理人

12 condemn [kən'dem] (v.) to criticize something or someone strongly, usually for moral reasons 責難

13 reproof [rɪ'pruːf] (n.) strong criticism or disapproval 申斥

Poor Mariana lived forlornly, waiting every day for the footstep of her stingy lover.

224

Claudio had a queer friend called Lucio, and Lucio saw a chance of freedom for Claudio if Claudio's beautiful sister Isabella would plead with Angelo.

Isabella was at that time living in a nunnery[14]. Nobody had won her heart, and she thought she would like to become a sister, or nun. Meanwhile Claudio did not lack an advocate[15].

An ancient lord, Escalus, was for leniency[16]. "Let us cut a little, but not kill," he said. "This gentleman had a most noble father."

Angelo was unmoved. "If twelve men find me guilty, I ask no more mercy than is in the law."

Angelo then ordered the Provost[17] to see that Claudio was executed[18] at nine the next morning.

14 nunnery ['nʌnəri] (n.) member of a female religious group which lives in a convent 女修道院

15 advocate ['ædvəkeɪt] (n.) somebody such as a lawyer, who pleads another's case in a legal forum 辯護者

16 leniency ['liːnjənsi] (n.) mercifulness 仁慈

225 After the issue of this order Angelo was told that the sister of the condemned man desired to see him.

"Admit her," said Angelo.

On entering with Lucio, the beautiful girl said, "I am a woeful suitor to your Honor."

"Well?" said Angelo.

She colored at his chill[19] monosyllable[20] and the ascending[21] red increased the beauty of her face.

"I have a brother who is condemned to die," she continued. "Condemn the fault, I pray you, and spare my brother."

"Every fault," said Angelo, "is condemned before it is committed. A fault cannot suffer. Justice would be void[22] if the committer of a fault went free."

She would have left the court if Lucio had not whispered to her, "You are too cold; you could not speak more tamely if you wanted a pin."

17 provost ['proʊvoʊst] (n.) a chief official or superintendent 監管者

18 execute ['eksɪkjuːt] (v.) to kill someone, especially legally as a punishment 處死

19 chill [tʃɪl] (a.) an emotional coldness or unfriendliness in the atmosphere or in somebody's manner 冷淡的

20 monosyllable ['mɑːnəˌsɪləbəl] (n.) a word or utterance of one syllable 單音節詞

21 ascending [ə'sendɪŋ] (a.) rising or increasing to higher levels, values, or degrees 上升的

22 void [vɔɪd] (a.) without result; in vain 徒勞的

She told him that nothing becomes power like mercy.

226 So Isabella attacked Angelo again, and when he said, "I will not pardon him," she was not discouraged, and when he said, "He's sentenced; 'tis too late," she returned to the assault[23]. But all her fighting was with reasons, and with reasons she could not prevail[24] over the Deputy.

She told him that nothing becomes power like mercy. She told him that humanity receives and requires mercy from Heaven, that it was good to have gigantic strength, and had to use it like a giant.

She told him that lightning rives[25] the oak and spares the myrtle[26]. She bade him look for fault in his own breast, and if he found one, to refrain[27] from making it an argument against her brother's life.

227 Angelo found a fault in his breast at that moment. He loved Isabella's beauty, and was tempted to do for her beauty what he would not do for the love of man. He appeared to relent[28], for he said, "Come to me tomorrow before noon."

She had, at any rate, succeeded in prolonging her brother's life for a few hours.

In her absence Angelo's conscience rebuked[29] him for trifling[30] with his judicial duty.

When Isabella called on him the second time, he said, "Your brother cannot live."

Isabella was painfully astonished, but all she said was, "Even so. Heaven keep your Honor."

But as she turned to go, Angelo felt that his duty and honor were slight in comparison with the loss of her.

23 assault [ə'sɔːlt] (n.) a violent physical or verbal attack 攻擊
24 prevail [prɪ'veɪl] (v.) to prove to be stronger and in the position of greater influence and power 勝過
25 rive [raɪv] (v.) to split or tear apart 劈開
26 myrtle ['mɜːrtl] (n.) evergreen shrub with sweet-smelling white flowers 桃金孃
27 refrain [rɪ'freɪn] (v.) to avoid doing or stop yourself from doing something 抑制
28 relent [rɪ'lent] (v.) to change your attitude and become less strict or cruel towards someone 變溫和；軟化
29 rebuke [rɪ'bjuːk] (v.) to speak to someone severely about something they have done wrong 訓斥
30 trifle ['traɪfl] (v.) act frivolously 玩弄

228 "Give me your love," he said, "and Claudio shall be freed."

"Before I would marry you, he should die if he had twenty heads to lay upon the block," said Isabella, for she saw then that he was not the just man he pretended to be.

So she went to her brother in prison, to inform him that he must die.

Isabella went to her brother in prison, to inform him that he must die.

At first he was boastful, and promised to hug the darkness of death. But when he clearly understood that his sister could buy his life by marrying Angelo, he felt his life more valuable than her happiness, and he exclaimed, "Sweet sister, let me live."

"O faithless coward! O dishonest wretch[31]!" she cried.

At this moment the Duke came forward, in the habit[32] of a friar, to request some speech with Isabella. He called himself Friar Lodowick.

229 The Duke then told her that Angelo was affianced[33] to Mariana, whose love-story he related. He then asked her to consider this plan. Let Mariana, in the dress of Isabella, go closely veiled to Angelo, and say, in a voice resembling Isabella's, that if Claudio were spared she would marry him. Let her take the ring from Angelo's little finger, that it might be afterwards proved that his visitor was Mariana.

Isabella had, of course, a great respect for friars, who are as nearly like nuns as men can be. She agreed, therefore, to the Duke's plan. They were to meet again at the moated[34] grange[35], Mariana's house.

They were to meet again at the moated grange, Mariana's house.

31 wretch [retʃ] (n.) someone who is unpleasant or annoying 可恥的人

32 habit ['hæbɪt] (n.) a distinctive attire (as the costume of a religious order) 神職人員的服裝

33 affianced [ə'faɪənst] (a.) to promise somebody or yourself in marriage to somebody else 訂婚的

34 moated ['moʊtɪd] (a.) surrounded by a moat 四周圍有壕溝的

35 grange [greɪndʒ] (n.) an outlying farm 莊園

230 In the street the Duke saw Lucio, who, seeing a man dressed like a friar, called out, "What news of the Duke, friar?"

"I have none," said the Duke.

Lucio then told the Duke some stories about Angelo. Then he told one about the Duke. The Duke contradicted[36] him.

Lucio was provoked[37], and called the Duke "a shallow, ignorant fool," though he pretended to love him.

"The Duke shall know you better if I live to report you," said the Duke, grimly[38]. Then he asked Escalus, whom he saw in the street, what he thought of his ducal[39] master.

Escalus, who imagined he was speaking to a friar, replied, "The Duke is a very temperate gentleman, who prefers to see another merry to being merry himself."

The Duke then proceeded to call on Mariana.

Isabella arrived immediately afterwards, and the Duke introduced the two girls to one another, both of whom thought he was a friar.

They went into a chamber apart from him to discuss the saving of Claudio, and while they talked in low and earnest tones, the Duke looked out of the window and saw the broken sheds[40] and flower-beds black with moss, which betrayed Mariana's indifference to her country dwelling.

231 Some women would have beautified their garden: not she. She was for the town; she neglected the joys of the country. He was sure that Angelo would not make her unhappier.

"We are agreed, father," said Isabella, as she returned with Mariana.

So Angelo was deceived by the girl whom he had dismissed from his love, and put on her finger a ring he wore, in which was set a milky stone which flashed[41] in the light with secret colors.

Some women would have beautified their garden.

36 contradict [ˌkɑːntrəˈdɪkt] (v.) to argue against the truth or correctness of somebody's statement or claim 反駁

37 provoke [prəˈvoʊk] (v.) to cause a reaction or feeling, especially a sudden one 挑釁；激怒

38 grimly [ˈgrɪmli] (a.) stern or forbidding in action or appearance 冷酷地

39 ducal [ˈduːkəl] (a.) of or connected with a duke 公爵的

40 shed [ʃed] (n.) small buildings 棚；小屋

41 flash [flæʃ] (v.) to reflect light suddenly or briefly 閃出；反射

232 Hearing of her success, the Duke went next day to the prison prepared to learn that an order had arrived for Claudio's release. It had not, however, but a letter was handed to the Provost while he waited.

His amazement was great when the Provost read aloud these words, "Whatsoever you may hear to the contrary, let Claudio be executed by four of the clock. Let me have his head sent me by five."

But the Duke said to the Provost, "You must show the Deputy another head," and he held out a letter and a signet. "Here," he said, "are the hand and seal of the Duke. He is to return, I tell you, and Angelo knows it not. Give Angelo another head."

The Provost thought, "This friar speaks with power. I know the Duke's signet[42] and I know his hand[43]."

He said at length[44], "A man died in prison this morning, a pirate of the age of Claudio, with a beard of his color. I will show his head."

The pirate's head was duly shown to Angelo, who was deceived by its resemblance to Claudio's.

The Duke's return was so popular that the citizens removed the city gates from their hinges[45] to assist his entry into Vienna. Angelo and Escalus duly presented themselves, and were profusely[46] praised for their conduct of affairs in the Duke's absence.

233 It was, therefore, the more unpleasant for Angelo when Isabella, passionately angered by his treachery, knelt before the Duke, and cried for justice.

When her story was told, the Duke cried, "To prison with her for a slanderer[47] of our right hand! But stay, who persuaded you to come here?"

"Friar Lodowick," said she.

"Who knows him?" inquired the Duke.

"I do, my lord," replied Lucio. "I beat him because he spake[48] against your Grace."

42 signet ['sɪgnɪt] (n.) a seal (especially one used to mark documents officially) 圖章

43 hand [hænd] (n.) somebody's handwriting 筆跡

44 at length: after some time or following a delay 終於；最後

45 hinge [hɪndʒ] (n.) a joint that holds two parts together so that one can swing relative to the other 鉸鏈

46 profusely [prə'fjuːsli] (adv.) in an abundant manner 豐富地

47 slander ['slændər] (n.) one who attacks the reputation of another by slander or libel 誹謗者

48 spake [speɪk] past tense of speak〔古〕speak 的過去式

234 A friar called Peter here said, "Friar Lodowick is a holy man."

Isabella was removed by an officer, and Mariana came forward. She took off her veil, and said to Angelo, "This is the face you once swore was worth looking on."

Bravely he faced her as she put out her hand and said, "This is the hand which wears the ring you thought to give another."

"I know the woman," said Angelo. "Once there was talk of marriage between us, but I found her frivolous[49]."

Mariana here burst out that they were affianced by the strongest vows. Angelo replied by asking the Duke to insist on the production of Friar Lodowick.

"He shall appear," promised the Duke, and bade Escalus examine the missing witness thoroughly while he was elsewhere.

Presently the Duke re-appeared in the character of Friar Lodowick, and accompanied by Isabella and the Provost.

235 He was not so much examined as abused and threatened by Escalus. Lucio asked him to deny, if he dared, that he called the Duke a fool and a coward, and had had his nose pulled for his impudence[50].

"To prison with him!" shouted Escalus, but as hands were laid upon him, the Duke pulled off his friar's hood, and was a Duke before them all.

"Now," he said to Angelo, "if you have any impudence that can yet serve you, work it for all it's worth."

"Immediate sentence and death is all I beg," was the reply.

"Were you affianced to Mariana?" asked the Duke.

"I was," said Angelo.

"Then marry her instantly," said his master. "Marry them," he said to Friar Peter, "and return with them here."

"Come hither[51], Isabel," said the Duke, in tender tones. "Your friar is now your Prince, and grieves he was too late to save your brother;" but well the roguish[52] Duke knew he had saved him.

49 frivolous ['frɪvələs] (a.) not serious in content or attitude or behavior 輕佻的

50 impudence ['ɪmpjudəns] (n.) showing a lack of respect and excessive boldness 厚臉皮

51 hither ['hɪðər] (adv.) to this place 來這裡

52 roguish ['roʊgɪʃ] (a.) mischievously playful 惡作劇的

236 "O pardon me," she cried, "that I employed my Sovereign in my trouble."

"You are pardoned," he said, gaily.

At that moment Angelo and his wife re-entered. "And now, Angelo," said the Duke, gravely, "we condemn thee to the block on which Claudio laid his head!"

"O my most gracious lord," cried Mariana, "mock[53] me not!"

"You shall buy a better husband," said the Duke.

"O my dear lord," said she, "I crave no better man."

Isabella nobly added her prayer to Mariana's, but the Duke feigned[54] inflexibility.

"Provost," he said, "how came it that Claudio was executed at an unusual hour?"

Afraid to confess the lie he had imposed[55] upon Angelo, the Provost said, "I had a private message."

"You are discharged[56] from your office," said the Duke. The Provost then departed.

53 mock [mɑːk] (v.) to ridicule 嘲弄
54 feign [feɪn] (v.) to pretend to feel something, usually an emotion 假裝
55 impose [ɪm'poʊz] (v.) to force someone to accept something 強加於
56 discharge [dɪs'tʃɑːrdʒ] (v.) to dismiss somebody from a job 解雇
57 stout [staʊt] (a.) fairly fat and heavy, or having a thick body 矮胖的

237 Angelo said, "I am sorry to have caused such sorrow. I prefer death to mercy."

Soon there was a motion in the crowd. The Provost reappeared with Claudio. Like a big child the Provost said, "I saved this man; he is like Claudio."

The Duke was amused, and said to Isabella, "I pardon him because he is like your brother. He is like my brother, too, if you, dear Isabel, will be mine."

She was his with a smile, and the Duke forgave Angelo, and promoted the Provost.

Lucio he condemned to marry a stout[57] woman with a bitter tongue.

Quotations from Shakespeare

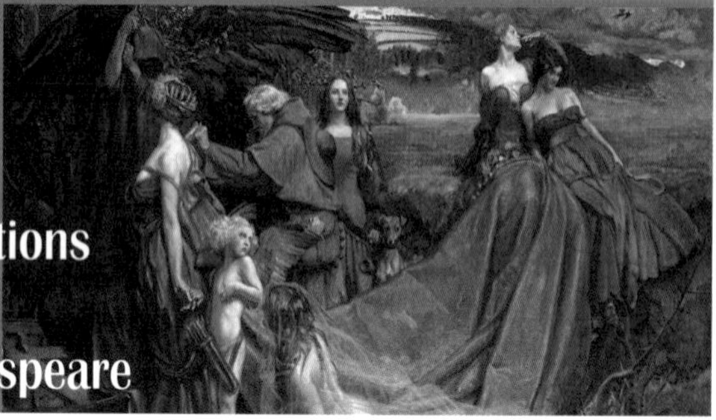

ACTION

Action is eloquence, and the eyes of the ignorant More learned than their ears.

Coriolanus—III. 2.

ADVERSITY

Sweet are the uses of adversity,
Which, like the toad, ugly and venomous,
Wears yet a precious jewel in his head.

As You Like It—II. 1.

That, Sir, which serves and seeks for gain,
And follows but for form,
Will pack, when it begins to rain,
And leave thee in the storm.

King Lear—II. 4.

Ah! when the means are gone, that buy this praise, The breath is gone whereof this praise is made:
Feast won—fast lost; one cloud of winter showers, These flies are couched.

Timon of Athens II. 2.

ADVICE TO A SON LEAVING HOME

Give thy thoughts no tongue,
Nor any unproportioned thought his act
Be thou familiar, but by no means vulgar.
The friends thou hast, and their adoption tried Grapple them to thy soul with hooks of steel;
But do not dull thy palm with entertainment
Of each new-hatched, unfledged comrade. Beware
Of entrance to a quarrel: but, being in,
Bear it, that the opposer may beware of thee.
Give every man thine ear, but few thy voice:
Take each man's censure, but reserve thy judgment, Costly thy habit as thy purse can buy, But not expressed in fancy: rich, not gaudy:
For the apparel oft proclaims the man;
And they in France, of the best rank and station, Are most select and generous, chief in that.
Neither a borrower, nor a lender be:
For loan oft loses both itself and friend;
And borrowing dulls the edge of husbandry.

This above all.—To thine ownself be true;
And it must follow, as the night the day,
Thou canst not then be false to any man.

Hamlet—I. 3.

AGE

My May of life Is
fallen into the sear, the yellow leaf:
And that which should accompany old age,
As honor, love, obedience, troops of friends,
I must not look to have; but, in their stead,
Curses not loud, but deep, mouth-honor, breath, Which the poor heart would feign deny, but dare not

Macbeth—V. 3.

AMBITION

Dreams, indeed, are ambition; for the very substance of the ambitious is merely the shadow of a dream. And I hold ambition of so airy and light a quality, that it is but a shadow's shadow.

Hamlet—II 2.

I charge thee fling away ambition;
By that sin fell the angels, how can man then,
The image of his Maker, hope to win by 't?
Love thyself last; cherish those hearts that hate thee;
Corruption wins not more than honesty.
Still in thy right hand carry gentle peace, To silence envious tongues. Be just, and fear not! Let all the ends, thou aim'st at, be thy country's, Thy God's, and truth's.

King Henry VIII.—III. 2.

ANGER

Anger is like
A full-hot horse, who being allowed his way,
Self-mettle tires him.

King Henry VIII.—I. 1.

ARROGANCE

There are a sort of men, whose visages
Do cream and mantle like a standing pond,
And do a willful stillness entertain,
With purpose to be dressed in an opinion
Of wisdom, gravity, profound conceit,
As who should say, " I am Sir Oracle,
And when I ope my lips, let no dog bark!"
O! my Antonio, I do know of these
That therefore are reputed wise
For saying nothing, when, I am sure,
If they should speak, would almost dam those ears, Which, hearing them, would call their brothers fools.

The Merchant of Venice—I. 1.

AUTHORITY

Thou hast seen a farmer's dog bark at a beggar?
And the creature run from the cur?
There thou might'st behold the great image of authority a dog's obeyed in office

King Lear—IV. 6.

Could great men thunder
As Jove himself does, Jove would ne'er be quiet, For every pelting, petty officer Would use his heaven for thunder: nothing but thunder—
Merciful heaven!
Thou rather, with thy sharp and sulphurous bolt,
Splitt'st the unwedgeable and gnarled oak,
Than the soft myrtle!—O, but man, proud man!
Drest in a little brief authority—
Most ignorant of what he's most assured,
His glassy essence,—like an angry ape,
Plays such fantastic tricks before high heaven, As make the angels weep.

Measure for Measure—II. 2.

BEAUTY

The hand, that hath made you fair, hath made you good: the goodness, that is cheap in beauty, makes beauty brief in goodness; but grace, being the soul of your complexion, should keep the body of it ever fair.

Measure for Measure—III. 1.

BLESSINGS UNDERVALUED

It so falls out
That what we have we prize not to the worth,
Whiles we enjoy it; but being lacked and lost,
Why, then we rack the value; then we find
The virtue, that possession would not show us
Whiles it was ours.

Much Ado About Nothing—IV. 1.

BRAGGARTS

It will come to pass,
That every braggart shall be found an ass.

All's Well that Ends Well—IV. 3.

They that have the voice of lions, and the act of bares, are they not monsters?

Troilus and Cressida—III. 2.

CALUMNY

Be thou as chaste as ice, as pure as snow,
thou shalt not escape calumny.

Hamlet—III. 1.

No might nor greatness in mortality
Can censure 'scape; back-wounding calumny
The whitest virtue strikes. What king so strong, Can tie the gall up in the slanderous tongue?

Measure for Measure—III. 2.

CEREMONY

Ceremony
Was but devised at first, to set a gloss
On faint deeds, hollow welcomes.
Recanting goodness, sorry ere 'tis shown;
But where there is true friendship, there needs none.

Timon of Athens—I. 2.

COMFORT

Men
Can counsel, and speak comfort to that grief
Which they themselves not feel; but tasting it,
Their counsel turns to passion, which before

Would give preceptial medicine to rage,
Fetter strong madness in a silken thread,
Charm ache with air, and agony with words:
No, no; 'tis all men's office to speak patience To those that wring under the load of sorrow;
But no man's virtue, nor sufficiency,
To be so moral, when he shall endure
The like himself.

Much Ado About Nothing—V. 1.

Well, every one can master a grief, but he that has it.

Much Ado About Nothing—V. 1.

COMPARISON

When the moon shone, we did not see the candle.
So doth the greater glory dim the less;
A substitute shines brightly as a king,
Until a king be by; and then his state
Empties itself, as does an inland brook
Into the main of waters.

Merchant of Venice—V. 1.

CONSCIENCE

Thus conscience does make cowards of us all;
And thus the native hue of resolution
Is sicklied o'er with the pale cast of thought;
And enterprises of great pith and moment,
With this regard, their currents turn awry,
And lose the name of action

Hamlet—III. 1.

CONTENT

My crown is in my heart, not on my head;
Not decked with diamonds and Indian stones,
Nor to be seen; my crown is called "content";
A crown it is, that seldom kings enjoy.

King Henry VI., Part 3rd—III. 1.

CONTENTION

How, in one house,
Should many people, under two commands,
Hold amity?

King Lear—II. 4.

When two authorities are set up,
Neither supreme, how soon confusion
May enter twixt the gap of both, and take
The one by the other.

Coriolanus—III. 1.

CONTENTMENT

'Tis better to be lowly born,
And range with humble livers in content,
Than to be perked up in a glistering grief,
And wear a golden sorrow.

King Henry VIII.—II. 3.

COWARDS

Cowards die many times before their deaths;
The valiant never taste of death but once.

Julius Caesar—II. 2.

CUSTOM

That monster, custom, who all sense doth eat Of habit's devil, is angel yet in this:
That to the use of actions fair and good
He likewise gives a frock, or livery,
That aptly is put on: Refrain to-night:
And that shall lend a kind of easiness To the next abstinence: the next more easy:
For use almost can change the stamp of nature,
And either curb the devil, or throw him out
With wondrous potency.

Hamlet—III. 4.

A custom
More honored in the breach, then the observance.

Hamlet—I. 4.

DEATH

Kings, and mightiest potentates, must die;
For that's the end of human misery.

King Henry VI., Part 1st—III. 2.

Of all the wonders that I yet have heard,
It seems to me most strange that men should fear;
Seeing that death, a necessary end,
Will come, when it will come.

Julius Caesar—II. 2.

The dread of something after death,
Makes us rather bear those ills we have,
Than fly to others we know not of.

Hamlet—III. 1.

The sense of death is most in apprehension.

Measure for Measure—III. 1.

By medicine life may be prolonged, yet death
Will seize the doctor too.

Cymbeline—V. 5.

DECEPTION

The devil can cite Scripture for his purpose.
An evil soul, producing holy witness,
Is like a villain with a smiling cheek;
A goodly apple rotten at the heart;
O, what a goodly outside falsehood hath!

Merchant of Venice—I. 3.

DEEDS

Foul deeds will rise,
Though all the earth o'erwhelm them to men's eyes.

Hamlet—I. 2.

How oft the sight of means to do ill deeds,
Makes deeds ill done!

King John—IV. 2.

DELAY

That we would do,
We should do when we would; for this would changes, And hath abatements and delays as many, As there are tongues, are hands, are accidents;
And then this should is like a spendthrift sigh, That hurts by easing.

Hamlet—IV. 7.

DELUSION

For love of grace,
Lay not that flattering unction to your soul;
It will but skin and film the ulcerous place;
Whiles rank corruption, mining all within,
Infects unseen.

Hamlet—III. 4.

DISCRETION

Let's teach ourselves that honorable stop,
Not to outsport discretion.

Othello—II. 3.

DOUBTS AND FEARS

I am cabin'd, cribb'd, confined, bound in
To saucy doubts and fears.

Macbeth—III. 4.

DRUNKENNESS

Boundless intemperance.
In nature is a tyranny; it hath been
Th' untimely emptying of the happy throne,
And fall of many kings.

Measure for Measure—I. 3.

DUTY OWING TO OURSELVES AND OTHERS

Love all, trust a few,
Do wrong to none; be able for thine enemy
Rather in power, than use; and keep thy friend
Under thy own life's key; be checked for silence, But never taxed for speech.

All's Well that Ends Well—I. 1.

EQUIVOCATION

But yet
I do not like but yet, it does allay
The good precedence; fye upon but yet:
But yet is as a gailer to bring forth
Some monstrous malefactor.

Antony and Cleopatra—II. 5.

EXCESS

A surfeit of the sweetest things
The deepest loathing to the stomach brings.

Midsummer Night's Dream—II. 3.

Every inordinate cup is unblessed,
and the ingredient is a devil.

Othello—II. 3.

FALSEHOOD

Falsehood, cowardice, and poor descent,
Three things that women hold in hate.

Two Gentlemen of Verona—III. 2.

FEAR

Fear frames disorder, and disorder wounds
Where it should guard.

King Henry VI., Part 2nd—V. 2.

Fear, and be slain; no worse can come, to fight:
And fight and die, is death destroying death;
Where fearing dying, pays death servile breath.

King Richard II.—III. 2.

FEASTS

Small cheer, and great welcome, makes a merry feast.

Comedy of Errors—III. 1.

FILIAL INGRATITUDE

Ingratitude! Thou marble-hearted fiend, More hideous, when thou showest thee in a child, Than the sea-monster.

King Lear—I. 4.

How sharper than a serpent's tooth it is
To have a thankless child

King Lear—I. 4.

FORETHOUGHT

Determine on some course,
More than a wild exposure to each cause
That starts i' the way before thee.

Coriolanus—IV. 1.

FORTITUDE

Yield not thy neck
To fortune's yoke, but let thy dauntless mind
Still ride in triumph over all mischance.

King Henry VI., Part 3rd—III. 3.

FORTUNE

When fortune means to men most good,
She looks upon them with a threatening eye.

King John—III. 4.

GREATNESS

Farewell, a long farewell, to all my greatness!
This is the state of man: To-day he puts forth
The tender leaves of hope, to-morrow blossoms,
And bears his blushing honors thick upon him;
The third day, comes a frost, a killing frost;
And,—when he thinks, good easy man, full surely
His greatness is ripening,—nips his root,
And then he falls, as I do.

King Henry VIII.—III. 2.

Some are born great, some achieve greatness,
and some have greatness thrust upon them.

Twelfth Night—II. 5.

HAPPINESS

O, how bitter a thing it is to look into happiness through another man's eyes.

As You Like It—V. 2.

HONESTY

An honest man is able to speak for himself,
when a knave is not.

King Henry VI., Part 2nd—V. 1.

To be honest, as this world goes, is to be
one man picked out of ten thousand.

Hamlet—II. 2.

HYPOCRISY

Devils soonest tempt,
resembling spirits of light.

Love's Labor Lost—IV. 3.

One may smile, and smile,
and be a villain.

Hamlet—I. 5.

INNOCENCE

The trust I have is in mine innocence,
And therefore am I bold and resolute.

King Henry VI., Part 2nd: IV. 4.

INSINUATIONS

The shrug, the hum, or ha; these petty brands,
That calumny doth use;—
For calumny will sear
Virtue itself:—these shrugs, these bums, and ha's, When you have said, she's goodly, come between, Ere you can say she's honest.

Winter's Tale—II. 1.

JEALOUSY

Trifles, light as air,
Are, to the jealous, confirmations strong
As proofs of holy writ.

Othello—III. 3.

O beware of jealousy:
It is the green-eyed monster, which does mock
The meat it feeds on.

Othello—III. 3

JESTS

A jest's prosperity lies in the ear
of him that hears it.

Love's Labor Lost—V. 2.

He jests at scars,
that never felt a wound.

Romeo and Juliet—II. 2.

JUDGMENT

Heaven is above all; there sits a Judge,
That no king can corrupt.

King Henry VIII, — III. 1.

LIFE

Life's but a walking shadow, a poor player,
That struts and frets his hour upon the stage,
And then is heard no more: it is a tale
Told by an idiot, full of sound and fury,
Signifying nothing.

Macbeth—V. 5.

We are such stuff
As dreams are made of, and our little life
Is rounded with a sleep.

The Tempest—IV. 1.

LOVE

A murd'rous, guilt shows not itself more soon, Than love that would seem bid: love's night is noon.

Twelfth Night—III. 2.

Sweet love, changing his property,
Turns to the sourest and most deadly hate.

King Richard II.—III. 2.

When love begins to sicken and decay,
It useth an enforced ceremony.

Julius Caesar—II. 2.

The course of true-love
never did run smooth.

Midsummer Night's Dream—I. 1.

Love looks not with the eyes,
but with the mind.

Midsummer Night's Dream—I. 1.

She never told her love,—
But let concealment, like a worm i' th' bud,
Feed on her damask check: she pined in thought
And, with a green and yellow melancholy,
She sat like Patience on a monument,
Smiling at grief. Was not this love indeed?

Twelfth Night—II. 4.

But love is blind, and lovers cannot see
The pretty follies that themselves commit.

The Merchant of Venice—II. 6.

MAN

What a piece of work is man! How noble in reason!
How infinite in faculties! in form, and moving,
how express and admirable! in action, how like
an angel! in apprehension, how like a god! the
beauty of the world! the paragon of animals!

Hamlet—II. 2.

MERCY

The quality of mercy is not strained:
it droppeth, as the gentle rain from heaven,
Upon the place beneath: it is twice bless'd;
It blesses him that gives, and him that takes:
'Tis mightiest in the mightiest: it becomes The throned monarch better than his crown:
His scepter shows the force of temporal power,
The attribute to awe and majesty,
Wherein doth sit the dread and fear of kings;
But mercy is above this sceptered sway;
It is enthroned in the hearts of kings;
It is an attribute to God himself;
And earthly power doth then show likest God's,
When mercy seasons justice.
Consider this,—
That, in the course of justice, none of us

Should see salvation: we do pray for mercy;
And that same prayer doth teach us all to render The deeds of mercy.

Merchant of Venice—IV. 1.

MERIT

Who shall go about
To cozen fortune, and be honorable
Without the stamp of merit! Let none presume
To wear an undeserved dignity.

Merchant of Venice—II. 9.

MODESTY

It is the witness still of excellency,
To put a strange face on his own perfection.

Much Ado About Nothing—II. 3.

MORAL CONQUEST

Brave conquerors! for so you are,
That war against your own affections,
And the huge army of the world's desires.

Love's Labor's Lost—I. 1.

MURDER

The great King of kings
Hath in the table of his law commanded,
That thou shalt do no murder.
Take heed; for he holds vengeance in his band,
To hurl upon their heads that break his law.

King Richard III.—I. 4.

Blood, like sacrificing Abel's, cries,
Even from the tongueless caverns of the earth.

King Richard II.—I. 1.

MUSIC

The man that hath no music in himself,
Nor is not moved with concord of sweet sounds,
Is fit for treasons, stratagems, and spoils;
The motions of his spirit are dull as night,
And his affections dark as Erebus:
Let no such man be trusted.

Merchant of Venice—V. 1.

NAMES

What's in a name? that, which we call a rose,
By any other name would smell as sweet.

Romeo and Juliet—II. 2.

Good name, in man, and woman,
Is the immediate jewel of their souls:
Who steals my purse steals trash; 'tis something, nothing.
'Twas mine, 'tis his, and has been slave to thousands:
But he, that filches from me my good name,
Robs me of that, which not enriches him,
And makes me poor indeed.

Othello—III. 3.

NATURE

One touch of nature makes the whole world kin.

Troilus and Cressida—III. 3.

NEWS, GOOD AND BAD

Though it be honest, it is never good
To bring bad news. Give to a gracious message
An host of tongues; but let ill tidings tell
Themselves, when they be felt.

Antony and Cleopatra—II. 5.

OFFICE

'Tis the curse of service;
Preferment goes by letter, and affection,
Not by the old gradation, where each second
Stood heir to the first.

Othello—I. 1.

OPPORTUNITY

Who seeks, and will not take when offered,
Shall never find it more.

Antony and Cleopatra—II. 7.

There is a tide in the affairs of men,
Which, taken at the flood, leads on to fortune;
Omitted, all the voyage of their life Is bound in shallows, and in miseries:
And we must take the current when it serves,
Or lose our ventures.

Julius Caesar—IV. 3.

OPPRESSION

Press not a falling man too far; 'tis virtue:
His faults lie open to the laws; let them,
Not you, correct them.

King Henry VIII.—III. 2.

PAST AND FUTURE

O thoughts of men accurst!
Past, and to come, seem best; things present, worst.

King Henry IV., Part 2nd—I. 3.

PATIENCE

How poor are they, that have not patience!—
What wound did ever heal, but by degrees?

Othello—II. 3.

PEACE

A peace is of the nature of a conquest;
For then both parties nobly are subdued,
And neither party loser.

King Henry IV., Part 2nd—IV. 2.

I will use the olive with my sword:
Make war breed peace; make peace stint war; make each Prescribe to other, as each other's leech.

Timon of Athens—V. 5.

I know myself now; and I feel within me
A peace above all earthly dignities,
A still and quiet conscience.

King Henry VIII.—III. 2.

PENITENCE

Who by repentance is not satisfied,
Is nor of heaven, nor earth; for these are pleased;
By penitence the Eternal's wrath appeased.

Two Gentlemen of Verona—V. 4.

PLAYERS

All the world's a stage,
And all the men and women merely players:
They have their exits and their entrances;
And one man in his time plays many parts.

As You Like It—II. 7.

There be players, that I have seen play,—
and heard others praise, and that highly,—
not to speak it profanely, that,
neither having the accent of Christians,
nor the gait of Christian, Pagan, nor man,
have so strutted, and bellowed,

that I have thought some of nature's journeymen
had made men and not made them well,
they imitated humanity so abominably.

Hamlet—III. 2.

POMP

Why, what is pomp, rule, reign, but earth and dust?
And, live we how we can, yet die we must.

King Henry V. Part 3rd—V. 2.

PRECEPT AND PRACTICE

If to do were as easy as to know what were good to do, chapels had been churches, and poor men's cottages princes' palaces. It is a good divine that follows his own instructions: I can easier teach twenty what were good to be done, than be one of twenty to follow mine own teaching. The brain may devise laws for the blood; but a hot temper leaps o'er a cold decree: such a bare is madness, the youth, to skip o'er the meshes of good counsel, the cripple.

The Merchant of Venice—I. 2.

PRINCES AND TITLES

Princes have but their titles for their glories, An outward honor for an inward toil;
And, for unfelt imaginations,
They often feel a world of restless cares:
So that, between their titles, and low name,
There's nothing differs but the outward fame.

King Richard III.—I. 4.

QUARRELS

In a false quarrel these is no true valor.

Much Ado About Nothing—V. 1.

Thrice is he armed that hath his quarrel just;
And he but naked, though locked up in steel,
Whose conscience with injustice is corrupted.

King Henry VI., Part 2nd—III. 2.

RAGE

Men in rage strike those that wish them best.

Othello—II. 3.

REPENTANCE

Men shall deal unadvisedly sometimes,
Which after-hours give leisure to repent.

King Richard III.—IV. 4.

REPUTATION

The purest treasure mortal times afford,
Is—spotless reputation; that away,
Men are but gilded loam, or painted clay.
A jewel in a ten-times-barred-up chest
Is a bold spirit in a loyal breast.

King Richard II.—I. 1.

RETRIBUTION

The gods are just, and of our pleasant vices
Make instruments to scourge us.

King Lear—V. S.

If these men have defeated the law,
and outrun native punishment,
though they can outstrip men,
they have no wings to fly from God.

King Henry V.—IV. 1.

SCARS

A sear nobly got, or a noble scar,
is a good livery of honor.

All's Well that Ends Well—IV. 6.

To such as boasting show their scars,
A mock is due.

Troilus and Cressida—IV. 5.

SELF-CONQUEST

Better conquest never can'st thou make,
Than arm thy constant and thy nobler parts
Against those giddy loose suggestions.

King John—III. 1.

SELF-EXERTION

Men at some time are masters of their fates;
The fault is not in our stars,
But in ourselves.

Julius Caesar—I. 2.

SELF-RELIANCE

Our remedies oft in ourselves do lie,
Which we ascribe to heaven: the fated sky
Gives us free scope; only, doth backward pull
Our slow designs, when we ourselves are dull.

All's Well that Ends Well—I. 1.

SILENCE

Out of this silence, yet I picked a welcome;
And in the modesty of fearful duty
I read as much, as from the rattling tongue
Of saucy and audacious eloquence.

Midsummer Night's Dream—V. 1.

The silence often of pure innocence
Persuades, when speaking fails.

Winter's Tale—II. 2.

Silence is the perfectest herald of joy:
I were but little happy, if I could say how much.

Much Ado About Nothing—II. 1.

SLANDER

Slander,
Whose edge is sharper than the sword; whose tongue
Outvenoms all the worms of Nile; whose breath
Rides on the posting winds, and doth belie
All corners of the world; kings, queens, and states,
Maids, matrons, nay, the secrets of the grave,
This viperous slander enters.

Cymbeline—III. 4.

SLEEP

The innocent sleep;
Sleep that knits up the raveled sleeve of care, The death of each day's life, sore labor's bath, Balm of hurt minds, great nature's second course, Chief nourisher in life's feast.

Macbeth—II. 2.

SUICIDE

Against self-slaughter
There is a prohibition so divine,
That cravens my weak hand.

Cymbeline—III. 4.

TEMPERANCE

Though I look old, yet am I strong and lusty:
For in my youth I never did apply

Hot and rebellious liquors in my blood;
Nor did not with unbashful forehead woo
The means of weakness and debility:
Therefore my age is as a lusty winter,
Frosty, but kindly.

As You Like It—II. 3.

THEORY AND PRACTICE

There was never yet philosopher,
That could endure the tooth-ache patiently;
However, they have writ the style of the gods,
And made a pish at chance and sufferance.

Much Ado About Nothing—V. 1.

TREACHERY

Though those, that are betrayed,
Do feel the treason sharply, yet the traitor
Stands in worse case of woe.

Cymbeline—III. 4.

VALOR

The better part of valor is—discretion.

King Henry IV., Part 1st—V. 4.

When Valor preys on reason,
It eats the sword it fights with.

Antony and Cleopatra—III. 2.

What valor were it, when a cur doth grin
For one to thrust his band between his teeth,
When he might spurn him with his foot away?

King Henry VI., Part 3rd—I. 4.

WAR

Take care
How you awake the sleeping sword of war:
We charge you in the name of God, take heed.

King Henry IV., Part 1st—I. 2.

WELCOME

Welcome ever smiles,
And farewell goes out sighing.

Troilus and Cressida—III. 3.

WINE

Good wine is a good familiar creature, if it be well used.

Othello—II. 3.

O thou invisible spirit of wine,
if thou hast no name to be known by, let us call thee—devil!. . . O, that
men should put an enemy in their mouths,
to steal away their brains!
that we should with joy, revel,
pleasure, and applause,
transform ourselves into beasts!

Othello—II. 3.

WOMAN

A woman impudent and mannish grown
Is not more loathed than an effeminate man.

Troilus and Cressida—III. 3.

WORDS

Words without thoughts
never to heaven go.

Hamlet—III. 3.

Few words shall fit the trespass best,
Where no excuse can give the fault amending.

The Rape of Lucrece

WORLDLY CARE

You have too much respect upon the world:
They lose it, that do buy it with much care.

Merchant of Venice—I. 1.

WORLDLY HONORS

Not a man, for being simply man,
Hath any honor; but honor for those honors
That are without him, as place, riches, favor,
Prizes of accident as oftas merit;
Which when they fall, as being slippery standers,
The love that leaned on them, as slippery too,
Do one pluck down another, and together
Die in the fall. But 'tis not so with me.

Troilus and Cressida—III. 3

TRANSLATION

前言

p. 004 莎翁的著作，一直被稱為「平凡天才所寫過最豐富、最道地、最美好的作品」，莎士比亞樂於受教，單單他一個人的劇作（只有在科學方面不足道哉）中所蘊含的真正智慧，即是集全體英國人的學識都無法企及。

他是諸善之師，讓我們認識了憐憫、慷慨、真勇和愛，他閃耀的才智可以經過各種「剪裁」，即使在小角色的身上都可看到，而其厚實淵博的知識也融入我們的口語和俗諺中，並因此廣為流傳，使得如今的英語世界中幾乎沒有一個角落不受到他的啟發，即使在窮鄉僻壤的茅屋瓦舍也因而豐富精采。

莎翁的惠贈就像大海一樣，雖然常未受到公認，但處處都能感受到，就像他的朋友班·強生對他的描述：「他的榮耀不單是屬於某個時代的，而是千秋萬世永垂不朽的。」他始終能保持人生的正途，不會在感情和心境上徬徨歧路。

在他的創作中，我們找不出道德上的攔路強盜、感情上的盜賊、有趣的惡棍，以及親切而高雅的女冒險家——也沒有微妙糾結的情勢，致使在隱身於時尚和感情方面膚淺魅力下的心靈面前出現最粗野的形象。

他沒有吹捧不適的情慾，不會假善名行惡之實，也不會蔑視合理而適切的原則。因此，他使我們不致於嘲弄癡愚，或是對罪惡打顫。莎翁使我們仍保有對人類的愛，以及懂得自重。

他熟識所有美麗的形式和影像，它們全都在大自然的單純面貌中，在對花草和芬芳不滅的愛中，以及在對露珠、清水、柔和的輕風和聲響、朗朗晴空和孤寥的森林，以及明月下的樹蔭等永無止盡的愛中，呈現出甜美又高雅的一面。這些都成了詩的素材，也讓我們敏銳地意識到它們和心智感情間那種無法界定的關係，而這就是它們的本質和其躍動的心靈，在他最忙碌和悲劇性的場景之中，它們的來臨就像是陽光灑落在岩上和廢墟上一樣，和一切的崎嶇險惡及拒斥形成鮮明的對比，並提醒我們有更純靜和更光彩奪目的要素存在著。

令人驚異之處在於，莎翁的作品被視為除了聖經之外，為所有英國古典文學最受到高度尊崇的。「所以莎翁筆下的人物性格，被藝術家、詩人和小說作家們廣泛的擷取，」一位美國作家曾說：「所以交織在一起的是英國文學主體中的人物性格，而對這些戲劇情節的無知，也往往會成為讓你無地自容的主因。」可是，莎翁的作品是為成人的男男女女而寫的，字裡行間是年幼者所無法了解的。

有鑑於此，本書係以一種極簡單的形式，讓莎翁劇作中那些有趣的故事得以再生，使年少的人也能了解並欣賞它們，這正是本書作者所期許的目的。

E.T.R.

p. 006 大家都說，莎翁的作品已在文明和經濟方面彙集出一套體系，讓我們懂得慎思明辨。後續的所有作家都爭相仿傚，大家也懷疑所有後繼者帶給其國家在理論知識上的箴言，以及實務上的嚴謹通則，恐怕都沒有他一個人來得多。

——山繆爾・強森

（Samuel Johnson）

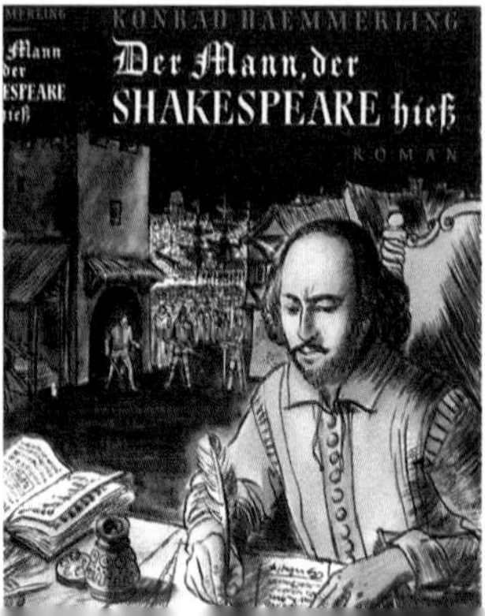

莎翁的簡短生平

p. 007 1564年4月26日這一天，英格蘭瓦威克州（Warwickshire）埃文河畔史特拉福這個市場小鎮的教區教會裡，有人登記受洗，受洗的人是約翰．莎士比亞（John Shakespeare）的兒子威廉（William），而且是以拉丁文「Gulielmus filius Johannis Shakespeare」登記。

一般而言，威廉．莎士比亞的生日應該是他受洗的前三天，不過這事缺乏確切的證據。莎翁的姓氏有各式各樣的拼法，而且這位劇作家本人也未曾自始至終都用同一種拼法。比方說，在受洗記錄上雖拼成「Shakespeare」，然而在他若干確認無誤的簽名中，卻用「Shakspere」，甚至在作品的初版中更印成「Shakespeare」。

哈利威爾（Halliwell）告訴我們，莎翁家族各個成員在寫這名字時，至少有三十四種不同的拼法。

莎士比亞父親雖貴為史特拉福的議員，卻顯然寫不出自己的名字，只是當時在十個人之中，就有九人心甘情願地以畫符號代替簽名，所以此事應不致於讓他特別蒙羞。

在各種傳說和其他資料來源中，對莎翁父親的職業有各個不同的講法，有的說是屠夫，也有的說是羊毛商或賣手套的。他同時或在不同時間從事所有的這些職業，並非絕無可能，當然，上述職業沒有一樣可以正確無誤冠在他頭上也不無可能。總之，他職業的性質可以很容易讓我們了解到，各式各樣的傳統是如何產生的。

莎翁的父親在婚前即是名地主，並且耕種他自己的土地，後來娶一位鄉紳的女兒瑪麗·艾登（Mary Arden）為妻，岳父也是地主，在亞斯拜士（Asbies）擁有五十六畝的廣大土地。

威廉是第三個孩子，上面是兩個女兒，可能都不幸在襁褓中夭折，在他之後又生了三個兒子和一個女兒。至少在莎士比亞出生後十或十二年，他父親仍繼續過著悠哉游哉的生活。1568年，他成了史特拉福的地方高級長官，或稱首長，而且在往後的許多年，都一如三年前那樣擁有議員一職。

因此到他十年任期結束時，我們就可以很自然地認定，威廉·莎士比亞應該會得到史特拉福當地所能提供的最好教育。該鎮的免費學校，已開放給所有男孩就讀，就像當時所有的公立中學一樣，是在大學畢業生的指導下運作，而這些畢業生也有資格傳播這種曾一度讓英格蘭誇耀的高深學識。

我們雖無莎翁在這間學校就讀的紀錄，但是對於他在那兒受教一事，卻不會有任何合理的懷疑。依據舊式的傳統論點，莎士比亞所受的教育十分有限，但對那些研究過他作品且不受上述傳統觀點影響的人來說，可謂握有豐富的證據，可以證明他一定在學識上建立起堅實的基礎，正確的說，一定曾在公立中學受教過。

史特拉福就像許多鄉下的城鎮一樣，並沒有自外於一般的世界，它是個交通要道，每一種商品的行商都經常會雲集於這兒的市場。這位詩人劇作家想必始終都是睜大著雙眼作觀察，可是從出生一直到1582年和安妮·哈瑟威（Anne Hathaway）結婚為止，有關他的事跡中沒有一件是為人所確切熟知的，直到約1589年在倫敦擔任演員，不過那時我們也僅僅知道他生了三個孩子。

我們始終無從得知，以表演為唯一職業的情況，究竟在莎翁的人生中持續了多久，不過最大的可能就是他在抵達倫敦沒多久，就立刻展開了編劇的工作，這時大家才知道他已展開了自己的寫作生涯。

改良和變更未臻標準的老舊戲劇以符合當時所需，是套極為常見的慣例，甚至在當時最棒的劇作家之間也不例外，而且莎翁的能力也很快地讓他冒出頭來，很明顯，他是相當適合這工作的。當變更原本由其他作家所著的劇本蔚為風尚後，改編的工作實際上就成為一種創作的工作了，而莎翁少數初期的作品的確就是這樣的案例，眾所皆知在較老舊的劇本中，都可以找到它們的蹤跡。

我們在此尚無需對這位全世界最偉大劇作家出版過的作品極盡吹捧之能事，因為對它們的批判聲音已消耗殆盡，而英國、德國和美國最優秀的知識份子，也已把他們的力量專注於闡述這些作品的價值上。

莎翁於1616年4月23日在史特拉福過世。莎士比亞在演藝圈和劇作圈的夥伴，以及以其他方式結識他的人們，不但一致表達出對他才賦的欽佩，而且還包括對他的尊敬及熱愛。班・強生就說：「我愛這個人，對他逝世後所獲得的令譽表達敬意，對他的崇拜也一如其他任何偶像。此君為人坦誠，而且具有開放和自由的特質。」

莎士比亞在死後第二天，即葬於史特拉福教堂的聖壇北側，在墓穴上立了塊平坦的石頭，上面鐫刻了由他自己親自寫下的墓誌銘：

朋友，看在上帝的份上，
切莫挖掘此墓，
愛惜墓石的會得庇佑，
移我屍骨者將受詛咒。

1 哈姆雷特

p. 012 哈姆雷特是丹麥國王的獨子，他深愛自己的父母親，並與美麗女孩歐菲麗亞相戀，沈浸在幸福裡。歐菲麗亞的父親波洛紐斯，則是國王的大臣。

在哈姆雷特遠赴異鄉威登堡深造時，父親突然去世。年輕的哈姆雷特聽說國王是遭到蛇吻致死，於是回家奔喪。年輕王子深愛著父親，卻發現母后在國王撒手之前的一個月，就決定改嫁，而且是嫁給叔父，這自然令他難以接受。

哈姆雷特不願為婚禮而延後服喪。

「我不僅要穿上黑衣服喪，一顆心更是為亡父哀慟不已。至少，他的兒子還惦記著他，而且悲痛逾恆。」

但叔父克勞狄斯對他說：「你不應該這樣悲傷過度，當然，失去父親是一定會難過的，但……」

哈姆雷特痛苦地喊道：「啊，我無法短短一個月就忘記自己的摯愛。」

p. 013 於是母后和克勞狄斯就撇下他，歡歡喜喜地去籌措婚禮，把待他們不薄的可憐國王忘得一乾二淨。

獨自一人的哈姆雷特這時開始滿心納悶與疑惑，不知道該如何是好，因為父親死於蛇吻的事令他難以置信。一切似乎顯得很明白，好像是惡毒的叔父殺害了國王，以便篡奪王位並迎娶母后。只是他無憑無據，難以指控。就在這時，一位叫何瑞修的同學剛好從威登堡來找他。

「你怎麼來了？」哈姆雷特親切地迎接好友。

p. 014「陛下，我是來參加你父王的喪禮的。」

「我想應該是參加我母后的婚禮的，」哈姆雷特難過地說道：「我父親……再也看不到像他這樣的人了。」

何瑞修回答：「陛下，我想我昨天晚上見到了他。」

哈姆雷特驚訝地聆聽著，何瑞修解釋他和兩位守衛是如何在城垛處看到國王的鬼魂。

於是哈姆雷特當晚就前往城垛。果然到了午夜時分，在冷冽的月光下，國王的鬼魂穿著他過去慣常披戴的盔甲，來到了城垛。

哈姆雷特的膽子很大，並沒有被鬼魂嚇得逃之夭夭。鬼魂招手將他引到一旁，他便跟著走過去。鬼魂跟他說，他的揣測是正確的。

p. 015 是惡毒的克勞狄斯趁著他在果園裡睡午覺時，把毒藥滴入他的耳朵裡，害死了他好心的國王兄長。

鬼魂說：「你一定要為我報這個仇，讓心狠手辣的叔父得到報應。但是，不可以傷害你的母后，因為她是我的愛妻，也是你的母親。要記住我的這些話。」

這時曙光將起，鬼魂就消失無蹤了。

p. 016「從現在起，我心裡頭只想報殺父之仇，我會記著您的話的！我要將一切都抛掉……什麼書本、歡樂、青春……全都抛掉……我現在一心一意只記得您的命令。」哈姆雷特說道。

於是當他的朋友們走過來時，他要他們發誓，決不會透露看到鬼魂的事。這時天際已經微微泛白，他們離開城垛走進屋內，思索著該如何報殺父之仇。

和父親的鬼魂會面之後，讓他激動欲狂，但為了不讓叔父起疑心，他決定裝瘋賣傻，假裝自己因為其他事發了瘋，以掩飾對叔父的不共戴天之仇。

而在歐菲麗亞的面前時，他表現得非常粗暴，讓歐菲麗亞不由得地也以為他發瘋了。歐菲麗亞很愛他，而他以前常常送她禮物，寫情書給她，對她講了很多深深款款的話。

p. 017 歐菲麗亞是如此深愛他，所以她相信，他一定是完全瘋掉了，不然是不可能這樣狠心對待她的。歐菲麗亞跟她父親說了這件事，還拿了一封很動人的情書給父親看，而那正是哈姆雷特寫給她的信。信裡頭有很多瘋言瘋語，不過卻有首很動人的短詩：

儘管懷疑星辰只是把火，
懷疑太陽會被移走，
懷疑真理竟成謊言，
卻不容懷疑我的愛。

從這件事以後，每個人都認定了哈姆雷特是愛得發狂了。

p. 018 可憐的哈姆雷特過得非常苦悶，他多麼想按照父親鬼魂的指示行動，但他生性溫和，並不想去殺人，即使是報殺父之仇。結果，他甚至有時候會懷疑起鬼魂所言是否真實。

就在這時，一批戲子來宮廷作表演，哈姆雷特便指定戲碼，要他們在國王和母后面前表演。而這齣戲碼所演出的故事，正是描述一個男人在自家花園被一位親人所殺害，而且凶手後來還娶了男人的妻子。

這位惡毒的國王高坐在王位上，他身邊坐著王后，一旁還有群臣，當他看著舞台上正演出自己曾經幹過的可怕勾當時，不難想像他心中會作何感受。

當劇情演到狠毒的親人把毒藥灌進沈睡男子的耳朵裡時，克勞狄斯突然站了起來，踉踉蹌蹌地走開，王后和群臣隨之跟在其後。

p. 019 這時哈姆雷特對朋友說：「現在我可以確定鬼魂說的是真的了！克勞狄斯要是沒有下這種毒手，那他看到這齣戲時就不會這麼難受了。」

這時母后派人來叫他去見她，這是克勞狄斯的意思，要她好好斥訓哈姆雷特，不應該安排這種戲碼等等的。克勞狄斯想知道到底是怎麼一回事，就暗中囑咐老波洛紐斯躲在王后房間的簾子後面，一探究竟。

當母子兩人談話時，哈姆雷特滿口狂言亂語，嚇得王后大喊救命，而躲在簾幕後面的波洛紐斯也跟著叫了起來。

p. 020 哈姆雷特以為躲在後面的就是國王，於是舉劍刺向簾子，但被殺死的並不是國王，而是可憐的老波洛紐斯。

這件事讓叔叔和母親非常地生氣，更悲慘的是，被他殺死的人，竟是愛人的父親。

「啊！你太魯莽，太狠毒了！」王后喊道。

哈姆雷特痛苦地回答道：「簡直和謀殺國王或是嫁給親王一樣地狠毒。」

接著哈姆雷特就明明白白告訴母后他所有的想法，以及他又是如何得知這樁謀殺事情的。末了他乞求母后至少不要再對克勞狄斯那麼好了，因為他是卑鄙之徒，殺害了一個好國王。

就在他們談話時，已故國王的鬼魂再度出現在哈姆雷特的面前，但母后看不見鬼魂。當鬼魂走後，母子倆就分開了。

p. 021 王后跟克勞狄斯陳述了剛剛所發生的事情，也說明了波洛紐斯是怎麼被殺死的。克勞狄斯說道：「顯然地，哈姆雷特已經瘋了，現在他殺了參謀大臣，所以為了他的安全著想，我們一切計畫要如期進行，並且把他送去英格蘭。」

於是國王派兩位親信將哈姆雷特送出國，並帶信給英國王室，要求他們把哈姆雷特處死。

但這件事被哈姆雷特給識破，他暗中把信給弄到手，再把那兩位準備背叛他的臣子名字給加進去。

當船駛抵英格蘭時，哈姆雷特就逃到一艘海盜船上，於是兩個狠心的臣子也不管他的死活了，繼續去迎接他們自己的命運。

p. 022 哈姆雷特匆忙趕回王宮，但在這同時卻發生了不幸的事情：紅顏薄命的歐菲麗亞，她在失去了心愛的人和父親之後，就得了失心瘋了。她在頭髮上插著花花草草，在宮裡頭瘋瘋顛顛地走來走去，哼哼唱唱地不知在唱什麼，滿嘴瘋言瘋語地也不知道在講什麼。

有一天，她走到溪邊的柳樹旁，想要把花環掛在柳枝上，結果整個人連同花朵不慎摔落水裡，因而溺斃了。

p. 025 哈姆雷特之前因為裝瘋，不得已冷落她，但他其實一直是很愛她的。而就在哈姆雷特逃回宮裡時，卻看到國王、王后和宮廷裡的人都在為心愛女友的葬禮而落淚。

歐菲麗亞的兄弟賴爾提斯也進宮了，他要為父親老波洛紐斯的死討個公道。這時，只見他悲痛地跳進墳墓裡，雙臂再次緊緊地抱住歐菲麗亞。

「就算歐菲麗亞有千萬個兄弟，他們對她的愛，還不及我一個人對她愛呀！」哈姆雷特喊道，也跟著跳進墳墓裡，然後兩個人就打了起來，直到被人拉開為止。

事後，哈姆雷特乞求賴爾提斯原諒，「是可忍孰不可忍，沒有任何人可以比我更愛她，就算是她的兄弟也不例外。」哈姆雷特說。

然而，狠毒的克勞狄斯是不會讓他們互相友好的。他告訴賴爾提斯，說哈姆雷特是如何殺了老波洛紐斯的，兩人並且設計了一場陰謀，打算謀害哈姆雷特。

p. 027 賴爾提斯向哈姆雷特下戰帖，要和他較量較量劍術，而宮廷裡的人也都來觀看比賽。

哈姆雷特所拿的是一把比較鈍的劍，那是比賽專用的。然而，賴爾提斯所拿的劍不但鋒利，而且劍尖還沾了毒液。

此外，惡毒的國王還準備一碗摻有毒藥的酒。他的用意是，當比賽愈來愈激烈時，哈姆雷特應該會叫酒來，這樣就可以派上用場了。

這時，賴爾提斯和哈姆雷特開始比起劍來。在幾個回合後，賴爾提斯鋒利的劍刺中了哈姆雷特。

哈姆雷特對於這種小人行逕感到很憤怒，因為他們是在擊劍，又不是在對決。這時，就在兩個人互相逼近對打時，雙方的劍都被擊落。兩人於是再把劍拾起來，可是哈姆雷特卻拿錯了劍，把自己那把較鈍的劍換成了賴爾提斯那支鋒利且有毒的劍。

這時哈姆雷特一擊，刺中了賴爾提斯，賴爾提斯隨之倒地而死，自食惡果。

此時，王后突然也尖叫了起來：「這酒……這酒！噢，親愛的哈姆雷特，我中毒了！」

原來，她誤喝了國王為哈姆雷特所準備的那碗毒酒。國王眼睜睜地看著王后倒下，她和自己一樣狠心，但他深愛著她，而她卻死於自己的卑劣陰謀之下。

p. 028 歐菲麗亞死了，波洛紐斯死了，王后死了，賴爾提斯死了，還有被派往英格蘭的那兩名臣子也死了——這讓哈姆雷特終於有了膽子完成鬼魂的命令，去報殺父之仇。要是他能早拿定主意殺了罪該萬死的惡毒叔父，那麼這一條條的人命就不會白白犧牲了。

哈姆雷特最後鼓起勇氣，做了自己所應做的事，將毒劍調頭朝篡位的國王刺去。

「這次，毒液終於發揮作用了！」他喊道，國王隨之嗚呼哀哉。就這樣，哈姆雷特終於實現了承諾，報了殺父之仇。所有的任務都完成了，而他也死得其所。

在一旁目睹他死去的人們，莫不為他祈禱，為他落淚，因為他的臣民都很愛戴他。丹麥王子哈姆雷特，他悲劇的一生，就此落幕了。

2 仲夏夜之夢

p. 030 荷蜜雅和賴桑德是對戀人，
可是荷蜜雅的父親卻希望她嫁給另一個男人狄米楚斯。

當時，他們所居住的雅典城有條惡法：任何婦女都必須遵從父命嫁人，如果不肯遵從，就要被處死。

荷蜜雅的父親見到女兒竟敢違抗自己的好意，就怒氣沖沖地跑到雅典公爵的面前，表示如果荷蜜雅仍違抗父命，就要求處死她。

於是公爵給荷蜜雅四天的時間考慮，四天之後她如果還是不肯嫁給狄米楚斯，就會被處死。

p. 031 賴桑德當然悲痛欲絕，這時對他來說，最好的解決辦法，似乎就是帶著荷蜜雅私奔到他姑媽家，只要到了那個地方，就不必理會這條殘酷的法律，可以和荷蜜雅成親了。而在動身之前，荷蜜雅把私奔的事告訴了好友海倫娜。

雖然狄米楚斯要娶的是荷蜜雅，但他早就和海倫娜交往許久了。海倫娜就和所有醋勁大發的人一樣糊塗，無法認清狄米楚斯琵琶別抱想娶荷蜜雅，錯並不在可憐的荷蜜雅。

海倫娜知道，如果把荷蜜雅要到雅典城外樹林私奔的事情告訴心上人，那他一定會追去的，「到時候，我就可以跟著他，最起碼還能看到他的人。」她這樣自言自語道。

p. 032 於是，海倫娜跑去找狄米楚斯，向他洩露了好友的秘密。

當時在賴桑德和荷蜜雅相約碰面，以及另一對男女決定尾隨於後的那片樹林裡，就像大多數叢林一樣，常有精靈出沒。當晚，這裡就來了仙王歐白朗和仙后蒂妲妮雅。

那時候的精靈都是很精明的人類，可是偶爾也會像凡夫俗子一樣，蠢態百出。歐白朗和蒂妲妮雅原本應該可以一直過著幸福的日子，但兩人寧可吵吵鬧鬧，也不願意愜意地過日子。

他們兩人只要一見面，就會拌嘴，大吵大鬧，嚇得隨從的精靈會爬進橡果殼裡躲起來。

因此，兩人常常各走各的，仙王帶著他的徒眾徘徊在樹林的這一頭，仙后則端起架子和隨從流連在另一頭，而不像一般的精靈國，能夠歡歡樂樂地在月光下晝夜歌舞。

p. 033 至於這次爭執的起因，是為了一個印度小男孩。蒂妲妮雅想收小男孩為貼身隨從，歐白朗則要小男孩跟著他，成為精靈武士。當然，仙后死也不願把孩子交給他。

在這個皓月當空的晚上，精靈王國的仙王和仙后在林子間一處遍布苔蘚的空地上碰面了。

「真是冤家路窄，又在月光下碰頭了，驕傲的蒂妲妮雅！」仙王說。

「怎麼，善妒的歐白朗，是你嗎？」仙后回答：「你什麼事情都要吵！來，仙子們，我們走！我現在不想理他！」

「吵架還不是因妳！」仙王說：「把那個印度小男孩給我，我就會乖乖地服侍妳，愛護妳。」

p. 034「你死了這條心吧！就算你拿整個仙國來交換，也休想把他搶走。仙子們，我們走！」

她和隨從們隨即在月光下離去。

「好，快滾吧！」歐白朗說：「不過只要妳待在樹林裡，我就會一直跟著妳。」

接著，歐白朗把他甚為寵幸的精靈潑克叫了過來，潑克是個很會惡作劇的精靈。

潑克常常溜進酪農那兒拿走奶油，有時候還鑽到攪奶器裡，讓奶油製作不起來；再不就是把啤酒弄酸，或是讓人們在黑漆漆的晚上迷路，然後再大聲嘲笑他們。更可惡的是，他會趁著人們要坐下時，冷不防地抽走下面的凳子，或是在他們舉杯飲酒時，把熱麥酒潑灑到對方的下巴，弄得他們一片狼藉。

p. 035 歐白朗對這小精靈說：「現在，快去替我採一朵叫做『在愛中懶散』的花來。那是一種紫色的小花，只要把它的汁液滴在熟睡者的眼睛上，那麼等他們醒過來，無論第一眼看到的是什麼，都會立刻愛上它。我要把這種花的汁液，滴在蒂妲妮雅的眼睛裡，等她一睜開眼，不管看到的是獅子、黑熊、大野狼、公牛，或是雞婆的猴子，還是一天到晚攀上跳下的人猿，她都會立刻愛上牠。」

在潑克離開時，狄米楚斯剛好經過那片林間空地，後面跟著可憐的海倫娜，仍不死心地對他傾訴衷腸，要他不要忘記他自己說過的那些山盟海誓。但狄米楚斯仍說自己並不愛她，也無法愛她，那些什麼山盟海誓早已是過眼雲煙了。

p. 036 歐白朗替可憐的海倫娜感到難過，當潑克帶著那朵花回來時，就命令他跟著狄米楚斯，把汁液滴到他眼裡，這樣等狄米楚斯醒過來，看到了海倫娜，就會馬上愛上她，就像她對他的愛一樣。

潑克於是出發，待在林子裡徘徊，然而，他找到的卻是賴桑德，而非狄米楚斯，因而陰錯陽差地把汁液滴到了賴桑德的眼裡。好巧不巧的是，當賴桑德醒來後，看到的並不是情人荷蜜雅，反而是在林子裡尋找狄米楚斯的海倫娜。於是，在這紫色花朵的魔力下，賴桑德愛上了海倫娜，對原來的心上人棄之不顧。

當荷蜜雅醒來發現賴桑德不見了，就在林子裡遊盪，想找尋心上人。潑克回去後，把事情經過告訴了歐白朗，歐白朗立刻發現潑克鑄下了大錯，於是命令他再著手尋找狄米楚斯。最後，潑克終於找到了狄米楚斯，把汁液滴進了他的眼裡。

p. 037 狄米楚斯醒來後，第一個看到的也是海倫娜，於是狄米楚斯和賴桑德一同尾隨她經過林子，而荷蜜雅也亦步亦趨地跟在愛人身後，一如之前海倫娜死心塌地跟著狄米楚斯一般。

最後，海倫娜和荷蜜雅開始吵了起來，而狄米楚斯和賴桑德也準備決鬥。歐白朗很難過，原本一片好心卻弄巧成拙。於是他告訴潑克說：

「這兩個年輕人要去決鬥了，現在你先用濃霧籠罩整個黑夜，讓他們迷失方向，誰也找不到誰。等他們精疲力竭睡去之後，再趁機把解藥花液滴在賴桑德的眼睛裡，讓他找回舊愛。這樣一來，兩個男人就會各自擁有熱愛他們的女子，而且會把這一切當成是一場仲夏夜之夢罷了，如此就能皆大歡喜了。」

於是潑克出發去完成仙王的指令，他看到那兩個互相迷路的男人沈沈睡去，就把汁液滴到賴桑德的眼裡，並且說道：

p. 038 當你清醒過來，
就會得到真愛，
只消一眼瞥見，
舊情人的眼神。
傑克娶了吉兒，
真是天作之合。

在這同時，歐白朗發現蒂妲妮雅在一處長滿野百里香、櫻草、紫羅蘭、忍冬、麝香薔薇和玫瑰的沙洲上睡著了。蒂妲妮雅每晚都會在這兒睡上一會兒，外面還蓋上似琺瑯般的蛇皮被子。

歐白朗這時彎下腰來靠近她，把汁液滴到她眼裡，並且這麼說：

在妳醒來後不管看到什麼，
都會把他當作情人。

當蒂妲妮雅醒來時，第一個看到的，竟然是一個奇蠢無比的鄉巴佬，當時他正打算進入林子裡彩排一場戲，好在派對上大顯身手。這名鄉巴佬曾遇見過潑克，調皮的潑克就把一個驢頭套在他肩膀上，彷彿那兒原本就長了個驢子腦袋。

p. 039 蒂妲妮雅醒來後發現這個可怕的怪物，就立刻說：「這是哪位天使啊！你的聰明才智，和你英挺的外貌一樣也超凡嗎？」

「要是我真聰明到能夠走出這林子的話，那我就心滿意足了。」這名愚蠢的鄉巴佬說。

「請不要離開這片樹林。」蒂妲妮雅說道。顯然，愛情汁液的魔力已在她身上起了作用，對她來說，這名鄉巴佬似乎已成了世上最美麗和最可愛的生物了。

「我愛你，」蒂妲妮雅繼續說道：「請跟我來，我會差遣精靈伺候你的。」

p. 040 於是她召喚了四個精靈前來，他們分別是豆花、蛛網、飛蛾和芥子。

「你們得好好伺候這位紳士，」仙后吩咐道：「把杏仁、懸鉤子、紫葡萄、青無花果和桑椹拿給他吃，從蜜蜂那兒偷蜜給他，再用色彩鮮艷的蝴蝶翅膀，將月光從他睡眼矇矓的眸子邊給搧走。」

「是的！」其中一名精靈說完，其他的精靈也都隨聲附和：「是的！」

p. 041「現在請坐到我身邊，」仙后對著鄉巴佬深情款款地說：「讓我撫摸著你那可愛的臉蛋，把麝香薔薇插在你柔滑又有光澤的頭上，並親吻那對漂亮的大耳朵，我的小親親！」

「豆花在哪兒？」這位套著驢腦袋的鄉巴佬問道。他並不怎麼在意仙后對他的款款深情，但是有這麼多精靈隨侍在側，倒是讓他很得意。

「我在這裡！隨時聽候您的吩咐。」豆花說。

「替我抓抓腦袋，豆花！」鄉巴佬猶不滿足的繼續說：「蛛網在哪兒？」

「我在這裡！隨時聽候您的吩咐。」蛛網說。

鄉巴佬說：「替我把那樹頂上的紅色蜜蜂給宰了，再把蜂蜜拿來，對了，芥子在哪兒？」

p. 042「我在這裡！隨時聽候您的吩咐。」芥子說。

「哦！我什麼都不需要了。」鄉巴佬說：「你只要幫著豆花，替我

抓抓腦袋就行了！我想我該去理個髮了，老覺得臉上毛茸茸的。」

「還想吃點什麼嗎？」仙后說。「我想來點上好的乾燕麥，然後再來點乾草。」鄉巴佬回答，原來他戴上驢腦袋後，口味也變得和驢子一樣了。

「要不要我派些精靈，從松鼠窩裡替你拿些新鮮的乾果來？」仙后又問。

「現在我倒想吃一兩把上好的乾豌豆，」鄉巴佬說：「可是請妳的人先不要來打攪我，我想睡了。」

仙后見狀說：「我要把你緊緊擁在懷裡。」

所以當歐白朗來到時，就發現他那美麗的仙后，正狂吻那個戴著驢腦袋的鄉巴佬，並不斷傾訴著愛意。

p. 043 歐白朗在替蒂妲妮雅解除魔法之前，他已經說服她把想據為己有的印度小男孩交給他。

等到男孩弄到手後，歐白朗憐憫起了蒂妲妮雅，便將解藥花汁滴到她動人的眸子中。不到片刻功夫，她就看到剛才所愛戀的驢頭鄉巴佬，發現了自己竟然這麼蠢。

歐白朗把驢頭從鄉巴佬的頭上取了下來，讓他的蠢腦袋靠在百里香和紫羅蘭上，繼續睡他的大頭覺。

p. 044 之後，一切又恢復了平靜，歐白朗和蒂妲妮雅比以往更加相惜了。至於狄米楚斯的心中除了海倫娜外，已不做第二人想，而海倫娜則至始至終都鍾情於狄米楚斯，除了他之外，心裡容不下其他任何一個男人。

至於荷蜜雅和賴桑德呢，他們仍是一對彼此熱愛的情人，一如你走在路上、或是行經精靈落腳的森林時所會碰到的那些情侶一樣。

這四個彼此相愛的凡人，於是回到雅典完成了婚事，而精靈王國的仙王和仙后也在這片林子裡，愉快地生活在一起。

3 李爾王

p. 046 李爾王上了年紀，心力交瘁之餘已厭倦了王國的政務，只希望在三位女兒身邊安詳地終老一生。

在三個女兒之中，有兩個分別嫁給阿爾班尼和康瓦爾的公爵，另外勃艮第公爵和法蘭西國王，在追求他的小女兒柯蒂莉亞。

李爾王把三個女兒一起叫過來，說他打算把王國分給她們。

「可是首先呢，」國王說：「我很想知道妳們究竟有多愛我？」

葛妮莉其是個十分惡毒的女人，一點也不愛她的父親，這時卻說她對他的愛已超過言詞所能表達的程度，要比視野、空間或自由更為珍貴，也非生命、恩典、健康、美麗和榮耀所能比擬。

「我愛你一如我的姊妹們，甚至更多，」蕾岡也表示：「因為除了父親的愛之外，我什麼都不在乎。」

p. 047 李爾王對蕾岡的表白十分高興，於是轉向最小的女兒柯蒂莉亞。

「小甜心，雖然妳是最後一個說，但相信美言絕不會少於兩個姊姊，」李爾王說：「我把王國中最好的一部分留給妳，現在妳會說些什麼呢？」

「什麼話都沒有，父王！」柯蒂莉亞回答。

「可能是由於妳對我沒有一絲的愛，才讓妳什麼話都說不出口，現在再說一遍。」國王說。

柯蒂莉亞這時回答：「我是依照做女兒的本分愛陛下，不多也不少。」

柯蒂莉亞這樣說，是因她不齒於兩個姊姊表達愛的手段，實際上她們對愛缺乏正確的認知，不知道應對老父盡到什麼樣的本分。

p. 048「我是你的女兒，」柯蒂莉亞繼續說：「你把我養育成人而且疼愛我，因此我會恰如其分地恪盡自己本分以回報您老人家，服從您、愛您，帶給您最大的榮耀。」

李爾王本來是最愛柯蒂莉亞的，希望她一番愛的表白能比兩個姊姊更誇大。

他說：「滾吧！對我和我的一顆心來說，妳只是個陌生人。」

肯特伯爵是李爾王最喜歡的弄臣和愛將之一，他想為柯蒂莉亞緩頰，可是李爾王聽不進去。

他把王國平分給葛妮莉和蕾岡，然後告訴她們他只要留下一百名武裝騎士，並輪流住在兩個女兒那兒即可。

當勃艮第公爵得知王國沒有柯蒂莉亞的份兒後，就放棄了追求，可是法蘭西國王比較聰明，於是對李爾王說：「國王，你分不到財產的女兒，會是我們以及偉大法蘭西的王后。」

p. 049「帶她走，帶她走，」李爾王說：「我永遠都不要再見到她那張臉。」

於是柯蒂莉亞成了法蘭西的王后，而肯特公爵則由於冒險幫柯蒂莉亞爭取財產而遭到放逐。

李爾王和女兒葛妮莉住在一起，不過她自從取得父親該交付的每樣東西後，就開始為了李爾王替他自己所保留的一百名騎士而和父親產生嫌隙。

p. 050 葛妮莉對父親極為苛刻，又不孝順，連她的僕人不是拒絕服從李爾王的命令，就是假裝聽不到他們一行人的話。

當肯特公爵遭到放逐後，言談舉止間就好像要前往另一個國家似的，不過暗地裡卻假扮成一位僕人回來，並侍候著李爾王。

李爾王只有兩個朋友，那就是他只知道如今身為自己僕人的肯特公爵，以及對他忠心耿耿的另一位弄臣。

後來葛妮莉明明白白告訴父親，他的騎士只會縱情吃喝，給她王宮帶來無比騷亂，於是央求他只留下極少數和他一樣的垂垂老者。

「我的隨從都是明白所有責任和義務的人，」李爾王說：「葛妮莉，我不會再打攪妳了……現在我要去找另一個女兒。」

p. 051 於是他跨上馬鞍和隨從們出發前往蕾岡的城堡，可是過去在表達對李爾王的依戀上都強過姊姊的蕾岡，如今似乎在大逆不道上也更勝一籌，竟表示以五十位騎士服侍李爾王仍嫌太多。這時葛妮莉已匆忙趕到那兒，防止蕾岡對老國王表現任何的善意，見到蕾岡這麼說，也表示即使只用到五位騎士都算太多，因為她的僕人也可以侍候他啊。

當李爾王認清，兩個女兒真正的意圖就是把他給趕走時，就離開她們了。

p. 052 那是個狂風暴雨的夜晚，他徘徊在荒原，痛苦下的他已陷入半瘋狂狀態，除了那名可憐的弄臣外沒有任何隨從。可是不一會兒，他的僕人也就是善良的肯特公爵即遇到了他，最後說服李爾王到一處破落的小茅草屋裡躺著休息。

到了黎明，肯特公爵把他的王室主人帶往多佛，並緊急趕往法蘭西的王宮，把所發生的事告訴柯蒂莉亞。

柯蒂莉亞的丈夫給她一支軍隊，她就率領這支軍隊登陸多佛，在那兒發現李爾王正躑躅在荒郊野外，還帶著一頂以蕁麻和雜草編成的王冠。

於是他們把他帶了回去，給他東西吃，讓他穿上衣服，接著柯蒂莉亞來到他面前並親吻父親。

「對我一定要多擔待些，」李爾王說：「過去的事就忘了吧，請原諒我，我又老又笨。」

p. 053 如今他終於知道哪個孩子最愛他，以及誰又值得他愛。

葛妮莉和蕾岡把她們的武力聯合起來和柯蒂莉亞的軍隊戰鬥，並取得了勝利，於是柯蒂莉亞和她的父親被捕下獄。

葛妮莉的丈夫阿爾班尼公爵是個好人，並不知道妻子有多麼惡毒，後來才聽到了整個故事的實情。

p. 054 當葛妮莉發現丈夫知道自己是個惡毒的女人後就自殺了，不過臨死前在嫉妒心的作祟下，又讓她妹妹蕾岡服下了致命的毒藥。

這對壞姐妹早已做好安排，柯蒂莉亞必須在獄中絞死，雖然阿爾班尼公爵立刻遣了信差企圖搭救，可是為時已遲。

只見年老的李爾王蹣跚地來到阿爾班尼公爵的營帳，手臂上擁著愛女柯蒂莉亞的屍體。

不久，在老王的雙唇傾吐出對女兒的愛後就倒地不起，柯蒂莉亞仍在他臂彎裡，而李爾王也在此時溘然長逝。

4 馴悍記

p. 056 帕度亞這地方住了一位名叫巴布提斯塔的紳士，他有兩個漂亮的女兒，大姊凱瑟琳暴躁易怒，行為粗魯，沒有人想娶她，可是她妹妹碧安卡不但美麗迷人，而且嘴巴又甜，因為追求者眾多，大家都央求她父親答應婚事。

可是巴布提斯塔說，大女兒一定要先嫁，於是碧安卡的眾多追求者決定找個倒霉鬼娶凱瑟琳，這樣她們的父親就肯聽聽他們的求親了。

於是大夥想到了維洛那有位名叫皮楚齊歐的紳士，他們半開玩笑地問他是否願意娶凱瑟琳那個嘮嘮叨叨、令人討厭的女人。

令人大出意外的是，他竟然說好，還說這種人最適合當他的妻子了，並且表示如果她長得好看又有錢的話，那他保證很快就會讓她服服貼貼的。

p. 057 皮楚齊歐於是去找巴布提斯塔，請求他准許自己去追求他溫柔的女兒凱瑟琳，而巴布提斯塔卻不得不向他坦白，要怎麼形容她女兒都可以，獨獨就是無法說她女兒是溫柔的。

就在這時，凱瑟琳的音樂老師衝進來，抱怨那個潑辣的女兒，只因為他糾正她彈錯了，她就用琴打他的腦袋，把琴都給打破了。

皮楚齊歐說：「別擔心，這倒讓我更愛她了，我很想找她談一談。」

p. 058 等凱瑟琳走進來時，他說：「早啊，凱特，我聽說這是妳的小名。」

「你話難道只聽一半的嗎？」凱瑟琳無禮地說。

皮楚齊歐說：「哦，不，人們說妳是『直爽的凱特』，『健康活潑的凱特』，有時候也說妳是『潑婦凱特』，我聽到每個城鎮的人都在誇讚妳溫柔又美麗，所以特來請求妳當我的妻子。」

凱特大叫：「你的妻子？你想得美！」接著她還對他說了些很難聽的話，很遺憾的是，她最後還呼了他一個巴掌。

「妳要是再打我一下，我也會回敬妳。」他平靜地說道，接著又講了許多奉承話，聲稱非卿莫娶。

當巴布提斯塔走進來時，他立刻問皮楚齊歐：「你可以多快娶我女兒？」

皮楚齊歐回答：「要我快點當然很好，只是……」

p. 059「那妳覺得如何，凱瑟琳？」做父親的繼續問。

凱瑟琳憤怒地說：「我才不想嫁人，你這個做父親的怎麼也摻上一腳，硬要我嫁給這個瘋瘋顛顛的惡棍。」

皮楚齊歐說：「啊，您和全世界的人都說錯了，您應該看看，我們兩個在獨處時，她對我是多麼地溫柔呀。總之，我要去威尼斯為我們的婚禮買些上好的嫁妝……吻吻我，凱特，禮拜天我們就要結婚了。」

聽到這些話，讓凱瑟琳氣得走出房間，皮楚齊歐則笑了笑，跟著從另一道門走出去。

p. 060 不管她是否愛上了皮楚齊歐，或者只是很高興碰到了一個不怕自己的男人，抑或皮楚齊歐無視於她的無禮和蠻橫，仍執意娶她為妻，讓她受寵若驚……總之呢，一如皮楚齊歐所打的包票，她真的在禮拜天嫁給了他。

為了要挫一挫凱瑟琳的粗野和傲氣，讓她懂得收斂，皮楚齊歐故意在婚禮時遲到，而且趕來時，還穿得一身邋遢，讓凱瑟琳羞於與他為伍。他的隨從也是穿得破破爛爛的，他們馬匹的模樣也沿途讓路人發噱。

p. 061 新婚後的第一頓早餐時間，皮楚齊歐把妻子拉走，不准她用餐，還說她現在是他的人了，他想怎麼對待她，就怎麼對待她。

他的態度很粗暴，在整個婚禮上都是一副瘋瘋癲癲的樣子，令人恐懼，讓凱瑟琳怕得發抖，只好乖乖地跟他走。

p. 062 他讓她坐上一匹瘦弱的老馬，走起路來還一瘸一拐的。他們走在顛簸泥濘的路上，往皮楚齊歐的家前進，而且整路上他又罵又吼的。

等到達夫君家的時候，凱瑟琳早已疲累不堪了。然而，當天晚上皮楚齊歐卻不讓她吃睡，因為他拿定了主意要好好調教這位悍妻，讓她畢生難忘。

皮楚齊歐和藹可親地帶她進門，可是當晚餐端上來時，他卻挑三揀四，直嚷嚷說肉燒得太焦，僕人也招待不周；還說他是這麼地愛她，除非是最上等的食物，不然他是不會給她吃的。到最後，一整天趕路下來已經疲憊不堪的凱瑟琳，只好空著肚子上床。

p. 063 這時丈夫仍不斷說著自己是如何愛著她，而且說他很擔心她會睡不好。他把她的床鋪扯亂，把枕頭和床罩扔在地上，讓凱瑟琳根本無法上床睡覺。皮楚齊歐不斷地對著僕人又叫又罵，好讓凱瑟琳明白，脾氣差的人是多麼倒人胃口。

第二天的情況也是一樣，送上來的食物都被嫌得一無是處，而且在她還沒來得及嚐上一口就被端走。最後，由於缺乏睡眠，她變得病懨懨的，感到頭暈目眩。

她於是對一位僕人說：「求求你給我弄點吃的來，什麼都好。」

「來份蹄膀子如何？」僕人問。

凱瑟琳急切地回答：「好啊！」可是僕人因為知道主人的用意，就說他怕蹄膀子對急性子的人不好，便問她來一份牛肚如何？

「沒關係，快拿來！」凱瑟琳說道。

「我想牛肚也是滿上火，也不是很好。」僕人說：「那麼來碟芥末牛肉如何？」

p. 065「太好了。」凱瑟琳說。

「可是芥末太辣了。」

「那牛肉就好，芥末就不用了。」
凱瑟琳喊道，肚子顯得越來越餓了。

僕人說：「不行，一定要配芥末，單吃牛肉是不行的。」

凱撒琳失去耐心地喊了起來：「那就兩樣都要吧，一樣也行啦，什麼都可以啦。」

僕人說：「那就單來一份芥末囉！」

這時凱瑟琳才明白僕人是在耍她，就打了他一個耳光。

就在這時候，皮楚齊歐拿了一些食物來給她，可是當她好不容易要開始填飽肚子時，他就叫裁縫把她的新衣服帶進來，並命令僕人把桌子的東西清一清，讓凱瑟琳仍舊餓著肚子。

裁縫為她製作的衣服和帽子，讓她很滿意，可是皮楚齊歐卻百般挑剔，把衣帽都扔到地上，還說決不會讓他親愛的妻子穿這麼蠢的衣服。

p. 066 凱瑟琳喊道：「我要穿，一般淑女都會戴這種帽子的。」

「等到妳變淑女時，妳也就可以戴這種帽子了，但是現在還不成。」他回答。

「來，凱特，我們就這麼一身破破爛爛地回妳的娘家吧！就如陽光在烏雲中綻放出來，布衣粗服也能展現出一個人的正直。現在才早上七點，我們不用趕路就可以在午餐時間抵達了。」

「現在都快下午兩點了，等到我們到達時都已經晚餐時間了。」凱瑟琳畢恭畢敬地說道，因為她發現自己不能拿在家裡的那種壞脾氣，來對待她的這位丈夫。

「我動身的時間，就是七點。」皮楚齊歐頑固地說：「為什麼不管我說什麼、做什麼，或是想什麼，妳都要跟我唱反調？今天不去了，如果要出發，我說幾點就是幾點。」

最後，他終於肯帶她回娘家了。

「瞧那月亮！」他說。

「那是太陽！」凱瑟琳糾正道。沒錯，那的確是太陽。

p. 067「我說它是月亮，怎麼又要和我唱反調啦！我說它是太陽就是太陽，我說是月亮就是月亮，總之我說它是什麼就是什麼，不然我就不帶妳回娘家了。」

凱瑟琳不想再和他爭了，她說：「你說啥，就是啥，我都依你。」

於是他們繼續回凱瑟琳的娘家，當他到達時，大家都齊聚在碧安卡的婚宴上，婚禮上還有另一對才結婚不久的新人——霍坦西歐和他的妻子。

大夥兒連忙歡迎兩人，並安排他們入座。

用過餐後，太太小姐紛紛退席，於是巴布斯提塔也加入陣容，一起揶揄起皮楚齊歐。他說：「我的女婿皮楚齊歐啊，你很不幸，恐怕你娶到了天字第一號的悍婦了。」

p. 068 皮楚齊歐說：「你們錯了，就讓我來證明給你們看吧！現在我們來下個賭注，我們就各自派人傳話給妻子，要她們立刻過來，如果誰的妻子來得最快最乾脆，那麼誰就贏得賭注了。」

大夥聽了欣然贊同，因為每個人都認為自己的妻子最溫順，都認為自己是贏定了。於是他們提議就以二十克朗來作為賭注。

「才二十克朗？」皮楚齊歐說：「又不是拿老鷹或獵狗來下賭，要賭我老婆的話，少說也得多個二十倍。」

「那就一百克朗吧！」碧安卡的丈夫盧森西歐說。

「同意！」其他人都叫了起來。

於是盧森西歐差了僕人到美麗的碧安卡那兒，吩咐她立刻來到他那兒。巴布斯提塔說他相信自己的女兒一定會過來。

誰知僕人回來後卻這麼說：「先生！夫人很忙，不能來！」

p. 069「難道這就是給你的答覆！」皮楚齊歐說。

「如果嫂夫人沒給你一個更不堪的答覆，或許閣下該覺得自己很幸運了。」盧森西歐對皮楚齊歐提出反擊。

接著霍坦西歐又說：「去懇請我妻子馬上來找我！」

「噢……還要用『懇請』的呀？」皮楚齊歐說。

「少說大話了，我就怕不管閣下如何乞求，尊夫人都不肯來呢！」霍坦西歐尖酸地說。

這時僕人走進來，說道：「她說你一定是在開玩笑，她才不要來呢！」

「這回更妙了，更妙了！」皮楚齊歐對他僕人說：「現在去夫人那兒，就說我『命令』她馬上過來。」

這讓大夥聽得哈哈大笑來，直說他們很清楚她會怎麼回答，而且她是不會過來的。

這時，巴布斯提塔突然驚呼道：「凱瑟琳走過來了！」

沒錯，正是凱瑟琳本人。

「你叫我來有什麼吩咐嗎，老爺！」凱瑟琳問她丈夫。

「妳妹妹和霍坦西歐的老婆哪兒去啦？」

「她們正在客廳的爐火旁聊天哪！」

「去！把她們給叫來！」

當她去叫她們來時，盧森西歐說：「真是怪事！」

「這是怎麼了？」霍坦西歐說。

p. 070 皮楚齊歐說：「這就是和睦相處，就是愛情，就是寧靜的生活囉。」

巴布斯提塔說：「那麼賭注是你的了，我還要額外加上兩萬克朗做她的嫁妝，就當做是給另一個女兒的，因為她已經完全變成了另外一個人了。」

於是皮楚齊歐拿到了賭注，而且還家有嬌妻。他讓凱瑟琳改掉了驕氣和壞脾氣，而他也很愛護妻子，兩人之間只有無盡的濃情蜜意，幸福一生。

5 暴風雨

p. 072 米蘭的公爵普洛斯帕羅是個博學又好學不倦的人，他成天在書堆裡打滾，把國政交給他完全信任的兄弟安東尼奧。

然而，這種信任卻落得不好的下場，因為安東尼奧早想篡位。為了達到這個目的，他本想殺了自己的兄弟，但因人民十分愛戴普洛斯帕羅而作罷。

然而在普洛斯帕羅的大敵，也就是那不勒斯國王艾隆索的幫助下，安東尼奧還是順利把魔掌伸進公爵的領地，獲得了所有的榮耀、權力和財富。

之後，他們把普洛斯帕羅帶到遠離陸地的海上，逼著他坐上一條沒有任何裝備、桅檣和帆篷的小舟。

他們憎惡地也把他不滿三歲的小女兒米蘭達一起扔到小舟上和他作伴，隨即揚長而去，留下父女倆自生自滅。

p. 073 不過，在追隨安東尼奧的弄臣中，卻有一個臣子仍對合法的主子普洛斯帕羅一片忠心。雖然要從沐猴而冠的仇敵手中救出公爵是不可能的，但還可以做其他的事，好讓公爵記得有位臣子對他的敬愛。

這位名叫龔札羅的可敬貴族，於是偷偷在船上藏了一些新鮮的飲水、乾糧、衣裳，以及普洛斯帕羅最看重的東西——幾本他視為珍寶的書籍。

後來，小舟漂蕩到一座島嶼，普洛斯帕羅和小女兒也安全著陸。當時，這座島嶼被一位邪惡的女巫席柯拉絲施了法，多年來一直處在她的魔咒之下，她把所有善良的精靈都禁錮在樹幹裡。

普洛斯帕羅被沖上岸時，女巫剛死去沒多久，可是精靈們仍然被囚禁著，而其中的精靈頭頭是艾瑞爾。

p. 074 普洛斯帕羅是個了不起的魔法師，他在當政期間，幾乎把全副精力都放在魔法的鑽研上，而把米蘭的大小事物委託兄弟管理。

普洛斯帕羅的法術不但讓禁錮的精靈得到自由，也能讓他們服從於他，而這些精靈也比普洛斯帕羅在米蘭的子民們，更加忠心不二。

普洛斯帕羅十分善待這些精靈，只要按照吩咐辦事便行，而且在權力的運用上，也顯得明智又適切。他發現只有一個精靈必須粗暴對待，那就是卡利班，他是個醜陋又畸形的怪物，樣子很可怕。他的母親，就是那名邪惡的老女巫，而他的種種習性既邪惡又粗暴。

p. 075 當米蘭達長大成甜美又楚楚動人的少女時，意外地遇到一件事，那就是安東尼奧、艾隆索、艾隆索的兄弟席巴斯提安、艾隆索的兒子費迪南，以及年老的龔札羅一起乘船出海，並且航行到離普洛斯帕羅不遠的地方。

普洛斯帕羅知道他們在那兒，於是用魔法掀起一場狂烈的暴風雨，連船上的水手都認為逃不過一劫了。後來，王子費迪南第一個跌落海裡，老父十分悲傷，認為愛子已經淹死。

然而，艾瑞爾卻把費迪南平安地帶上岸。其他的船員雖然被沖出船外，但也毫髮未傷地分別在這座島嶼的不同地方著陸，至於所有人都認為已經失事的那艘船，仍完好如初，並在艾瑞爾的引領下，下了錨安穩地停靠在港口。當然，這些奇蹟都是靠普洛斯帕羅和他的精靈們才能夠完成的。

p. 076 當暴風雨正在肆虐時，普洛斯帕羅讓女兒看到這艘華麗的船，是如何在波濤洶湧下費力前進，並告訴她，船上載滿了像他們一樣活生生的人類。

對這些感到悲憫萬分的米蘭達，立刻央求掀起這場暴風雨的父親平息它。她的父親要她別怕，因為他打算拯救其中所有人的生命。

p. 077 之後，他首度把兩人的身世告訴女兒，並表示他之所以要引起這場暴風雨，無非就是要把在船上的仇敵——安東尼奧和艾隆索給弄到手。

說完之後，一直為他做事的艾瑞爾剛好出現，普洛斯帕羅就向女兒施魔法，讓她入睡。

一直渴望完全自由的艾瑞爾這時開始訴苦起來，覺得自己一輩子都在做些單調而辛苦的工作，可是普洛斯帕羅卻提醒他，別忘了席柯拉絲統治這島嶼時所遭遇的一切苦難，以及他還虧欠主人的那份恩情，因為讓這些苦難告終的，正是普洛斯帕羅。艾瑞爾聞言，便不再抱怨，並且忠實的答應，不管普洛斯帕羅有何命令，都會盡力辦到。

「那就這樣做吧！」普洛斯帕羅說：「兩天內，我就會釋放你。」

p. 078 接著，他吩咐艾瑞爾化身為水中之神，並差遣他找那位年輕的王子。不久，艾瑞爾就停留在費迪南身旁，只是費迪南無法看到他。只見艾瑞爾這樣吟唱著：

請來到這處黃色沙灘，
然後再把手兒牽，
等你們親親嘴，行過禮，
驚濤駭浪也會靜下去。
你們不妨到處輕盈的跳著，
並請各位齊聲唱和！

p. 079 歌聲把四周的氣氛轉變得嚴肅起來，費迪南也隨著這奇幻的歌曲而行。歌曲的字裡行間，讓他心中悲傷不已，淚流滿面，因為它們是這樣流瀉出來的：

你的父親沈睡在五噚的海底深淵，
骨骼化身為珊瑚，
珍珠即是他的眼睛。
他全身沒有一處腐爛，

只是在大海的風雲變幻中，
顯得富麗又珍奇。
海洋女神時時敲著喪鐘，
聽！如今我聽到了——叮叮噹噹的鐘聲。

p. 080 就這樣唱著唱著，艾瑞爾把這個被咒語所困的王子，帶到普洛斯帕羅和米蘭達的面前。

瞧呀！接下去所發生的事，都一如普洛斯帕羅所期待，米蘭達自從初有記憶以來，就未曾見過除了父親之外的其他人類，只見她帶著崇敬的目光，望著眼前這位年輕的王子，愛苗不由得悄悄地生起。

「我會稱他為聖物，因為自然界裡我所見過的東西，都沒有他來得高貴。」

至於費迪南則帶著驚奇與喜悅，注視著她的美貌，然後驚呼：「一定是仙女下凡！」

在米蘭達的鼓舞下，他並不打算隱藏自己的熱情，兩人幾乎沒有交談幾句，費迪南就發下誓願，只要米蘭達願意，就可以成為他的皇后。

普洛斯帕羅雖然心裡暗自高興，可是仍假裝憤怒地說：「你一定是來這兒打探什麼的，我會把你脖子和腳綑在一起，讓你啃貝殼、嚼樹根、飲海水，快跟我來！」

p. 082「不！」費迪南說完就拔出了劍，可是普洛斯帕羅立刻對他施以魔法，王子就像雕像一樣站在原地，宛如石頭一樣動也不動。米蘭達在驚駭之餘，立刻請求父親大發慈悲，饒了自己的心上人。

然而，父親還是無情的拒絕了她，並命令費迪南跟著他進入牢房。他在那兒指派王子賣力的工作，搬動好幾千根沈重的木頭，把它們堆疊起來。費迪南很有耐心地聽令行事，而且能博得甜美的米蘭達無限同情，他覺得一切的勞苦都很值得。

米蘭達很同情王子的遭遇，想盡量幫助他完成這些粗重的活兒，但王子並沒有讓她動手，只是愛苗已燃的秘密，再也藏不住了。聆聽完王子細訴衷腸後，米蘭達喜不自勝，並且答應要做他的妻子。

p. 083 後來，普洛斯帕羅解除了王子的勞役，並且滿心歡喜地答應小倆口的婚事。

「帶她走吧！」普洛斯帕羅說：「她是你的了！」

在這同時，安東尼奧和席巴斯提安則在小島的另一端，密謀殺害那不勒斯國王艾隆索，因為他們認為費迪南已死，在心患既除下，如果艾隆索一死，那麼席巴斯提安就可以順利繼承王位。兩人打算趁著艾隆索熟睡時下毒手，可是艾瑞爾卻適時地喚醒他。

艾瑞爾向他們變了許多戲法，比方說在他們面前擺出盛宴，不過當他們正要吃時，他就在雷電交加中化身為鳥身人面的女妖，而且豐盛的酒席也瞬間消失不見。接著，艾瑞爾數落他們的種種罪狀，然後消失不見。

p. 084 普洛斯帕羅藉著魔法，把他們帶到沒有屋子的樹叢中，而自己則在那兒候駕。對方在顫抖畏懼之餘，終於痛徹前非。

普洛斯帕羅決定把自己的魔力做最後一次的運用，「之後我會折斷魔杖，然後讓魔法書都葬身在深不可測的大海之中。」

接著他讓四周響起了美妙的音樂，並且以最適當的模樣，也就是米蘭公爵的身分，出現在大家面前。由於他們已經悔改，所以他就原諒了這些人，並且道出自從他們殘酷地把這對父女放諸風浪手中後，所發生的所有事情。

他們全都為過去的罪行感到後悔不已，其中最難過的就是艾隆索了，因為他還為失去子嗣而慟哭。

然而，普洛斯帕羅抽開了簾幕，讓他們看到費迪南和米蘭達正好端端地下著棋。只見艾隆索興高采烈的迎接摯愛的兒子，當他聽說與費迪南對奕的那位美麗少女，正是普洛斯帕羅的女兒時，又再次向愛子致意，接著這對年輕的戀人宣布他們已互許終身，艾隆索便說：

p. 085「把你的雙手給我，我真心希望你喜悅，否則就讓悲痛和感傷持續佔據我的心靈吧！」

於是一切都有了幸福的結局，這艘船早已安全地停靠港邊。第二天，一行人起航前往那不勒斯，費迪南和米蘭達就要在那兒結為連理。艾瑞爾賜給他們平靜無波的大海與好兆頭的強風，而很多人也都高高興興地來參加了婚禮。

p. 086 接著，離去多年的普洛斯帕羅，終於回到他自己的公爵屬地，並受到忠心子民的熱情歡迎。

他不再使用魔法了，可是人生仍十分快樂，不僅是因為他找回了自己，最主要的，是對於那些恩將仇報、罪大惡極的仇人們，他不但沒有施加報復，而且很高貴地原諒他們。

至於艾瑞爾，普洛斯帕羅最後釋放了他，好讓他可以無拘無束地雲遊四海，並以暢快無比的心，吟唱出那甜美的歌聲：

蜜蜂採蜜的地方，我也在那兒駐足。
我躺在櫻草的花冠裡休息，
一直睡到貓頭鷹啼叫時，
再騎上蝙蝠的背部四處遨遊，
快活地追逐著炎夏的尾巴。
如今我要快樂地，
在五彩繽紛的花叢底下生活。

6 辛白林

p. 088 辛白林是不列顛的國王，育有三子，其中兩個兒子在很小時就被別人從他身邊偷偷抱走，只留下唯一的女兒伊莫珍伴著他。

後來國王梅開二度，並代為撫養摯友的兒子李奧納圖斯。李奧納圖斯是伊莫珍的兒時玩伴，當他長大後，伊莫珍就祕密嫁給他。這使得國王和王后十分生氣，國王為了懲罰李奧納圖斯，便將他逐出不列顛。

可憐的伊莫珍在和李奧納圖斯分開時心都要碎了，而李奧納圖也一樣傷心，因為他們不單是戀人和夫妻，而且打從幼年開始就一直是朋友兼親密夥伴。

二人在熱淚盈眶和頻頻親吻中互道再見，還承諾永遠不會忘掉彼此，只要他們活著就永遠不再愛上任何人。

p. 090「這顆鑽石是我母親的，吾愛！」伊莫珍說：「拿去，我的甜心！只要你愛我就請留著它。」

李奧納圖斯回答：「最甜美的吾愛，請為我戴上這手鐲。」

伊莫珍一邊拭淚一邊哭喊著：「啊！我們要到何時才能再度聚首？」

就在兩人仍依偎在對方的臂膀裡時，國王趕來了，於是李奧納圖斯必須立刻離開，無法再次互道珍重。

當他前往羅馬投靠父親的一位老友時，白天一直思念他心愛的伊莫珍，晚上也不斷夢見她。

有一天在一場宴會上，一些義大利和法國貴族正談到他們的心上人，並發誓她們是全世界最忠實、最榮耀以及最美麗的女孩。

這時一位法國人想起李奧納圖斯曾多次提到，他的妻子伊莫珍要比任何法國女孩都來得更美麗、聰明和忠貞不渝。

「現在我仍這麼說。」李奧納圖斯表示。

「她未必像你說的那麼好，有可能她會說一套做一套。」有一名義大利貴族伊阿基摩說。

p. 091「她從不會騙人。」李奧納圖斯說。

伊阿基摩說：「我可以打賭，如果我到不列顛，就可以說服你妻子按照我的意願辦事，即使違逆閣下的意思她也會聽從我。」

「你永遠都不可能辦到，」李奧納圖斯說：「我可以用手上的這枚戒指打賭，」它就是伊莫珍在分別時送給他的，「我妻子會信守對我所做的所有誓言，閣下永遠也說服不了她做其他事情。」

於是伊阿基摩就以自己的半數家產和李奧納圖斯的戒指對賭，並立刻起程前往不列顛，不久就在一封信的引見下見到了李奧納圖斯的妻子。

當他到達那兒時，雖受到殷勤的款待，可是他仍決心要贏得賭注。

p. 092 他告訴伊莫珍，她的丈夫已不再思念苦守寒窯的妻子，並繼續說了些有關李奧納圖斯的殘酷謊言。

起初伊莫珍有在聆聽，可是不久就察覺伊阿基摩是個不正派的人，於是命令他立刻離開她。

接著他說：「原諒我，美麗的女士，剛才我所說的全都是謊言。告訴妳這些只是想知道妳是否相信我，或是否真如妳先生所想的那樣值得信任，妳會原諒我嗎？」

「我會很爽快的原諒你。」伊莫珍說。

p. 093「那麼或許妳可以證實這一點，」伊阿基摩繼續鼓起如簧之舌，「我有個皮箱得請人看管，裡面有許多珠寶，都是你丈夫、我和其他一些紳士買來當作送給羅馬皇帝的禮物。」

「我當然會竭盡所能幫助我丈夫和他的朋友，如果把那些珠寶拿到我房間，我一定會好好看管它們。」

「只要一個晚上就好，」伊阿基摩說：「明天我就要離開不列顛了。」

就這樣那只箱子送到了伊莫珍的房間，而且那天晚上她也和平常一樣上床睡覺，當她很快進入夢鄉時，皮箱蓋突然打開了，只見一個人跳了出來，那傢伙赫然就是伊阿基摩。

有關珠寶的事和他所說的其他內容都是假的，他只是想混進她房間好贏得那筆靠下三濫手段得來的賭注。

他四下張望並注意傢俱的擺設，然後偷偷溜到伊莫珍睡的那張床旁邊，從她手臂上悄悄取下她丈夫的離別贈禮，也就是那只金手鐲，再爬回皮箱裡，第二天上午立刻航向羅馬。

p. 094 當他碰到李奧納圖斯時就說：「我到過英國而且贏得賭注了，因為你老婆已不再掛念你，她一整晚都待在臥房和我談心，她房間掛著繡帷，還有一個精雕細琢的玻璃燈罩和銀製的柴架，上面的造型就是兩個眨著眼的愛神丘比特。」

「我不相信她會忘了我，不相信她會待在房間和你談話，一定是你從僕人那兒聽到她房間的描述。」

「哦，但她從手臂取下這個手鐲送給我了呀！」伊阿基摩說：「我看到了她，她優雅動人的舉止更勝過她的禮物，而且也使得這禮物更有價值。總之她把這給了我，還說曾一度把它視若珍寶。」

「把這戒指拿走吧，」李奧納圖斯泣道：「你贏了，也贏了我的生命，如今知道妻子已經忘了我，世上再也沒有一樣東西讓我眷戀了。」

p. 095 在憤怒下李奧納圖斯陷入瘋狂，於是寫信給不列顛的老僕畢薩尼歐，命令他把伊莫珍帶到密爾福特港，然後把她給殺掉，因為她已經忘了他，並且把他的禮物胡亂送給別人。

在此同時他又寫信給伊莫珍，囑咐她和他的老僕畢薩尼歐一起前往密爾福特港，這樣他這個做老公的就可以和她在那兒會合了。

畢薩尼歐雖然接到來信，可是心地善良的他卻無法執行裡面所交付的命令，而且他也很有智慧，心想絕對不能讓夫妻倆單獨在一起，於是他就把李奧納圖斯寫給她的信交給了伊莫珍，並且和她一起動身前往密爾福特港。

p. 096 在畢薩尼歐離開前，惡毒的王后給了他一瓶飲料，然後囑咐說生病時服用的話會很有效。她希望他會把這交給伊莫珍，並且希望伊莫珍去見閻王，這樣惡毒王后的兒子就可以當上國王了。只不過，王后認為是毒藥的這瓶飲料，實際上卻是安眠藥。

當畢薩尼歐和伊莫珍來到密爾福特港附近時，他就告訴她實情，好讓她明白李奧納圖斯在寫給他的信中究竟交代了些什麼。

「我得繼續前往羅馬，要見他本人。」伊莫珍說。

接著畢薩尼歐幫她穿上男孩的衣服，並送她啟程前往羅馬，自己則回到王宮。在他離開之前，就把王后送給他的那瓶飲料交給了伊莫珍。

伊莫珍繼續前行，不過越來越感到疲累不堪，最後終於來到一處洞穴。似乎有人住在那兒，然而當時卻無人現身，於是她走了進去，就在幾乎餓死時，看到洞裡有些食物，便拿起來據案大嚼，不過就在此時，一名老人和兩個年輕男孩進入洞穴中。

p. 097 她看到他們感到十分害怕，認為對方一定會為了食物被拿而對她大發雷霆，儘管她原本打算吃完後留些錢在桌上，但現在似乎百口莫辯。

只是讓她驚訝的是，對方居然親切地歡迎她，只見男裝下的她看起來帥氣十足，一張臉既和善又美麗。「閣下不妨把我們當成兄弟，不要客氣。」那兩位男孩說，於是她就在那兒待了下來，幫他們作飯，把一切打點得舒舒服服的。

可是有一天當那名叫比拉瑞優斯的老先生和兩名男孩一起外出打獵時，伊莫珍突然覺得不舒服，心想應該服用畢薩尼歐給她的那瓶藥。

於是她服用了它，沒想到立刻就像一具死屍般躺在那兒。當比拉瑞優斯和男孩們打獵回來時，見狀認為伊莫珍已死，於是淚眼滂沱地唱起喪歌，然後把她抬走並放進林子裡，同時在她身上鋪滿了花朵。

p. 098 他們對她唱起了甜美的歌，把各式各樣的花撒滿她身上，其中有灰白色的櫻草花、蔚藍色的風信子、多花薔薇以及有毛的苔蘚，然後滿懷哀傷的離開了。

他們剛一離開伊莫珍就醒了，她不知道自己究竟是怎樣來到這兒，也不知道身在何處，於是漫無目的地穿過樹林。

當伊莫珍住在洞穴裡時，羅馬人已決定進攻不列顛，而且派出大軍殺了過來，對伊莫珍使出惡毒手段的李奧納圖斯感到越來越後悔，於是也跟隨部隊一起回來，不過這回他並不是站在羅馬人那兒和不列顛作戰，而是打算和不列顛人聯手對抗羅馬。

在伊莫珍獨自徘徊時，遇到了羅馬將軍魯西阿斯，他就收留她為侍從以伺候自己。

當羅馬人和不列顛人之間的戰爭開打時，比拉瑞優斯和他的兩個孩子即為他們自己的國家而力戰，至於李奧納圖斯則假扮成英國鄉下人和他們並肩作戰。

p. 099 辛白林不幸成了羅馬人的階下囚，於是老比拉瑞優斯偕同兒子和李奧納圖斯奮勇拯救了這位國王。

後來不列顛人贏得了戰爭，一干囚犯被帶到國王面前，裡面有帶著伊莫珍的魯西阿斯、伊阿基摩，以及穿了羅馬士兵制服的李奧納圖斯。

由於李奧納圖斯殘忍地下令老僕殺了妻子，所以對生命早已厭倦，希望被他們當成羅馬士兵而處以極刑。

當他們被帶到國王面前時，魯西阿斯就朗聲說：「我是個羅馬人，擁有一顆羅馬人赤誠的心，即使斧鉞加身也再所不惜。如果必須一死，就讓我慷慨赴義吧！我只乞求一死，不過我身旁的孩子卻生而為不列顛人，因此就讓他獲得贖身的機會吧！從沒有一個主人擁有像他這麼善良、盡忠職守、勤奮又真誠的侍從，雖然服侍過羅馬人，可是卻沒有做出一件傷害不列顛人的事，救救他，閣下！」

p. 101 辛白林看了看這位侍從，雖然他就是自己的女兒伊莫珍，可是在女扮男裝下並沒有認出她。一股仁慈油然自辛白林內心升起，他不但赦免了這個「男孩」，而且還說：「不管他向我要什麼，都會得到我的賞賜，即使要求饒了哪位俘虜一命，我也會答應。」

伊莫珍說：「我要求的恩賜就是要這位先生老實說出，他手指上的那枚戒指是從誰那兒拿來的？」說完就指向伊阿基摩。

「趕快說出來，」辛白林說：「你是怎麼弄到那枚鑽石的？」

於是伊阿基摩就把他惡行的全部真相給說了出來。這時，李奧納圖斯再也無法控制自己了，立刻拋開所有繼續隱瞞下去的念頭，並且走向前去，高聲咒罵自己愚昧無知，竟然相信伊阿基摩的謊言，還一再呼喚他認為已經身亡的妻子。

「哦，伊莫珍，我的愛，我的生命！」他哭喊道：「哦，伊莫珍！」這時伊莫珍忘了自己已喬裝為男人，立刻跟著喊：「和平，吾王……讓和平降臨這兒！讓和平降臨這兒！」

仍是侍從身份的伊莫珍正要舉步向前，飽受折磨的李奧納圖斯轉身一把抓住她，伊莫珍因而受到了阻擋。接著李奧納圖斯看出對方即是他的妻子伊莫珍，於是雙方跌入彼此的臂彎裡。

p. 102 國王很高興地再次見到他親愛的女兒，而且對救他的人（如今大家才發現他就是李奧納圖斯）滿懷感謝。接著國王轉向比拉瑞優斯和兩個男孩。

此時比拉瑞優斯開口說：「我就是您的老僕比拉瑞優斯，一直只效忠於您，可是您卻指控我叛國，在處處受到懷疑下，我就不再忠誠了，於是偷了您兩個兒子，瞧……他們就在這兒。」

說完他就帶兩個男孩上前。其實先前這兩兄弟還認為伊莫珍和他們一樣是男孩，因此義結金蘭，誰知道他們竟是親兄妹。

惡毒的王后最後死於她自己的毒藥，國王在三個孩子相伴下快樂地一直活到老，就這樣，惡人受到了懲罰，善良和真誠的人則從此之後一直快樂地生活著。所以說，惡人會飽受苦難，正直的人卻會枝繁葉茂，直到地老天荒。

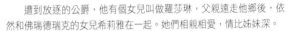

7 皆大歡喜

p. 104 從前有個惡毒的公爵，叫做佛瑞德瑞克，把本屬於他兄弟的王國給篡奪過來，然後把自己的手足驅逐出境。

那位可憐的兄弟，便進入亞登森林，在那兒縱情山水，過著無拘無束的日子，就像俠盜王子羅賓漢在英國的雪伍德森林一樣悠哉。

遭到放逐的公爵，他有個女兒叫做羅莎琳，父親遠走他鄉後，依然和佛瑞德瑞克的女兒希莉雅在一起。她們相親相愛，情比姊妹深。

有一天，王宮裡舉辦一場角力大賽，羅莎琳和希莉雅相偕前往觀賞，與賽的一方是位馳名的角力好手查爾斯，曾在這類競賽中擊斃過許多對手。

而這次和他出賽的則是個年輕人，名叫奧蘭多，身材細瘦，人又稚嫩。羅莎琳和希莉雅認為，他就像其他選手一樣必死無疑，於是兩人便苦口婆心地要求他不要從事這麼危險的活動。然而，她們的好言相勸，卻只換來一種結果，讓奧蘭多的心意更加堅定，他想在比賽中漂亮地勝出，以贏得兩位甜美少女的讚美。

p. 106 這位奧蘭多也像羅莎琳的父親一樣，有個貪婪的兄弟，為了家業的繼承而把他逐出家門。他也是對手足的無情，感到無比傷心。因此在遇到羅莎琳之前，奧蘭多一直心灰意冷，置自己的生死於度外。

可是現在，美麗的羅莎琳出現了，她溫柔的凝視，給了他力量和勇氣，於是他奮力出擊，最後竟把查爾斯打得讓人抬出場。

佛瑞德瑞克公爵十分欣賞他的勇氣，連忙請教他的名字。

「我叫奧蘭多，是羅蘭·特·鮑埃斯爵士最小的兒子。」這位年輕人說。

p. 107 羅蘭．特．鮑埃斯爵士生前和遭放逐的那位公爵，一直維持良好的友誼，所以佛瑞德瑞克一聽到奧蘭多竟是他的兒子，便覺得十分痛惜，並決定不再支助對方。

可是羅莎琳聽後十分高興，這位英挺的年輕陌生人，竟是父親老友的愛子。所以當大夥兒離開時，她還頻頻回頭望著奧蘭多，又對這位勇敢的年輕人說了些其他的話。

「先生，請為我配戴這個，」她把脖子上的項鍊給了對方，「本來我可以給你更多東西，只是手頭不大方便。」

當羅莎琳和希莉雅獨處時，就會開始談到這位英俊的角力選手，羅莎琳坦承從第一眼起，就愛上了他。

「好好控制妳的感情吧。」希莉雅說。

「哦，感情戰勝了我的理智呀。妳看！公爵來了。」羅莎琳答道。

「雙眼還飽含怒火。」希莉雅說。

「妳立刻給我離開王宮。」他對羅莎琳說。

「為什麼？」她問道。

「別管為什麼，妳已經遭到放逐，」公爵回答：「十天後，如果還有人在我王宮的方圓二十英哩內看到妳，就準備受死吧！」

p. 108 於是羅莎琳出發前往亞登森林，尋找遭到同樣命運的父親。

希莉雅深愛羅莎琳，不忍見她隻身前往，更何況這趟路很危險，於是她毅然決定同行。身材較高的羅莎琳，裝扮成年輕的莊稼漢，而希莉雅則做成鄉下姑娘的打扮。羅莎琳說她要改名為蓋尼密，並把希莉雅取名為愛蓮娜。

最後，當她們終於來到亞登森林時，已累得人仰馬翻，於是坐在草地上。這時，忽然一個莊稼漢打從這條路經過，於是蓋尼密向對方要些食物充飢。

對方慨然應允，並告訴她們，有位牧羊人的羊群和房子想要賣掉，於是姊妹倆便把它們買了下來，並假扮成牧羊人和牧羊女後，在林子裡安頓下來。

在此同時，奧蘭多的兄弟奧立佛出現，他打算取走手足的性命。而奧蘭多也在亞登森林徘徊，後來並在那兒遇上了落難的合法公爵。公爵好心收留了他，並帶在自己身邊。

p. 109 奧蘭多的心頭除了羅莎琳外，已容不下任何東西。他走到森林裡，在樹上刻下她的芳名，並寫下充滿愛意的詩句，然後掛在樹枝上，並且被羅莎琳和希莉雅給瞧見了。

有一天，奧蘭多遇上了她們兩人，但羅莎琳穿著男人的衣服，他沒認出來。不過，由於羅莎琳和蓋尼密十分相像，使得奧蘭多充滿著幻想，並因而喜歡上這個帥氣的年輕牧羊人。

「這兒出現了一個呆頭呆腦的癡情郎，經常在林子裡出沒，還在樹上留了些詩句。」羅莎琳說：「如果我能找到他的話，就可以立刻治好他的愚蠢。」

p. 110 奧蘭多承認自己就是那個呆頭呆腦的癡情郎，羅莎琳接著說：「如果你每天都來看我的話，我就會裝成羅莎琳，並表現出她難以捉摸和固執的那一面，就像一般的女孩子那樣，直到你對自己癡愚的愛感到羞愧為止。」

於是他每天都到羅莎琳的屋子報到，把想向羅莎琳傾訴的衷腸，都一股腦地說給她聽，並從中得到不少歡樂。至於羅莎琳，她也知道情郎的傾吐對象其實就是自己，因此暗自竊喜。就這樣，許多日子便在歡樂中悄然逝去。

一天上午，正當奧蘭多前來探訪蓋尼密時，忽然看見一個男子躺在地上睡著了，一隻母獅子蜷伏在附近，據說獅子不會獵捕任何死去或睡著的動物，因此看來牠是在等著這個傢伙醒來，然後據案大嚼。

奧蘭多端詳了這個男子一眼，看出對方正是自己那個歹毒的兄弟奧立佛，原來他一直想要取奧蘭多的性命，所以來到了這兒。奧蘭多不計前嫌，奮力迎戰這頭母獅，並把牠給殺了，救回手足一命。

就在奧蘭多奮戰母獅時，奧立佛醒了。看到曾被自己惡毒相待的弟兄，不惜冒著生命危險，把他從野獸手中給拯救出來。

p. 112 他不禁對自己的邪惡行徑，感到懊悔不已，並請求奧蘭多原諒他。於是從這時開始，他們又成了相親相愛的兄弟。

那頭母獅重創了奧蘭多的手臂，使得他無法前去探望那位「牧羊人」，於是差請自己的兄弟出馬，要求蓋尼密前來與自己一晤。

奧立佛於是動身前往，把整件事情一五一十地告訴蓋尼密和愛蓮娜。愛蓮娜對這種坦白認錯的男子漢行徑，感到傾心不已，立刻愛上了他。

可是當蓋尼密聽到奧蘭多當時所經歷的危險後，立刻暈倒在地。當她甦醒後，情真意切地說：「我應該恢復女兒身才對。」

p. 113 奧立佛回到兄弟那兒，把一切告訴了對方，然後說：「我很愛愛蓮娜，可以把家產都讓給你，然後娶她，在這兒做個牧羊人。」

「就把婚禮安排在明天吧，」奧蘭多說：「我會要求公爵和他朋友前來的。」

當奧蘭多告訴蓋尼密，他的兄弟會如何地在明天完成婚事時，又說了這麼一句話：「唉！從別人眼中看見幸福，滋味是多麼苦澀啊！」

仍穿著蓋尼密衣裳的羅莎琳，裝出男生的嗓音：「如果這麼真心愛著羅莎琳，那麼在你兄弟娶愛蓮娜時，你也會和羅莎琳結為連理。」

第二天，公爵、隨從們、奧蘭多、奧立佛和愛蓮娜，都為了這場婚禮而共聚一堂。

蓋尼密隨後走出來，對公爵說：「如果我把令嬡羅莎琳帶來，你會把她許配給奧蘭多嗎？」

「是的！」公爵開口說：「我願意把所有的王國都給她作嫁妝。」

p. 114「你是說，只要我把羅莎琳給帶來，你就會娶她嗎？」她又轉頭對奧蘭多問道。

只見奧蘭多朗聲回答：「即使我是統治許多王國的君王，也願意這麼做。」

接著，羅莎琳和希莉雅走了出去，羅莎琳再度換上玲瓏有緻的女人服飾。不一會兒，兩人相偕回來。

只見羅莎琳轉身走向父親，「現在我要把我自己交給你，因為我本來就是你的寶貝女兒。」

「如果眼見為真的話，」他說：「那妳就是我的女兒了。」

接著，她又對奧蘭多說：「我也把我自己交給你，因為我也是屬於你的。」

p. 115「如果眼見為真的話，」奧蘭多說：「那妳就是我的羅莎琳了。」

「如果你不是我父親，那我就是無父的孤女。」她對公爵這樣說，然後又轉頭對奧蘭多說：「如果你不是我丈夫，那我就一輩子不嫁。」

於是奧蘭多和羅莎琳，以及奧立佛和希莉雅兩對佳偶，一起完成了婚事，然後和公爵一起回到原來的王國，從此以後就過著快樂的日子。

p. 116 佛瑞德瑞克對自己的惡毒行徑，後悔不已，於是做了聖潔的隱士，並把王國還給兄弟，然後一個人跑到修道院祈求上蒼的原諒。

那是場愉快的婚禮，在森林中長滿苔蘚的空地上舉行，把自己裝扮成牧羊人的羅莎琳，以及與她一直十分要好的「牧羊女」，在同一天完成終身大事，而且每個人都享受到一頓盛宴，賓主盡歡。這是在四面高牆的華屋美廈裡所享受不到的賞心樂事，只有在碧草如茵的美麗樹林裡，才能見到這一幕。

8 連環錯

p. 118 伊吉恩是西西里海港錫拉谷的一名商人，妻子名叫愛蜜麗雅，他們一直過著十分幸福的生活，直到伊吉恩的合夥人去世，他才不得不隻身前往一個叫葉皮丹的地方。

等到愛蜜麗雅能力許可，就迫不及待地追隨丈夫而去，夫妻倆一起在那兒過了一段時日，生下兩個小寶寶，他們長得很像，即使穿上不同的衣服看起來也完全一樣。

現在你一定要相信一件十分奇怪的事，在這兩個小寶寶出生的同一間小旅館的同一天，另一對比愛蜜麗雅和伊吉恩還窮的夫妻也生了兩個小寶寶，他們是那麼的窮困，所以雙親只好把他們的雙胞胎賣給了伊吉恩夫妻。

愛蜜麗雅急著帶孩子給錫拉谷的親朋好友瞧瞧，於是不顧天候的危險，帶著四個小寶寶偕同伊吉恩搭船返鄉。他們的船在距離錫拉谷還很遙遠的地方突然漏水了。

愛蜜麗雅把自己的一個孩子綁在桅杆上，並把其中一個奴隸孩子綁在自己身上，伊吉恩也按照妻子的作法弄妥好剩下的兩個孩子，之後他們把自己固定在同一根桅杆上，盼求能安全獲救。

p. 119 然而這艘船卻在突然間撞上一塊礁石，斷成了兩半，愛蜜麗雅和她所綁住的兩個孩子就在大海上漂浮著，並逐漸遠離了伊吉恩和另外兩個孩子。

愛蜜麗雅和她所保護的兩個孩子被葉皮丹的一些人給救起，不過柯倫茲地區的一些漁人卻強行把兩個孩子從她身邊帶走，她只好孤伶伶地回到葉皮丹，狀況十分悽慘。後來，愛蜜麗雅就在小亞細亞一個著名的城市夷斐斯安頓下來。

p. 120 伊吉恩和他所保護的兩個孩子也獲救，而且際遇比愛蜜麗雅還幸運，可以回到錫拉谷撫養兩個孩子，直到孩子都長大到了十八歲。

他把自己的孩子取名叫安提弗斯，奴隸的小孩叫卓米歐，奇怪的是，在海上漂流不知去向的那兩個孩子雖然和他失散，但也取了相同的名字。

跟隨伊吉恩長大的那個兒子到了十八歲就越來越焦躁不安，很想找他兄弟，於是伊吉恩讓他偕同那位奴僕孩子啟程，以下就稱這兩個年輕人為「大安提弗斯」和「大卓米歐」(譯註：原文作「錫拉谷的安提弗斯」和「錫拉谷的卓米歐」)。

伊吉恩因為自己一個人住很孤單，於是在外旅行了五年。在他離家的這段期間就像斷了線的風箏，有關錫拉谷的消息全都無從得知，而且從未到過夷斐斯。

伊吉恩憂鬱地旅行在外，最後來到了夷斐斯，不過他才進城，就被抓了起來。

p. 121 後來他才知道，錫拉谷的公爵對待不幸落入他手中的夷斐斯人十分暴虐，於是夷斐斯政府氣得通過了一條法律：任何來到夷斐斯的錫拉谷人，除非能繳出一千鎊的罰款，否則就得處以死刑。

就這樣伊吉恩被帶到夷斐斯的公爵蘇里紐斯面前，公爵告訴伊吉恩，如果不能在當天結束前交出一千鎊就必須一死。

當我告訴你，被柯倫茲漁民綁架的那兩個孩子如今已成了夷斐斯的公民，而且在那兒被蘇里紐斯公爵的叔叔梅納方公爵養育成人時，你一定會認為命運之神在這故事裡面的安排真是奇妙。至此，我們就稱這兩個年輕人為「小安提弗斯」和「小卓米歐」(譯註：原文作「夷斐斯的安提弗斯」和「夷斐斯的卓米歐」)。

p. 122 此外，就在伊吉恩被捕的那一天，大安提弗斯也在夷斐斯上了岸，還假裝自己是從葉皮丹來的，以免遭到處罰。

他把錢交給僕人大卓米歐，吩咐他把錢帶到「半人馬旅館」，然後留在那兒等他回來。在不到十分鐘的時間裡，他兄弟的奴僕小卓米歐竟在市場遇見了他，他立刻把對方誤認為是自己的奴僕。

「為什麼這麼快就回來了？你把錢放在哪兒？」大安提弗斯問。

眼前的這位小卓米歐除了上星期三從主人那兒接到六個便士並把它交給馬具商外，根本不知道有什麼錢，只曉得男主人沒有回去吃午餐而惹得女主人大發雷霆，於是要求大安提弗斯趕緊回到叫做「鳳凰」的宅第。

p. 123 他的這番話惹惱了大安提弗斯，要不是對方飛快的逃走，他一定會鞭打他。大安提弗斯後來回到半人馬旅館，發現他的金子就寄放在那兒，於是走出這家旅館。

當兩位美麗的女士向他舉手示意時，他正在夷斐斯閒逛著。她們是兩姊妹，名字是安德安娜和露西安娜，其中安德安娜是他兄弟小安提弗斯的妻子。

安德安娜在聽到小卓米歐那些奇怪的敘述後，心中就認定她的丈夫更喜歡其他女人勝過自己，「喂，你怎麼看起來一副不認識我的樣子！」她對眼前這位其實是她小叔的男子說：「可是我還記得，話要說出來才會讓人愉悅，肉要切開才顯得出美味。」

p. 124「妳是在對我說話嗎？」大安提弗斯拘謹地說：「我不認識妳呀！」

「呸！姊夫！」露西安娜說：「你清楚得很，她派卓米歐請你回去用午餐。」

安德安娜這時也說：「來啊！來啊！我已經被你愚弄得夠久了，你這個一味逃避責任的老公就和我一起用餐吧，坦白從寬，只要承認這是套愚蠢的惡作劇，我就會原諒你。」

她們是意志堅定的女子，大安提弗斯又已對雙方的爭執不下感到厭煩，於是順從地跟著她們來到鳳凰這間屋子，那兒有一頓十分晚的「午餐」在等著他們。

當小安提弗斯和奴僕小卓米歐要求進屋時，他們正在用餐。

「毛德、布瑞吉、瑪麗安、西西莉、吉利安、吉安！」小卓米歐大叫，他早已記住所有奴僕的名字。

p. 125 沒想到屋裡竟傳來這樣的回答：「笨蛋，只會運貨的雜種馬、花花公子、呆子。」這下子大卓米歐倒是在不知情下出言侮辱了他的兄弟。

屋外的主人小安提弗斯和那名奴僕使盡全力想要進屋去，可是少了鐵橇，於是悻悻然離開。小安提弗斯對妻子十分惱火，於是把曾答應要送給她的一串金項鍊轉贈另一個女人。

在鳳凰這棟屋子裡，露西安娜一直認為大安提弗斯就是姊夫，於是就趁著和他獨處時以韻文說起教來，希望他能對安德安娜好些。

大安提弗斯回答自己未婚，但這時他也發現自己竟愛上了眼前這位女孩，如果露西安娜是條美人魚，他就很願意枕著她那頭飄然的金色秀髮倘佯在海裡，那種感受一定無比甜美。

露西安娜這時心頭一震，於是離開了他，並把他愛的表白告訴安德安娜，雖然安德安娜非常喜歡自己的丈夫，可是嘴硬的她卻說自己的丈夫又老又醜，實在不適合出現在別人面前，難聽的聲音也不宜讓人聽到。

p. 127 沒多久大安提弗斯接待了一位訪客，對方是金匠安吉羅，原來小安提弗斯曾答應要給妻子一串項鍊，就向這位訪客訂購，只是後來在　怒之下打算送給另　個女人。

這時金匠把項鍊交給了大安提弗斯，大安提弗斯說：「我沒有訂購啊！」可是金匠只是把這當作玩笑話而已，使得大安提弗斯一頭霧水，認為這項鍊的事簡直和被強拉到安德安娜家吃午餐一樣荒謬可笑。他出價打算買下，可是安吉羅傻呼呼地表示還會再來拜訪。

這事所帶來的影響就是，當一位債主一句廢話不說的站在安吉羅面前，威脅他如果不立刻付清債務就要逮捕送官時，這位可憐的金匠實在掏不出錢來。

後來債主果然帶了一個衙吏來，情況危急的安吉羅突然看到小安提弗斯從鳳凰這間屋子走來，於是鬆了一口氣。小安提弗斯以前都在鳳凰用餐，可是如今卻被鎖在外面。

當小安提弗斯否認自己收過那項鍊時，安吉羅沮喪極了，那份苦澀不知向誰傾吐，不過他可以請母親代替自己坐牢，只要她老人家開口即可，當然，他也報官緝拿了小安提弗斯。

p. 128 此刻大卓米歐來了，告訴被他誤認的小安提弗斯說，船已經把他的貨運走了，而且又颳起了順風，這話聽在小安提弗斯耳中真是一派胡言。

他很想痛毆那奴僕一頓，可是這時只要自己能夠順利脫身就心滿意足了，於是急忙告訴大卓米歐趕快回去找安德安娜，囑咐她到他書桌上找出那包錢，好搭救她被捕的丈夫。

雖然安德安娜認為丈夫已愛上了妹妹而對他火冒三丈，但仍沒有阻止露西安娜去拿錢包，並吩咐大卓米歐立刻把主人帶回家。

不幸得很，就在大卓米歐來到官府門前就遇到了真正的主人，當然對方從未遭到逮捕，也不了解大卓米歐給他那袋錢是什麼意思。

後來當一位他不認識的女士出現，向他索取曾答應送她的　串項鍊時，大安提弗斯更是驚訝萬分。

p. 129 很顯然，當這位女士和小安提弗斯一起用餐時，他的兄弟大安提弗斯卻在他住處據案大嚼。於是大安提弗斯回答：「滾！你這個狐狸精！」她大吃一驚，不過對這個封號卻欣然接受。

在此同時，小安提弗斯苦苦等候會讓他獲釋的那筆錢，在徒勞無功後，就不再是個好脾氣的人了，因此當小卓米歐出現時，自然怒急攻心，幾乎要瘋了。當然這位可憐的奴僕並未接到指示去拿那袋錢，而且身上除了一根繩子之外一樣有用的東西都沒有。

於是小安提弗斯當街痛毆小卓米歐，連衙吏的勸阻也不顧了。後來當安德安娜、露西安娜和一位醫生趕來時，他仍餘怒未消，三人都認為他已經瘋了，而且好像非要得到他的錢包不可。

他的狂怒讓大夥都一哄而上，把他給緊緊綁起來，可是好心的安德安娜卻讓他免除這種羞辱，她答應支付他所需要的那筆錢，並要求醫生帶他回到鳳凰。

p. 130 和安吉羅在生意往來上的那位債主也收到了錢，於是兩人和好如初，沒多久大家就看到這兩人在一座修道院前，聊著小安提弗斯種種怪異行徑。

「噓，小聲點！」最後那位債主說：「我想那就是他耶！」

來的人並不是他，而是帶著奴僕大卓米歐的大安提弗斯，頸子上還赫然掛著安吉羅的那條項鍊。

重修舊好的兩人於是一把抓住他，想要知道他究竟是什麼意思，明明否認收到那條項鍊，現在卻明目張膽地戴著它。

大安提弗斯脾氣上來了，於是抽出劍來，但就在此刻，安德安娜和其他人也出現了。

悶悶不樂的安德安娜說：「住手，不要傷害他，他已經瘋了，把劍拿開，再把人給綁起來……還有卓米歐也要綁起來。」

p. 131 大卓米歐並不想被綁，於是對主人說：「快跑，主人！趕快跑到修道院裡，不然就會被搶劫了。」於是兩人退到修道院裡。

安德安娜、露西安娜和群眾依舊在外面，不久修道院的女院長就出來了，並且說：「各位，為什麼要聚在這兒呢？」

「要接回我那精神錯亂的可憐丈夫。」安德安娜回答。

安吉羅和那位債主說他們並不知道他已經瘋了，而安德安娜則把身為妻子的種種憂慮都一股腦地告訴了修道院女院長。因為修道院女院長似乎認為安德安娜是個潑婦，而且如果丈夫精神錯亂的話，那麼最好還是暫時不要回到她身邊。

p. 132 於是安德安娜決定向蘇里紐斯公爵控訴。哎呀，你瞧！還真巧呢！才一盞熱茶功夫這位大人物就帶了一些官吏和兩個人出現了，他們分別是伊吉恩和劊子手，原來一千個馬克並沒有籌措到，伊吉恩的命運似乎已經確定了。

公爵還沒經過修道院，安德安娜就已跪在他面前，訴說著那悲慘的故事，包括她發瘋的丈夫冒冒失失地偷了珠寶，而且還拔出劍來想要傷人，末了還補充，修道院的女院長拒絕讓她把丈夫帶回家。

公爵於是吩咐手下傳喚女院長，不過還沒來得及下令，「鳳凰」的一位奴僕就跑到安德安娜面前，說他的主人竟把醫生的鬍子給燒了。

「豈有此理！」安德安娜說：「他還在修道院裡呢。」

「我說的都是事實，就和我現在是活的一樣千真萬確。」那位奴僕說。

p. 133 大安提弗斯還沒有走出修道院，他在夷斐斯的兄弟就精疲力竭地倒在公爵面前，並且大聲叫：「我要求正義，最仁慈的公爵，要防備這個女人。」他指著安德安娜說：「她在我家把其他男人當成自己丈夫一樣的款待。」

就在他說話時，伊吉恩也開腔了：「除非我精神錯亂，要不然一定是看到了我的兒子安提弗斯。」

可惜沒有人看他一眼，小安提弗斯繼續侃侃而談，他把醫生叫做「老套的騙子」，還說對方是幫派份子之一，把他和奴僕卓米歐給綁在一起，然後推到地窖裡，直到他們咬斷捆綁的繩子才得以脫逃。

公爵實在納悶，為什麼和他說話的人竟被瞧見跑進修道院裡，當伊吉恩問小安提弗斯是否就是他兒子時，公爵仍然滿腹狐疑。

後來小安提弗斯說：「我這輩子從未見過父親。」可是他實在太像伊吉恩所撫養的那個兄弟，所以連伊吉恩都受到了矇蔽，於是說：「一定是我不幸落難了，你才羞於承認我這個父親。」

p. 134 不過沒多久，修道院女院長就帶著大安提弗斯和大卓米歐走上前來。

安德安娜於是喊了起來：「我看到了兩個丈夫，不然就是我的眼睛欺騙了我。」大安提弗斯在發現了父親後也說：「你就是我父親伊吉恩，否則就是他鬼魂。」

這真是意外連連的一天，因為這時修道院女院長也說：「我會繳出他的罰金釋放這個人，而且也得到自己失散已久的丈夫，說話啊，伊吉恩，我是你的妻子愛蜜麗雅啊！」

公爵深受感動，他說：「他不用罰金就可以自由了。」

所以伊吉恩和愛蜜麗雅又再度聚首，而安德安娜和她丈夫也重修舊好。可是沒有一個人要比大安提弗斯更快樂了，只見他當著公爵的面走到露西安娜那兒說：「我告訴過妳我愛妳，願意成為我妻子嗎？」

她的答案一望便知，因此用不著贅述了。

至於那兩位卓米歐也很高興的認為，他們今後再也不會受到任何責打了。

9 羅密歐與茱麗葉

p. 136 從前在維洛那住了兩大家族，分別是蒙塔古和卡普萊特。雙方都很富有，據我推想，他們也像其他有錢人一樣，對大多數事情都很明理，可是在一件事上卻顯得絕頂愚蠢：從很久很久以前，這兩大家族之間就有了紛爭，不過他們並沒有像理性的人們那樣想辦法調和雙方的不愉快，而是不斷鬧著彆扭，無法讓雙方的不和平息。

所以一個蒙塔古家族的人如果在街上碰到了一個卡普萊特家族的人，是不會和他交談的，反過來說，卡普萊特家族的人也不會找上蒙塔古家族的人，即使雙方談起話來，也都是說些無理和令人不悅的事，所以通常到最後都會大打出手。

另外他們的親戚和僕人也都愚不可及，使得這兩大家族之間的紛爭越演越烈，街頭上演的打架鬧事、決鬥以及種種不愉快都層出不窮。

卡普萊特家族的大家長卡普萊特爵士這天舉辦一場宴會，那是頓豐盛的晚宴，還有舞會助興。卡普萊特爵士十分好客，因此表示只要不是蒙塔古家族，任何人都可以來到那兒。

p. 137 可是蒙塔古家族有個年輕人叫羅密歐，由於愛上了受邀出席的羅莎琳，自然十分渴望參加那場宴會。

這位女孩對羅密歐從沒好言好語過，而他也沒有愛上她的理由，事實上羅密歐雖然很想獻出他的愛，但始終沒有遇到適合的意中人，於是只好愛了一個不該愛的女孩。這次羅密歐是偕同朋友莫卡提歐和賓佛利歐，前去參加卡普萊特家族的盛宴。

p. 138 老卡普萊特非常親切地歡迎羅密歐和他的兩位朋友，不久年輕的羅密歐就穿梭在穿著天鵝絨和綢緞的眾賓客之間，只見他們渾身散發著出身宮廷的不凡氣派，男士們的刀柄和衣領都鑲著珠寶，女士們的胸膛和手臂也配戴著閃閃發光的首飾，連美麗的束腰都鑲著貴重的寶石。

羅密歐亦盛裝出席，他心想最好戴上黑色面具遮住自己的眼睛和鼻子，好讓每個人就只能看到他嘴巴和頭髮，這個方法可以讓他看起來比屋內的其他人英俊上十二倍。

不久，他忽然在舞者之中發現一個女孩是這麼的美麗和可愛，使得從那一刻開始，就完全忘了那個過去一直認定是自己所愛的羅莎琳。

p. 139 他仔細端詳著這另一位美麗的女子，看著她輕移蓮步，舞動著緞子衣服和珍珠，對羅密歐來説，即使把全世界拿來和她相比也似乎毫無意義，而且一點價值也沒有。

當卡普萊特夫人的姪子提伯特聽到他的聲音，並認出他就是羅密歐時，羅密歐還兀自説著這些或是其他類似傾慕的話。

提伯特十分憤怒，於是立刻走到叔叔那兒，告訴他有個蒙塔古家族的人，竟然在沒有受邀的情況下貿然前來參加這場盛宴，可是老卡普萊特是個心腸好的謙謙君子，不會粗魯地對待來到自家屋簷下的人，於是命令提伯特閉嘴，可是這個年輕人卻只想等待機會大大指責羅密歐一番。

p. 140 在此同時，羅密歐走向這個美麗的女孩，以甜言蜜語訴説愛意，並且吻了她，這時恰好她母親叫人請她過去，羅密歐才發現讓他魂縈夢繫的女孩竟是茱麗葉，也就是他一再詛咒的那位仇敵卡普萊特爵士的女兒。於是他走開了，真是痛心疾首，可是對她的愛卻沒有一絲減損。

後來茱麗葉對奶媽説：「沒有在跳舞的那位紳士是誰？」

「他叫羅密歐，是蒙塔古家族的人，也是你們最大仇敵的獨子。」奶媽回答。

接著茱麗葉回到自己房間，透過窗戶往外看去，外面是片美麗的灰綠色花園，一輪明月十分皎潔。沒想到羅密歐就隱藏在樹林間的這片花園裡……因為他打算再見到她，不能就這樣一走了之。

茱麗葉並不知道他就在那兒，就大聲說出她不足為外人道的一些想法，告訴寂靜的花園她是多麼地愛羅密歐。

p. 141 羅密歐聽到後喜悅已非筆墨所能形容，於是躲在下面抬頭仰望，在月光下看到她美麗的臉蛋，正在長滿蔓藤的窗戶邊凝思著。當他仰望和聆聽時，覺得自己就好像是在夢中被人帶走，然後被一些魔法師安置在這個美麗且被施過魔咒的花園裡。

「啊，為什麼你要叫羅密歐？」茱麗葉說：「我愛你，你叫什麼會有多重要？」

「只要把我喚作妳的愛，我就重新受洗和命名，從今以後，就永遠不再叫羅密歐了。」

羅密歐喊道，並從遮蔽他的柏樹和夾竹桃樹蔭處走到潔白的月光下。

茱麗葉起初有些害怕，可是當她看到那是羅密歐本人而且沒有其他陌生人時，也高興了起來。只見他就站在下面的花園，而她則倚在窗邊，兩人一起傾訴了許久，每一方都試著找出全世界最甜蜜的話語，好讓談話內容討得對方歡欣，當然這些都是情人之間慣常使用的。

p. 142 他們談的所有話語和聲音所共同譜出的甜美音樂，都記載在一本絕妙的好書裡，有朝一日你們或許就會讀到它。對彼此相愛而且有幸聚首的人們來說，時光總是過得那麼飛快，當要分離的時刻來臨，兩人就好像早已相識許久……而且真的幾乎不知如何分手道別。

「明天我會派人找你的！」茱麗葉說。

就這樣在躊躇再三和滿懷憧憬下，他們終於道了再見。茱麗葉進入她房間，黑色的簾幕遮蔽了明亮的窗戶，羅密歐也穿過寂靜且露濕的花園離開了，一切都好像一場夢。

p. 144 第二天一大早，羅密歐就來到勞倫斯修士那兒，告訴這位神職人員整個事情的來龍去脈，並祈求對方立刻為他和茱麗葉主持婚禮，雙方交談一陣後，修士終於同意這麼做。

所以當那天茱麗葉差遣老奶媽來找羅密歐，並得知他打算這麼做後，這位老婦就帶來一個訊息：茱麗葉那兒一切安好，而且會為第二天上午茱麗葉和羅密歐的那場婚禮打點好所有事情。

年輕人本應把婚事稟告雙親，以徵求他們的同意，可是由於卡普萊特和蒙塔古這兩大家族之間由來以久的愚蠢紛爭，使得這對年輕戀人很怕徵求他們雙親的同意。

勞倫斯修士願意祕密協助這對年輕的戀人，因為他認為兩人一旦成婚，他們的雙親就會立刻得知，或許這段良緣會讓一場由來以久的紛爭就此有了圓滿的結局。

p. 145 所以第二天一大早，羅密歐和茱麗葉就在勞倫斯修士的小房間結了婚，然後雙方就在淚眼婆娑和親吻中道別。羅密歐答應那天晚上會來到花園，而奶媽也會準備好一副繩梯，然後從窗戶垂下，使羅密歐得以爬上去，在寧靜的環境下單獨向他親愛的妻子傾訴衷腸。

可是就在這天發生了一件可怕的事。

對羅密歐當天參加卡普萊特家族盛宴一事始終耿耿於懷的那名年輕人提伯特，這天在街上巧遇羅密歐和他兩位朋友莫卡提歐以及賓佛利歐，於是罵羅密歐為惡棍，並要求和他決鬥。

羅密歐本來不希望和茱麗葉的表兄弟決鬥，可是莫卡提歐卻拔出了劍，和提伯特打了起來，不久莫卡提歐就被殺了。

當羅密歐看到朋友遇害，除了對殺害他的人感到義憤填膺外，早已忘記了一切，於是也和提伯特打了起來，直到對方倒地而亡。

p. 146 就這樣羅密歐在自己婚禮的這一天，竟殺了愛妻茱麗葉的表兄弟，並被判放逐。

可憐的茱麗葉和他年輕的丈夫在那天晚上碰了面，他爬上群花之間的繩梯，找到她的窗戶。只可惜這是場哀悽的會面，而且也在苦澀的熱淚和沈重心情下分開，因為他們無法知道何時會再度聚首。

當時茱麗葉的父親自然不知道女兒已婚，於是希望他嫁給一位名叫派瑞斯的男士，當被女兒拒絕時覺得十分憤怒。茱麗葉也急著前往勞倫斯修士那兒，請教他自己到底該怎麼做。

p. 148 他建議她假裝同意，然後修士説：「我會給妳一小瓶藥水，讓妳在兩天內都好像死了一樣，他們就會把妳帶到教堂準備下葬，這樣就沒人娶妳了。最後他們會把妳放進墓穴裡，在醒來之前，羅密歐和我會趕到那兒照顧妳……妳願意這麼做嗎，還是會感到害怕？」

「我願意，別跟我説害怕這個字。」

茱麗葉説完便回到家裡，告訴父親她願意嫁給派瑞斯。如果她大聲告訴父親真相……呃，那麼這個故事就會有所不同了。

卡普萊特爵士眼看目的已達覺得十分高興，於是開始廣邀親朋好友，並著手準備婚宴事宜。家族每一個人都通宵達旦的忙碌，因為有太多的事要做，可是時間卻少得可憐。

p. 150 卡普萊特爵士見到茱麗葉怏怏不樂，於是急著讓她成婚，當然實際上她是為丈夫羅密歐的事在發愁，可是父親卻認為她是為了表兄弟提伯特的死而悲傷，因而認為婚姻或許會讓她有其他的事可想。

那天一大早奶媽就來叫茱麗葉，打算替她穿上婚紗好進行婚禮，可是茱麗葉卻沒醒來，之後奶媽便突然叫起來……

「哎呀！哎呀！快來幫忙！快來幫忙！小姐死了！嗚……嗚……打從我出生起就沒碰過這種事。」

卡普萊特夫人跑了進來，接著卡普萊特爵士和新郎派瑞斯公爵也急奔而至。只見茱麗葉全身發冷而慘白地躺在那兒，已無生命跡象，所有人的哀悽都無法喚醒她，所以當天他們就以喪禮取代了婚禮。

在此同時，勞倫斯修士差遣一名信差，並帶著一封信來到曼圖瓦找羅密歐，告訴他所有的事。一切計畫看來都是那麼的完美，只是那名信差因事延誤而無法動身。

壞消息總是傳得比較快些，羅密歐的僕人雖然知道這樁祕密婚姻，可是卻不知道茱麗葉裝死的消息，所以一聽到她的喪事，立刻急著前往曼圖瓦，告訴羅密歐他的年輕妻子是如何地死去和躺在墓穴中。

p. 151「是這樣嗎？」羅密歐心碎地哭喊：「那麼今晚我也要躺在茱麗葉的旁邊。」

他親自買了毒藥，然後直奔維洛那，再匆忙趕到茱麗葉所躺的墓地。那並不是墳，而是一處墓穴。

他破門而入，下了石階來到墓穴。只見那兒躺的全都是卡普萊特家族死去的人，這時，羅密歐聽到身後有一個聲音指明要他站住。

那是派瑞斯伯爵，也就是要在這一天娶茱麗葉的人。

「你膽敢來到這兒騷擾卡普萊特家族的故人屍骨，你這個蒙塔古家族的卑鄙傢伙！」派瑞斯喊道。

可憐的羅密歐在傷痛欲絕下已陷入半瘋狂狀態，這時仍試著謙恭有禮的回答：

「閣下已經被告知，」派瑞斯說：「如果回到維洛那就必須一死。」

「我一定會死的，」羅密歐說：「我是為了別的事才到這兒來的，好了！溫和有禮的年輕人……別管我！快走……在我帶給你傷害之前快走！我愛你勝過我自己……走……別管我。」

派瑞斯接著說：「我要向你挑戰，並當成重罪犯把你逮捕。」憤怒和絕望的羅密歐立刻抽出劍來。

p. 152 他們打了起來，不久派瑞斯即命喪黃泉。當羅密歐的劍刺穿他時，派瑞斯曾喊道：

「哦，我竟然被殺了！如果閣下大慈大悲的話，那就打開墓碑，讓我和茱麗葉合葬在一起。」

這時羅密歐說：「事實上我才要這麼做呢！」

他帶著已死的派瑞斯進入墓裡，然後把他放在親愛的茱麗葉身旁。

只見羅密歐彎腰跪在茱麗葉旁邊，柔聲對著她說話，把她摟在臂膀裡，吻著她冰冷的雙唇，終於相信茱麗葉已經死了。雖然她越來越接近甦醒的時刻，可是他卻在這時飲下了毒藥，死在他的甜心兼愛妻身旁。

p. 153 當勞倫斯修士趕來時已經太晚了，並且看到所發生的一切事情……，接著可憐的茱麗葉從睡夢中醒來，發現丈夫和朋友雙雙死在自己身邊。

方才打鬥的吵雜聲也把其他人引到這兒，勞倫斯修士聽到他們趕來就立刻溜之大吉，獨留茱麗葉在那兒。

她看到盛了毒藥的杯子，立刻明白這一切是如何發生的，由於已經沒有毒藥留下，茱麗葉只好拔出羅密歐的匕首，猛然刺向自己的心臟……就這樣她也倒落在地，死時頭還倚在羅密歐的胸膛上。

這是對忠貞不渝但卻最不快樂的戀人，他們的故事就在此時劃下句點。

p. 154 當兩大家族的老人們從勞倫斯修士那兒得知所發生的所有事情後，不禁哀慟逾恆，也終於認清由於他們的爭執所鑄成的一切傷害，於是他們為此懊悔不已。最後這兩大家族終於跨過他們孩子的屍體，在友誼和寬恕中緊握著彼此的手。

10 威尼斯商人

p. 156 安東尼奧是個富裕的威尼斯商人，生意興隆，他的船幾乎航遍五湖四海，和葡萄牙、墨西哥、英格蘭以及印度都有生意往來。

雖然以坐擁財富為傲，可是卻十分慷慨，很喜歡拿它們來賙濟朋友以紓貧解困，在眾多朋友中又以巴薩尼歐和他關係最好。

巴薩尼歐也像其他許多紳士一樣喜歡五光十色和趕時髦，加上個性鹵莽衝動又揮霍無度，因此最後發現自己不僅床頭金盡，而且面對債主也無力償還，於是去找安東尼奧尋求進一步的協助。

p. 158 他說：「安東尼奧，我虧欠你的金錢和愛都多得無法數計，現在我想到了一個計畫，只要你肯出手相助就可以償還我所虧欠你的一切。」

「請說說我能做些什麼？我一定辦到。」他的朋友回答。

接著巴薩尼歐又說：「在貝爾蒙有一位小姐繼承了萬貫家財，來自世界各地有名望的追求者都絡繹不絕地上門求親，因為她不僅富裕，而且美麗又善良。上回相遇時，她還含情脈脈地望著我，看出來當時是向我示好，因此我很肯定，如果能夠擁有足夠的財力前往她所居住的貝爾蒙，就一定能夠戰勝所有對手而贏得她的愛。」

「我的所有財產如今都在海上，」安東尼奧說：「所以身邊沒什麼現錢，但幸好我在威尼斯信用良好，一定會借到你所需要的那些金額。」

p. 159 當時在威尼斯住了一位專門放高利貸的有錢人夏洛克，安東尼奧對他充滿了鄙視和厭惡，總是以最疾言厲色的態度對待他，還不時加以責罵。他曾把夏洛克當成野狗一樣踢出門外，甚至還吐他口水。

夏洛克只是很有耐心地聳聳肩，默默承受這一切無理的舉動，可是在內心深處卻懷有一種期待，那就是要狠狠報復這個有錢又自鳴得意的商人。

p. 160 對安東尼奧來說，上門借錢既傷他的自尊又損及自己的事業，而且夏洛克還想：「我應該比安東尼奧更富裕五十萬個硬幣才對，不管在市場上以及在什麼地方，他都會指責我索取的利息太高，而且更糟的是，這小子還會不要利息地把錢給借出去。」

所以當安東尼奧偕同巴薩尼歐來找夏洛克，要求借給他三千個硬幣而且為期三個月時，夏洛克掩蓋了自己的敵意，對安東尼奧說：

「雖然你對我是那麼地不假辭色，但我仍願意與你為友並擁有你的愛。所以我會把錢借給你，而且不收取任何利息，可是為了增加些樂趣，你要簽一張字據，同意如果三個月後沒有償還這筆錢，我就有權割下你一磅肉，而且不管切下什麼部位都任由我選擇。」

「不，絕對不要為我冒這種危險。」巴薩尼歐對朋友叫道。

「為什麼不呢？別怕！」安東尼奧說：「我的船在期滿前的一個月就會回來，我要簽這個字據。」

p. 161 於是巴薩尼歐有了足夠的財力前往巴爾蒙，可以在那兒向秀麗動人的玻希雅求婚。

可是就在他動身的那晚，夏洛克的漂亮女兒潔西卡帶著情人從父親的家私奔，還帶了從父親密窖那兒偷來的好幾袋硬幣和珠寶。

夏洛克的哀傷和憤怒是可以想見，而且對她的愛也轉化為恨。「要是她戴著耳朵上的珠寶死在我腳邊那該有多好啊！」

如今他唯一的慰藉就是聽到安東尼奧的船隻遇難，因而損失慘重。「讓他留意那張字據吧！」夏洛克說：「讓他好好留意那張字據吧！」

p. 162 在此同時巴薩尼歐來到貝爾蒙，拜訪了明豔的玻希雅。他發現一切都和他告訴安東尼奧的一樣，有關玻希雅財富和美麗的傳聞招來了不分遠近的追求者。

可是玻希雅對他們所有的人就只是一個回答：只有誓言遵從她父親遺囑上的條款，她才會接受這人的求婚。

遺囑上的條件嚇跑了許多熱切的追求者，因為要想全然地贏得玻希雅，就必須猜出她的三個首飾盒中究竟哪一個放了她的肖像畫，如果猜對了，那麼玻希雅就會成為他的新娘，但如果猜錯了，就一輩子被這條誓約所限制：永遠不得洩露到底選了哪個首飾盒、永遠不得結婚，而且要立刻離開。

p. 164 首飾盒分別為金、銀、鉛所製，而且上頭都有刻字，其中金製的那只上面寫著：

「誰選了我就會得到許多男人所想要的。」銀製的那只為：

「誰選了我就會得到他應得的。」而鉛製的那只則是：

「誰選了我就必須交出他所擁有的一切東西去賭賭運氣。」

摩洛哥王子的勇氣一如其他黑人一樣，是所有追求者之中第一個接受這考驗的，他選擇了金製的首飾盒，因為他說銀和鉛都是低賤的金屬，絕不可能放她的肖像畫。

於是他選擇了金製的那只，並發現裡面是許多人想要的死亡畫像。

p. 165 在他之後來的是阿瑞岡那位傲慢的王子，他說：「就讓我擁有自己所應得的吧……這位小姐一定是我應得的。」他選擇了銀製的那只，結果裡面是一個傻瓜的頭部畫像。

「難道我所應得的只是個笨蛋的腦袋？」他喊道。

最後來的是巴薩尼歐，玻希雅實在害怕他做出錯誤的選擇，於是故意拖延，因為她愛他至深，甚至和他對她的愛不相上下。

「不過請讓我馬上選擇好嗎？」巴薩尼歐說：「因為我就是靠折磨而活。」

p. 166 接著玻希雅吩咐僕人把樂師帶來，並在她這位愛時髦的情人做選擇時演奏音樂。只見巴薩尼歐起了誓，走到三個首飾盒那兒，此時樂師們已奏起柔美的音樂。

「只有浮誇的外表是會遭到鄙視的。」他說：「全世界到現在仍會被虛飾所騙，但我眼中既沒有俗豔的金子，也沒有閃閃發光的銀子，所以我選擇鉛製的首飾盒，而且欣然接受結果。」

說完他就打開首飾盒，發現玻希雅明豔照人的肖像畫果然在裡面，於是轉身走向她，問她是否真的屬於他。

「沒錯，」玻希雅說：「我是屬於你的，這房子也是你的，而且我還會把這只戒指一起給你，你可千萬不要讓它離身。」

p. 167 巴薩尼歐表示，他快樂的幾乎說不出話來，最後總算找到一些詞語來宣誓，只要還活著就戒指不離身。

突然間，他所有的喜悅都在哀傷中破滅，因為威尼斯的使者這時來到，告訴他安東尼奧已傾家蕩產，而且夏洛克也要求公爵主持公道，請安東尼奧履行那份字據，按照上面的約定，他有權取安東尼奧身上的一磅肉。

玻希雅聽到巴薩尼歐的朋友飽受這種危險的威脅，也和巴薩尼歐一樣感到難過。

她說：「首先，請帶我到教堂，讓我成為你的妻子，然後立刻前往威尼斯幫助你朋友，還有，錢一定要帶得足夠支付他欠款的二十倍。」

可是當新婚夫婿離開後，玻希雅也跟在後面，不但假扮成一名律師抵達威尼斯，還得到著名律師比拉瑞奧的引見。夏洛克要求安東尼奧身上的一磅肉，於是威尼斯公爵就請來比拉瑞奧，以裁決夏洛克所提出的法律問題。

p. 168 當兩造在法庭碰頭時，巴薩尼歐拿出兩倍的借款，相信夏洛克一定會撤回他的要求。

不過這位放高利貸的傢伙只回答了這麼幾句話：

「即使六千個硬幣中的每個硬幣分為六份，且每份又可換回一個硬幣，我也不會接受……我只要依約賠償。」

不久玻希雅就假扮律師抵達法庭，甚至連她丈夫都認不出來。由於玻希雅有名律師比拉瑞奧的引見而獲得公爵的歡迎，並把這案子交給她，讓玻希雅來裁定。

只見玻希雅以崇高的話語勸夏洛克慈悲為懷。可是他對玻希雅的好言好語充耳不聞。

他只是一個勁的回答：「我只要那磅肉。」

「你怎麼說？」玻希雅問威尼斯商人安東尼奧。

p. 169「我無話可說，」他回答：「我已經做好了準備。」

「那麼法庭裁定把安東尼奧身上的一磅肉給你。」玻希雅又對放高利貸的夏洛克說。

「真是廉明公正的法官啊！」夏洛克高聲叫：「快宣判吧，來，快準備好。」

「慢著，這份字據只規定把安東尼奧的肉給你，閣下可沒權要他的血哦，如果你讓他的血流出一滴，那麼所有的家產就要被國家沒收，這是法律的規定。」

夏洛克害怕極了，於是說：「那我還是拿巴薩尼歐所提供的那筆錢吧！」

「不行！」玻希雅嚴厲地說：「除了那份字據上所寫的之外你什麼都別想得到，現在趕快拿走你的那磅肉，但要記住，如果多一點或少一點的話，哪怕重量只有一根頭髮那樣，你也會失掉全部的財產和妻子。」

害怕的夏洛克說：「只要把我借給他的三千個硬幣給我就好了，讓他走吧！」

巴薩尼歐正要付錢給他，可是玻希雅卻說：「不行，除了那份字據上所寫的之外，他什麼都別想得到。」

p. 170 她又説道：「你這個外國佬，一直想要取走一個威尼斯公民的生命，因此依照威尼斯的法律，你的生命和財物都要被沒收，趕快下去乞求公爵開恩吧！」

至此局面整個反轉，對安東尼奧全無半點慈悲之心的夏洛克也嚐到同樣的苦果，就這樣，這位放高利貸的傢伙不但有一半的家產要被國家充公，並把另一半分配給她女兒的丈夫，而且更得對此心甘情願。

巴薩尼歐為了感謝這位聰明的律師，終於經不起百般勸誘而把妻子給他的那枚戒指送給對方，可是當初他曾答應戒指不離身的。當他回到貝爾蒙後就全向玻希雅坦白交待，她似乎很生氣，並發誓除非能夠再得到她的那枚戒指，否則再也不會和他要好了。

但最後她終於告訴他，假扮成律師救他朋友一命的正是她，而且從他那兒拿到了那枚戒指，最後她原諒了巴薩尼歐。

等到巴薩尼歐瞭解到從首飾盒「抽中籤王」後所得到的戰利品有多麼豐厚時，就顯得更樂不可支了。

11 馬克白

p. 172 如果請一個人説説馬克白的傳説，他可能會告訴你兩個故事，其中之一是敍述一個叫馬克白的人雖然在一〇三九年靠著犯罪登上蘇格蘭的王位，不過大致上仍公正且有效地治理著國家，前後至少達十五年。

至於另一則故事則來自於一個叫做「想像力」的地方，那兒陰鬱而非比尋常，以下你所聽到的就是這則故事。

在「懺悔者聖愛德華」（Edward the Confessor）開始統治英格蘭的前一兩年，蘇格蘭和挪威王打了一仗，蘇格蘭靠著馬克白和班柯兩位將軍取得勝利。

戰事結束後，兩位將軍一起步行前往蘇格蘭王鄧肯所在的埃爾金郡佛瑞斯鎮這地方，而鄧肯則正在那兒候駕。

當他們越過一處偏僻的荒原時，忽然看見三個留了鬍鬚的女人，只見這三個姊妹手牽手，相貌憔悴，穿著十分古怪。

p. 173「説，妳們是誰？」馬克白詰問。

「啊，馬克白，葛萊密斯的指揮官！」第一個女人説。

「啊，馬克白，考特的指揮官！」第二個女人説。

「啊，馬克白，未來的國王！」第三個女人説。

p. 174 然後班柯就問：「那我呢？」只見第三個女人回答：「你會成為眾王之父。」

「多告訴我一些吧！」馬克白説：「在父親死後我就是葛萊密斯的指揮官了，可是考特的指揮官如今還健在呀，而且國王和他的子女也都活得好好的。説！現在我命令你！」

這三個女人並沒有回答，而是憑空消失不見，就好像突然化為一縷輕煙似的。

班柯和馬克白這才知道，和他們説話的是女巫。正當他們討論起這些預言時，兩位貴族走了過來，其中一人奉國王之名感謝馬克白，讚譽他功勛彪炳，另一人則説：「國王吩咐我要稱呼閣下為考特的指揮官。」

p. 175 這時馬克白才了解到，身為考特指揮官的那傢伙昨天因叛國而被殺，於是不禁想到：「第三名女巫不是叫我『未來的國王』嗎！」

他説：「班柯，你也看到那些女巫對我所説的都是真的，難道不相信你的兒孫都會成為國王嗎？」

只見班柯皺皺眉頭，鄧肯有兩個兒子馬爾康和唐納班，因此班柯認為，如果希望自己的兒子佛烈安斯統治蘇格蘭的話，那是大逆不道的，於是就告訴馬克白，女巫們是打算假藉有關王位的一些預言來引誘我倆做壞事。

不過，馬克白卻得意忘形得無法保守這個祕密，以致於在寫給妻子的一封信中提到此事。

p. 176 馬克白夫人是蘇格蘭國王的孫女，不過後來國王卻在王位保衛戰中因對抗鄧肯之前的那任國王而死，且對方還下令處死她唯一的兄弟。

因此對馬克白夫人來説，鄧肯會讓她想起那些苦澀不堪的不法行徑。她的丈夫具有皇室血統，所以當她看到他的信時，就堅信丈夫一定會當上國王。

當一位信差抵達她那兒，並通知她鄧肯要在馬克白的城堡過一夜時，馬克白夫人就提起精神打算採取一項十分卑劣的行動。

她幾乎一看到馬克白回來就告訴他，一定要讓鄧肯度過一個沒有太陽的明天，她的意思是鄧肯必須一死，而且不會被人發現是他們夫妻幹的。

「以後再説吧！」馬克白不安地説，到了晚上，他的回憶裡滿滿都是鄧肯善意的言語，因此即使要他饒這位貴客不死相信也會欣然從命的。

p. 177「難道你要當個懦夫而活？」馬克白夫人質問起來，看來她似乎把道義和懦弱劃上了等號。

「我敢去做一個男子漢會去做的任何事，」馬克白回答：「絕對沒有一個人要比我更有勇氣。」

「為什麼要寫那封信給我？」她凶巴巴地盤問，然後以充滿痛苦的言詞煽動他謀害國王，並以一些狡詐的話語告訴他該如何進行。

p. 178 鄧肯用過餐後就上床睡覺，另外有兩個侍從官站在臥室的門邊守衛著。馬克白夫人要兩位侍從喝了許多酒，直到昏昏沈沈地睡去為止。

接著她取出他們的短劍，要不是國王那張沈睡的臉像極了她父親，馬克白夫人一定會親手弒君的。

馬克白稍後趕來，看到短劍扔在侍從官身邊。不久，他就雙手血紅地出現在妻子面前，並且說：「我剛才好像聽到一個聲音叫道：『別再睡啦！這一覺都被馬克白給破壞了。』」

「快洗洗你的手，」她說：「為什麼不把短刀扔到那兩個侍從官旁邊？趕快帶著短劍回去，然後把血抹在那兩個傢伙身上。」

「我不敢！」馬克白說。

可是他的妻子卻敢，不久就回到馬克白身邊，雙手也和他一樣紅通通的，可是一顆心卻沒有他來得潔白。她嘲笑他畏首畏尾，還驕傲的告訴他事情經過。

p. 179 此刻這兩個殺人犯突然聽到一陣敲門聲，馬克白多麼希望這陣敲門聲可以叫醒死者，不過後來才發現這是費夫地區指揮官麥克達夫的敲門聲，原來早先鄧肯曾告訴麥克達夫要去拜訪他。於是馬克白走向他，並帶他來到國王的房門外。

麥克達夫走了進去，不久就大叫著跑出來：「哦，太悽慘了！太悽慘了！」

馬克白也和麥克達夫一樣表現出飽受驚嚇的樣子，並裝作一副義憤填膺狀，表示實在無法容忍謀害鄧肯的兇手竟然還在這世上逍遙。說完他就趁著侍從官還未能陳述自己的無辜之前，就手起刀落殺害了他們。

p. 180 謀殺的罪行並未敗露，馬克白順利在司康登基，鄧肯有一個兒子避走愛爾蘭，另一個則遠赴英格蘭。

馬克白如今已身為國王，可是仍不滿足，有關班柯的預言讓他心情沉重無比，如果佛烈安斯統治了這個國家，那就代表馬克白的兒子不在王位上，因此馬克白決意殺害班柯和他的兒子。

他雇了兩個惡棍，並設宴招待貴族們，再叫兩人趁著班柯隨同佛烈安斯赴宴的途中殺害了班柯，不過佛烈安斯卻乘隙逃脱。

在此同時，馬克白和王后十分殷勤地接待他們的賓客，席間馬克白表達了一個打從他登基開始就已經表示過數千回的願望：「願諸位胃口大開，消化良好，並敬祝二者齊備！」

p. 181「我們懇請陛下和我們同坐！」一位蘇格蘭貴族林諾克斯説。可是馬克白還未來得及回答，班柯的鬼魂就進到宴會廳，並坐在馬克白的位子上。

馬克白並未察覺到那鬼魂，還表示如果班柯也能夠出席這場盛會，那真可以説連蘇格蘭最精挑細選的騎士都齊聚一堂了，然而麥克達夫卻早已斷然回絕了他的邀請。

此時看不見班柯鬼魂的林諾克斯再度把國王強推入座，並指了指鬼魂所坐的那張椅子，示意國王坐在那兒。

p. 182 可是具有魔眼的馬克白卻看到了鬼魂，看到它形似薄霧，滿身是血，於是暴躁地質問：「這到底是你們之中哪個人幹的？」

可是除了他之外仍沒有人看到鬼魂，馬克白就面向鬼魂説，「你可不能説是我幹的哦！」

鬼魂轉眼消逝無蹤，馬克白這才肆無忌憚地舉起一杯酒説：「願全桌的人都高高興興，再敬我們親愛的朋友、也就是錯過此次歡聚的班柯。」

當班柯的鬼魂第二次進來時，大家已經乾杯了。

「走開！」馬克白大叫：「你是沒有感覺又沒有頭腦的傢伙，隱身在泥土裡，你這個可怕的影子！」

這次還是一樣，除了他沒有一個人看到鬼魂。

「陛下究竟看到了什麼？」一位貴族問。

p. 183 王后不敢給這問題一個答案，只是急著央求賓客們離開這個病人，如果國王不得已而說話的話，情況一定會更加嚴重。

然而第二天馬克白又好了，於是決定找那些女巫談談，她們的預言竟讓他情況惡化到這般田地。

這天雷雨不斷，馬克白在一處洞穴找到了她們，這些女巫正圍繞著一個大鍋旋轉，鍋子裡正熬煮著許多奇怪又可怕的動物小屍塊。在馬克白抵達之前，她們就知道他會來。

「不管我問妳們什麼都要回答。」國王說。

「您願意從我們這兒還是我們主人那兒聽到答案？」第一個女巫問。

p. 184「那就召喚它們。」馬克白回答。

女巫們立刻把血倒入鍋中，油脂瞬間化成火焰捲燒著，然後一個戴著頭盔的腦袋出現了，臉上還蒙著副面具，所以馬克白只能看到它的雙眼。

第一位女巫嚴肅地說：「它可以知道你的想法！」馬克白就在這時對那腦袋開腔了，而從那顆腦袋裡也立刻傳出一個聲音：「馬克白！要小心費夫的指揮官麥克達夫！」說完那腦袋就下降到鍋子裡，直到消失不見。

「再多說一些。」馬克白懇求道。

「它是不會聽令於人的。」第一個女巫說，接著又有一個戴著皇冠的小孩自鍋中升起，手上還拿了一棵樹，只見這孩子說：

「在伯南的樹林爬上鄧西納山之前，馬克白是無敵的。」

「這種情況永遠不會發生。」馬克白說。接著他又要求那小孩告訴他，班柯的後代子孫是否會永遠統治著蘇格蘭。

p. 185 不過此時鍋子已沈入地下，馬克白接著又聽到音樂聲，只見一排國王的幽靈依序經過馬克白面前，排在最後的赫然就是班柯的鬼魂。

馬克白看到每一個國王都很像班柯，數數一共有七位，然後在一瞬間，那兒就只剩下他一個人了。

馬克白的第二步行動就是派遣殺手前往麥克達夫的城堡，他們並沒發現麥克達夫，於是詢問麥克達夫夫人他在哪兒，麥克達夫夫人的回答充滿揶揄，質問他下落的那名兇手就把麥克達夫稱為賣國賊。

「你這個騙子！」麥克達夫的小兒子高聲喊道，於是他立刻被刺殺，死前還趁著有最後一口氣時央求母親快逃，可是那批兇手毫無人性，城堡內的人只要有一個活口他們就不會離開。

當麥克達夫的朋友羅斯前往英格蘭，告訴他妻兒都已遭到殺害時，他正偕同馬爾康聆聽懺悔者聖愛德華在講述一位醫生醫治病人的故事。

p. 186 起初羅斯不敢說出真相，以免充滿同情心且可以在高貴情操下讓苦難得到紓解的麥克達夫，轉而成為飽受哀傷打擊又滿懷恨意的人。

可是當馬爾康說英格蘭已派遣一支軍隊前往蘇格蘭攻打馬克白時，羅斯終於衝口說出不幸的消息，麥克達夫聞言痛哭失聲。「你是說全都死了？我所有可愛的孩子和他們的母親都撒手人寰了？你是說全都死了？」

他的可悲期望就是報仇雪恨，但如果能到馬克白在鄧西納山的城堡一探究竟，就可以看到一股遠比復仇更莊嚴的力量正發揮作用。

原來是報應來了，馬克白夫人瘋了，她不斷做著可怕的夢，而且還夢遊著。

p. 188 此外她不停地洗手，十五分鐘就一次，可是不管怎麼洗，皮膚上仍然可以看到一處紅色的血痕。

後來只見她鎮日狂呼，所有的阿拉伯香水也都無法讓她的小手變香，聽到她的呼號更令人同情。

「你難道不能照料精神病患嗎？」馬克白質問起醫生，但醫生回答，他的病人必須照料好自己的精神狀況。

這個回答讓馬克白嘲笑起那些藥來，「把藥拿去餵狗！」他說，「任何一種藥我都不會扔的。」

有一天他聽見女人的哭泣聲，一名官員趨前對他說：「陛下，王后死了！」

「出去，短短的蠟燭這麼快就熄滅了。」馬克白喃喃說，意思是人生就像一支蠟燭，任由輕風的擺佈。馬克白並沒有哭泣，因為他太熟悉死亡了。

不久一位信差就告訴馬克白，他看到伯南的樹林在踏著步伐前進，馬克白於是叫他騙子和奴隸，並威脅對方如果說錯的話就把他給吊死，「如果你說的沒錯，大可以吊死我。」馬克白又加上一句。

p.190 從鄧西納堡塔樓的窗戶往外看去，伯南的樹林看起來的確像是在行軍一樣。其實英格蘭軍隊的每個士兵都奉令在伯南的樹林找棵樹砍下大樹枝，然後高高舉起，使得遠遠看去就像一棵棵人形大樹爬上鄧西納山一樣。

馬克白仍勇氣十足地前去戰鬥，反正不是征服對方就是戰死沙場，他頭一件做的就是在一場戰鬥殺了英格蘭將軍的兒子。

馬克白這時覺得沒有一個人可以在和他交手之後還能活著，當麥克達夫來到他面前，雙目冒火嚷著要復仇時，馬克白就對他說：「回去，我已經讓你們家族流了太多的血。」

「我要說的話都在這支劍上！」麥克達夫回答，然後掄起刀劈向他，並命令他不要做無謂的抵抗。

「我不會放棄的！」馬克白說，可是他最後的時辰已到，不久就倒了下去。

當麥克達夫拎著馬克白國王的腦袋來到馬爾康面前時，馬克白的人馬隨即退去。

「歡迎國王！」他歡呼道，新的國王瞧了瞧已死的舊國王。

就這樣，馬爾康在馬克白之後君臨天下，在往後的歲月，班柯的子子孫孫都成了國王。

12 第十二夜

p. 192 伊利里亞的公爵歐西諾深愛著美麗的女伯爵奧莉薇亞，然而她卻對他的追求不屑一顧，讓歐西諾空痴情一場。後來，在奧莉薇亞的兄弟過世時，她把公爵遣來的信差斥回，要他回去告訴主人，說在未來的七年之內，就是大自然也見不到她的容顏，她會像修女那樣蒙起面紗，以追悼死去的兄弟，讓兄弟的愛得以永遠鮮活地留駐在自己哀傷的記憶中。

公爵渴望有人能傾聽他的悲傷，讓他能不斷地傾訴衷曲。這時，他剛好就遇到了這樣的人選。

因為就在此時，一艘大船在伊利里亞的海岸發生船難，而在被救上岸的人當中，包括了船長和一名叫做薇兒拉的美麗少女，但少女並沒有慶幸自己被救起，因為她擔心自己的雙胞胎兄弟席巴斯安已經溺斃。對她來說，席巴斯安就如她心頭上的肉一樣，他們兩人長得十分相像，除了服飾上男女有別外，外人很難分辨出他們。

p. 194 為了讓她寬心，船長說他有看到席巴斯安把自己綁在一根結實的船桅上，漂浮在海面上，因此可能已經被救起來了。

薇兒拉打聽了這一地的統治者，得知是由年輕的公爵歐西諾所治理，而且公爵人如其名，性格高貴。於是她決定女扮男裝，想要找機會去當公爵的侍從。

結果一切如她所願，如今，她每天都得聽歐西諾訴說他的衷腸。

起初，她很同情公爵的遭遇，可是沒過多久，同情卻滋生成愛苗。後來公爵突然想到，如果能夠差遣這位儀表出眾的小伙子替他勸服奧莉薇亞的話，原本毫無希望的追求，搞不好會成功。

薇兒拉只得心不甘情不願地接下這份差事，不過當她來到奧莉薇亞的住處時，奧莉薇亞就謊稱生病，並吩咐自負又愛多管閒事的管家馬沃里奧擋駕，不讓這位信差進門。

p. 195 但現在化名成西薩里奧的薇兒拉不肯罷休，誓言一定要和女伯爵好好談談。

奧莉薇亞聽到有人竟敢違抗自己的命令，就很好奇是誰這麼大膽，她說：「我們就再聽聽歐西諾的信使有什麼說法吧！」

p. 196 當薇兒拉獲准出現在她面前時，僕奴們都已退下，女伯爵很有耐心地聽著這位大膽的公爵信差在數落自己的不是，一邊聽著，竟一邊就愛上了這位假扮的西薩里奧。

等西薩里奧離開後，奧莉薇亞渴望送些定情物給他，於是叫喚馬沃里奧，吩咐他去跟蹤這位青年。

「就說他把這個戒指忘在這兒了，」她邊說邊從手指上脫下一枚戒指，「但不要告訴他這是我的。」

馬沃里奧照著她的吩咐做了，薇兒拉當然心知肚明得很，自己並沒有把什麼戒指忘在她那兒，她也見識到了女人墜入情網之迅速，奧莉薇亞竟這麼快就愛上了她。不久她就回到公爵那兒，內心裡對心上人、對自己或是對奧莉薇亞，都深感憂傷。

她能給歐西諾的，只是不著邊際的安慰。那天晚上，在公爵聆聽甜美動人的音樂來療傷止痛時，西薩里奧就站在旁邊。

「哦！看來你也戀愛啦！」公爵這樣對自己的隨從說。

「多少有一點兒！」薇兒拉回答。

p. 197「她是哪樣的女人？」他又追問。

「就像你這樣。」她回答。

「真的？那麼她多大年紀了？」公爵又問。

答案十分有趣，「和您歲數差不多，殿下。」

「那太老了，老天！」公爵叫道：「我看還是讓她找個大一點兒的男人吧！」

薇兒拉柔順地說：「我會好好考慮的，殿下。」

p. 198 不久，歐西諾又再次央求西薩里奧探訪奧莉薇亞，並為自己表明心跡。可是她想勸阻他，於是說：

「要是有個女孩她愛上了你，一如你愛奧莉薇亞那樣的話，你會怎樣？」

「哦！那是不可能的。」公爵回答。

「但我知道女人也會對男人心生同樣的愛，」薇兒拉繼續說：「我父親有個女兒就這樣愛上了一個男人，」後來她又臉紅地補充：「如果我是一個女的，或許也會愛上閣下。」

「那她結果如何？」他問道。

「到頭來還是一場空，殿下！」薇兒拉回答：「她從未表白過自己的愛，只是讓這個埋藏在心裡的秘密侵蝕她粉紅的雙頰，就像花兒裡的蛀蟲一樣，她在相思愁苦中憔悴，一如堅忍的雕像（譯註：古時的墓碑常刻有象徵的人物像，而「忍耐」即為其中最常見的象徵之一）對著悲悽苦笑，這不就是愛嗎？」

「那你姊妹的愛澆熄了嗎？」公爵問道。此時，一直以這種不著痕跡的方式對他傾吐愛意的薇兒拉答道：

「父親就只有我一個女兒，而且我的兄弟都……閣下，還要我去找那位女士嗎？」

p. 199「快去找她！」薇兒拉所說的事隨即就被公爵置之腦後，「然後把這串珠寶給她。」

於是薇兒拉啟程前往。這一次，可憐的奧莉薇亞再也無法隱藏愛意，她向薇兒拉告白了自己的愛慕。薇兒拉於是趕緊離開，並說道：

「我不再為主人對妳所灑下的熱淚感到哀慟了！」

薇兒拉在說這話的同時，並沒有想到自己對別人所受的苦，是很容易心軟的。

於是，當為情所困的奧莉薇亞派人去乞求西薩里奧來看她時，西薩里奧無法忍心拒絕。

p. 200 然而，奧莉薇亞對西薩里奧這名僕人的愛意，讓安德魯・奧古齊特爵士感到很吃味。這位爵士是個愚蠢的傢伙，他很喜歡奧莉薇亞，但奧莉薇亞並不領情，當時，他正偕同奧莉薇亞那位性情愉快的老叔父托比爵士，一起待在奧莉薇亞的家。

同樣身為爵士的托比很喜歡惡作劇，而且他也知道安德魯爵士是個聲名狼藉的懦夫，於是也心想，如果能夠在安德魯爵士和西薩里奧之間挑起決鬥，那想必會是一場難得一見的好戲。

就這樣，他慫恿安德魯爵士下戰帖，而且還親自去找西薩里奧。可憐的侍從西薩里奧真是嚇壞了，他說：「我要回到屋裡了，我不是戰士。」

「你休想，」托比爵士說：「除非閣下先和我較量較量。」

托比這位老人家看起來很好鬥。薇兒拉心想，還是等安德魯爵士來了再說吧。最後，爵士終於出現，各位要是心知肚明的話，就會知道他當時也是嚇懷了。薇兒拉抽出劍時直打著哆嗦，安德魯爵士也是一樣。

p. 201 這時，來了王宮的一些官吏，他們制止了這場被設計了的決鬥，讓決鬥的兩個人鬆了好大一口氣。薇兒拉趁機溜煙似地逃走，而托比爵士則在她身後叫喊著：

「真是個沒有用的小子，比兔子還膽小。」

就在這些事情發生之際，席巴斯安逃離了凶險的大海，毫髮未傷的在伊利里亞上岸，然後決定前往歐西諾的王宮。

當薇兒拉忙不迭地離開奧莉薇亞家時，席巴斯安正巧路過，而且撞見了安德魯爵士和托比爵士，安德魯爵士誤以為席巴斯安就是懦弱的西薩里奧，便壯了膽子走過去，準備飽以老拳，他嚷道：「都是你惹的禍。」

「什麼我惹的禍？你給我說清楚，講明白！」席巴斯安一邊說道，一邊回敬好個幾大拳，直到托比爵士出手拯救朋友。

p. 202 托比爵士抓住席巴斯安，席巴斯安掙脫出來，他抽出劍，準備和兩人拼鬥。這時，奧莉薇亞聽到爭吵聲立刻跑出來，將托比爵士和安德魯爵士罵得落荒而逃。

接著，奧莉薇亞轉身向席巴斯安，也把他誤認為是西薩里奧，於是對他說了不少深情款款的話，並央求他一起進屋。

奧莉薇亞的美麗和優雅，讓席巴斯安目眩神迷，令他求之不得。於是兩人就在當天共結連理，而且結婚之後奧莉薇亞才發現如意郎君不是西薩里奧，而席巴斯安也才搞清楚是怎麼一回事。

在此同時，歐西諾在得知可惡的西薩里奧很快就勾搭上奧莉薇亞之後，就帶著西薩里奧去找奧莉薇亞。

p. 203 這時奧莉薇亞在門口前碰到他們兩人，她誤以為西薩里奧就是自己的丈夫，於是先指責他始亂終棄，接著又對公爵表示，他的追求簡直愚蠢極了，好像琴聲結束後的嗡嗡哀號聲一樣。

p. 204「妳還是這麼地殘忍無情？」歐西諾說。

「一路走來，如終如一。」她答道。

這讓歐西諾聽得老羞成怒，他說他一定要報復她，要把她心愛的西薩里奧給殺掉。

「過來，小子！」他對西薩里奧說。

薇兒拉乖乖地跟著離開，並說道：「為了讓你安心，死一千次我都願意。」

但奧莉薇亞嚇壞了，她喊道：「西薩里奧，親愛的老公，不要走！」

「老公？」公爵憤怒的問。

「不，殿下，不是我！」薇兒拉說。

「快去叫神父來！」奧莉薇亞喊道。

當初為席巴斯安和奧莉薇亞主持婚禮的神父走了進來，他宣稱西薩里奧就是新郎。

「哦，你這個扮豬吃老虎的傢伙！」公爵吼道：「再見！把他給帶走，以後再也不要讓我看到他。」

這時王冠上還淌著血的安德魯公爵走過來，控訴西薩里奧把他腦袋給打破，還弄傷了托比爵士。

「我沒有，」薇兒拉很肯定地說：「拔出你的劍和我較量較量，不過事先聲明，你得光明正大，我是不會傷害你的。」

p. 205 薇兒拉自己在那兒一個勁地表明，但沒有人相信她；就在這時，走來了席巴斯安，讓大家都疑惑了起來。

「很抱歉！夫人，」他對愛妻說：「我傷害了妳的親人，請原諒，甜心，為了不久之前我們彼此許下的誓言，請原諒我。」

「這兩個人怎麼會長得一模一樣，連聲音和動作也都一樣！」公爵先是望著薇兒拉，然後看著席巴斯安驚呼道。

「把一個蘋果剖成兩半，也不會像眼前這兩人那樣長得那麼相像，到底誰才是席巴斯安？」一位認識席巴斯安的人問道。

「我沒有什麼兄弟來著，」席巴斯安：「我只有個姊妹，不過她被無情的狂濤巨浪給吞沒了。」

接著他轉向薇兒拉說：「如果你是個女子，那我一定會讓自己的熱淚灑在你的臉頰上，並說『再三歡迎已遭滅頂的薇兒拉！』」

看到親愛的兄弟還活著，薇兒拉欣喜萬分，立刻承認她就是席巴斯安的姊妹薇兒拉。

p. 206 當薇兒拉說話時，歐西諾對她又憐又愛。

「孩子！」他說：「你曾對我說過千百回，你對女人的愛，將永遠比不上對我的愛。」

「這些話雖然是過分誇大的誓言，」薇兒拉回答：「但我是真心的。」

「把妳的手給我，」歐西諾愉悅地說：「請做我的妻子，我夢寐以求的皇后。」

溫柔的薇兒拉聽了很高興，而奧莉薇亞也了解到席巴斯安是個忠貞的情人和好丈夫，而他也找到了一個真實又可愛的妻子。

13 奧賽羅

p. 208 四百年前威尼斯住著一個叫做伊阿高的海軍軍官，由於他的將軍奧賽羅摒除了已獲大力舉薦的他，而選擇能言善道並曾幫助奧賽羅贏得黛絲蒙娜芳心的麥可．卡西歐為副官，因而對奧賽羅懷恨在心。

伊阿高有位朋友叫做羅德里高，曾提供伊阿高金錢，而且覺得除非能娶到黛絲蒙娜為妻，否則自己絕對快樂不起來。

奧賽羅是個摩爾人，但皮膚黝黑，因此仇敵都把他叫做黑人。他一生艱苦，際遇也充滿了刺激，曾吃過敗仗，並被當做奴隸賣掉，不過卻是個了不起的旅行家，見多識廣，曾看到肩膀比腦袋還要高的人。

p. 209 不過勇猛如獅的他卻有個很大的毛病，那就是嫉妒心重，他的愛十分自私，愛一個女人即意味著絕對地佔有她，好像佔有一個沒有生命和不會思考的物品一樣，而奧賽羅的故事則是一篇講述嫉妒的故事。

有天晚上，伊阿高告訴羅德里高，奧賽羅要瞞著黛絲蒙娜的父親布拉班提奧帶走她。

於是伊阿高說服羅德里高，把布拉班提奧叫醒，當這位元老出現時，伊阿高就告訴他黛絲蒙娜已在最糟的情況下私奔了。雖然伊阿高是奧賽羅手下的軍官，可是仍稱奧賽羅為竊賊和巴巴利（譯註：北非的蠻族地區）的野馬，野蠻而下賤。

p. 211 布拉班提奧就在威尼斯公爵的面前，指控奧賽羅利用巫術迷惑了他女兒，但奧賽羅表示，他所用的唯一巫術他的聲音，透過這聲音把歷險和間不容髮的逃亡經過告訴了黛絲蒙娜。

接著黛絲蒙娜被帶到元老院，她說：「我在奧賽羅高貴的心靈中看到了他的臉。」以解釋她是如何不顧奧賽羅近乎全黑的臉龐而愛上他。

當奧賽羅娶了黛絲蒙娜時，她很高興地成了他的妻子，不會說半句違逆丈夫意思的話，尤其當公爵希望他能前往賽普路斯抵禦土耳其人的侵略時更是如此。

奧賽羅已準備出發，黛絲蒙娜很想與他一起出征，最後終於獲准成行，在賽普路斯和他碰頭。

奧賽羅在賽普路斯島登陸時見到這情形喜不自勝，「哦，我的甜心！」他對偕同伊阿高、伊阿高妻子和羅德里高一同抵達的黛絲蒙娜說：「真不知道該對妳說些什麼，只是我很喜歡這種快樂的感覺。」

p. 212 不一會兒消息傳來，土耳其的艦隊失去了戰鬥力，於是他宣布，從晚上五點到十一點要在賽普路斯舉辦歡宴。

卡西歐要在奧賽羅統治賽普路斯所在的城堡內值勤，於是伊阿高決定猛灌對方酒，卡西歐知道酒一下肚就會直衝腦門而壞了大事，因此伊阿高的計謀就有些困難，可是當僕人們把酒帶到卡西歐的房間時，卡西歐就有些把持不住了。同時伊阿高又唱起了行酒歌，於是卡西歐頻頻舉杯，為將軍的健康一飲而盡。

酒意正濃的卡西歐變得喜歡爭論，伊阿高趁機要羅德里高說些不中聽的話給卡西歐聽，卡西歐因此掄起棍棒要打羅德里高，而羅德里高就跑到前總督蒙塔諾面前。

p. 213 蒙塔諾謙恭地為羅德里高求情，可是卻從卡西歐口中得到一個十分無理的回答：「得了吧，得了吧，你喝醉了！」

接著卡西歐還弄傷了他，伊阿高於是趁機派羅德里高出去高喊有人叛變，好把這城市給嚇得惶惶不安起來。

喧囂聲吵醒了奧賽羅，在得知原委後就說：「卡西歐，我愛你，可是以後永遠別想做我副官了。」

當卡西歐和伊阿高兩人獨處時，遭貶黜的卡西歐不禁對自己的聲譽悲嘆起來，伊阿高表示聲譽不過就是些騙人的玩意兒。

「哦，老天！」對對方毫無戒心的卡西歐大喊時，「人們居然會把仇敵放進嘴裡，好讓他偷掉自己的腦筋。」

伊阿高建議他向黛絲蒙娜求情，以求奧賽羅原諒自己。

p. 214 卡西歐很喜歡這個建議，第二天上午就在城堡的花園裡向黛絲蒙娜提出要求。

善良的黛絲蒙娜就說：「看開一點，卡西歐，我寧願死也不會置你的問題於不顧。」

此刻卡西歐又見到奧賽羅和伊阿高走了進來，於是立刻退下。

伊阿高說：「我實在不想這樣。」

「你說什麼？」奧賽羅問，他覺得伊阿高大概會提些令人不悅的事，可是伊阿高卻假裝自己什麼也沒說。

「剛從我妻子那兒離開的不是卡西歐嗎？」奧賽羅問。伊阿高知道那就是卡西歐，而且為什麼會前來這兒，可是嘴巴卻說：「我實在無法相信，卡西歐竟然這麼內疚地溜掉。」

黛絲蒙娜向奧賽羅解釋，是悲痛和羞辱讓卡西歐自覺有罪地退避，接著黛絲蒙娜又提醒他，當她還未陷入愛情的漩渦並且對奧賽羅百般挑剔時，卡西歐是如何善盡他好朋友的角色。

p. 215 奧賽羅這時為柔情所溶化，於是説：「我不會拒絕妳的任何要求。」黛絲蒙娜順勢告訴他，她要求他做的會和三餐一樣對他大有幫助。

黛絲蒙娜離開了花園，伊阿高趁機問道，卡西歐是否真的在黛絲蒙娜婚前便已認識她。

「沒錯！」奧賽羅説。

「果然沒錯！」伊阿高口氣中彷彿以前讓他感到困惑的一些事情如今終於豁然開朗。

「難道他不誠實？」奧賽羅問。只見伊阿高充滿懷疑的不斷重覆他那句形容詞，好像欲言又止不敢説出那個「不」字。

「你究竟是什麼意思？」奧賽羅堅決要求對方説出。

伊阿高這時的言談與當初在卡西歐面前的話可説完全相反，他曾告訴卡西歐，聲譽不過是些騙人的玩意。

他對奧賽羅這麼説：「竊取我錢囊不過是偷到些廢物，可是竊取我的好名聲卻會讓我身敗名裂。」

奧賽羅這時思緒馳騁著，伊阿高信心十足，認為奧賽羅的嫉妒一定會警告他小心防範。

p. 216 沒錯，除了伊阿高之外又有誰能喚起那嫉妒心來呢？嫉妒是個綠眼妖魔，無論誰成了餵食它的肉，都要受它的嘲弄。

伊阿高讓嫉妒心帶給人們一場大災難，只見他又以下面的論點火上加油：黛絲蒙娜和奧賽羅私奔等於蒙蔽了她父親。「如果她蒙蔽了他，又何嘗不會蒙蔽你呢？」伊阿高心裡頭真正想説的就是這句話。

一會兒黛絲蒙娜又進來了，告訴奧賽羅晚餐已經準備好了。她看到奧賽羅有些心神不寧，奧賽羅則解釋他頭有點痛，於是黛絲蒙娜拿出一條過去奧賽羅送給她的手帕。

p. 217 這條手帕大有來頭，是一名兩百歲的女先知用神聖的蠶絲編織，接著用來自於處女心臟的鮮血染色，最後再繡上草莓圖案而成。

溫柔的黛絲蒙娜並沒有多想什麼，只把它當成一件柔軟又冰冷的東西，剛好可以蓋在陣陣作痛的額頭上，她也知道這條手帕根本沒施過什麼咒語，弄丟了它並不會讓自己家破人亡的。

p. 218「讓我把它放在你頭上，」她對奧賽羅說：「這樣一個小時就會好了。」

可是奧賽羅怒氣沖沖地說手帕太小，並任由它掉落在地。

不久黛絲蒙娜就和他進屋內用晚餐，愛蜜麗雅順勢撿起了那條手帕，原來伊阿高過去曾屢次要求她把它給偷來。

當伊阿高進來時，愛蜜麗雅把手帕端詳了一番，兩人交談幾句後，伊阿高就把手帕從她手上一把搶來，然後吩咐她離開。

他和奧賽羅在花園相遇，奧賽羅似乎很渴望能夠從伊阿高口中聽到些最惡毒的謊言。因此伊阿高就告訴奧賽羅，他曾見到卡西歐用一條手帕擦嘴，由於它有草莓圖樣，因此猜測這就是奧賽羅送給妻子的那條。

怏怏不樂的這名摩耳人怒髮衝冠，幾乎快發狂了，伊阿高立刻對天發誓，他會獻出一切，包括自己的雙手、一顆心以及頭腦，任由奧賽羅差遣。

「我接受你的忠誠，」奧賽羅說：「讓我在三天內聽到卡西歐的死訊。」

p. 219 伊阿高的下一步就是把黛絲蒙娜的那條手帕放到卡西歐的房間，卡西歐後來看到了它，知道不是屬於自己的，可是又喜歡上面的草莓圖案，於是送給心上人碧安卡，並要求她為自己仿製一份。

伊阿高於是又進行下一步，那就是誘使因手帕一事不斷威嚇黛絲蒙娜的奧賽羅，去偷聽卡西歐和他之間的談話，他的用意是藉此談到卡西歐的心上人，並讓奧賽羅認為開口說話的女人就是黛絲蒙娜。

「你好嗎？副官！」當卡西歐出現時伊阿高問道。

「糟糕的是現在我已經不是副官了，」卡西歐沮喪地說。「繼續提醒黛絲蒙娜，不久你就會官復原職了，」伊阿高說完又壓低嗓門加了一句，好讓奧賽羅聽不到，「如果碧安卡能夠出面把事情給搞定，很快就有轉圜餘地了！」

p. 220「唉！這可憐的小淘氣，」卡西歐說：「我真的以為她愛我。」接著他就像平常那樣成了一個多嘴的花花公子，在誘導下開始吹噓碧安卡是多麼喜歡他。躲在一旁偷聽的奧賽羅滿懷怒氣，猜測卡西歐一定是在談黛絲蒙娜，於是心想「我看見了你的鼻子，可是不知道應該把它丟給哪一條狗吃。」

當碧安卡進來時，奧賽羅仍在偷聽，已視卡西歐為禁臠的碧安卡一聽說卡西歐要求她仿製那條手帕的圖案，還以為它是卡西歐的新情人所有，怒急攻心之餘便把手帕甩向他，並說些嘲弄他的話，於是卡西歐憤而離去。

奧賽羅見到碧安卡不論在地位、美貌和言談上都遠不如黛絲蒙娜，就不由得開始向眼前的這名惡棍讚美起自己妻子，他稱讚她針線的技巧、可以「唱出大熊凶殘」的甜美嗓音、機智、溫柔，以及皮膚的細緻滑嫩。

p. 221 每當他讚美她時，伊阿高就說些不中聽的話，讓奧賽羅又記起了自己的憤恨，並粗暴地一吐胸中怒火。但最後他還是不得不讚美起黛絲蒙娜，並說：「真可惜，伊阿高，哦！伊阿高，真可惜，伊阿高！」

壞事做絕的伊阿高發起狠來從沒有片刻的猶豫，如果硬要說有，就是在這時他有些拿不定主意。

「那就勒死她！」他說，「很好，很好！」那個可悲的呆頭鵝也說。

當黛絲蒙娜帶著父親家族的一名親戚出現時，他們倆仍在談論謀殺的事。那名親戚叫做羅鐸維科，替威尼斯公爵捎來一封信給奧賽羅，信中要把奧賽羅從賽普路斯召回，並把總督職位交到卡西歐手上。

p. 222 不幸的黛絲蒙娜抓住這令人不悅的時刻，再次催促奧賽羅答應卡西歐的請求。

「畜牲！」奧賽羅咆哮著。

「或許是這封信激怒了他。」羅鐸維科向黛絲蒙娜解釋，並順便把信中內容告訴了她。

「我很高興，」黛絲蒙娜說。就是這番令人難堪的話讓奧賽羅的無情在她身上爆發開來，更何況這還是頭一遭發生呢！

「我也很高興妳動了怒。」奧賽羅說。

「為什麼？溫柔的奧賽羅！」她挖苦地說。奧賽羅於是摑了她一巴掌。

如今黛絲蒙娜到了該分居一段時間以拯救自己人生的時候了，可是她毫不明白自己所面臨的危險，只知道她的愛徹底受到重創。

「我不該受到這種待遇。」她說道，兩行熱淚緩緩滑落臉頰。

p. 223 羅鐸維科十分震驚，一股厭惡感湧上心頭，「我的天，」他說：「這種事在威尼斯簡直讓人難以置信，快給她賠罪。」

可是奧賽羅就像一個瘋子在夢魘中開口說話一樣，以醜陋的言語把他污穢的想法一股腦地渲洩而出，並且大吼：「別再叫我看到妳！」

「我不會繼續待在這兒惹你嫌的。」他妻子雖然這樣說，可是卻仍躊躇再三，只有當他大吼一聲「滾！」後，黛絲蒙娜才離開他丈夫和眾賓客。

接著奧賽羅邀請羅鐸維科用餐，不過卻補充了這樣一句：「閣下，歡迎來到賽普路斯，你們這群山羊和猴子。」說完不等這位夥伴回答就離開了。

高貴的訪客們實在不喜歡被迫看到別人的家庭糾紛，也不想被罵作山羊或猴子，於是羅鐸維科要求伊阿高解釋。

p. 224 這回伊阿高終於真實地面對自己，以迂迴的說法表示，實際上奧賽羅要比表面更糟，然後建議他們好好觀察他的行為，並避免再提出任何問題以免引起奧賽羅的不快。

伊阿高接著著手吩咐羅德里高殺害卡西歐，羅德里高其實和這位朋友貌合神離，因為他曾交給伊阿高許多珠寶，想透過這傢伙轉送給黛絲蒙娜，以討得她歡心，可是卻沒有任何效果。由於伊阿高把所有珠寶都據為己有，所以黛絲蒙娜連一顆也沒見著。

當卡西歐離開碧安卡的家時，伊阿高就以謊言讓他平靜下來，後來羅德里高把他給打傷了，可是自己也在卡西歐反擊時受了傷。

這時只見卡西歐大叫，羅鐸維科和一個朋友立刻跑過來，卡西歐指出羅德里高正是攻擊他的人，伊阿高心想這位朋友只會帶來麻煩，很想擺脫對方，於是就叫道：「你這惡棍！」然後用刀朝羅德里高猛刺，可是對方卻沒死。

p. 225 黛絲蒙娜在城堡中十分哀傷，她告訴愛蜜麗雅她必須離開她，因為這是她丈夫的意思。

「要把我給打發走！」愛蜜麗雅叫道。

「這是他的命令，」黛絲蒙娜說：「如今我們一定不能惹他生氣。」

說完又唱了一首歌，那是一位女孩在遭到情人卑劣的對待後所唱的，歌詞描述那位少女在樹旁哭泣著，這時只見大樹的樹枝也低垂著，好像在為女孩的遭遇垂淚，唱完後黛絲蒙娜便上床入睡。

她醒來時見到丈夫狂亂的雙眼緊盯著她。

「今晚祈禱了嗎？」他問道，接著又告訴眼前這個無罪的甜美女人，他會祈求上帝原諒她在良心上所犯的任何罪惡。

「我不會扼殺妳的靈魂。」

他說完又告訴她，卡西歐已經招認了，可是黛絲蒙娜知道卡西歐絕不會招認和她有關的任何事，還表示卡西歐不可能說出任何會傷害她的話來。此時奧賽羅才說，卡西歐的嘴已無法再說話了。

p. 226 黛絲蒙娜飲泣著，可是暴怒的奧賽羅仍惡言相向，不理會她的任何辯解。

奧賽羅最後掐住她的喉嚨，給她帶來致命的傷害。

心生不祥預兆的愛蜜麗雅來了，在門邊苦苦央求著要進來。奧賽羅開了門，這時只聽見一個聲音從床上傳了過來：「我是無罪而死的。」

「是誰幹的？」愛蜜麗雅哭了起來，那個聲音又傳了過來，「沒有別人……是我自己做的，再會吧！」

「她是我殺的！」奧賽羅說。

他站在那張令人悲痛的床旁邊，向跑進來的眾人滔滔不絕地說出他的證據，伊阿高也在其中，可是當他談到那條手帕時，愛蜜麗雅就道出了實情，奧賽羅這時才了解真相。

「除了雷霆外，上天難道沒有石頭可以砸向那惡棍嗎？」他邊叫喊邊奔向伊阿高，只見伊阿高給了愛蜜麗雅致命的一擊後就飛奔而逃。

p. 227 但不久他們就把他給押回來，後來並把他給處死，算是減輕了一些傷痛。

他們要把奧賽羅帶回威尼斯，並在那兒審判他，可是他卻仗著自己的劍脫逃了。

「在你們離開前我要說一兩句話，」他在房間對那些威尼斯人說：「當你們談到我時，請老老實實的說，不要美言，也不要惡意構陷。就說我連最好的珠寶都棄若敝屣，而且到了傷心處，鐵石心腸的我也會潸然淚下。多年前我在阿勒坡曾看到一個土耳其人毆打一個威尼斯人，於是我就一把掐住他的喉嚨並殺了他。」

說完就舉刀往自己的心臟猛刺，死前還帶著絕望的愛意以雙唇輕觸黛絲蒙娜的芳顏。

14 冬天的故事

p. 230 西西里國王李昂提斯有個最要好的朋友，也就是波西米亞的國王波利克賽尼斯，兩人曾一起受教，直到長大成人而且得各自回去統治他們的王國，才依依不捨的分開。

經過多年之後，兩人都結了婚並育有一子，於是波利克賽尼斯前往西西里找李昂提斯，並留宿在那兒。

p. 231 李昂提斯是個性情暴烈的人，而且生性愚蠢，後來他的笨腦袋竟認為老婆赫米歐妮喜歡波利克賽尼斯的程度，要超過她自己的丈夫。

一旦這個想法深入腦海，就再也沒有一樣東西能夠消除它了，於是李昂提斯命令手下一位貴族卡密羅，在波利克賽尼斯的酒中下毒。

卡密羅試圖說服國王打消此舉，可是卻發現他心意已決，無可動搖，於是假裝同意，然後把李昂提斯打算對付波利克賽尼斯的計畫，告訴了波利克賽尼斯。當晚，他們就從西西里的王宮脫逃回到波西米亞，卡密羅也在那兒住了下來，成為波利克賽尼斯的好友兼顧問。

至於李昂提斯則把王后打入大牢，她的兒子也就是王位的繼承人，在看到母親受到這麼不公平和殘忍的待遇後，竟傷痛至死。

王后繫獄時生了一個小孩，她的朋友寶莉娜幫小寶寶作最好的打扮，然後抱給國王瞧。她認為國王只要看到他無助的小女兒，就會軟化對王后的惡毒心腸，更何況王后從沒有做過任何對不起國王的事，而且愛他的程度遠超過他所該得到的。

p. 232 可是國王連瞧都沒有瞧這寶寶一眼，就命令寶莉娜的丈夫乘船把這小娃兒給帶走，並扔到他所能找到最荒涼可怕的地方，寶莉娜的丈夫在無可奈何下不得不聽命行事。

可憐的王后以叛國的罪名被帶到法庭審判，指控她寧可讓波利克賽尼斯出任國王，可是實際上除了她丈夫李昂提斯外，王后從不認為任何人具有這種資格。

李昂提斯後來差遣幾位使者去詢問天神阿波羅，看看李昂提斯對王后的殘酷想法是否正確，可是卻沒有耐心靜待他們回來。不過好巧不巧的是，這些使者終於在審判時返抵國門，只見神諭上說：

p. 233 赫米歐妮是無辜的，波利克賽尼斯也沒有罪，卡密羅是忠實的臣子，李昂提斯則是個猜疑的暴君。如果失去的仍沒找回，國王就會活在沒有繼承人的痛苦中。

接著來了一個侍從，告訴他們小王子死了，可憐的王后一聽到這不幸的消息便突然倒地不起，國王終於了解到過去他是多麼惡毒和不對。

於是他命令寶莉娜和王后左右的侍女們把她帶走，想盡辦法恢復她健康，可是沒多久寶莉娜回來，告訴國王赫米歐妮死了。

p. 234 如今李昂提斯的雙眼終於睜開了，看到自己的愚蠢，原本可以安慰他的小女兒也被自己趕走，淪為野狼和老鷹的腹中肉。

如今生命裡什麼都沒為國王留下，於是他萬念俱灰，鎮日生活在悲痛中，使得往後的每一年李昂提斯都在祈禱和痛悔自責中度過。其實小公主被遺棄在波西米亞的海岸邊，那是屬於波利克賽尼斯統治的王國。

寶莉娜的丈夫永遠都沒有機會回家告訴李昂提斯他把小寶寶扔到

什麼地方，因為當他回到船上時遇到一隻大熊，當場被大卸八塊，就這樣送了命。

可是這名遭到遺棄的可憐小寶寶後來被一名牧羊人發現了，當時只見小公主盛裝打扮，服飾不但名貴還配戴了些珠寶，另外在披風上也別了一張紙，上面說她名叫帕蒂塔，來自於高貴的雙親。

牧羊人心地善良，於是把這名小寶寶帶回家交給妻子，夫妻倆就這樣把她視如己出地撫養長大。

p. 235 她就像普通牧羊人的孩子一樣，沒有接受更多的教育，可是卻從出身於王室的母親那兒遺傳到不少優雅氣質和魅力，所以和她那處村莊的其他少女相比顯得十分與眾不同。

有一天，波西米亞那位好國王的兒子佛洛利澤王子在牧羊人住家的附近打獵，看到了帕蒂塔，如今她已成長為一位嫵媚動人的女人。

他和牧羊人做了朋友，可是卻沒有告訴對方自己是王子，只說他叫多瑞克里斯，是位平民士紳。後來又深深愛上了美麗的帕蒂塔，幾乎每天都會來看她。

國王無法理解究竟是什麼原因讓王子幾乎每天離家，於是派人監視他，這才發現波西米亞國王的繼承人已愛上了美麗的牧羊女帕蒂塔。波利克賽尼斯希望了解這段愛情是否是真誠的，於是把自己和忠實的卡密羅假扮起來，一起前往老牧羊人的家。

p. 236 兩人抵達時適逢剪羊毛節的慶典，雖然是陌生人，但卻受到隆重的歡迎，只見眾人不斷地跳著舞，還有一名小販出售緞帶、蕾絲和手套，好讓年輕男孩買來送給他們的心上人。

然而佛洛利澤和帕蒂塔卻無視於這五光十色的場景，只是靜靜地一起談心。

國王注意到帕蒂塔迷人的風采和無人能及的美貌，卻永遠都猜不到她就是老朋友李昂提斯的女兒。

他對卡密羅說：「在綠草地上奔逐的貧賤牧羊女中，她算是最美麗的，雖然出身寒微，但渾身卻散發出勝過她自己家世的味道……或許高貴得和這地方一點也不相襯。」

卡密羅回答：「老實說她可算是畜牧之后呢！」

p. 237 可是當還不認得自己父親的佛洛利澤要求兩位陌生人見證他和這位美麗牧羊女的訂婚典禮時，國王就吐露自己的真實身份，不但禁止了這場婚禮，還說如果她再和佛洛利澤相見就會殺掉她和牧羊人老父，說完就離開他們。

可是卡密羅依然留在原地，因為他已被帕蒂塔深深吸引，且想和她作朋友。

p. 238 長久以來卡密羅一直都知道，李昂提斯是如何為他愚不可及的瘋狂行徑感到懊悔，而且渴望回到西西里探望他的老主人，因此當時就提議這對年輕人不妨到那兒去，要求李昂提斯保護他們。

於是他們出發了，牧羊人也帶著帕蒂卡的珠寶、娃娃服，和別在她披風上的那張紙條同行。

李昂提斯好心地收容了他們，他對佛洛利澤王子很有禮貌，可是所有的目光卻都集中在帕蒂塔身上，他發現她是那麼地像王后赫米歐妮，並且一再說：

「如果當年沒有殘忍地拋棄我女兒，大概她今天也會出落地這般美麗脫俗了。」

p. 239 當老牧羊人一聽到國王曾失去了小女嬰，而且又被遺棄在波西米亞的海岸時，就很篤定地認為，自己所撫養的小孩帕蒂塔一定是國王的女兒。當老牧羊人說出了他所碰到的那段故事，並出示珠寶和紙條時，國王終於意識到帕蒂塔的確就是自己失散多年的孩子，於是滿心喜悅地歡迎她，並獎賞了好心的牧羊人。

波利克賽尼斯曾匆忙追在兒子身後好阻止了他和帕蒂塔的婚事，可是當這位國王發現她就是老友的女兒時，立即十分高興地同意了這門親事。

然而李昂提斯卻快樂不起來，他想起了美麗的王后，此刻她應該站在自己身邊分享他對女兒幸福的喜悅，如今卻慘死在自己的刻薄之下。在觸景傷情下他久久無法言語，只是喃喃說：

「哦，妳的母親！妳的母親！」說完還要求波西米亞國王原諒他。只見李昂提斯一再親吻女兒後，又親了親佛洛利澤王子，同時感謝老牧羊人所付出的一切善心。

p. 240 寶莉娜對已故王后赫米歐妮的善心義舉這些年來一直贏得國王的關照，因此地位始終崇榮，這天她說：

「我有個雕像是由義大利傑出藝術家裘里奧・羅曼諾耗時多年完成的，和已故的王后十分相像，我把它保存在一間單獨的密室中，自從你失去了王后以來，我每天都到那兒兩三回，現在可否請陛下去見見那雕像？」

於是李昂提斯、波利克賽尼斯、佛洛利澤和帕蒂塔、卡密羅，以及他們的隨從們就一起來到寶莉娜的家，那兒有個厚重的紫色簾幕，隔開了一個壁龕，只見寶莉娜把手放在簾幕上說：

「它栩栩如生的樣子真可謂絕世無雙，我確信和王后的近似程度超過你們所看到的任何一樣東西，或人類巧手所能雕琢出的任何事物。因此我把它給單獨地保存著，遠離其他東西，可是它……瞧……真是精雕細琢呀！」

p. 241 說完，她就拉起了簾幕，讓大家看到那座雕像，國王凝視了這座已故愛妻的美麗雕像良久，但什麼話都沒說。

「我喜歡你的沈默，」寶莉娜說：「這更能誇示你的驚奇，請坦白說這像不像她？」

「幾乎就是她本人了，」國王說：「但是寶莉娜，赫米妮歐臉上沒有那麼多皺紋，而且看上去一點也沒它那麼老。」

「哦，並沒有老很多耶！」波利克賽尼斯說。

「呃，」寶莉娜說：「這就是雕刻家高明的地方，能讓我們看到現在的赫米妮歐，要是她還活著的話……」

李昂提斯一動也不動地凝視著這雕像，簡直無法把目光給移開。

p. 242「如果知道這個可憐的影像會激起你這麼多悲傷和愛的話，」寶莉娜說：「我就不會讓你看到它了。」

可是他只回答：「不要放下簾幕！」

「不，不應該看下去了，」寶莉娜說：「否則你會認為它是可以動的。」

「就讓它動吧！就讓它動吧！」國王說：「妳不覺得它在呼吸嗎？」

「我要放下簾幕了，」寶莉娜說：「不然你認為它會馬上成為活人。」

「哦，可愛的寶莉娜，」李昂提斯說：「就讓我在往後的二十年都這麼認為吧！」

「如果你受得了的話，」寶莉娜說：「我還可以讓這雕像動起來，讓它走下來握著你的手，不過這只會讓你以為我在使妖術。」

「不管妳能叫它做些什麼，我都樂於看看。」國王說。

接著，在場所有人都一邊讚美一邊注視著，那座雕像真的從座墊上動了起來，然後走下階梯，用手臂繞著國王的脖子，而國王則端起她的臉並親吻多次，因為這不是雕像，而真的是活生生的王后赫米歐妮本人。

p. 244 原來在寶莉娜的好心幫助下，這些年來她一直隱居著，而且不想讓丈夫發現，儘管她知道他已經懊悔，但卻無法徹底饒恕他，直到獲知自己小女兒的下落。

如今帕蒂塔找到了，她原諒了丈夫所作的一切，對夫妻倆來說，這又像一場全新而美麗的婚姻，他們再度攜手同行了，佛洛利澤和帕蒂塔也成了婚，並一直愉快地生活著。

歷經長期的懊悔和痛苦，李昂提斯終於覺得真愛的雙臂又再度圍繞著自己，對他來說，多年的創痛已在此刻得到美好的報償。

15 無事生非

p. 246 故事開始於某個晴朗的日子，當時西班牙阿拉貢王子唐・佩德婁剛打敗了敵人取得勝利，至於前往什麼地方作戰則記不清了！

總之，在經過一場精疲力竭的大戰後，他感到十分快樂，想要好好玩玩，於是來到梅西那渡個假，隨從中有他的異母兄弟唐・約翰，以及兩位年輕的義大利貴族班奈迪克和柯勞狄歐。

班奈迪克是個生性快活的話匣子，已下定決心打一輩子光棍，不過另一方面，柯勞狄歐才剛踏上梅西那這片土地，就愛上了梅西那總督李奧納多的女兒希蘿。

七月的這一天，一位叫鮑拉齊歐的香水商在李奧納多家一間發霉的屋子裡焚燒乾薰衣草，這時一些對話聲透過開啟的窗戶飄了過來。

p. 247「談談你對希蘿的意見，有話不妨直說。」柯勞狄歐央求著。

「她太矮了，而且又是褐色頭髮，不值得讚美，」班奈迪克回答：「只有改變髮色或身高才行，你真把她給寵壞了。」

「在我眼中，她簡直是普天下最甜美可愛的女人！」柯勞狄歐又說。

「可是在我眼裡卻不是，而且也不需要配戴什麼眼鏡便可瞧出。」班奈迪克回嘴道：「如果把她放在她表姊妹身旁一比，就會發現希蘿已是美人遲暮，簡直就像十二月的最後一天，而對方卻正值青春年華，有如五月的第一天，可是很不幸，她表姊妹碧翠絲是個兇婆娘。」

碧翠絲是李奧納多的外甥女，喜歡以尖酸刻薄的話嘲弄或批評班奈迪克來自娛，班奈迪克叫她做「親愛的傲慢小姐」。

p. 248 在唐・佩德婁來到那兒開始幽默的對談時，柯勞狄歐和班奈迪克仍在交談，「先生們，你們在說什麼悄悄話？」

班奈迪克答道：「我熱切盼望閣下的雍容大度能命我說出。」

「我命你一秉忠誠的心告訴我。」唐．佩德婁風趣地說道。

班奈迪克回道：「柯勞狄歐愛上李奧納多那個五短身材的女兒希蘿了。」

唐．佩德婁聽了很高興，因為他很欣賞希蘿，而且也喜歡柯勞狄歐。於是當班奈迪克離去後，唐．佩德婁就對柯勞狄歐說：

「希望你對希蘿的愛能永遠堅貞不移，我會幫你贏得她芳心的。今晚她父親要辦場化裝舞會，我會假扮你，告訴她你有多麼愛她，如果她也願意的話，我就會找她父親，要求他同意你們共結連理。」

p. 249 然而柯勞狄歐有個表面上稱兄道弟的敵人，也就是唐．佩德婁的異母兄弟唐．約翰，這個壞胚子看見唐．佩德婁比較喜歡柯勞狄歐，不由得妒意大起。

而鮑拉齊歐把他在無意中聽到的那段有趣對白都告訴了唐．約翰。

「看來化裝舞會上有好戲可看了。」當鮑拉齊歐說完之後，唐．約翰回道。

於是在舉行化裝舞會的那天晚上，唐．佩德婁戴起面具假裝成柯勞狄歐，並問李奧納多是否可跟他女兒出去走走。

兩人就這樣相偕離去，而唐．約翰則來到柯勞狄歐面前說：「我想你就是班奈迪克先生吧？」

「正是！」柯勞狄歐撒了個無傷大雅的小謊。

p. 250「如果閣下能夠運用對我兄弟的影響力，來醫治他對希蘿小姐的愛，我一定會感激不盡的，她的身份配不上他。」

「你怎麼知道他愛上了希蘿小姐？」柯勞狄歐問。

「我聽到他以誓言表明自己的愛意。」唐．約翰這樣回答，這時，鮑拉齊歐在旁齊聲附和：「我也聽到了。」

兩個壞蛋說完就揚長而去，把柯勞狄歐一個人留在那兒。柯勞狄歐覺得他的王子背叛了自己。

「再會了，希蘿！」只聽他喃喃自語：「我真是個笨蛋，竟然對這麼一個說客掏心掏肺。」

在此同時，碧翠絲和戴著面具的班奈迪克正神采奕奕的交換意見。

「班奈迪克曾讓你發笑嗎？」她問道。

「誰是班奈迪克？」他問道。

「就是王子身旁的那個弄臣呀！」碧翠絲回答。她的話十分銳利，惹得班奈迪克老大不高興，他事後還這麼宣稱：「即使她擁有伊甸園，我也不會娶她的。」

不過，這場化裝舞會上最主要的演說者既非碧翠絲，也不是班奈迪克，而是唐．佩德婁，只見他完成了計畫，並且帶著李奧納多和希蘿來到柯勞狄歐面前，瞬時之間，柯勞狄歐原本悽慘的臉又恢復了明亮。「柯勞狄歐，你希望什麼時什候上教堂？」佩德婁問。

p. 251「就明天，」柯勞狄歐忙不迭地回答：「在娶希蘿之前真叫我度日如年。」

「給她一個禮拜的時間，親愛的孩子！」李奧納多說，此時柯勞狄歐欣喜若狂，一顆心還砰砰地跳著。

「至於現在嘛，我們還得為班奈迪克先生找個妻子，」和藹可親的唐．佩德婁說：「不過這卻是只有天神海克力斯才能達成的使命。」

「我會幫助你的，」李奧納多說：「只是必須連續十個晚上不眠不休才行。」

接著希蘿又說：「殿下，我會竭盡所能去幫碧翠絲找個好丈夫。」

鮑拉齊歐為了鼓舞懊喪的唐．約翰，就在他面前獻出一計：鮑拉齊歐有信心說服柯勞狄歐和唐．佩德婁，好讓兩人相信希蘿是個腳踏兩條船的女孩，用情不專。唐．約翰同意了這個惡毒的奸計。

p. 250 另一方面，唐・佩德婁則想出了一個愛的計畫，於是對李奧納多說：「如果我們在談話中假裝班奈迪克正渴慕碧翠絲的愛，並趁著她走近時故意讓她聽到，那麼碧翠絲就會同情班奈迪克，看到他好的一面，愛上他。然後趁著班奈迪克在旁邊時假裝不知道他在偷聽，說什麼美麗的碧翠絲竟然愛上像他這麼一個無情又愛嘲弄別人的傢伙，真是件大不幸……這樣不出一個禮拜，他一定會跪在她面前的。」

於是，這一天，當班奈迪克在一座涼亭裡看書時，柯勞狄歐就故意和李奧納多坐在外面，然後有意無意地說：「你女兒告訴我碧翠絲寫了封信。」

「她晚上總會起來個二十次，寫些只有上帝才知道的玩意兒，不過有一次希蘿瞧到信紙上寫著『班奈迪克和碧翠絲』，然後又看到碧翠絲把它給撕掉。」李奧納多驚呼道。

柯勞狄歐順勢說：「希蘿告訴我，碧翠絲曾叫喊『噢，班奈迪克甜心！』」

p. 253 這個不大可能發生的事深深觸動了班奈迪克，只是他實在難以相信，他自言自語道：「她美麗又善良，我不能那麼高傲，我覺得我愛她，當然人們會取笑我，但言語上的攻擊又傷不了我。」

這時碧翠絲也來到了涼亭，她說道：「我原本不想來的，但還是勉為其難地過來告訴你一聲，晚餐已經準備好了。」

「美麗的碧翠絲，謝謝妳，」班奈迪克說。

「看來向我道聲謝所帶給你的痛苦，比起到這兒來所帶給我的痛苦只會多不會少。」碧翠絲有意用這句回答來潑他冷水。

不過班奈迪克不但沒有感到被潑到冷水，心裡頭反而覺得暖暖的，他推論出，她講話這麼粗魯，正代表著她很高興能來叫他。

p. 254 另一方面，承擔溶化碧翠絲芳心這項任務的希蘿，也順利找到了一個時機，這天她對女僕瑪格麗特說：「趕快到客廳去悄悄告訴碧翠絲，就說我和烏蘇拉正在果園裡談著她的事。」

希蘿篤定地認為，只要這樣說，碧翠絲一定會跑來偷聽個究竟，這就好像是兩位表姊妹事先約好要來你說我聽那樣地確定。

果園裡有處樹蔭，忍冬樹隔開了豔陽，瑪格麗特出去辦這差事沒多久，碧翠絲就進來了。

p. 255「可是妳確定嗎，」希蘿的女侍烏蘇拉問：「班奈迪克真的一心一意愛著碧翠絲？」

「王子和我未婚夫也這麼說。」希蘿回答：「他們希望我告訴她，可是我卻這麼說：『不！這得靠班奈迪克自己去克服萬難。』」

「為什麼妳要這麼說？」

「還不是因為碧翠絲太狂傲了嘛，她目中無人，根本不屑去愛別人。我才不想看到她去嘲弄可憐的班奈迪克，我還寧願班奈迪克的熱情趕快消退。」

「我不同意妳的說法，」烏蘇拉說：「我認為妳的表姊妹慧眼獨具，不會看不到班奈迪克的優點的。」

「說實在的，除了柯勞狄歐之外，在義大利就算他最有男子氣概了。」希蘿說。

接著這兩人就離開了果園，碧翠絲興奮極了，人也變得溫柔起來，在步出涼亭時還對自己說：「可憐又可愛的班奈迪克，為什麼不老實跟我講呢？你的愛會馴服我這顆狂野的心的。」

p. 256 現在我們再把話題轉回到那個惡毒的計畫上。

商妥柯勞狄歐婚事的前一天晚上，唐．約翰進入唐．佩德婁和柯勞狄歐正在談話的那間屋子，並問柯勞狄歐是否打算在明天成婚。

「你也知道他很想結這個婚囉！」唐．佩德婁說。

「他或許可以知道些不一樣的事，」唐．約翰說：「只要跟我來，我就會讓他看到。」

於是他們就跟著他進入花園，看到一位女孩斜倚在希蘿的窗戶，和鮑拉齊歐談情說愛。

柯勞狄歐認為這女孩就是希蘿，於是說：「明天我會為這件事當眾羞辱她。」唐．佩德婁也認為她就是希蘿。可是這女孩並非希蘿，而是瑪格麗特。

當柯勞狄歐和唐．佩德婁離開花園時，只見唐．約翰低聲輕笑了起來，他賞給鮑拉齊歐一個錢包，裡面裝了一千個硬幣。

這筆不義之財讓鮑拉齊歐遍體舒暢，所以當他和朋友康拉德走在街上時，就誇耀起自己的財富和撒錢的人來，並且把他所幹的勾當都說了出來。

p. 257 一位守夜人在無意中聽到他們的談話，心想幹了壞事竟能得到一千硬幣的報酬，把這人給收押起來就一定沒錯，於是立刻逮捕了鮑拉齊歐和康拉德，當晚他倆就在牢中熬過漫漫長夜。

第二天還沒正午，梅西那有一半的貴族都來到了教堂，這是希蘿大喜的日子，只見她身著婚紗喜形於色來到那兒，美麗的臉蛋看不到一絲罩頂的烏雲，眉宇間還散發出坦率而明亮的神色，主持婚禮的神職人員為修道士法蘭西斯。

修道士轉身面對柯勞狄歐說：「到這兒來，閣下，你願意娶這位女士嗎？」

「不！」柯勞狄歐表示異議。

李奧納多認為他是在說些俏皮話以娛眾嘉賓，於是對法蘭西斯說：「修道士，你應該這麼說，『請來這兒把她給娶回家。』」

修道士法蘭西斯又轉向希蘿問：「女士，到這兒來，妳願意嫁給這位伯爵嗎？」

「我願意。」希蘿回答。

p. 258「你們兩人要是有哪一方有所猶豫，請直言無諱。」修道士說。

「妳有嗎？希蘿！」柯勞狄歐問。

「沒有。」她說。

「那你有嗎，伯爵？」修道士又問。

「我敢替他回答『絕沒有！』」李奧納多搶先說。

柯勞狄歐痛苦地大叫：「哦！沒有一個人敢這樣說，神父！」說完又繼續問李奧納多：「你會把令嬡交給我嗎？」

「悉聽尊便，」李奧納多回答：「就像上帝把她交給我一樣。」

「那我能回報你什麼？」柯勞狄歐問：「有什麼禮物能夠與之相比？」

「沒有，」唐・佩德婁說：「除非你退還給贈送者。」

「好心的王子，幸虧有您教導我，」柯勞狄歐說：「那拿去吧，李奧納多，把她給帶回去。」這些殘忍話就從柯勞狄歐、唐・佩德婁和唐・約翰那兒脫口而出。

p. 259 教堂霎時變得不再神聖莊嚴，只見希蘿儘可能的替自己解釋，然後昏了過去。

最後除了希蘿的父親以外，所有迫害她的人都離開了教堂，而那些對他女兒的指控，也讓李奧納多飽受嘲弄，人們大叫：「把她帶走，讓她去死吧！」

然而修道士法蘭西斯目光銳利，可以查探出靈魂的善惡，因此看出希蘿是不該蒙受這些指責的。

「她是無辜的，」他說：「有一千個徵候這麼告訴我。」

在他善心的凝視下，希蘿甦醒了過來。原先陷入慌亂且暴跳如雷的父親，這才知道事情不是他想的那樣。這時修道士說：「他們撇下了希蘿不管，任由她一個人羞愧而死，現在在真相揭露之前，我們就假裝她真的死了，那些造謠者一定會轉而痛悔自責的。」

「修道士的建議很好。」班奈迪克說。

p. 260 接著希蘿就被帶往一間休養所。這時教堂只留下碧翠絲和班奈迪克。

班奈迪克知道碧翠絲哭得很難過、很久了，於是說：「我相信妳那美麗的表姊妹一定受到了委屈。」

碧翠絲仍悲泣著。

「這不是很奇怪嗎，」班奈迪克忽然柔聲說：「除了妳之外，這世上再也沒有我愛的東西了？」

「我也會說，對你的愛已超過世間萬物，」碧翠絲說：「但我為我表姊妹的遭遇感到很難過，所以沒有心情說這些。」

「告訴我，該為她做些什麼事？」班奈迪克說。

「殺了柯勞狄歐！」

「啊！世界這麼大，何苦呢！」班奈迪克說。

「你的拒絕，等於殺了我，」碧翠絲說：「再見！」

「夠了！既然這麼說，我會向他挑戰的。」班奈迪克狂喊。

p. 261 現在再把場景拉回，當鮑拉齊歐和康拉德還關在獄中時，由一個叫杜拜瑞的治安官審問。

那名守夜人提出了證據，大意是説鮑拉齊歐曾表示他因為密謀對付希蘿而收到一千個硬幣。

在審訊時，李奧納多雖然沒有在現場，但還是徹頭徹尾地相信希蘿的清白，另一方面，他也把自己那個痛失愛女的父親角色扮演得入木三分，後來當唐·佩德婁和柯勞狄歐前來友善的拜訪他時，就對那位義大利人説：「你誹謗了我的孩子，讓她羞憤而死，所以現在我要向你挑戰，咱們比劃比劃吧！」

「我不能跟一個老人家對打。」柯勞狄歐説。

「那你就能讓一個女孩白白送命？」李奧納多冷笑道，而柯勞狄歐則滿臉羞紅。

p. 262 在雙方一陣唇槍舌戰後，李奧納多負氣離開房間，唐·佩德婁和柯勞狄歐的心裡都覺得一陣刺痛，這時班奈迪克進來了。

柯勞狄歐説：「看來那個老頭子氣得想要把我的鼻子給咬斷。」

「你真是個惡棍！」班奈迪克不耐煩地説：「快和我打一場，時間和武器都由你挑，否則我會叫你懦夫。」

柯勞狄歐一愣，説道：「我會和你交手的，還沒有人説我不能把一個二楞子的腦袋給剁下來。」

班奈迪克笑著，此時已到了唐·佩德婁接見官員的時刻，只見王子坐在一張有踏腳墊的椅子，整理好思緒準備裁決。不久門開啟了，杜拜瑞和人犯們獲准進入。

「你們告發了這些人什麼罪？」唐·佩德婁説。

p. 263 這時鮑拉齊歐全招了，他感到很痛快。他把整個過錯都歸咎到落跑的唐·約翰身上，他説：「希蘿小姐已經死了，除了接受謀殺犯所應得的懲罰外，我別無他求。」

在旁聆聽的柯勞狄歐陷入極度痛苦，並且深感後悔，見到李奧納多又進來屋內，就對他說：「這奴隸澄清了令嫒的清白，閣下要怎樣向我報復，都悉聽尊便。」

唐．佩德婁也很低姿態地說：「李奧納多，我也隨你處置了。」

「我要求兩位聲明我女兒是清白的，並在墳前歌頌以榮耀她。至於你呢，柯勞狄歐，我還有話對你說，我兄弟有個女兒很像希蘿，可說是她的翻版，如果娶了她，我復仇的意念才會平息。」

柯勞狄歐說：「高貴的閣下，我是屬於您的，任您差遣。」

p. 264 接著柯勞狄歐就回到他的房間，譜出了一首莊嚴的曲子，然後偕同唐．佩德婁及其隨從們一起來到教堂，在李奧納多家族的紀念碑前獻唱。

當結束時，柯勞狄歐又說：「晚安，希蘿，以後我每年都會這麼做。」

莊嚴肅穆的他此時已成了心為希蘿所屬的謙和紳士，並準備娶一個他不愛的女孩。柯勞狄歐被告知要在李奧納多的家中見那女孩，他打算忠實地履行約定。

他被引進一個房間，李奧納多的兄弟安東尼奧和若干蒙面的女孩也跟隨著他走進去。只見修道士法蘭西斯、李奧納多和班奈迪克已在那兒候駕，這時安東尼奧領著一位女孩走向柯勞狄歐。

年輕人說：「甜心，讓我看看妳的臉。」

「先要發誓娶她才行。」李奧納多說。

「把手給我，」柯勞狄歐對那女孩說：「在聖潔的修道士面前發誓，如果願意成為我妻子，我一定會娶妳的。」

「我還活著的時候就是你妻子了。」女孩脫下了她的面具。

p. 266 「真是另一個希蘿！」柯勞狄歐驚呼。

「只要造謠中傷還未平息，」李奧納多解釋：「希蘿就活不下來。」

接著修道士就要替這對已經和解的新人進行結婚儀式，可是班奈迪克突然打斷了他，「等等！修道士，這些女孩之中哪一位是碧翠絲？」

於是碧翠絲卸下了面具，班奈迪克順勢說：「妳愛我嗎？」

「普通而已，」沒想到回答竟是這樣，「那你愛我嗎？」

「普普通通，」班奈迪克答道。

「有人告訴我，你為了思念我幾乎快死了。」碧翠絲說。

「別人也告訴我同樣的話，妳為我憔悴得差點和死神相會。」班奈迪克回嘴。

「這是你親筆寫的，足以證明妳的愛。」柯勞狄歐邊說邊亮出班奈迪克寫給心上人的一首十四行詩。

「這兒也有呢！」希蘿說：「這是給班奈迪克的禮物，是我從碧翠絲的包包裡拿到的。」

「真是個奇蹟，」班奈迪克驚呼：「我們怎麼心口不一呢，來！我要娶妳，碧翠絲。」

「為了救你一命，就讓你做我丈夫吧！」碧翠絲回答。

於是班奈迪克吻了她，修道士在主持完柯勞狄歐和希蘿的婚禮後，就順勢宣布他倆結為夫妻。

p. 268「已婚的班奈迪克，你覺得如何？」唐．佩德婁問。

「真是太快樂了，以至於讓我忘記了憂傷。」班奈迪克回答：「不管開什麼玩笑都無妨，至於你，柯勞狄歐，過去真希望永遠追隨著閣下，可是如今你已是我連襟了，就和碧翠絲的表姊妹終生廝守並永遠愛她吧！」

「直到今天我都喜歡用棍棒追著你打，班奈迪克，你真欠揍！」柯勞狄歐說，可是班奈迪克用話打斷了他：「來，來，讓我們跳舞吧！」

於是他們就跳起了舞，沒有一件事可以讓這兩對快樂的戀人停下飛舞的腳步，即時這時候傳來了唐．約翰被捕的消息（儘管對無法得逞的壞蛋施懲也並不是什麼好事）。

16 一報還一報

p. 270 許多世紀之前，維也納在位的公爵維辛提奧秉性善良，不願意看到子民因違法而陷入哀悽，因此以寬大為懷的作風統治該地。

所帶來的影響就是當他的首席大臣拿一份違法亂紀者的名單給他看後，維辛提奧才知道名單上的維也納人多得足以讓他大搖其頭。

p. 271 因此公爵決定凡是做錯事的人都必須接受處罰，可是他又珍惜自己的聲望，知道如果在紀律鬆散後突然嚴明起來，就會遭惹民怨，使得人民都會叫他暴君。為了這個理由維辛提奧告訴樞密院，說他必須前往波蘭處理重要的國家大事。

「我已經選擇安哲魯在我離開時治理維也納。」他說。

現在再談談安哲魯，雖然他看起來一副高貴的樣子，但實際上卻是個卑鄙的傢伙。

p. 272 他曾答應要娶一個叫做瑪麗安娜的女孩，但後來卻因為她的嫁妝弄丟了而對她不理不睬。

於是可憐的瑪麗安娜無助地活著，每天都等待著吝嗇愛人的腳步，並且依舊愛著他。

在任命安哲魯代理職權後，公爵就找上一個名叫湯瑪斯的化緣修士，要求對方拿一套化緣修士的服裝，再指導他如何發揮宗教諮商的技巧，因為他根本無意前往波蘭，而是想留在當地看看安哲魯的政績。

安哲魯在位還不到一天，就以一個叫柯勞狄歐的年青人有魯莽自私的行為而判他死罪，在當時，這種犯行只會懲以嚴厲的申斥。

p. 274 柯勞狄歐有個神經大條的朋友叫做路西歐，這朋友發現有個機會可以讓柯勞狄歐重獲自由，只要柯勞狄歐那位美麗的姊妹伊莎貝拉向安哲魯懇求即可。

當時伊莎貝拉正住在一家女修道院，沒有一個人曾贏得她的芳心，而且她也認為自己會希望成為一位修女，在這其間柯勞狄歐則不乏擁護者。

年老的貴族伊斯卡魯斯要求安哲魯寬大為懷，「稍加責打以示薄懲即可，不必造成殺戮，」他說：「更何況這位紳士還有位最高貴的父親。」

可是安哲魯對此仍無動於衷，並且心想：「即使只有十二個人判我有罪，我也不會要求法外開恩。」

安哲魯後來下命令給典獄長，要讓他在第二天上午九點看到柯勞狄歐被行刑。

p. 275 在這道命令發布後有人告訴安哲魯，該死囚的姊妹想要見他。

「請她進來！」安哲魯說。

這名美麗的女孩和路西歐一同進入，然後說：「我以哀悽的心情向閣下請願。」

「哦？」安哲魯說。

安哲魯冷酷的話讓她一陣羞紅，益增她容顏的豔麗，「我有個兄弟被判了死刑，」她繼續說：「我譴責錯誤，可是求求你赦免我兄弟。」

安哲魯說：「每一個過錯在犯下之前就已受到譴責了，錯誤無法忍受，如果犯錯者得到自由，正義將無從伸張。」

此時要不是路西歐對她附耳說道：「妳表情太冷淡了，即使向人討一根針也得說得更溫順些才行啊！」伊莎貝拉一定扭頭就走。

p. 276 接著她再次對安哲魯展開溫情攻勢，雖然安哲魯表明不會原諒她兄弟時，伊莎貝拉仍毫不沮喪，後來安哲魯又說：「現在為時已遲，他一定會被行刑的。」她才回復言詞攻擊。雖然她這一切的拼搏都是有道理的，可是仍未能讓伊莎貝拉對這名公爵的職務代理人佔有優勢。

她告訴他，世上沒有一樣東西能像慈悲一樣產生這麼大的威力，人性會接受並需要來自於上帝的仁慈，具有無與倫比的力量是椿美事，但也得像一名大力士那樣妥於運用它。

接著伊莎貝拉又告訴安哲魯，雷電會劈裂高大的橡樹以救助柔弱的桃金孃。她要求他不妨先看看自己的內心是否有瑕疵，只要找到其中一項就要節制自己，以避免做出反對她兄弟活下去的論點。

p. 277 這時，安哲魯貪戀起伊莎貝拉的美色，為了她的美貌，安哲魯已不顧一切的要去做玷辱人性之愛的事。於是他故作憐憫地說：「明天正午之前來找我。」

至少，她已成功地延長兄弟幾小時的生命。

當伊莎貝拉離開後，安哲魯的良知立刻指責他怠忽了自己在司法判決上的職責。

當伊莎貝拉第二次探訪他時，安哲魯就說：「妳的兄弟是無法活下去了。」

伊莎貝拉一陣晴天霹靂，心中痛苦極了，不過嘴裡只說：「即使如此，也願上帝能維持你的榮耀。」

可是當她轉身要走時，安哲魯突然覺得相較於失去她，職責與榮耀竟顯得是那麼微不足道。

p. 278「只要把妳的愛給我，」他說道：「柯勞狄歐就會得到自由。」

伊莎貝拉則說：「在我嫁給你之前，即使他有二十個腦袋放在斷頭臺上也應該一死。」她終於認清安哲魯並不像他外表所假裝的那樣大公無私。

於是她來到獄中找柯勞狄歐，告知他必須一死。

起初他還說大話，並答應自己會緊緊擁抱死亡的黑暗，可是當他充分明白伊莎貝拉可以嫁給安哲魯以換取自己的生命時，就覺得自己的生命要比伊莎貝拉的快樂更重要，於是就呼喊：「親愛的姊妹，讓我活下去吧！」

「你這沒有信心的懦夫！你這不誠實的卑鄙傢伙！」她喊道。

就在這時穿著修士衣服的公爵來了，要求和伊莎貝拉談談，他自稱為化緣修士羅鐸維克。

p. 279 公爵告訴她，安哲魯曾和瑪麗安娜訂過婚，並對他倆愛的故事做了一番敘述。然後公爵就要求伊莎貝拉考慮他的計畫，讓瑪麗安娜穿著伊莎貝拉的衣服，把臉用面紗緊緊遮住然後去找安哲魯，並模仿伊莎貝拉的聲音說，只要柯勞狄歐獲得饒恕就會嫁給他。當然還得讓瑪麗安娜趁機取下安哲魯小指上的戒指，這樣事後就可以證實他的訪客的確是瑪麗安娜。

化緣修士就像男人中的修女，伊莎貝拉當然對他們有無比的尊敬，於是同意了公爵的計畫，不久他們就在以壕溝圍成的一處農莊那兒，也就是瑪麗安娜的家再度聚首。

p. 280 在大街上公爵看到路西歐，而路西歐瞧見一個穿著像是化緣修士的男人走來，就高聲叫：「修士，有公爵的消息嗎？」

「沒有耶！」公爵說。

路西歐告訴公爵一些有關安哲魯的事，接著又說了一件有關公爵的事。

公爵提出反駁，路西歐就怒指公爵為「一個膚淺又不學無術的笨蛋」，只是外表仍裝著愛他。

「如果我能夠活著把你的話報告給公爵，那麼他一定會更加的認識你。」公爵嚴肅地說。

接著公爵又在街上看到伊斯卡魯斯，於是詢問對方覺得公爵到底是個什麼樣的人。伊斯卡魯斯還認為自己是在對一位化緣修士說話，於是就回答：「公爵是個十分溫和的紳士，寧願見到他人快樂也不願獨自快活。」

說完公爵就繼續拜訪瑪麗安娜。

伊莎貝拉也隨後趕到，公爵就介紹兩位女孩互相認識，此時，她們還都認為他是化緣修士。

除了公爵之外，兩個女孩這時來到一個房間，討論拯救柯勞狄歐的事宜，當她們以低沈且誠摯的語調談話時，公爵就透過窗戶往外瞧，看到了破損的棚子和黑漆漆又長著苔蘚的花壇。很顯然，遭到男友背叛的瑪麗安娜對自己在鄉下的住所已漠不關心。

p. 281 有些婦女會美化她們的庭園，可是卻不包括瑪麗安娜在內。看來她久居城市，忽略了鄉下的樂趣，因此公爵確信，安哲魯不會讓她更不快活的。

「我們都同意了，神父。」當伊莎貝拉偕同瑪麗安娜出來時說道。

就這樣，安哲魯被他所忘掉的那個女孩矇蔽了，並把自己的戒指戴到對方手指上，只見那戒指上鑲了顆乳白色的寶石，可以在光亮下閃耀著神秘的色彩。

p. 282 聽到她事成後，公爵就在第二天來到獄中，準備聽聽釋放柯勞狄歐的那道命令。不過公爵在等待時卻發現，等到的不是那道命令，而是一封被繩子捆好並打算呈給典獄長的信。

當典獄長大聲唸出其中的字句時，公爵不由得大驚，只見內容是這樣寫的：「不管你聽到什麼矛盾的話，都得在鐘跑到四點時處死柯勞狄歐，並在五點把他的項上人頭交到我這兒來。」

可是公爵對典獄長說：「你一定要向代理公爵職位的安哲魯出示另一顆人頭。」接著又拿出一封信和一個圖章，然後說：「這兒是公爵的手書和印信，他就要回來了，我只告訴你，安哲魯並不知道，現在就把另一個人頭給安哲魯。」

典獄長心想：「這名化緣修士講起話來很有權威，更何況我又認得公爵的圖章和筆跡。」

典獄長又鉅細靡遺地說：「今天上午監獄裡死了一個人，他是個海盜，年紀和柯勞狄歐相近，而且鬍子顏色也相同，我就把他的腦袋給呈上去。」

於是這個海盜的腦袋就準時出示於安哲魯，而安哲魯則被這個酷似柯勞狄歐的東西給矇騙了。

公爵回來的消息大受民眾歡迎，維也納的公民們都把城門從鉸鏈那兒移開，好協助他順利進入維也納。安哲魯和伊斯卡魯斯準時現身，並且都由於在公爵出國時協助處理公務而大受讚揚。

p. 283 因此，當伊莎貝拉被安哲魯的不忠所惹惱而跪在公爵面前乞求正義時，安哲魯的不快是可想而知。

在伊莎貝拉敘述自己的遭遇時，公爵不禁呼喊：「竟然有人帶她進入監獄，還公然侮辱我的左右手！等等，是誰說服你來這兒的？」

「是化緣修士羅鐸維克。」她說。

「有誰認識他？」公爵問。

「我認識，大人，」路西歐回答：「我曾揍過他，因為這人出言不遜，有負您的大恩大德。」

p. 284 一名叫彼得的修道士這時說：「羅鐸維克修士是個聖人。」

這時一名官員帶走伊莎貝拉，而瑪麗安娜則走上前來，卸下她的面紗，對安哲魯說：「這就是你曾一度發誓值得好好端詳的那張臉。」

當她伸出手說「你想把戒指送給別人，但最後卻戴在這隻手上」時，他終於勇敢地面對她。

「我知道這個女人，」安哲魯說：「我倆曾一度論及婚嫁，可是我發現她十分輕佻。」

瑪麗安娜衝口說出，他們曾在最強烈的海誓山盟下訂了婚，安哲魯的回應則是要求公爵一定要找出羅鐸維克修士這個人來。

「他會現身的。」公爵答應道，並吩咐伊斯卡魯斯在他離開後徹底盤問這名行蹤不明的證人。

不久扮演羅鐸維克修士的公爵就再度現身，並由伊莎貝拉和典獄長陪同。

p. 285 伊斯卡魯斯盤問沒多久，就發現他並不是個會誹謗別人並帶來威脅的人，另外路西歐由於曾把公爵叫做笨蛋和懦夫，還說要揪下公爵的鼻子以懲罰他的傲慢，所以這時也要求羅鐸維克替自己開脫。

「到監獄的就是他，」伊斯卡魯斯突然驚呼，可是當幾雙手才按住公爵，他就立刻脫掉修道士的頭巾，以公爵的身份出現在所有人面前。

「現在，」他對安哲魯說：「如果你還有任何傲慢可供差遣，那就讓它產生作用以發揮其所有價值。」

「我只乞求立刻審判並把我處死。」安哲魯回答。

「你不是和瑪麗安娜訂過婚嗎？」公爵問。

「是的！」安哲魯說。

「那就立刻娶她，」安哲魯的主人說完就吩咐彼得修士：「替他們成婚，然後和他們一起回到這兒。」

「到這兒來，伊莎貝拉，」公爵柔聲說：「妳的修道士如今成為妳的王子了，他想拯救你的兄弟，可是讓人難過的是為時已遲。」可是淘氣的公爵心裡清楚得很，他已經救了柯勞狄歐。

p. 286「哦！請原諒，」她喊道：「我竟然利用一國之君解決自己的麻煩。」

「你已獲得原諒。」他興高采烈地說。

就在這時安哲魯和他的妻子再度進來，公爵嚴肅地說：「安哲魯，我們就判你在柯勞狄歐送掉腦袋的斷頭台上受刑！」

「哦，我最仁慈的大王，」瑪麗安娜喊道：「不要愚弄我！」

「你會換得到一位更好的丈夫。」公爵說。

「哦，我親愛的大王，」她說：「我不想要什麼更好的男人。」

高貴的伊莎貝拉這時挺身而出，和瑪麗安娜一起乞求，可是公爵仍假裝不為所動。

「典獄長，」他說：「柯勞狄歐為什麼會在一個不尋常的時刻被判處死刑？」

典獄長害怕供出他欺騙安哲魯的謊言，於是說：「我曾私底下接到個訊息。」

「你被免職了。」公爵說，典獄長於是離開。

p. 287 安哲魯說：「我很抱歉引發這些不幸的事，現在寧願一死以求你的憐憫。」

不久群眾之中即出現一陣騷動，原來典獄長又偕同柯勞狄歐再度現身，典獄長像個大孩子似的說：「我救了這個人，他很像柯勞狄歐。」

公爵很開心，並對伊莎貝拉說：「因為他很像你兄弟，所以我原諒了他。親愛的伊莎貝拉，如果你是屬於我的話，他也會像我的兄弟。」

她嫣然一笑，算是答應公爵的要求，公爵接著原諒了安哲魯，並獎勵典獄長。

至於路西歐則被判娶了一個舌頭很毒的矮胖女人。

莎翁作品佳言錄

p. 288 Action 行動

行動勝於雄辯，老百姓的眼睛要比他們的耳朵還要精明。
(Coriolanus: III. 2.)

Adversity 逆境

逆境也是有好處的，
就像其貌不揚又有毒的癩蛤蟆，
腦袋上卻頂著顆價值連城的珠寶。
(As You Like It: II. 1.)

為謀利才前來投效的人，
會拘泥於虛禮和身段，
但一下雨就要捲舖蓋走人，
把你給撇在暴風雨裡。
(King Lear: II. 4.)

唉！花費無數鈔票才買到人家的這聲讚美，
一旦錢財散盡，就會隨之消失。
酒肉朋友來得快，去得也快；冬天的烏雲一出現，蒼蠅即銷聲匿跡。
(Timon of Athens: II. 2.)

Advice to A Son Leaving Home
寫給離家遠行的孩子

不要一想到什麼就脫口而出，
凡事務必三思而後行。
與人為善，但不可流於粗鄙。
相知已久的好友，就用鋼箍緊扣在靈魂上；
但切不可濫結每個泛泛之交，
小心，避免與人紛爭，可是萬一爭端已起，
就應該讓對方知道自己是不可輕侮的。
傾聽每個人的觀點，可是只對極少數人發表自己的高見，
接受每個人的批評，可是卻要保留自己的判斷。
在衡量自己的荷包下不妨多購置華服，
但不可標新立異，可以高貴有品味，但不可流於俗豔，
因為服裝往往可以表現出自己的格調，
像法國的名流仕紳，就在這點上顯得最為出類拔萃和慷慨大度。
不要向人告貸，也不可把錢借與他人，
否則錢借了出去往往會賠了本錢，而且還失去朋友，
至於向人告貸則容易養成因循怠惰的惡習。
最最重要的是，必須忠於自己；
正像有了白晝才有黑夜一樣，對自己忠實，才不會欺詐別人。
(Hamlet: I. 3.)

p. 289 Age 歲月

我的人生旅程已邁入凋零，化做黃葉；
即使歲月催人老，也應當與高齡相伴，
尊寵、惠愛、恭順、友眾——不可以指望擁有這些，
但卻可代之以……
悄然而深沈的憤怒，
和徒託空言的尊敬——那貧困者寧可不說但卻不敢不說的空話。
(Macbeth: V. 3.)

Ambition 野心

野心是那麼虛浮的東西，所以我認為它不過是幻影中的幻影。
(Hamlet— II 2.)

我囑咐你，放棄野心，
為了這項罪惡，天使都墮落了，那麼，
造物者依自己形象所創造出來的人類，
又如何能希望憑藉野心而贏得勝利？
要懂得珍惜恨你的人，最後才愛自己，
腐化不可能比誠實贏得更多，
永遠都要用右手遞出和平的橄欖枝，
去撫慰嫉妒的口舌，要公正無畏，
立身行事的目的是為了國家、上帝和真理。
(King Henry VIII.—III. 2.)

Anger 憤怒

怒火像匹烈馬，如不加駕馭就會精疲力竭。
(King Henry VIII.—I. 1.)

Arrogance 傲慢

有一種人臉上會裝出一副心如止水的樣子，故意緘默不語，為的是得到智慧、嚴謹及思想博大精深的美名，好像他因此便可以說：「我乃聖經，說的話都是金玉良言，只要一啟雙唇連狗都不准在旁亂吠！」
啊！我的安東尼奧，我曉得這樣的人，只因為閉口不言而得到聰明的美譽；可是他們一旦開口，那我敢斷言，聽到的人都會罵他們傻瓜，並認為污染了自己的雙耳。
(The Merchant of Venice: I. 1.)

p. 289 Authority 權力

你見過農夫飼養的狗向乞丐唁唁而吠，乞丐就立刻飛奔躲狗嗎？
在這種地方你便可看出權勢的表徵，狗仗人勢，
即使在權位中的狗也可以叫人俯首舔耳。
(King Lear: IV. 6.)

世上的大人物如果都能像天神一樣讓雷電交作，
那麼天神將永遠得不到寧靜，
因為到時候每個芝麻綠豆大的官員都會耀武揚威，
讓天空中只聽見雷電聲……上天是慈悲的，
寧願把雷霆萬鈞的火力用去劈碎一棵枝繁葉茂又壯碩無比的橡樹，
也不願去損傷嬌柔的鬱金香……可是人類啊！傲慢的人類！
哪怕只掌握一丁點短暫的權力，
便忘了自己如琉璃般易碎的原本面目，而像隻盛怒的潑猴，
在上帝面前做出種種醜態，使得天使們也因為憐憫他們的痴愚而垂淚。
(Measure for Measure: II. 2.)

Beauty 美貌

造物者的手使得你美，同時也使得你善，
有了美而不重視善，那美也不得長久，
在我們整個人的結構中，美德是其中的靈魂，
可以使肉體維持永恆的美。
(Measure for Measure: III. 1.)

Blessings Undervalued
珍惜手上所擁有的

事情總是這樣的：
在享用自己已經到手的東西時往往對它不屑一顧，
但是一旦少了它或弄丟了，
就會誇大其價值，同時也會發現過去在享用時所看不出來的好處。
(Much Ado About Nothing: IV. 1.)

Braggarts 吹噓

每一個愛說大話的人，
到頭來都會被人發現是頭蠢驢。
(All's Well that Ends Well—IV.3.)

他們有獅子的吼聲和熊的舉止，難道不算是怪物嗎？
(Troilus and Cressida: III. 2.)

Calumny 誹謗

任憑你像冰一樣堅貞，像雪一樣純潔，還是逃不過讒人的誹謗。
(Hamlet: III. 1.)

人們的任何權力和尊榮都逃不過他人的譏讒，
哪個強而有力的君王可以讓最純潔的德行免除背後的中傷？
(Measure for Measure: III. 2.)

p. 290 Ceremony 禮節

一切禮節都是為了文飾那些虛矯的行為、
言不由衷的歡迎和出爾反爾的殷勤而設立的，
但如果有真正的友誼，這些身段就通通不再需要了。
(Timon of Athens: I. 2.)

Comfort 撫慰

人們自己沒有感受到悲苦才能夠寬慰他人，一旦親身體嚐到悲苦的滋味，
他們的勸誡就會轉化為激情。在這之前他們曾用格言療治激憤，
用一根根銀線束縛瘋狂、用空話來迷惑痛楚。
不！不！誰都會勸慰一個在悲哀的重擔下輾轉呻吟的人，
可是誰也沒有那樣鎮定自持的修為和勇氣，能夠叫自己忍受同樣的痛苦。
(Much Ado About Nothing: V. 1.)
每個人都能療傷止痛——只要傷痛沒有襲向他們自己
(Much Ado About Nothing: V. 1.)

Comparison 比較

月光照耀大地的時候，我們便看不見燭火，
所以較大的榮耀也能掩蓋較小的，
代替國王的人會和國王同樣耀眼，直到真的國王出現，
那時他的威嚴便頓時消逝，猶如開啟的溪河注入汪洋大海。
(Merchant of Venice: V. 1.)

Conscience 良心

正是這種重重顧慮使我們全變成了懦夫，
決心的赤熱光彩被審慎思維蒙上灰暗的陰影，
本可以敢作敢為的大幹一番，
也為了這緣故而偃旗息鼓，失去了行動的意義。
(Hamlet: III. 1.)

p. 291 Content 滿足

我的皇冠是在自己心中，而不是在頭頂上，
它沒有飾之以鑽石和印度寶石，也沒人看得見，
我的皇冠叫做「滿足」，只是鮮少有國王會喜歡這種皇冠的。
(King Henry VI., Part 3rd: III. 1.)

Contention 爭論

一個屋簷下的許多人若令出多門，
又如何能夠融洽共處呢？
(King Lear: II. 4.)

當兩個威權互爭雄長時，是不會有任何一方勝出的，
而且毀滅很快的就會趁虛而入，
利用一方去打擊另外一方。
(Coriolanus: III. 1.)

Contentment 知足

出身寒微並且平平安安的與貧賤人士為伍，
要比身著錦繡、頭戴金冠但卻滿懷悲愴好得多。
(King Henry VIII.: II. 3.)

Cowards 怯懦

懦夫在真正步入死亡之前，就已經死過好多次了，
可是英雄豪傑一生中只死一次。(Julius Caesar: II. 2.)

Custom 習慣

習慣雖然是個可以使人失去羞恥的魔鬼，但也可以做個天使，
對於勉強向善的人，它會用潛移默化的手段讓他去惡從善。
要是今晚加以抑制，下一回就會覺得這種自制的功夫並不太難，
慢慢即可習以為常了。因為習慣簡直有種改變氣質的神奇力量，
它可以制服惡魔，或是把它從人們心靈中給驅逐出去。
(Hamlet: III. 4.)

習俗嘛，
革除要比恪遵不渝還來得體面些。
(Hamlet: I. 4.)

Death 死亡

國王和最有權勢的人也必須一死，
因為這才是人們苦難的結束。
(King Henry VI., Part 1st: III. 2.)

在我所聽過的所有怪事中，最讓人拍案驚奇的就要算是貪生怕死了，
死亡是人們逃避不了的結局，它要來的時候誰也阻止不了。
(Julius Caesar: II. 2.)

對於死亡後的恐懼，
使我們寧可忍受現有的苦難，而不敢輕易嚐試那不可知的災害。
(Hamlet: III. 1.)

死亡的感覺會在憂慮不安中達到頂點。
(Measure for Measure: III. 1.)

藉助藥物或許可以延年益壽，
然而死神也會抓走醫生的。
(Cymbeline: V. 5.)

p. 292 Deception 欺瞞

魔鬼也會引用聖經裡的話以遂其目的，
邪惡的心靈若引經據典，就好像笑臉迎人的小人，
是外表美麗但裡面卻爛掉的蘋果，啊！虛偽的人有多麼堂皇的外表！
(Merchant of Venice: I. 3.)

Deeds 行爲

罪行必將敗露，
即使用大地遮蓋也不能盡掩天下人耳目。
(Hamlet: I. 2.)

一見到可以為惡的工具，便會真的把壞事幹出來，
這是多麼常有的事啊！
(King John: IV. 2.)

Delay 遷延

我們想要做一件事，
在想做時便應該下手去做，因為這個「想要」是會變的，
會有各式各樣的折扣延宕，如世人的舌頭、世人的手和世事的變幻，
到了那時，這個「應該」就只能像敗家子的一聲嘆息一樣讓我們徒然自怨自艾罷了。
(Hamlet: IV. 7.)

Delusion 錯覺

為了祈求上天的慈悲，
請不要在你心靈塗上自慰的膏油，
這只能在瘡疤上面敷層皮膜，
而臭惡的膿水卻已在裡面潰爛並暗中蔓延。
(Hamlet: III. 4.)

Discretion 慎思明辨

我們自己要曉得適可而止，
不要逾越分寸才好。(Othello: II. 3.)

Doubts and Fears 疑惑和恐懼

我被惱人的疑惑和恐懼所包圍束縛。
(Macbeth: III. 4.)

p. 293 Drunkenness 醉態

毫無節制的縱慾是一種暴政，
它曾顛覆了不少王位，
無數君王也因而沈淪。
(Measure for Measure: I. 3.)

Duty Owing to Ourselves and Others 對我們自己和他人的義務

泛愛眾，但只有對少數人推心置腹。
對任何人都不可虧欠，應該有能力和敵人抗衡，
但不要因爭強好勝而炫耀自己的能力。
坦誠交友，保持友誼，寧可被批評為木訥寡言，
也莫多言賈禍而讓人責怪你。
(All's Well that Ends Well: I. 1.)

Equivocation 模稜兩可

我不喜歡聽那個「不過」，這會使以前的好消息為之失色：
好可惡的一聲「不過」，它像是一個獄吏帶領著一個重刑犯。
(Antony and Cleopatra: II. 5.)

Excess 不知節制

最甜美的食物若攝取過量也會讓胃狂嘔。
(Midsummer Night's Dream: II. 3.)
每一個過量的杯子都是受到詛咒的，杯裡的東西就是惡魔。
(Othello: II. 3.)

Falsehood 虛偽

虛偽、怯懦和沒有良好的家世，
是女人所最憎惡的三件事。
(Two Gentlemen of Verona: III. 2.)

Fear 畏懼

畏懼會帶來混亂失序，而混亂失序則會帶給人創傷，
這是我們應該要小心的。
(King Henry VI., Part 2nd: V. 2.)

畏懼並不能免於一死，戰爭的結果大不了也是一死，
奮戰而死，是以死亡摧毀死亡，但畏怯而亡，卻只做了死亡的奴隸。
(King Richard II.: III. 2.)

Feasts 宴樂

酒餚即使寒酸，但只要主人熱情招待，也一樣可以盡歡。
(Comedy of Errors: III. 1.)

Filial Ingratitude 做子女的不孝

忘恩負義啊！你這鐵石心腸的鬼，
你在一個孩子身上出現的時候，簡直比海怪還可厭哩！
(King Lear: I. 4.)

一個不知感恩的孩子要比毒蛇的利齒還要尖銳許多。
(King Lear: I. 4.)

p. 294 Forethought 先見之明

好好決定一個計畫，不要盲動躁進，
以致在半途中碰上意外的危險。(Coriolanus: IV. 1.)

Fortitude 剛毅

對於命運的軛，你不必引頸承受，
要鼓起大無畏的精神，
不顧一切惡運，乘勝邁進。
(King Henry VI., Part 3rd: III. 3.)

Fortune 財富

當命運之神最想加惠於人時，
就會對他們怒目而視。
(King John: III. 4.)

Greatness 高貴

別了，長久的別了，我的一切權勢！
這就是人生：今天他滋長出希望的嫩葉，明天開花，
渾身花團錦簇，
第三天霜降，肅殺的寒霜。

這得意的人正以為可以一帆風順的達到全盛時期，
但突然從根部受到摧殘，於是他倒了下去，
像我現在這樣。
(King Henry VIII.: III. 2.)

有些人生而尊貴，有些人是贏得尊貴，
更有些人的尊貴是從前者手上硬逼來的。
(Twelfth Night: II. 5.)

Happiness 幸福

唉！從別人眼中看見幸福是多麼地苦澀啊！
(As You Like It: V. 2.)

Honesty 誠實

誠實的人就是在刀斧加身時仍能夠為自己辯護。
亨利六世中篇
(King Henry VI., Part 2nd: V. 1.)

像這樣的世界，誠實的人在一萬人裡頂多只能挑出一個來。
(Hamlet: II. 2.)

Hypocrisy 僞善

魔鬼往往會化為光明的天使引誘世人。
(Love's Labor Lost: IV. 3.)

一個人可以滿臉堆笑，但骨子裡卻是個殺人不眨眼的惡徒。
(Hamlet: I. 5.)

p. 295
Innocence 純眞

我信賴的是自己的清白，所以我大膽而堅決。
(King Henry VI., Part 2nd : IV. 4.)

Insinuations 奉承

聳聳肩，或哼哼哈哈的，這些無關宏旨的表情是誹謗所使用的，
誹謗會把最貞潔的美德給烙傷。
這些聳聳肩和哼哼哈哈會在你剛說完「她很漂亮」，
但還未能說出「她很貞潔」之前就橫攔進來。
(Winter's Tale: II. 1.)

Jealousy 嫉妒

輕如空氣的瑣碎事物，
對於嫉妒的人來說卻會像聖經上的證據一般確鑿有力。
(Othello: III. 3.)

噢！要當心嫉妒之心：它是青眼妖怪，總是戲弄牠所要吞噬的肉。
(Othello: III. 3.)

Jests 嘲弄

嘲弄者的話能否得逞係取決於聽者的耳朵。(Love's Labor Lost: V. 2.)
從沒受過傷的人才會嘲笑別人的疤痕。(Romeo and Juliet: II. 2.)

Judgment 審判

蒼天高於一切，一位真神即坐鎮其中，
祂不是任何一個國王能夠賄買的。
(King Henry VIII, : III. 1.)

Life 人生

人生不過是個行走的影子，
一個在舞台上比手畫腳但卻演技拙劣的演員，
登場片刻，便在無聲無息中悄然退下。
(Macbeth: V. 5.)

我們人類的本質和夢一樣，短促的一生也是在睡夢中走完。
(The Tempest: IV. 1.)

p. 295 Love 愛

愛比殺人重罪更難隱藏，連黑暗中的愛也有正午的陽光。
(Twelfth Night: III. 2.)

甜蜜的情愛一旦變質，就會轉化為最惡毒和最可怕的怨恨。
(King Richard II.: III. 2.)

當愛開始讓人生厭並消褪時，總是會出現矜持的禮貌。
(Julius Caesar: II. 2.)

真愛的道路向來崎嶇不平。
(Midsummer Night's Dream: I. 1.)

愛情不用眼睛觀看事物，但憑心靈。
(Midsummer Night's Dream: I. 1.)

她從未表白自己的愛，讓隱匿耗盡原本豔紅的腮幫子，
像蓓蕾裡的小蟲子般，
她在沈思中憔悴了，憂鬱得臉色蠟黃，就像坐在墓碑上的「忍耐」二字般對著愁苦微笑，這不就是真愛嗎？

(Twelfth Night: II. 4.)

愛情是盲目的，情人眼裡是看不見他們所做的荒唐事。
(The Merchant of Venice: II. 6.)

Man 人類

人是何等巧奪天工的一件上帝傑作呀！理性是何等的高貴！
智慧是何等的浩瀚無垠！儀態是何等的優雅！
一舉手一投足是多麼地像個天使！
悟性是多麼像個神明！真是集世界之美，稱得上萬物之靈！
(Hamlet: II. 2.)

Mercy 慈悲

慈悲的特質是無一絲勉強的，它像甘霖自天而降，
有雙重的福佑，賜福給那施者和受者；
它在最有威嚴的人手中是最有威嚴的，比皇冠更適宜於帝王的身份，
它的寶杖是人間威權的象徵，而威權即是帝王尊嚴的標記，
也是帝王所以令人敬畏的緣由。不過，慈悲卻在王權之上，
它佔住國王的心頭，是上帝的象徵，在以慈悲調和法律時，
帝王是最近似上帝的了。
不妨想想：
如果真的要公平，那麼我們死後誰也不能得救，所以我們祈求慈悲，
而這番祈禱也教訓我們要做慈悲的事。
(Merchant of Venice: IV. 1.)

p. 296 Merit 長處

如果沒有一點長處，誰能夠欺騙命運而獲得榮耀？
誰也別妄自擺出非分的威儀！
(Merchant of Venice: II. 9.)

Modesty 謙遜

假裝不知道自己的優異處正是卓越的證明。
(Much Ado About Nothing: II. 3.)

Moral Conquest 以德服人

勇敢的征服者，因為你們的確是，
你們要對由自己的情感和世俗慾望所組成的大軍作戰。
(Love's Labor's Lost: I. 1.)

Murder 謀殺

偉大的萬王之王早已在祂的誡律中命令你不可殺人，
當心！上帝手中握有懲罰的工具，以打擊那些違反祂誡律的人。
(King Richard III.: I. 4.)
這血就像是向上帝獻祭的亞伯的血一樣，
甚至從並無喉舌的土壤深窟裡湧出。
(King Richard II.: I. 1.)

Music 音樂

內心沒有音樂為伴的人，若再不受美妙音符的感動，
那就只適合做賣國、耍權謀和巧取豪奪的勾當。
這時，他靈魂的一舉一動必如夜晚一樣黑暗，
情感也必如地獄一樣陰幽，當然這樣的人是不可信的。
(Merchant of Venice: V. 1.)

Names 姓名

姓名裡有什麼？被我們叫做玫瑰的那種花，
要是換上其他任何名字，還不都擁有同樣的芬芳？
(Romeo and Juliet: II. 2.)

好名聲是靈魂中的無上之寶，無論男女皆然。
偷我錢囊的人不過是竊走了一些臭銅錢，
那都是虛無的東西，只是不斷地在你我手裡來來去去，
況且更曾做過千萬人的奴隸。
但無論是誰偷去了我的名譽，那麼他雖然並不因此而富足，
我卻由於失去它而淪為赤貧。
(Othello: III. 3.)

Nature 順其自然

動之以情，大家即全無異議。
(Troilus and Cressida: III. 3.)

p. 297 News, Good and Bad 好消息和壞消息

雖然是據實以告，但把壞消息帶來總不是件好事。
好消息多說無妨，但壞消息卻最好留待大家感覺出來的時候再自行呈現。
(Antony and Cleopatra: II. 5.)

Office 官職

服役的就這麼倒楣，升遷要靠關說和私情，
並不會循慣例依序遞補。
(Othello: I. 1.)

Opportunity 機會

一個追求好運的人在鴻運當頭時如果沒有接受，
那就永遠不會再有這樣的機會了。
(Antony and Cleopatra: II. 7.)

人生在世如潮起潮落，
把握住高潮的時機便可導致成功，
失去良機，人生的航程必觸礁擱淺，終生顛沛。
(Julius Caesar: IV. 3.)

Oppression 壓迫

不要把一個快要倒下去的人擠壓得太厲害，這也是美德，
他的罪過自有法律制裁，就放手由法律懲治他，而非藉由你。
(King Henry VIII.: III. 2.)

Past and Future 過去與未來

噢！人們的想法是多麼討厭呀！
過去的和未來的看來都是最好的，只有目前的東西看起來最糟。
(King Henry IV., Part 2nd: I. 3.)

Patience 耐心

缺乏耐心的人是多麼可憐啊！
什麼創痛不是漸漸痊癒的？
(Othello: II. 3.)

Peace 和平

和平即是勝利的本質，
因為雙方都很有顏面的被征服了，
沒有一方是失敗者。
(King Henry IV., Part 2nd: IV. 2.)

我會一面使用橄欖枝，一面揮動自己的刀劍，
戰爭孳生和平，使和平制止戰爭，
讓兩者的相處有如彼此的醫生。
(Timon of Athens: V. 5.)

我現在終於認識自己了，
在內心深處感到一種超脱世間一切榮華的祥和，一種寧靜感。
(King Henry VIII.: III. 2.)

Penitence 懺悔

一個人若能懺悔，天地都會為之動容，若還不表滿意，便有違天理人情，
一個人若能做贖罪的苦行，上天的震怒都會為之平息。
(Two Gentlemen of Verona: V. 4.)

p. 298

Players 演員

整個世界都是座舞台，所有的男男女女不過是上面的演員罷了，
他們有的上場，有的下場，一個人一生要扮演好幾種角色。
(As You Like It: II. 7.)

我曾見過一個別人讚不絕口的戲班子在演戲，
說句不算是褻瀆的話，他們的口音簡直大異於基督徒，
走台步時不像基督徒，也不像異教徒，更不像世間的凡夫俗子，
他們奔騰咆哮使我想到這些大概是上帝門徒所造的，
只是沒有造好，所以這樣令人厭惡的略具人形。
(Hamlet: III. 2.)

Pomp 華麗

什麼氣派、權勢、威風，又算得了什麼？
到頭來都不過是一坯黃土罷了！
不論生前活得多麼美好，都必須一死。
(King Henry VI. Part 3rd: V. 2.)

Precept and Practice 坐而言和起而行

若行和知一樣容易，那麼小土地公廟早就變成大教堂了，窮人的茅草屋也早就成為帝王的宮殿了。能遵奉自己教諭的便是個好牧師，教二十個人行善，要比做奉行教諭的二十人之一容易多了。頭腦儘管給血性訂下了規律，但衝冠一怒卻往往會躍過冷酷的戒條；血氣方剛下的狂妄就像隻狡兔，能跳過由忠告所構築成的破網。
(The Merchant of Venice: I. 2.)

Princes and Titles 王公貴族和頭銜

王公貴族無非是把稱號頭銜當作尊榮，
以虛浮而表象的聲譽換取心靈的勞苦，
不過為了虛無飄渺的空想，往往嚐遍無盡愁煩，
原來在他們的尊號和一些賤名之間，除了湧現的浮華的虛名外，
其他是毫無分別的。
(King Richard III.: I. 4.)

Quarrels 紛爭

在一番無謂的爭執中，必無真勇可言。
(Much Ado About Nothing: V. 1.)

理直氣壯的人好比披著三重盔甲，
但那種不公不義、喪盡天良的人即使穿戴鋼甲，也如同赤身裸體般。
(King Henry VI., Part 2nd: III. 2.)

Rage 憤怒

人在盛怒下往往會傷了最希望見到他好的人。
(Othello: II. 3.)

p. 299 Repentance 懊悔

人們有時會魯莽行事，
事後才有餘暇懊悔。
(King Richard III.: IV. 4.)

Reputation 聲譽

無瑕的名譽是人世間最純的珠寶，
失去了它，人類不過是堆鍍金的糞土、染色的污泥，
我忠貞的胸膛中有顆勇敢的心靈，
就像藏在十重鎖箱中的珠寶。
(King Richard II.: I. 1.)

Retribution 報應

神是公正的，
以我們在男歡女愛方面的罪惡作為懲罰我們的工具。
(King Lear: V. 3.)

如果有些人廢止了法律，掙脫國內的處罰，
那麼他們縱使能凌駕於其他人之上，
也必無雙翅飛離上帝那兒。
(King Henry V.: IV. 1.)

Scars 創傷

光榮得來的傷疤是榮譽的標記，
(All's Well that Ends Well: IV. 6.)
吹噓傷疤的人，會理所當然的受到嘲笑。
(Troilus and Cressida: IV. 5.)

Self-Conquest 征服自己

現在所能贏得的最大勝利莫過於把自己的良知武裝起來，
去抵禦那些虛無飄渺的誘惑。
(King John: III. 1.)

Self-Exertion 自我發揮

人們有時可以支配自己的命運，要是受制於他人，
那錯並不在我們的命運，而在於我們自身。
(Julius Caesar: I. 2.)

Self-Reliance 靠自己

許多事常是事在人為，
但我們偏愛往上天的身上推，
命運給我們自由，
只因為我們自己懶惰，
計畫才會遭到掣肘和挫折。
(All's Well that Ends Well: I. 1.)

Silence 沈默

在這靜默之中我也感到歡迎之意，
這種惶恐敬畏的羞怯，
讓我領受同樣的真誠，
更勝於雄辯滔滔與娓娓的口才。
(Midsummer Night's Dream: V. 1.)

當語言無效時，無言的天真往往能打動人心。
(Winter's Tale: II. 2.)

沈默是快樂的最佳前導，
如果我說得出自己有多麼快樂，便沒有什麼快樂可言。
(Much Ado About Nothing: II. 1.)

p. 301 Slander 中傷

中傷，它的鋒刃比刀劍更銳利，它的長舌比尼羅河中所有的毒蛇還毒，
它的呼吸駕著疾風，向全世界的每個角落散播惡意的誹謗，
任何國王、王后、國家、未婚少女或高潔的老婦都難逃其毒手，
甚至包括墳墓裡的祕密。
(Cymbeline: III. 4.)

Sleep 睡眠

那天真無邪的睡眠，把憂慮的亂絲編織起來的睡眠，那日常的死亡，
疲勞者的沐浴，受創心靈的油膏，大自然的第二個行程，
生命盛筵上的主要營養。(Macbeth: II. 2.)

Suicide 自殺

自殺之事，被上天所嚴禁，
使我軟弱的手不敢造次。
(Cymbeline: III. 4.)

Temperance 節制

我雖像是老了，但還是很強壯的，因為年輕時從未飲過刺激的熱酒，
也從未厚著臉皮去追求足以讓人耗弱的娛樂，
所以我的暮年好比生氣勃勃的冬天，雖結著嚴霜，卻不慘淡。
(As You Like It: II. 3.)

Theory and Practice 理論和實踐

從未出現過能耐心忍受牙痛的哲學家，
無論他們是怎樣自詡為超凡入聖，
看不起偶而的意外和苦痛。
(Much Ado About Nothing: V. 1.)

Treachery 背叛

雖然遭到背叛的可憐人心中無比苦楚，
但對方也擺脫不了更刺痛的良心譴責。
(Cymbeline: III. 4.)

Valor 勇猛

慎思明辨是勇氣中較好的一面。
(King Henry IV., Part 1st: V. 4.)

有勇無謀之輩只會浪費他的武器。
(Antony and Cleopatra: III. 2.)

一條狗呲牙咧嘴的話，把牠一腳踢開即可，
若硬是要把手指放進牠森森利齒之間，
那又算什麼勇敢呢？
(King Henry VI., Part 3rd: I. 4.)

p. 302 War 戰爭

留心！
你怎麼喚醒了沈睡的戰爭之劍，
我們以上帝之名命你小心。
(King Henry IV., Part 1st: I. 2.)

Welcome 歡迎

歡迎是永遠含笑的，而告別卻總是帶著嘆息。
(Troilus and Cressida: III. 3.)

Wine 醇酒

若能善加利用，美酒就是有用的東西。
(Othello: II. 3.)
啊！你這看不見的酒神，若是沒人知道你的尊姓大名，
那就讓我們叫你一聲惡魔吧！……
人們居然會把仇敵放進嘴裡，好讓他偷掉自己的腦筋！
我們竟然在狂歡中讓自己搖身一變成野獸。
(Othello: II. 3.)

Woman 女人

一個娘娘腔的男人要比一個魯莽粗野的男人婆更為可憎。
(Troilus and Cressida: III. 3.)

Words 言詞

不是出自肺腑的空話永遠上不了天國。
(Hamlet: III. 3.)

關於這番罪行實在沒有多少話好講，
任何藉口都不能寬恕這種過錯。
(The Rape of Lucrece)

Worldly Care 世俗的罣礙

你對於人生太過認真了，
用過慮的人去購買人生，是反倒會失去它的。
(Merchant of Venice: I. 1.)

Worldly Honors 世俗的榮耀

人本身沒有什麼榮譽可言，而是由於身外的浮名而感到榮耀的，
例如地位、財富、名聲等，時常是意外獲得的，因此是不穩的，
總有一天要垮下來。
至於趨炎附勢的人情也是靠不住的，
會互相牽連而同歸於盡，不過我並沒有這種情形。
(Troilus and Cressida: III. 3.)

國家圖書館出版品預行編目資料

品味莎士比亞英文名作選(合訂本) / E. Nesbit著；李璞良譯. -- 初版. -- 臺北市：寂天文化, 2016.05印刷

面；　公分

ISBN 978-986-184-681-1(25K平裝附光碟片)
ISBN 978-986-184-686-6(25K平裝)
ISBN 978-986-318-455-3(25K精裝附光碟)
ISBN 978-986-318-611-3　(平裝附光碟片)

1.英語 2.讀本

805.18　　105006830

品味莎士比亞英文名作選
(精裝典藏版)

改寫	E. Nesbit
翻譯	李璞良
編輯	謝雅婷
主編	黃鈺云
封面設計	林書玉
內頁排版	謝青秀 / 林書玉（中譯本）
製程管理	洪巧玲
出版者	寂天文化事業股份有限公司
電話	02-2365-9739
傳真	02-2365-9835
網址	www.icosmos.com.tw
讀者服務	onlineservice@icosmos.com.tw
出版日期	2017 年 09 月　初版再刷　500101
郵撥帳號	1998620-0 寂天文化事業股份有限公司

劃撥金額 600（含）元以上者，郵資免費。
訂購金額 600 元以下者，加收 65 元運費。
〔若有破損，請寄回更換，謝謝。〕

語言程度

CEF國際語言能力指標	GEPT 全民英檢	TOEIC 多益測驗
B1 (進階級) Threshold	中級	550